Emilion

EMILION

A.J. Joseph

The Book Guild

First published in Great Britain in 2026 by
The Book Guild Ltd
Unit E2 Airfield Business Park,
Harrison Road, Market Harborough,
Leicestershire. LE16 7UL
Tel: 0116 2792299
www.bookguild.co.uk
Email: info@bookguild.co.uk

The manufacturer's authorised representative in the EU
for product safety is Authorised Rep Compliance Ltd,
71 Lower Baggot Street, Dublin D02 P593 Ireland (www.arccompliance.com)

Typeset in 11pt Minion Pro

Printed and bound in Great Britain by CMP UK

ISBN 978 1835744 024

British Library Cataloguing in Publication Data.
A catalogue record for this book is available from the British Library.

For my wife, Louise, for her love and encouragement, and for her endless joie de vivre.

PROLOGUE

Rendezvous at Saint-Emilion, SW France

8th June 1944, 02:00 hours

It starts with a minor irritation, like a mosquito bite; that is how it is with the loss of memory. Françoise knows this.

It is a little thing, but it irritates her nevertheless, like the low drone of the Dakota aircraft that slowly approaches, drawing all malicious eyes towards them, but she cannot remember the name of the agent they are supposed to meet.

Not his real name, she could never forget that, although it would be fatal to utter it. For the life of her, she cannot remember his code name.

A silly little thing; why would her memory fail her now? There have been so many code names and she remembers them all. She has excellent recall; her life has depended upon it. She has always taken pride in her ability to remember every detail of a scene, and complex sequences of numbers, so why has she forgotten this one simple name? Perhaps it is the excitement of seeing him again.

'Raymond,' she whispers to the man waiting with her at the rendezvous point. 'Raymond.'

'What?' he snaps back.

He is not an unkind man, but he would prefer silence, and she instantly regrets her ill-discipline. He watches the night sky intently as he has done so many times, waiting for the drop from the unseen aircraft. With his head craned back his prominent Adam's apple is fully displayed. It seems to move of its own accord, as if he constantly gulps. How unattractive the lump of cartilage is, she thinks, and she idly wonders why she had never noticed it before. It is the first disingenuous thought she has ever entertained about Raymond, and she wonders what it signifies. He is a few years older than her, approaching his thirtieth year, and the couple are considered unusually attractive. To do their work they have often had to adopt disguises that play down their looks. A dull and unremarkable face better suits a spy.

When she does not reply Raymond throws up his hands in exasperation and turns to look at her, but when he speaks his tone is kinder. He knows they are both on edge. There are so many quislings and collaborators amongst the vintners and clergy; they could be betrayed at any moment.

'What is it, my love?'

'The code name, do you remember it?'

He looks at her quizzically, his face showing amusement and concern. 'Of course.'

'Tell me. What is it? I can't recall.'

He shakes his head in disbelief and resumes his vigil, but he takes hold of her hand and squeezes it reassuringly and replies gently, 'Look to the heavens, my love, you will remember it soon enough.'

*

The aircraft banks alarmingly before beginning its rapid descent. The lone passenger feels like his stomach has been left behind. It is as well he didn't eat before the flight. His heart races and his palms sweat. It will not be long now until he has to face the terrifying drop. Despite the deafening drone, in his headset he hears with crystal clarity the pilot's final command. It is as short and terse as every other command he has delivered: 'Get ready to jump.'

No further details, no expression of admiration for the risks being taken, no encouragement or good luck wishes. The pilot makes no effort to hide his resentment.

The jovial co-pilot is more forthcoming. 'We should see the beacon soon. We're approaching Saint-Emilion as far as I can tell, but hey ho! You never know; this night flying is tricky business.'

The airwaves resound with his avuncular laughter.

'Let's hope those Frenchie friends of yours get the fire alight, otherwise we could end up dropping you in the Dordogne river or right on top of the German garrison at Libourne!'

More unwarranted laughter.

'Right, old man, get ready. I think I see the light. Don't mind the skipper. It's nothing personal. Dropping civilians into France just isn't his cup of tea; he'd rather be dropping bombs on civilians.'

For the third time there are peals of laughter. The passenger supposes the crass remark is meant to be reassuring.

Awkwardly, he stands up and edges his way towards the oval-shaped door. He is a large, powerfully built man and it will be a tight squeeze to make it through the aperture. It always is. He performs one final check on the parachute harness, tests the clips and checks his bag is secure. With the explosives, fuses, timers and grenades it contains, it weighs a ton. He fears he will drop like a stone, or like a hanged man through a trap door.

'Seriously, old man,' says the co-pilot, adopting a valedictory tone, 'two days ago we were dropping paratroopers into Normandy. We're keen to get back to the action. We don't know what the top brass is thinking using this valuable crate to ferry you here, not when the beachheads are still vulnerable. That's why the skipper is a bit narked. To tell you the truth, I'm green with envy. I wouldn't mind seeing out the war in the wine-making centre of the world myself! I just wish we could land and pick up a crate or two of Bordeaux.'

He does not reply, and there are no further communiqués. The incongruous laughter dies away. As the jump light turns green he closes his eyes, takes a deep breath and launches himself through the narrow opening and out into the void. He does not breathe again until the rip cord is pulled and the parachute unfurls, and he begins his poorly controlled fall from the heavens.

As he hangs in the air, a kaleidoscope of thoughts races through his mind. He thinks about the first time he worked with Françoise, at the Berlin Olympics in 1936. Given her gift for languages and intelligence, she was already working as a spy, despite her young age. He thinks about her ambition to one day compete in the Games. She was a talented athlete, a good endurance runner and a keen shot. Ancient sports had ever been essential training for war – archery, mastery of horse, missile throwing and unarmed combat – but modern warfare is different, more impersonal and far more destructive, and largely fought at a distance, rendering sports anachronistic. He thinks about his own sporting talents, and he thinks about his young son. *Will he have the chance to represent his country one day, or will the greater game thwart his ambition too?*

He looks down towards the beacon and, despite the darkness, he begins to make out something of the familiar and subdued landscape. From the air, the endless fields of vines resemble Napoleonic troops on parade, the regimented rows forming vast geometric battalions that stand proud and erect and unyielding. To the east he begins to discern the modest summit adorned by the medieval bell tower of the monolithic church of Saint-Emilion, which, in its day, acted as a beacon of its own, guiding pilgrims towards Santiago de Compostela. *Wine and religion*, he thinks, *have ever been a source of wealth and conflict*. The town, like much of the region, is built on limestone. It is riddled with fractures, natural lines of weakness which, over time, running water has exploited and excavated, carving out extensive cave systems. The water has abandoned and forgotten many of the channels it made, leaving them high and dry. Some of the labyrinthine passageways are known to him. They have proved useful in the past, and they must do so again.

*

As she strains her eyes to the heavens, Françoise eventually catches sight of the single parachute falling gracefully through the clear night sky. The sound of the Dakota engine recedes, and the night regains an anxious stillness. She wonders how many other eyes are watching. The parachutist's descent is slow and uneven, and at times he hardly seems to be moving. His parachute expands and contracts, as if it were alive and breathing, as if it were a ghostly jellyfish moving lazily through the depths of the sea. She thinks there is almost something peaceful in the vista, like watching a bauble gently rotate on the branch of a Christmas tree, or a sycamore seed spiral down to earth, but Raymond squeezes her hand tightly, and she senses his growing agitation.

'He's taking too long and he's veering away from the beacon.'

She knows how vulnerable they are – how vulnerable and how exposed. She looks around furtively for signs of danger. The rendezvous point is a field that adjoins an abandoned farmhouse, one which was burnt to the ground by the occupying German soldiers. The field has long since turned to weed. It is surrounded by vineyards, and just beyond those, on the upper slopes of the broad valley, there are pine forests. She has always loved the woods, but just now they seem ominous and threatening.

'What's taking so long?'

She has never seen Raymond so nervous. He has an instinct for danger; something must be wrong. He slings his rifle from his shoulder and cocks the trigger, aiming it at the falling man.

She looks up and sees that the parachutist has drawn level with the treetops. For a brief moment he is caught in the glow of the firelight, and she thinks he resembles an angel hovering over them, then she laughs to herself, for she finally remembers his code name. He is the Angel – the Angel of Saint-Emilion.

Her relief and joy are short-lived. Just before the parachutist lands, all hell breaks loose. A powerful search light is switched on and all three of them are fully caught in the beam, like startled debutants upon a stage. A pack of ferocious Alsatian dogs begin to bark; there are whistles and cries and shouts of alarm all around them. She hears the unmistakable sound of gunfire, and the ground beneath her feet begins to churn as bullets rip into it.

'Gendarmes!' cries Raymond, throwing himself to the ground and into firing position in one fluid movement. 'We are betrayed!'

He fires three times in rapid succession and the searchlight goes out. He rolls away and finds a modicum of cover behind a low but derelict stone wall. Françoise takes a pistol from her belt just in time to shoot two Alsatian dogs that run and jump at her, their vicious teeth snapping.

They will not be taken without a fight.

'Help the Angel!' cries Raymond. 'I will cover you.'

He fires indiscriminately into the dark, hoping his bullets will find a mark, and deliberately drawing the gendarmes towards him. She turns and runs towards the spot where the parachutist landed. He overshot the mark, but he has already released his harness and begun crawling back towards her, shoving his heavy bag before him.

'No!' she cries. 'Leave that. There is no time. We must run for the woods.'

He knows she is right. There is nothing for it now but to try to escape.

'Raymond!' she implores. 'Raymond, come now, for the love of God.'

They stare at each other for a brief moment. He smiles sadly and shakes his head. 'Go now,' he says. 'Go now, my love, and I will hold them off for as long as I can.'

'No!' she screams, and tries to make her way back to him. But the Angel has her now, taking her by the arms and pulling her back across the abandoned field and into a patch of well-tended vines, where they lie low and try to catch their breath. Bullets fly all around them. Some of the gendarmes have torches, and they begin to train their beams towards them. She cannot take her eyes from Raymond, from the low wall where he lies. He fights on bravely, although she knows he has little ammunition. She imagines she hears him cry out in pain, as if he has been hit.

'Raymond,' she weeps, 'why don't you run? Run, my love, just run.'

'Françoise,' says the Angel, his tone urgent and fearful, 'it is we who must run. We must run like we have never run before. We must run like the wind.'

Damn them; damn the betrayers. He will not die here.

They find strength in their anger. She gathers herself together, sends a final kiss towards her beloved and darts forward, running hell for leather for the pine trees. The Angel has never seen anyone move so fast, and she effortlessly outpaces him. By the time he is halfway through the field of vines she has already made it to the cover of the woods. Behind him he can hear the gendarmes closing in. He won't make it. He hears a shot and a cry in the dark, and then Raymond falls silent. He knows it will be his fate too. He must run faster, he must concentrate only on that. There is no time to be afraid. He must set aside his breathlessness and his leaden-footed fatigue; he must fight the irritation he feels. Why does Françoise not run by his side? He had never appreciated her speed; he had never thought she would abandon him.

But then his heart leaps for joy because she is before him, emerging from the edge of the woods. He imagines she is waving and encouraging him on, like a fanatic spectator at a race. But instead, she aims her pistol straight at him. She is no longer crying. In the betraying moonlight, he can see the unreadable expression upon her face. He stops running and stares back at her in disbelief. As if in slow motion, he sees her take studied aim and expertly apply pressure to the trigger. A bullet explodes from the barrel of the pistol and hurtles towards him with fatal velocity.

1

Lost Property

Great Malvern, Worcestershire, January 1979

How much longer must he wait? The boy has already waited over an hour, but no one has come to collect him. Not that he minds; he is used to waiting and used to being alone. He prefers it that way.

It wouldn't be so bad if he had something to read, or a little money to buy refreshment, or if the Great Malvern railway station were a more interesting place to be, or if it wasn't so cold. He has walked the entire length of the station ten times trying to look inconspicuous. He has read all the plaques and information boards three times, feigning an interest in the architecture and history of the station's buildings. He has finally plucked up the courage to enter the Lady Foley tearooms on platform one. He found the grandiose name off-putting. He bided his time and waited until an elderly couple entered, and then he swiftly followed them in, hoping he wouldn't be noticed.

He hurriedly made his way to a table in a discreet corner and sat down in front of the large and heavily steamed-up window.

From the outside, he found the simple Gothic design of the Victorian-age railway station homely and comforting, but on the inside, he finds the exposed iron girders austere and the ornate floral capitals gaudy. And yet the information boards extolled their virtue. He supposes he must lack taste and is ignorant of art, as he seems to be ignorant of most things. He has read and re-read the headlines displayed at the newspaper kiosk, but he has no idea what they refer to. They mention something about 'a winter of discontent'.

He avoids making eye contact with the oversized, middle-aged lady with the severe countenance who commands the serving counter, but he knows she is eyeing him with suspicion, for he is not a paying customer. He expects to be asked to leave at any moment. It will not be his first eviction.

He looks down at the floor and pretends to adjust his fraying laces. Poor people have a way of seeing the poverty of others, however proudly they try to hide it. No doubt she can tell that his ill-fitting duffle coat is second hand, that his cheap trousers were purchased from a market stall and are too short for his frame, that there are holes in the soles of his shoes and that his knitted cricket sweater is threadbare. But then he thinks that it is his luggage that gives him away. Everything he possesses he carries in a small, battered suitcase. He thinks it may have once been coloured blue, but it is so creased and crumpled he can no longer be sure. The lock and handle broke a long time ago, before he took possession of it. The case is held together by an old leather belt which doubles as a handle. He wonders what Lady Foley's luggage would have been like. By all accounts, the tearoom was once her private waiting area, and she had a private tunnel built to connect it to the Imperial hotel, so that wealthy Victorians like Charles Darwin, who came to idle the day away or to undertake hydrotherapy, using the town's famous restorative waters to revive their ailing spirits, didn't have to risk contamination by mingling with the unwashed masses. Rich people have always had the means to command spaces.

He looks up and is startled to see the tea lady standing over him. For a big woman, she moves with stealth.

'Are you alright, my dear?' she asks.

There are six other people in the tearoom: two elderly couples, a studious-looking young woman bedecked in a conspicuous university scarf and the stationmaster. They all turn and stare at him. He has seldom felt less welcome.

He nods once, and then looks away, hoping she won't embarrass him further by asking him to leave.

The tea lady looks concerned. It is not his clothes or luggage that worry her but his pallid complexion, the gauntness of his face, the grease and dandruff visible in his long, curly and uncombed black hair, the dirt beneath his fingernails and the haunted look in his eyes. Everything about the boy speaks of neglect.

'Are you waiting for someone?' Her tone is not unkind.

'Yes,' he replies in a quiet, croaked voice, 'a friend of my aunt's is supposed to be meeting me.'

She does not look convinced. The stationmaster, full of his own self-importance, decides to butt in. He has a florid face, thick moustache and a mean, cynical look.

'And I suppose you had a ticket for the train you got off? It was the mail train from London, wasn't it?'

The boy resents the question and the accusation.

'Yes. My dad works… my dad worked for British Rail.'

'As do I,' says the stationmaster bullishly. 'It's a disgrace, and when the Tories get in they will privatise it, and then work-shy little herberts like you will no longer be afforded free travel at the tax payers' expense just because their old man worked for British Rail. Now, show me your pass.'

He reaches into the pocket of his duffle coat and retrieves the well-worn pass. The stationmaster takes it from him reluctantly, pinching it between his forefinger and thumb as if it were something befouled. The pass is little more than a folded piece of card held in a disintegrating plastic wallet. The stationmaster places it upon the table, dons a pair of rounded spectacles and uses a pen to open it, studying it intently, hoping to catch him out. The boy is only entitled to a limited number of journeys each year, and the dates and times of each trip must be recorded and stamped at a ticket office for the pass to be valid. Fortunately for him, everything is in order. But that does not prevent the stationmaster from goading him. He reads aloud and deliberately mispronounces his name:

'Benedick Harrison aged sixteen, from London.'

'Benedict,' replies the boy quietly and in a neutral accent.

'Oh, my apologies, *Benedick*,' says the stationmaster, now adopting what he imagines to be an upper-class accent, before adding, 'What kind of poncy name is that?'

And then he notices something that makes him rejoice, and he says with disbelief, 'I see the last trip you made was from Stranraer to Larne. You went to Northern Ireland despite all the troubles? What are you, Benedick, an imbecile or a terrorist?'

The two elderly couples look shocked by this revelation and the student shakes her head, showing nothing but disdain and contempt for the boy; how could anyone be so naïve or foolish as to willingly travel to Northern Ireland?

The boy does not reply. During the long journey back from Larne to London, and then onwards to Great Malvern, he has spoken to precisely no one. He prefers it that way.

'Perhaps he has family there,' says the tea lady, coming to his aid. She can see how shy and timid the boy is, and how he turns crimson with embarrassment. She feels guilty for having drawn him to the attention of the stationmaster.

By the momentary look of confusion on his inquisitor's face, the boy can tell that the possibility of anyone having family connections in Ireland had not occurred to him.

'You should kick the little tyke out, Margaret,' he says as he reluctantly hands the boy his pass back. Out of spite, he deliberately treads on his foot as he does so.

The boy does not react, although a familiar rage begins to build inside him. He wills himself not to cry. He imagines himself knocking the pugnacious stationmaster to the ground, and that thought brings him comfort.

If he knew anything about his aunt, what she looked like or where she lived, he would walk there right now, despite the cold, however far it was, rather than wait a moment longer in the tearoom. Benedict Harrison learnt a long time ago not to depend on other people.

'Oh well, no rest for the wicked,' says the stationmaster, looking pleased with himself as he heads for the exit. 'Unlike lazy, good-for-nothing students, some of us have real work to do.'

The young woman looks affronted, and the tea lady shakes her head.

'Never you mind him,' she says after the stationmaster has gone, 'he's just a bitter little man who wasn't good enough to get into the grammar school.'

'A little Hitler,' offers one of the pensioners.

'A professional jobsworth,' says another.

'What an unpleasant oaf,' says the student, salving her agitation by inhaling deeply on a cigarette and blowing smoke into the air in what she imagines is an alluring manner.

They all look at the boy and wait for him to pass judgement, but he remains mute. He would like to say, 'He's a bit like my father', but for reasons he cannot explain, he finds himself tongue-tied.

'Here you are, my dear, you drink this, it will do you good.'

Margaret hands him a cup of strong tea, with a biscuit resting on the side of the saucer. He can't help but notice how badly her hands shake.

It is wrong to expect or accept charity; he knows this, it is something his mother drummed into him. And yet the tea looks hot and the biscuit sweet, and he has not eaten a thing since leaving Ireland.

*

The man Benedict was supposed to meet at the railway station arrived more than two hours late. He breezed into the waiting room with an enviable air of confidence, the stationmaster hard on his heels like a faithful dog. If he had been wearing a cap, Benedict was convinced he would have doffed it. He said:

'Here he is, Dr Goodman, like I said. We've been keeping an eye on the boy for you.'

'Please, call me Cyril,' the man replied, taking the stationmaster's deference for granted and casting Benedict an uncertain look.

The tea lady scowled.

She was surprised to discover that the boy had told her the truth, and even more surprised to learn the identity of his aunt. Dr Goodman was well known to her, and she too adopted a fawning manner whilst in his presence. Even so, she was reluctant to give up her care for the boy, and as he left the tearoom, she surreptitiously thrust a pack of sandwiches, wrapped in greaseproof paper, into his hands.

'Had a bit of a prang, old boy,' said Dr Goodman, explaining his tardy arrival as they hurriedly made their way towards his car. 'Ruddy tyre popped just as I was crossing Castlemorton common. Damn sheep everywhere. Tried to avoid one of the blighters and bang! Wheel hits a pothole and the tyre bursts.'

Benedict had never met someone so well spoken. Dr Goodman sounded every bit like he belonged to the Royal Family, but his instincts told him the tale was only partly true. He wondered why the man would tell a lie.

'Are you a real doctor?' he had asked.

He looked mildly affronted by the question. 'If you mean am I a medical doctor, then no. I am a doctor of… engineering,' he replied, taking Benedict's suitcase without asking and throwing it unceremoniously into the back of his Land Rover, as if impatient to leave. 'I've known your aunt for years.'

*

Benedict wonders if the Land Rover is a military vehicle. It is as battered as his suitcase and as ancient as Dr Goodman. Noxious plumes of black smoke escape from the exhaust pipe every time they accelerate, and the engine is so noisy he can barely hear himself speak. Dr Goodman has to use excessive force to change gear, and the whole car jolts and clanks every time he does so. The suspension is shot, and every bump in the road causes him to bounce around uncontrollably in his seat, banging his head and shoulders against the ceiling and side door. He half expects to be jettisoned from the vehicle at one of the turns because the door rattles alarmingly, as if it were not properly shut or the latch was unsecure. He does not wish to appear frightened or ungrateful. It is the first car he has ever travelled in, and he finds the journey terrifying. It is not like he imagined and not like the car chases he has seen in movies, where the getaway drivers always make exaggerated turns of the steering wheel. Dr Goodman hardly seems to turn the wheel at all and seems oblivious to the dangers ahead. He drives carelessly and far too fast. Benedict finds himself pressing his foot to the floor as if applying an imaginary brake.

It begins to drizzle. Dr Goodman flicks a switch and the squeaky wipers reluctantly come to life, smearing grime across the chipped windscreen. The view is badly obscured.

'That's blown it,' he says, chuckling to himself. Without looking in the mirror, he presses heavily on the brakes, which squeal in protest. Benedict is thrown forward and narrowly avoids hitting his head on the windscreen. The car judders to a halt in the middle of the road and the engine stalls. Startled by the unexpected manoeuvre, the impatient man in the Ford Cortina behind them gives an angry blast of his horn and makes rude hand gestures as he passes by. Embarrassed, Benedict sinks down in his seat, wishing he were invisible, but Dr Goodman appears not to notice. 'The washer jets are blocked,' he explains, 'or the pump has gone.' Unabashed, he casually exits the car and begins to leisurely wipe the windscreen with a handkerchief, taking care not to get filth on his clothes.

Unlike the car, Dr Goodman is elegant and well dressed, dapper even. He wears a pristine trench coat, and his brown leather shoes are immaculately polished. His short white hair has a sharp, neat parting and he is clean-shaven, although his cheeks are now sunken and lined, and Benedict thinks he is far too thin. On his left wrist he wears an expensive watch, and on his wedding finger, a real gold ring. Despite his age, he is energetic and agile.

He finishes wiping the windscreen, but before he jumps back into the car he carefully rearranges a blanket across the driver's seat. Benedict had not noticed it before, but he can see its purpose: the car seats are covered in layers of wiry animal hair. He can't help but notice that a familiar odour follows Dr Goodman into the car. He smelt it when they first met, the unmistakable reek of alcohol and cigarettes. It is how his father smelt, especially after a good day at the races. Sure enough, before they set off, the driver begins to light up. He doesn't offer the cigarette packet to Benedict, but he asks:

'Do you smoke?'

He shakes his head.

'Quite wise,' says Dr Goodman. 'Filthy bloody habit. Better open the window, old boy, your aunt can't abide the smell of tobacco.'

*

Despite the reckless abandon with which Dr Goodman drives, the white-knuckle ride lasts the best part of twenty minutes. He insists on pointing out the geography, regardless of the lack of visibility, and Benedict pretends to listen attentively. It is a trick he learnt at school.

'We are heading south towards Castlemorton and Wellend, closer to Ledbury and the Gloucester border; that's where your aunt lives, old boy. Red Marl country.'

It would have been a long walk, thinks Benedict, but he would have made it; he has walked a lot further in the past and he can be obdurate. He wonders what red marl is, but he does not ask; best not to interrupt a man when he is spouting knowledge. It is another lesson he learnt at school.

'That's the Malvern Hills to your right. They run in a thin line for about nine miles or so, north to south. There are several summits. To the north you have End Hill and North Hill. Great Malvern sits on their eastern flank. Then there are the Worcester Beacon and the Hereford Beacon…'

He says something else, but Benedict does not catch it. He wonders if he fell asleep for a moment. He is so tired, and it is becoming uncomfortably hot inside the vehicle. The heating system seems to be the one thing that works properly, and it belts out a torrent of warm, oily-smelling air. He feels as if he is suffocating.

'…there are the remains of an Iron Age fort on one of the hills, if you're interested in that sort of thing, old boy. Your aunt likes to walk up there sometimes. The old girl is surprisingly fit for her age. She takes her easel and pallet with her, of course. There are some of the best vistas in the country from the top. If you look to the east, on a clear day you can see right across the River Severn valley to the Cotswold hills. Local legend has it you can see the Urals, but that's codswallop. To the west you can make out the Welsh hills… the "brooding and sombre Welsh hills" as your aunt calls them.'

He cannot help himself; before he knows it, the question leaves his lips.

'My aunt paints?'

His voice is weak and quiet. He has always been a reticent speaker.

'What was that?' asks Dr Goodman. 'You'll have to speak up, old boy, my hearing is not what it was. And your aunt can be as deaf as a post, when it suits her.'

He gives him an equivocal look and chuckles.

He takes a deep breath and puts more volume into his voice. 'Is my aunt a painter?'

Dr Goodman seems genuinely surprised by the question. 'Yes, and a first-class one, although she is better known for her sculpture. She is an artist of some renown. Didn't your parents tell you that?'

*

They leave a narrow, winding country lane and take a sharp left turn which is almost hidden by a dense stand of pine trees. They appear to be in the middle of nowhere. After a short journey along a track, an old farmhouse comes into view. Benedict notices there is an expensive-looking motorcar in the courtyard, parked next to an old rusty motorbike and sidecar. He hopes his aunt does not have company; he thought she lived alone. He is not in the mood to deal with more strangers.

'This is it, old boy,' says Dr Goodman, bringing the Land Rover to an indelicate halt. He reads relief in the boy's face, but also anxiety.

'My aunt lives here?' he asks in disbelief, overwhelmed by the apparent grandeur of the property and its extensive grounds.

'Yes, and if you must know, the farmhouse is seventeenth century and it's worth a tidy sum, although it's not my cup of tea. Far too remote from civilisation for my liking, but it suits a recluse. And to be frank, these half-timbered black and white buildings could do with a bit of modernisation. Not everything that's old is good.'

Without further ado, he jumps from the car and heads towards the house, whistling a merry tune to himself. 'Bring your case, old boy,' he calls out jovially behind him.

Benedict hears dogs barking and whining and scratching frantically at the porch door, not angrily and not in alarm, but more in welcome, as if they are keen to greet an old friend. There are cats everywhere, obstructing the path to the house, sitting on the window ledges and in the cottage garden, and emerging from the barns, the stands of trees and the surrounding fields; he has never seen such a motley selection.

The door of the front porch is unlocked. As Dr Goodman lets himself in, two enormous Alsatian dogs spring at him and all but knock him over. He laughs good-naturedly and makes a fuss of them.

'This is Romulus and Remus,' he says by way of introduction, 'but don't ask me which one is which. They are friendly enough, once you get to know them. They never forget your scent, you know. They have fantastic recall.'

Benedict has always been frightened of dogs and they sense it. They start to snarl and bark aggressively, and snap their way towards him.

'Romulus, Remus, sit!' shouts Dr Goodman in a surprisingly sharp and commanding voice. The dogs instantly obey and drop to the floor.

'Perhaps I'd better put them in the kennels for now,' he says, looking a little flustered, 'until you have a chance to get acquainted.'

He hurriedly leads the dogs around the back of the building. 'Do go in, old boy,' he calls out. 'Make yourself at home. There is some stew on the range if you're hungry, but don't let the cats in, they tiddle everywhere.'

He stands staring open-mouthed at the entrance porch. Not for the first time in his life, he feels abandoned. His aunt does not appear to be in. She did not bother to collect him from the station, and she could not be bothered to welcome him to her home. It is not an encouraging start.

Not knowing what else to do, he hesitantly enters the porch. It is so untidy and cluttered there is barely room to negotiate his way through it, not without disturbing something. There is a coat rack running its entire length, and every inch of it is filled with all manner of coats, hats and waxed jackets, piled one on top of another, three or four deep. Below it is a low wooden bench, and the space around it is littered with shoes and boots, all of which have been carelessly discarded. The disorder disturbs him. Boots and shoes should always be placed together, left toe pointing to right toe, always. It is something his mother insisted on.

There are clumps of dry grey mud scattered all over the tiled floor, and in one corner, sheets of old newspaper, which has been used by the dogs as a toilet. It would seem

Romulus and Remus are not permitted inside the house. He can see the fresh scratch marks on the inside of the external door, and in places, they have almost clawed their way through it. The single-pane windows of the porch are dirty and covered in dog drool, smeared no doubt by their inquisitive, wet, black noses. The wooden frames are badly rotted and the putty dried, cracked and all but fallen out. The windowpanes rattle in the wind. There is a desolate lightbulb hanging by a long cord from the high ceiling, but there is no lampshade. The ceiling mount is broken and the wires are exposed. The bulb is blackened, as if it blew a long time ago but has never been replaced. There is a dark brown Bakelite switch on the wall next to the internal door. The wiring looks ancient and lethal. The ceilings and windows are covered in tangles of cobwebs and dead flies.

The internal door is latched. It is old, and the metal-studded wood warped and poorly fitting in its frame. It takes quite an effort to push it open as the door sticks. He has to apply his foot to it to get it to yield. It opens directly into a large kitchen which has a low ceiling, exposing part of the timber frame of the house. There is little natural light, but he can see well enough to note that the room is every bit as cluttered, untidy and uncared for as the porch.

The kitchen is dominated by a large rectangular table. Its wooden surface is mostly covered by piles of old books, magazines and kitchen utensils, which include an ancient set of brass weighing scales. There are several bags of clay stacked at one end and objects he can only assume are abstract works of art. At the other end, a small space has been left clear; this is where his aunt sits and eats. He sees half a loaf of bread left out on a plate next to a jar of honey and a butter dish. The jar lid has not been replaced, and a knife, heavily laden with butter and honey, rests on top of it, dripping its contents onto the table. A half-full mug of coffee has been left to go cold next to the plate, and a multitude of coffee rings cover the tabletop.

The Belfast sink by the window is stacked full of unwashed plates and pots. The floor is covered by red quarry tiles. They are cracked and uneven, and they are adorned in places by a scattering of flour and vegetable peelings. There is a large Welsh dresser replete with delicate pieces of china, all coated in a layer of dust. The worktops are covered by wooden chopping boards, more discarded mugs, pots and plates, an ancient coffee-making machine and a redundant, white metal bread bin.

Taking up one side of the kitchen is a cast-iron range. It would appear to be lit, because the room is warm and a pot of stew simmers away on the hob. On one side of the range there is a half-full coal scuttle and two wicker baskets. One basket is piled high with logs, and in the other there is an open packet of firelighters, a box of cook's matches, a pile of old newspapers and a bag of kindling wood. The space on the other side of the range is taken up by a companion set of cast-iron fire tools, including pokers, tongs, shovels and brushes. They have all seen much use and far better days.

In another corner there is a rocking chair, its cushions covered in cat hair. Next to it is a rubbish bin, overflowing with bags of waste, and behind that, resting on a bench, is a large lidded metal tank with a tap at its base. A long, uncovered strip light runs along the centre of the ceiling, and there is another Bakelite switch by the door. He tries it. Nothing happens.

'Another power cut, I'm afraid,' says Dr Goodman, entering the kitchen with a box of candles in his hand. 'You'd better light some of these.'

He opens the door to the range and adds coal and logs to the fire with a practised familiarity. Impatient to be gone, he issues a quick list of instructions:

'Keep this burning low but don't let it go out, there's a good chap. Your aunt seldom lights any other fires. She prefers the cold. If you need hot water, boil a pan on the range; it's cheaper than boiling a kettle. The house is not connected to the mains, I'm afraid. The sewage waste goes into a cesspit which is buried in the garden, but heaven knows where. Let's hope you don't discover it by accident. You get water from the well. It is just around the back of the house; I'll show it to you later. Use the water that's stored in that metal tank for now. There is a standalone immersion heater outside the bathroom, which is on the first floor, next to the WC. I filled it up earlier and plugged it in. When the power comes back on, give it a couple of hours to heat up and then you can use it to fill a bath. I've fed the dogs, and the cats will look after themselves as cats are wont to do.'

'You are not staying?' asks Benedict in surprise. 'I thought you'd wait here until my aunt returns.'

'What?' he says, a look of confusion crossing his face. And then he bursts out laughing. 'I'm sorry, old boy, I should have explained. Your aunt *is* at home. She's in her studio. It's up in the attic. Under no circumstances must you disturb her, not when she is working, that's the golden rule. She's been up there all day and she will probably be up there all night too. Once she gets an idea for a piece of art she will keep working until it is complete. She loses track of time. Maybe you'll see her tomorrow.'

2

The Loose Hinge

Benedict looks dolefully around the kitchen. He shouldn't have come here; he should have stayed in Ireland or London. He is nothing but a burden; he is nothing but a burden to everyone. Perhaps the family tales about his aunt are true. He supposes there is a reason his father never spoke about her, and his mother just used to roll her eyes and refer to her as the 'awful aunt'. To be exact, she is his great-aunt, the sister of his paternal grandfather, but everyone in the family just calls her the 'awful aunt'. The family likes alliteration. His two grandmothers are nicknamed 'Nutcase-Nutty Nan' on his mother's side, and on his father's side, 'Silver-Sherry Nan', which was a shortened form of 'Silver-is-it-time-for-a-sherry Nan', which later became 'Silver-it-is-always-time-for-a-sherry Nan'. In sixteen years his 'awful aunt' has never once bothered to visit him, never sent a birthday wish or Christmas present; there has never been so much as a letter or a postcard sent to the family. It is as if she has disowned them and cast them adrift, although on what grounds, no one is prepared to say. Not for the first time, he wonders why she has invited him to stay with her now.

'Chin up, old boy,' says Dr Goodman, recognising the signs of despondency. 'I know the place is a bit of a mess, but it's all superficial.'

Dr Goodman's assumptions are wrong, thinks Benedict; he has lived with far worse mess than this.

Cyril feels the need to explain. 'Your aunt doesn't believe in wasting time on menial tasks like housework, and she's too stubborn and proud to hire a cleaner. You can kip down here tonight. I made the stew myself. It's not bad, and the rocking chair is quite comfortable once you get used to it. I'd stay and keep you company, but I have to get back for an emergency meeting in town. As it happens, I invited your aunt along, but she wouldn't be seen dead entering the Conservative Club.'

'You are a Tory?' asks Benedict, not really knowing what the label implies.

'Actually, no, old boy,' says Dr Goodman, once more looking mildly affronted by the question. 'Party politics doesn't overly interest me, but I like to keep an eye on what's going on. The country is in a bit of a pickle. The dustmen, water workers, sewage workers, ambulance drivers, gravediggers and "Uncle Tom Cobley and all" are all out on strike. Can you imagine, dead bodies are piling up in the morgues because the gravediggers are on strike? And these damn power cuts are happening too often. We are becoming a failed state. Tomorrow, you had better take that rubbish out and burn it because it is unlikely to be collected anytime soon.'

'The winter of discontent,' says Benedict, finally beginning to get an inkling of what the newspaper headlines were about.

'I don't know about winter, it feels more like a ruddy lifetime of discontent to me,' replies Dr Goodman with uncharacteristic bitterness. 'I sometimes wonder what we fought the war for. We had bread rationing in November because the bakers went on strike, and there was panic buying. I would have thought people would have had enough of rationing for one lifetime.'

'Why is everyone going on strike?' asks Benedict, eager to keep Dr Goodman from departing and suddenly fearful to be left alone in the large uninviting house with his awful aunt.

'Desperation and agitation,' he replies. 'Inflation and prices are rising, but wages are stagnant. Do you know what that means?'

'The poor are getting poorer.' It is a phrase he overheard a man use on his journey to Ireland.

'Everyone is getting poorer. The government has capped pay rises at five per cent. The tanker drivers are demanding a twenty-five per cent pay increase and threatening strike action if they don't get it. If that happens, we really will have a national crisis on our hands. It will cripple the country. The Tories are calling for a state of national emergency to be declared and for the army to be deployed. The unions are demanding the introduction of a minimum wage and a thirty-five-hour working week. They've got the government by the balls. Callaghan should resign.'

'Who is he?'

'James Callaghan, the Labour Prime Minister. Honestly, old boy, don't you follow the news?'

He doesn't answer directly. He is loath to admit that his father brought home newspapers only so that he could study the form of the horses, that their black and white television set was repossessed two years ago, that they could never afford batteries for his transistor radio and that, when she left, his mother, out of spite, took the radio's electric lead with her, as she took most other things too.

'If people are struggling to make ends meet then they should go on strike and force the fat cats to pay them a decent living wage,' he says, repeating something he once heard his father say.

'You think so, old boy? Are you a militant socialist, perchance?'

'A what?'

'A ruddy socialist. Don't tell me you don't know what a socialist is? What do they teach you in school these days?' He chuckles to himself, his good humour apparently restored. 'Ask your aunt. I think the two of you will get along famously. And now, I really must dash.'

'I don't think you could dash anywhere in that Land Rover. It is slower than a snail.'

Dr Goodman laughs aloud. 'Very droll, old boy, very droll. Alas, that crate is not mine. It is your aunt's pride and joy, so don't say a bad word about it to her face. I drive it now and again to keep the battery charged. The gearbox bearings are worn and the seals are leaking. Remind her to add some oil. The other car is mine.'

Benedict supposes he should be impressed. 'It's looks very… expensive.'

'It is, it's an Aston Martin V8 Volante. I bought it whilst I was in the States last year. Isn't she a beauty?'

He doesn't answer. It is not that he is envious, it is just that he has never coveted material things because the idea of owning anything is so alien to him, and so he cannot understand the pleasure people get from buying expensive and ostentatious objects that merely serve to remind other people of their poverty. He has never liked those who show off and flaunt their wares; he considers it ill-mannered somehow.

'And is the motorbike yours, too?'

'I wish it were. That rust bucket – the iron horse as your aunt calls it – is an original Triumph Tiger, used by dispatch riders during the war. Your aunt rides it out now and again. She stashes her art equipment in the sidecar and lets the Alsatians chase after her.'

And then he turns away and mutters something to himself. Benedict thinks it sounded like: 'Her whole life she's had dogs chasing after her.'

*

After Dr Goodman left, he had lit three candles and stationed them in strategic positions around the kitchen, sluiced out a bowl and spoon in the sink with cold water drawn from the metal tank, and helped himself to the stew.

It was delicious, the best he had ever tasted. Dr Goodman was clearly a modest man and a far better cook than his own mother had been. Her favourite dish was liver, coated in flour and fried with onions. He hated liver.

He had made himself a black chicory coffee and ladled eight teaspoons of sugar into it. He liked to eat the sugary residue once he had drunk the coffee. The milk in the fridge had gone off, presumably as a consequence of the frequent power cuts. He wondered how his aunt managed to work in her attic without electricity; he wondered how anyone managed to do anything without electricity. He settled down in the rocking chair and promptly fell into a deep sleep.

He had a vivid dream, or rather, he recollected in great detail an incident from his past. It is a memory that often surfaces, unbidden, to haunt his sleep. He has tried to forget it, or to reimagine it, but every time it appears, the dream-memory ends the same way. He cannot control what visions creep into his head. In the dream he had half-heartedly invited a school friend to tea and, much to his horror, he had unexpectedly accepted. His mother spent longer than usual tidying up. Every surface was scrubbed clean and polished. Everything had to be pristine and sparkling. She was excessively house proud. He shared a bunk bed, sleeping below his elder brother, and his younger brother slept in the same room. Every morning his mother would enter their bedroom early, uninvited and unannounced, and begin hoovering. At mealtimes, she frequently removed their plates and began washing up even before they had finished eating. She could rarely sit still for long and was always fussing around, like an irritating fly.

His mother liked to tell stories, and during the meal she had dominated the conversation. It was her usual embarrassing monologue of increasingly tall tales. She hardly paused for breath and gave no openings for anyone else to make a contribution. His father was absent, as usual, but his two brothers dutifully sat in silence and laughed on cue.

Predictably, she had served liver and onions. The liver was overcooked and leathery and difficult to chew. At one point, his friend had caught his eye and, thinking his mother could not see, made a well-known hand gesture, indicating that he thought she was a lunatic. They had laughed like conspirators. Later, when the friend had departed, she built herself into a fury. She exploded at him, a familiar ranting and raving about how there was nothing more sacred than family and how he should never show disloyalty by siding with others. He was nothing but an ingrate, and he had better not invite any more friends to her home. How could he have such little respect for his own mother?

He had sat in the kitchen and said nothing. He let her rant; it is what his father did. In her blind fury she had run at him waving a carving knife in his face. He had fought her off and disarmed her. They had not spoken much after that, and a few weeks later, she had left.

*

When the power eventually returns, the kitchen strip light flickers and hums and begins to emit a dull yellow light.

It wakes Benedict up. He wonders how long he has been asleep. It is pitch black outside. He wakes up in alarm, fearing the fire in the range may have gone out, but when he checks it, he finds that it is still going strong and that someone has fed it more logs. It is then that he notices he has a blanket draped around him. He does not recall seeing it before. Someone must have covered him up whilst he slept in the rocking chair.

'Dr Goodman? Auntie?' he calls out, but the house remains ghostly quiet.

He notices that the lid has been replaced on the honey jar and that the bread has disappeared.

As he extinguishes the candles, he senses something moving behind him. He wheels around in fright, but it is only a ginger cat, licking at an empty saucer.

Someone has let the cats in, he thinks. *How could I have slept through that?*

The kitchen has a second door, and he sees it has been left slightly ajar. It was definitely closed when he fell asleep. Cautiously, he opens it wider and discovers that it leads out into a long hallway which terminates in a dramatic flight of stairs. The landing light has been left on. There are several doors on either side of the hallway, but when he tries them, he finds them locked. He feels like a burglar. There is a grandfather clock standing against one of the walls and he notes the time: 2 am.

There are two things on his mind: he desperately needs the lavatory, and he thinks he ought to unplug the immersion heater. It could be a fire risk, and he dislikes the idea of wasting money needlessly; he has no intention of having a bath now. His mother used to unplug every electrical appliance in the house before she retired to bed, and she would check that she had done so at least three times. He hopes he is not becoming like his mother.

He tells himself he must be silent because he does not wish to disturb his aunt, but he deludes himself; in truth, he does not wish to alert her to the fact that he is awake and exploring her house. He is slight of build and fleet-footed, and he thinks he can move around quietly. But that is another delusion. The floorboards and stair treads creak alarmingly, and the ancient banister all but gives way when he leans on it, causing him to cry out in fear. He half expects to hear the attic door fly open and his awful aunt to descend the stairs in anger and demand to know why he is disturbing her by making such a racket.

But the house remains eerily quiet.

He can't help but notice that the walls and stairwell are crammed full of picture frames, none of which have been hung straight, and all of which house grainy, black and white photographs. The images are almost entirely devoid of people. They are barren landscapes or townscapes taken in foreign countries. He recognises a few of the famous landmarks of Rome, Paris, Berlin and Moscow, but many of the scenes are unknown to him. The images have been taken in winter and in the snow. He finds them desolate.

In one photograph there is a picture of a young man wearing a military uniform. He looks oddly familiar. He is sitting on the end of a hospital bed, as if he is about to be discharged, but he does not look well. He holds a cigarette in one hand and a book in the other. He points to its title, and Benedict reads: *Goodbye to All That* by Robert Graves. The picture is signed: *'To Helen, the flag bearer, with love and thanks, B.B., remember Barcelona, 1938.'*

The next photograph also takes his interest. It shows a long-jump pit and an athletics track in a cavernous but empty stadium. There is another handwritten message from B.B.: *'To Jeanette, remember Berlin, '36: may you make your own long-leap one day.'*

He wonders who B.B., Helen and Jeanette are, and why his aunt has these pictures hanging on her walls.

On the first floor he discovers more locked doors. The bathroom, when he discovers it, is freezing. There is no carpet or lino covering the wooden floorboards. There is a single-pane window which should contain a small, circular, hand-pulled extractor fan. The fan has broken and fallen out. A towel has been shoved into the hole. Frost has formed on the inside of the window. There is an old bath and washbasin. The ceramic is badly discoloured and cracked in places. He is surprised to see that they have taps. He turns them on, but no water flows out. There are two metal buckets, one to presumably transfer hot water from the immersion heater, which he satisfies himself is now unplugged, and one half full of cold water for filling the washbasin.

The WC is next door. The small closet has no natural light, and the room is even colder than the bathroom. He closes the door as quietly as he can, but the house is so still and the door so heavy, it seems as if he has deliberately slammed it shut. The quiet seems to amplify the noise somehow. He grits his teeth and braces himself in the expectation of a visitation from his aunt, but all remains quiet. The walls of the WC are decorated with woodchip, and they are covered in black mould. The toilet roll is damp and hangs from a holder whose Rawlplugs are halfway out of the wall. The toilet bowl is an ancient Armitage Shanks construction. There is a hand pull on a chain above his head, but it is clearly defunct. There is another bucket full of water beside the toilet, which is presumably used for flushing.

I am flushing the bog with Malvern Hills water, he thinks, *the water that is drunk by the Queen.*

*

He returns to the kitchen; he is wide awake now. There is an old wireless set on the table, and he wonders if it would disturb his aunt if he switched it on. He wonders if it will give him an electric shock if he tries.

He turns the volume control down and adjusts the dials, trying to find something interesting to listen to. He mostly picks up static, but, despite the late hour, he eventually tunes in to a station that is broadcasting news. The accent of the presenter is American, but he is addressing the dire political situation in Britain. He plays a recording of an interview with a union representative who insists that more public sector workers will go on strike and that there will be mass demonstrations in the major cities. Unfortunately, he says – but not sounding particularly regretful – there will be school closures, cancelled trains and disruption to hospitals. Another recording is aired, and this time it is the Prime Minister making a statement in the Houses of Parliament, insisting there is no national crisis and appealing for calm. He does not sound very convincing, and he is drowned out by gleeful jeering and a chorus of hectoring voices. Benedict feels sorry for him, in the way he has natural sympathy for any underdog.

Then the recording of an opposition politician is played. To wild cheers of approval, she calls for a vote of no confidence in the government and a general election. Benedict finds her voice shrill and grating, her manner carping and belligerent, and her words chilling and vicious, like his mother's could be when she was ranting, or wanting her own way.

Irritated, he changes station.

He finds one playing punk rock music. It reminds him of his two best friends at school. They dressed as punks because they could afford to do so and because they wanted to outrage people, especially their middle-class parents. It was just a convention they were following, like any other: adorning a uniform of protest. *It is odd*, thinks Benedict, *how so-called trendsetters are people who really just follow other people's fads*. His friends sported Mohican haircuts, and they had their ears and nose pierced. He thought they looked ridiculous but held his tongue. They repaid his loyalty by publicly castigating him for being 'a square' and unfashionable, which he found humiliating. They grew apart.

In reality, he could ill-afford to dress fashionably, whatever the latest fad may be, and he relied on hand-me-downs from his older brother and whatever his mother could salvage from local jumble sales. He seldom went out, partly because he had no money and partly because he had nothing to wear, but mostly because he didn't really care for other people's company. He never much cared for punk rock music either, finding it crass and overly loud, and he had no time for people who spat everywhere. At least his friends didn't become skinheads, unlike some of the boys in his year group. They frightened him. He detested their mindless violence and the hatred they spewed. He did his best to avoid them. He greatly admired the braver boys in the year that stood up to them and fought with them. He wished he could be like them, but he wasn't cut that way. He wondered if he was a coward at heart; his instinct was always to run from trouble. He heard a story about one of the skinheads who was expelled on his first day at college, the principal taking exception to his Nazi regalia and frog-marching him from the premises, saying something about how he had fought a war to defeat 'little thugs like you'. He doubted the truth of the tale, but the story had brought him comfort, for it felt like justice had been served.

He turns off the radio and begins to examine the books on the kitchen table instead, thinking he might read a while. He is intrigued to find that they are mostly written in foreign languages, a few of which he recognises, even if he doesn't understand them: French, German, Italian and Russian. Only a few are written in English, mostly weighty political or philosophical tomes, or books about fine art, all of them as dry as stale bread. The books and plays he had been encouraged to read at school were more to his taste: *Shane*; *The Kon-Tiki Expedition*; *Julius Caesar*; *The Guns of Navarone*; *Cry, the Beloved Country*; *All Quiet on the Western Front*; and his favourite, *The Red Badge of Courage*. He tries the magazines, but he finds them equally dull, as they are concerned with country pursuits, birds or gardening. He is on the point of giving up when he espies an unusual book cover. It depicts three elf-like men, one of whom is sitting on a leaf and fishing by a river. The title reads: *The Little Grey Men*. He wonders why his aunt would have an illustrated children's book on her kitchen table, but what really intrigues him is the name of the author; it simply reads: 'by BB'.

He settles into the rocking chair and begins to read, and he does not stop until he has finished the book.

3

The Boy With the Bat

After finishing the book, he fell asleep. He was not sure exactly what he expected to discover, but he felt disappointed to find nothing revelatory in the tale. The dust cover gave no further details about the author, and merely pointed out that the original illustrator had been someone called Denys Watkins-Pitchford.

The story itself was charming, and he admired it greatly. It revolved around four brothers, all of different dispositions, who are the last of their kind: little grey men who live in the woods. One, named Cloudberry, sets out seeking adventure and is never heard from again. He is cast as a rebellious and carefree spirit, and Benedict envies him. The others decide to build a boat and go in search of him. The eldest, Dodder, is reluctant and initially stays behind. He is cantankerous, partly because he has one false leg which gives him pain, and partly because he is fearful of change. He spends much of his time grumbling and fishing. He reminds Benedict of his father. He wonders if his own brothers would ever set out to search for him.

When he wakes up it has grown light outside, the book has fallen to the floor, and he is shivering with cold. His limbs ache.

He is surrounded by cats. They stare at him hungrily. His first thought is once more of the range. He is horrified to find that it has all but gone out. In something of a panic, he opens the vents, rakes the grate, blows on the embers, and tosses a handful of bunched-up newspaper and kindling onto the fire. He is relieved when the paper and wood ignite. It is with anxiety that, a while later, he feeds a little coal and a few more logs onto the fire, but he is gratified when they catch alight.

There, I have rescued it, he thinks.

He stretches and yawns and wipes sleep from his eyes. He helps himself to another sugary black coffee and banks up the fire. There is still no sign of his aunt. Through the window, he can see the ground is covered by a thick layer of fresh snow.

Feeling excited and keen to explore, he puts on his duffle coat and goes outside. He imagines he is Cloudberry. The air is fresh and sharp and it causes him to catch his breath. The sky is brilliantly clear and there is not a breath of wind. The winter sun is already quite high and he realises it must be late morning. The Malvern Hills are draped in snow and they stand in proud magnificence above the subdued landscape. He imagines them to be an Alpine range. He can make out tiny black dots: not skiers, but families playing in the snow together. He envies them.

He walks around to the kennels, expecting to be greeted by much angry barking, but he is surprised to find the gate to the compound open and the kennels empty.

Where the hell are the dogs? he thinks, looking around him in panic.

He can see paw prints in the snow, and he notices they lead to the back door of the house. His aunt must have rescued them earlier, but where are they now?

There are several outbuildings surrounding the house. For want of something better to do, he decides to explore them, but he is disappointed to find the doors bolted and locked. He tries each one in turn, but only the last one yields. Feeling like an intruder, he slips inside.

The outbuilding is an old barn, but it has a power supply and he switches on the light. He is surprised to see a long, sturdy workbench, replete with all manner of machinery, and shelves stacked high with tools and pots of paint. He recognises a few of the machines, including an engineering lathe and band saw. The well-equipped workshop smells of oil. The back of the barn has been used for storing junk: pieces of dilapidated furniture, bits of twisted metal, abandoned or broken sculptures and boxes of unwanted household items. He spends a while rummaging through them. In one box he finds a deflated rugby ball, a tattered Union Jack, a selection of boys' books covered in mildew, a pair of cricket boots – the leather decaying and half the studs missing – and an old cricket bat.

He removes the bat and examines it, almost reverentially. The rubber on the handle has peeled away and the willow has turned dark brown. It still smells of linseed oil, and he finds the aroma nostalgic. The face of the blade is cracked in multiple places and is held together with tightly woven, cream-coloured tape.

He has always loved cricket. It is the one sport he excels at; it is the one thing he excels at. His father had been a keen cricketer too, playing at a good level and, whilst completing his National Service, representing the army first eleven. But the father had never encouraged the son. Indeed, he did little but make disparaging remarks.

He notices that there is an inscription carved into the back of the bat. It reads: '*Knock them for six B.B.*' Benedict had once owned a bat of his own, a rare Christmas gift from Silver-Sherry Nan the year she was feeling flush after a substantial win on the football pools. That same year, not to be outdone, Nutcase-Nutty Nan had knitted him his cricket sweater. It was two sizes too large, and the V-neck hung down to his navel. Still, as his mother had said, 'There's plenty of growing room and it's the thought that counts.' B.B.'s cricket bat feels light in his hands, much lighter than the bats he used at school or that he borrowed from other members of the cricket club he played for. He wondered whether the bat remembered all the people who had wielded it; whether it remembered the edges as well as the shots it hit in the middle.

On the workbench he finds a pair of lightly soiled gardening gloves. He puts them on, imagining they are cricket gloves, with thick, padded, sausage fingers. He goes out into the yard and, despite the snow, begins to play an imaginary game of cricket, swishing the bat about and playing all sorts of shots. It is how he has spent much of his youth when he has been alone. He invents teams and games, and he takes on the role of each batsman, playing out their allotted innings and keeping a running commentary in his head. He has a prodigious memory and recalls all the scores, tallying totals quickly together as each batsman comes and goes. He has always been quick with numbers. He can lose himself in the game for hours at a time.

He thinks about his two brothers and the singular pursuits they follow. His younger brother often spends his time in imaginary worlds of his own, inventing characters and conversations, as he runs backwards and forwards along the landing, waving his arms about like a conductor. Or he simply does what their father does: he goes fishing. He sits for hours, a forlorn figure on the desolate riverbank, trying to catch something for their tea.

When their mother left, she took the younger brother with her. He has not seen him since.

His elder brother prefers to sit on the sofa and pull the stuffing out of the seats, scrunching it into a ball whilst he sucks his thumb. When they had a television, he would happily sit in front of it all day 'snuggling', as he called it.

He loses track of time and place. He is a famous batsman at Lord's cricket ground hitting the winning runs in a thrilling Test match. It is an impossible innings he has played. He is a genius, a champion – a superhuman. He raises his bat aloft and acknowledges the admiration of the crowd. It is then he notices the face in the kitchen window.

His aunt has been watching his antics for some time.

He is mortified, embarrassed beyond measure. He hastily drops the bat and walks towards the house, trying to appear casual, as if it were the most normal thing in the world for him to be playing an imaginary game of cricket by himself in a stranger's yard, and in the snow.

I am the boy with the bat, he thinks. *The batty boy with the bloody batty bat.*

He feels like all his darkest secrets have been exposed.

When he enters the kitchen he sees the two dogs lying obediently and silently by the range, warming themselves. They look up expectantly when he enters, but they do not move to greet him. Nor does his aunt. She leans against the sink and pulls her cardigan around her, crossing her arms, as if warding off the chill. She has her back to the window, and she stares at him for a long time. He cannot read her expression. It is not exactly stern, and he wouldn't say she was scowling, but neither does she rejoice to see him. He can only imagine what she must be thinking.

The first thing he notices about her is her height. She is nearly as tall as him, and he is already over six feet tall. Like him, she carries no weight about her, but hers is a healthy skinniness. She is lithe and graceful, like a ballerina. He knows she must be in her sixties, at least, but although she wears no makeup, she looks much younger, despite her hair turning grey. Then he realises the hairstyle probably adds to the illusion of height, for she has scrunched it up into a high bun, presumably so it doesn't get in the way whilst she is working.

The second thing he notices about her is her casual attire. She wears a pair of loose-fitting and faded dungarees, which are bespattered by paint and clay, a pair of blue moccasin slippers with a fleece lining, and a long, black, woollen cardigan. He notices she wears no jewellery or rings. Her features are sharp and her eyes appraising, although he thinks she looks tired, exhausted even. She exudes an air of despondency. Perhaps she is displeased with her finished piece of art? Perhaps she is displeased with him?

When she speaks her voice is surprisingly soft, and she is every bit as well spoken as Dr Goodman, although he detects a slight accent, something exotic that he cannot place. It sounds almost foreign.

'You play with a straight bat, but you need to keep your left elbow higher. And you are too static at the crease. Either take a big step forward to counter the swinging ball, or take a large step back to give you more time to play the spin and fast bowlers. And you need to bend your left leg more when you play the cover drive.'

He stares at her, half in amazement and half in admiration. He is utterly lost for words. A dissection of his batting prowess was the last thing he expected to hear from her. All he can think to say is: 'You know about cricket?'

She arches her eyebrows. 'Do you think women should only fix your teas and wash your whites?'

He was not aware that women even played cricket, and at his local club that is exactly what the women did: made the teas and washed the whites. He looked forward to the food the army of volunteer mothers supplied, although his own mother never ranked amongst their number; it was his favourite meal of the week. And when he opened the batting for his team, he tried to make sure he was still at the crease at the drinks interval. It is the only time he got to taste Robinson's barley water. He was shamefaced to admit that he hid away when it was time for the secretary to collect the match fees. To his astonishment, no one ever mentioned that he owed them money.

When he does not reply, she scoffs, and says, 'Well, we shall have none of that nonsense here. You will have heard of Donald Bradman?'

'"The Don". Yes, of course. My dad saw him bat at Colchester in 1948. He said he was the greatest batsman that ever lived, despite being an Australian.'

She looks unimpressed. 'You will rise above the casual racism of your father, Benedict, at least while you are under my roof. Is that understood? Perhaps the Don's record would have been less impressive if so many talented young men had not died in the wars. He may have faced sterner competition. Even so, he was clearly exceptional. Do you know how Bradman spent much of his youth?'

He shakes his head.

'He spent it alone, throwing a small ball against a wall and catching it. The ricochet was unpredictable. That is how he sharpened his reflexes and honed his hand–eye coordination. As from tomorrow, you will put away your imaginary games. Such things become habitual and are wont to unhinge us. If you must practise, then at least do so in a meaningful way. Now, tell me, how do you intend to make a living?'

He has no idea, and the uncertainty shows on his face. He imagined his aunt would look after him, at least for a while, at least until the situation with his father became clearer.

'What are you good at? Aside from cricket, what do you enjoy doing? You never know what interests and hobbies can be turned to a profit.'

He sighs and answers glumly, 'My teachers thought me "decidedly average" at everything.'

'Like Charles Darwin then,' she replies. 'As I recall, he proved his idiotic teachers wrong. I trust you have sufficient ambition to do the same.'

He supposes the comment is meant to be encouraging. 'My older brother is an apprentice welder and he is good at fixing things, but I am not so good with my hands. My woodwork teacher always complained he needed to carry out major surgery on anything I made.'

He has learnt that the self-deprecating comment usually invokes appreciative laughter, or a wry smile at the very least, but his aunt remains stony-faced. 'You are the product of one of Margaret Thatcher's comprehensive schools?'

He has no idea who Margaret Thatcher is, and again, the uncertainty shows on his face.

'She was the Minister for Education in the last Conservative government. She closed a record number of grammar schools and opened more comprehensives, which is rather ironic as they were a Labour Party initiative.

She also abolished the free school milk quota, which is a shame, as you look like you would have benefited from it. She is now the leader of the opposition. You were listening to a speech of hers on my radio last night.'

The hectoring woman with the chilling voice, he thinks.

'Did you sit the eleven plus exam?'

'Yes.'

'Did you pass it?'

'Yes and no. I was borderline but passed on appeal. It didn't matter anyway, Auntie; they closed the grammar school before I could go there.'

A look of pain crosses her face. 'You will call me Gail, Gail Miller; that is the name I am known by in the art world. You will never refer to me as your nan, gran, auntie, great-aunt or the "awful aunt".'

Once again, he looks astounded.

Her tone hardens and becomes severe. 'Oh yes, I know what the family calls me. Know this: I do not care. I do not care a fig what anyone thinks of me, is that understood?'

'Yes, Au… I mean Gail.' Somehow, it feels awkward and unnatural to pronounce her name. It is like calling his father 'Stan' instead of Dad. It is as if she wishes to deny they are related.

'And you should know that the radio is very dear to me. The set is an original Art Deco Bakelite. It was given to me as a present by a… a very close friend. It served me well during the war. I would have you leave it be. Do not adjust the dials again.'

'No, Au… of course not, Gail.' He almost chokes on the word.

She stares at him a while longer, and then nods slowly. She is unused to having people in her home, Dr Goodman aside, and she is not sure she will be able to adjust to it now. But she must; duty demands it, and she has always done her duty.

'I have few rules, Benedict, and, thankfully, you have already shown that you can comply with the most important: do not disturb me whilst I am working. I am neither your mother nor your keeper.'

No, thank God, he thinks to himself.

'You are free to leave whenever you wish, but whilst you are here you will earn your keep. Until we can find you paid employment, you will help out around the house. You can start by chopping more wood. There is an axe and chopping block behind the kennels, and a large pile of wood. Then you can fill up the coal scuttle and empty the ash from the range. Then you can take these bags of rubbish to the incinerator, which is at the bottom of the garden, and burn what you can. After that, I expect you to wash these pots and dishes, and sweep the floor. To be frank, I am surprised you have not shown more initiative. Do you expect to be waited on hand and foot? Can you not see what needs to be done? Do you need constant instruction? When I saw you had contributed nothing to the house, and that you left a precious book upon the floor and drank the last of my Camp coffee, and that you had eaten all the stew Dr Goodman had left for me, I wondered if you were as witless and selfish as your father.'

He bites his tongue. *What do you expect me to be?* he

thinks. *Cinderella, or a live-in maid? Is that why you invited me here, to be your dogsbody?*

'How do you know my father is witless and selfish? You've never wanted anything to do with our family.'

His words come out sharper than he intended, but he does not care. He dislikes her rudeness. Who the hell does she think she is? When have invited guests ever been expected to tidy up someone else's pigsty? He has spent enough of his life tidying up other people's mess. And it is not her place to criticise his father, whatever his faults. He had not come here uninvited; she had sent a letter. It had arrived out of the blue, the only letter he had ever received. She said to let her know the date and time of his arrival, and, if she wasn't able to come in person, her 'very good' friend Dr Goodman would collect him from the station. He had sent a reply, from Ireland, but now he sees just why she wanted him here.

He will show her how decisive he can be. He picks up his suitcase, which is where he left it, by the porch door, and makes to leave. He half expects her to call him back, but she lets him go. When he is halfway through the door she says:

'It is seven miles to the railway station. I wish you luck finding it. Take the cricket bat with you if you like. You can play more pretend games by yourself.'

He turns and stares at her. His look is full of anger and contempt. It seems to say: 'No, you keep it. Throw it on the fire, that's all it is fit for – firewood. I don't need anything from you. I don't want anything from you, not ever.'

He turns back around and strides out into the snow, making sure he slams the door shut behind him.

4

‘When a poor man came in sight’

By the time he makes it to the main road, the light is already fading. It has clouded over and the wind has picked up. The sky over the Malvern Hills looks ominous; a storm is brewing.

He tells himself he doesn’t care. He has an excellent memory for places, and once he has travelled a route once, he never forgets it. He will find his way. He throws his suitcase across his back and marches on. He thinks he might get a lift if he hitchhikes, but unfortunately there is no traffic. He can just make out a few tyre tracks in the road where a tractor has ploughed its way through the snow and he walks in the furrows. The road is tree-lined and hemmed in by hedgerows. They add to the gloomy feel. His feet are freezing and wet through. He wears freezer bags inside his socks, but even so, the melting snow finds its way through the holes in his shoes and through the bags too. He feels his resolve ebbing away. Even if he makes it to the railway station, he has no idea where to go. Despite the rage he feels, he wonders if he should turn back.

He is saved from making that decision by the three forgotten objects he finds in his duffle coat pockets. They were gifted him by Margaret the tea lady: a packet of sandwiches, a bobble hat and a pair of fingerless mittens. She said the hat and gloves were unclaimed items from lost property and so, 'he might as well have them', but he suspected she had knitted them herself. He puts them on and instantly feels warmer. He is famished and decides to eat one of the sandwiches. It is white bread smeared with cheap margarine and filled with a thin slice of processed cheese topped by a dab of rancid pickle. The sandwich has become frozen, and it sets his teeth on edge. He eats one half and saves the other for 'emergency rations'.

He walks on, humming to himself a few Christmas carols to keep his spirits up: 'Silent Night', 'In the Bleak Midwinter', 'Good King Wenceslas'. He thinks about the stories that were told within the family circle about his 'awful aunt'. Now he comes to think of it, little was ever substantiated; it was mostly unqualified aspersions and unkind rumours. The main source of gossip had been Silver-Sherry Nan. On the few occasions the family visited, he and his brothers would play Ludo with her, competing eagerly for the kitty of copper coins that the victor claimed; it seemed to them like a veritable fortune. Sometimes, she started early on the sherry and became quite tipsy. She would begin to talk wistfully about her late husband. 'What did Grandad do in the war?' they would ask, their mother sending them warning looks and discreetly shaking her head. Silver-Sherry Nan always gave the same answer: 'He died.'

Nothing more was forthcoming, and they were too polite to pry. But she would add that their 'awful aunt' had never wanted them to marry, that she tried to poison their relationship, that she was haughty and flighty, considering herself to be too good for them; that she was not patriotic and preferred the company of foreigners. She wanted nothing to do with their son and had not even attended his christening. She had taken herself off to live abroad with one of her 'fancy men'. She had not even attended her own brother's funeral. She was 'awful, truly awful'.

Eventually, after several more wearisome miles, he is relieved to see buildings, pavements and streetlights, and he knows he has made it to the edge of the town. He is just in time. It begins to snow heavily, a real blizzard, and the way becomes obscured.

*

'For heaven's sake, Gail, don't tell me you let the boy go, not in this weather? What were you thinking? He could die out there; conditions are atrocious.'

Dr Goodman finds it hard to hide his irritation. He puts down her latest sculpture without really studying it.

'Please don't lecture me, Cyril,' she replies, yawning. 'I am not in the mood for a sermon. And anyway, when did you become so soft-hearted? Tell me, what do you think of the piece? Be honest now.'

Petulantly, he picks the object up from the kitchen table and examines it once more, albeit perfunctorily. 'When I am ever untruthful?' he asks.

She does not answer.

'It is not your best work. It is derivative and you have presented pieces like this before: tortured and agonised angels falling from the heavens; angels at war with one another. It will sell, of course; wealthy Americans will lap it up, but it is not very original. It doesn't inspire me. Frankly, I find it insipid.'

She yawns again, and nods. 'I agree. I was thinking of taking the hammer to it. I feel I have lost my touch, Cyril. I no longer know what it is I am trying to do. I feel bereft of ideas. I never wanted my art to be constrained and placed into one box, one genre, as if that is all I could ever produce, if that was all I could ever be. So many artists have just one box we remember them by. But these days, I find I cannot break out of the box I have put myself in. I was thinking of going back to painting for a while.'

'Not more abstract twaddle?' he asks, looking up in alarm. 'You know that was never my cup of tea. *Sombre Welsh Hills* – a few black and red squiggles on a blank canvas; pretentious nonsense and you know it. Honestly, a child of three could have painted it. Or an elephant.'

She cannot be bothered to argue. In truth, they both know why she returns again and again to the image of fallen angels, why she cannot get such visions out of her mind, and why she finds comfort in moulding the clay the way she does. She replies, 'My abstract work was highly regarded. It won prizes, which is more than this sculpture will do.'

'You still harken after accolades?' he asks in surprise. 'Haven't you had enough adoration for one lifetime?'

'It is nice to have one's efforts appreciated, Cyril, and there is a bigger market for such work.'

He shakes his head in amazement; how can she be so wrapped up in her art when the boy is missing?

'And what about Benedict?' he asks.

'What about him?'

'Don't you have any sympathy for his plight?'

She yawns for a third time. She looks spent; her art is killing her. 'Naturally, but sympathy will not help him. He has a temper, but he needs to learn to stand and fight rather than run away. He is too sensitive, and too quick to take offence. Such a sensitive stem will not withstand the hard rains and bitter droughts of this world. No doubt he will sulk, like his father. From what little I know of the boy, he is supposed to be something of a genius, sharp-witted, and an actor capable of playing a part. That is, after all, why I invited him here. But then I heard that tale from his mother some years ago, and you know how little her word can be trusted.'

Cyril recalls the letter that arrived out of the blue eight years earlier. In it, Benedict's mother begged for a loan to help her through a 'tricky patch'. He recalls Gail's ire at receiving the plea. She disliked the chummy tone of the note, written as if she were a confidant and a best friend, rather than the 'obnoxious stranger' the family usually cast her as.

She laughs ironically. 'In her letter to me, the mother so extolled the virtues of her children I am frankly amazed they have risen to so little! Benedict has much to learn.'

'He is a boy, not yet seventeen,' replies Dr Goodman in exasperation.

He knows what she is thinking: when she was just two years older than Benedict is now she won a scholarship to study at Cambridge University, although women were not permitted to read for degrees. That is where she had first met Cyril, and, like him, she had been recruited by the intelligence services. At a young age, she had gone to war; she has been at war ever since. They both have.

'He is a boy that lives too much in his own world. I am not sure he will be able to complete the task.'

He shrugs his shoulders. 'You will never know if you abandon him now.'

*

The railway station is deserted. A thick cover of snow blankets the roof, the platform and the tracks, and through the glow of the yellow streetlamp, he can see that great flakes continue to drift from the sky. The snow on the rails is undisturbed; there has not been a train in some while. He is disappointed to find that the tearooms and waiting rooms are closed up and the lights extinguished, but he is relieved to find that the stationmaster is absent. There is not another soul about. The whole town seems to be shut up and wrapped in an eerie silence.

Perhaps the whole world is on strike? thinks Benedict.

The station clock shows it is 7.15pm.

There is nothing for it, he will have to wait until the morning. It will not be the first time he has spent the night in a railway station.

He finds a bench beneath the eaves of the roof. It offers a little shelter from the wind and the snow. He unpacks his nylon sleeping bag. It is tatty and lightweight, but it gives the illusion of warmth. He puts on dry socks and zips himself into the bag, like an insect in a cocoon, and lies down on the bench.

It is not long before the cold begins to bite and his teeth begin to chatter. He imagines the forthcoming headlines graphically displayed at the newspaper kiosk:

'Unknown boy found frozen to death on Great Malvern station; awful aunt to blame.'

It is no good, he thinks, he will have to move. With great effort, imagining himself to be Houdini, he extracts himself from the sleeping bag. He walks swiftly to the end of the platform and then runs back again. He repeats the exercise five times, until some colour returns to his cheeks and he begins to feel warm.

He notes the time; it is only 7.45pm. Time has decelerated. The snow continues to fall.

He has a long and uncomfortable night ahead of him. *Maybe I should explore the town*, he thinks. *Perhaps there is a more sheltered spot.*

For the next two hours he wanders around aimlessly. He becomes disconsolate. Everywhere is closed and there is hardly anyone about. The only people he sees are two drunks exiting a pub, arm in arm, and singing 'Merry

Xmas Everybody' loudly, and very badly, and an angry taxi driver whose car has skidded into a stationary vehicle.

Eventually, he finds himself standing outside the Conservative Club. The lights are on, but it does not look inviting. He wonders if Dr Goodman is inside. He hurries on past.

He spends a few moments standing beneath the unnatural and threatening blue lamp of the police station. He recalls a travel journal one of his teachers insisted they read about a young man, barely eighteen, who walked from England to Constantinople. On his travels through pre-war Germany, he often spent the night sleeping in a police station. Benedict wonders if the British police would be as friendly and accommodating to a vagrant. Before he risks entry, he studies the noticeboard nailed to an external wall, looking for a photograph of any of the constables. There is a poster of a well-dressed man wearing a fedora. He looks old and tired. The poster reads: 'DO YOU KNOW THIS MAN?' It says he suffers from amnesia. He was found on Bristol railway station, with no identification. There is a number to contact. Benedict wonders if anyone would be able to identify the man from such a grainy black and white image. The poster must be quite old, he thinks, for it seems faded. Next to the poster are mugshots of the police station's constables: PCs Barnes, Hackett and Stoneman. They are doppelgangers for the railway stationmaster. Benedict decides to move on.

He tries the doors of two churches, but they are both locked. *Are the vicars on strike too? And the priests?* he wonders. *What would Nutcase-Nutty Nan say to that?*

He thinks about his maternal nan and her strong religious faith. Her husband had also died in the war. He was a fireman, killed during the Blitz. She had raised her daughter alone. Later in life, long after her daughter had left home, she remarried and moved with her husband to Ballycastle, in Northern Ireland. There, despite their advancing years, they had run an orphanage. They seemed genuinely happy together, although his mother took every opportunity to point out the faults and failings of Nan's new husband.

Benedict had never considered his nan to be nutty, not really. She was just extrovert and scatterbrained, apt to forget names and dates and events. She had a penchant for wearing flamboyant clothes and costume jewellery, which he and his brothers ridiculed in private, and found embarrassing in public, but they forgave her that, for she was always well intentioned and kind-hearted. Of all their relatives, they looked forward to seeing Nutcase-Nutty Nan the most, not least because their mother would be on her best behaviour.

He had recently travelled to Ireland to visit his nan, hoping he might stay a while. But he found her moribund. She sat in a high-back chair in her tiny, cluttered sitting room, the life draining out of her, whilst the air filled with cigarette smoke, children played noisily outside, and her husband, unable to sit and watch her die, excused himself and disappeared 'for a walk'.

She did not seem to recognise Benedict, and her greeting was unusually cold. He supposed his mother had told her tall tales about him. Not knowing what else to say, he had asked, 'How are you, Nan?'

'Mustn't grumble,' she replied, before subsiding into a coughing fit.

Mustn't grumble, he thinks. *A tumour is killing her, she is in great pain, she must be angry with the world, and she will never see her beloved orphans grow up, but all she can say is 'mustn't grumble'.* He wonders if all her generation share a similar stoicism. He wonders why his own mother does nothing *but* grumble.

He had not stayed long, just long enough to finish a cup of tea and eat a piece of stale fruit cake. He would not invade upon their grief or stay in the house of the dying.

*

There is nothing for it. He makes his way back to the railway station. It is 9.50pm by the time he arrives. It has finally stopped snowing.

There is someone sitting on his bench, sipping coffee from the white plastic lid of a tartan vacuum flask. He is wearing an expensive overcoat, the collar turned up, snow boots, leather gloves and a Russian-style furry hat. It takes him a moment to recognise Dr Goodman.

'Good to see you, old boy,' he says by way of cheerful greeting. 'Here, drink some of this.'

He offers him the cup. Benedict hesitates before he takes it. His natural instinct is to trust the man, but he is not sure he wants to be drawn back into his aunt's world. 'What do you want from me?'

The question seems to surprise him. 'I don't want anything from you. I came to offer you a lift back to your aunt's. Whether you accept or not is entirely up to you. I'm afraid there won't be any trains tonight; it is the wrong type of snow. Apparently, the points are all frozen. Maybe try again tomorrow?'

He takes the cup. The coffee is milky and warming and tastes delicious.

'Benedict,' says Dr Goodman, adopting a serious tone, 'I do not doubt your fortitude, but I am not sure you will survive a night on this platform. It feels colder than a Moscow winter. Won't you come back with me to your aunt's?'

He sighs. 'I don't know. My aunt is… awful.'

He nods, as if in sympathy. 'Gail can be spiky, I grant you, especially when she is tired, but perhaps you two just got off on the wrong foot. What you have to understand is that she has never had children of her own. She is not used to dealing with young men such as yourself. There are ways to ask for things, aren't there? I am sure you don't really mind doing a few chores around the house to help out now and again, do you? It is only natural that we want to be helpful when we stay with someone, isn't it?'

'What did her last slave die of, exhaustion?'

Dr Goodman laughs aloud. 'Very droll, Benedict, very droll. It won't be like that, old boy, trust me. You'll have plenty of free time to do as you please, you'll have food in your belly and a roof over your head, and, if you are wise, there is a heck of a lot you could learn from your aunt.'

The prospect of learning anything from his aunt had not occurred to him. 'What? What can I learn from her?'

Dr Goodman speaks with an urgency and seriousness he has not heard before. 'She may look ancient to you,

Benedict, as I am sure I do, but please don't write us off because of that. Gail has great skills and vast knowledge.'

'And what about you? I don't even know what you do. Are you retired?'

'Yes and no. I still do a little freelance work, mostly working with computers and making my own small contribution to the space race.'

'I've read about computers. They are clever.'

Dr Goodman laughs again. 'Your aunt doesn't think so. She says they are easily fooled; that they have no active memory, only a working memory. She says they cannot create, they can only replicate what a clever programmer tells them to.'

It is Benedict's turn to look surprised. 'I am amazed she has even heard of computers. We only studied them in the last year at school.'

'My boy, she was using computers before you were born.'

He is startled; perhaps he has underestimated his aunt.

'And do you agree with her? Are computers stupid and easily fooled?'

He shrugs his shoulders. 'Yes and no. It partly depends on the cleverness of the programmer. We are experimenting with building more memory by finding ways to connect individual computers together. We are trying to build a hive mind if you will; they will get smarter the more memory we create. But to replicate the human brain they will have to learn how to make use of that memory, how to process the information at an emotional and intellectual level before they make choices, but that kind of machine learning seems like an impossible task at this juncture. As for now, they are little more than a speedy calculating tool and a limited memory box. There is no machine on earth more complicated than the living machine inside your head, Benedict, and your aunt's brain is more complicated than most.'

He laughs aloud at his own witticism.

'Dr Goodman,' he says, a thought suddenly occurring to him, 'could I come and work for you?'

He looks apologetic, sad even to have to dampen the boy's enthusiasm. 'I am sorry, Benedict, but the work I do is… well… erm… secretive stuff.' He taps his index finger against the side of his nose to emphasise the point. 'I am not allowed to talk about it.'

He sees the disconsolate look on his face.

'But chin up, old boy, I am sure between me and your aunt we can find you some useful work to do.'

5

The Memory Box

An instruction to my solicitors, Anderson, Morgan and Pratt, 8th June 1944:

> Sirs,
> I trust this message reaches you. Circumstances dictate I send it with all haste from an undisclosed airfield in southern England. If you do not hear from me before the New Year, then assume that I have fallen; execute my Will as previously arranged. The enclosed letter is sealed. It is for the attention of my son, Stanley, for him and him alone, but I hereby give instruction that he is forbidden to open it until his eighteenth birthday.
> Captain Kenneth B.B. Harrison, DSO

*

From the Exequatur to Raymond of Saint-Emilion: London, 7 June 1944, 06:00 hours

A coded message follows.
The vehicle has the green light but the engine leaks badly. Expect The Angel 02:00 hrs tonight at the usual drop. Be advised: he may be unfaithful to his wife. Adultery runs in the family. Proceed with caution: eliminate waste as necessary. Put Françoise in a box and bury her. Leave no trace; no record. Be advised: the Angel is sympathetic to the Bear; he sees red. He was a Cambridge recruit.

*

A coded message from Françoise to the Exequatur: Saint-Emilion, 8 June 1944, 04:00 hours

Cover blown. Request immediate extraction. They are dead, all dead. Ghosts everywhere. They will come for me soon. For the love of God, get me out.

*

A letter to Stanley Harrison Esq, to be delivered at the request of his late father by the solicitors' firm of Anderson, Morgan and Pratt.

Dear Stanley,
Son, if you are reading this then happy eighteenth

birthday. By my calculations, it should be 12th April 1952. I am sorry I could not be with you. I am sorry I could not see you grow to manhood. I never wished to leave you, but duty demanded it.

I do not have much time and I fear I am betrayed. Please forgive my brevity. There are things I would have you know.

A solicitor should have handed you this letter, along with a strong box. The key to the lock is attached to the reverse of the envelope. Everything you need to know about me is inside the box. It has been sitting in the vault of a bank ever since I deposited it there two weeks ago.

People are seldom what they seem, Son; I hope that is a lesson you have already learnt. Be guarded with strangers. I do not say 'trust no one' – that would make life impossible – but choose your allies wisely.

I am waiting for an aeroplane to fly me to France. It is 8th June 1944. Do you know the significance of that date, Son? It is D-Day plus two. Is D-Day a European-wide day of celebration? I do hope it is. Deliverance Day; the invasion of Europe; the Normandy landings – the day we began to push Hitler back. We have prayed for it for so long – an end to war.

But tonight, I am not flying to Normandy. I am part of another operation entirely, but one that, should it succeed, might end the war all the sooner. The plan is to open up another front; to invade France along its Atlantic coast. Bordeaux is a strategic port; much of Germany's supplies are shipped through it. If we can cut it off, and take control of the Bay of Biscay, then we will cripple the German war machine. Then, in France, we can squeeze them along two fronts at once and I believe they will crack. It will then be a race for Berlin, a race between the Eagle and the Bear; between the West and the East. I am to co-ordinate the Resistance forces in the Bordeaux area. We shall sabotage key installations and railway lines. And then will follow the paratrooper drops and the naval assaults, and before long, the arrival of an invasion fleet. It is work I am familiar with. After all, my life has been one of deception. I have been fighting fascism since 1935.

It sounds so simple, doesn't it, Son, but in reality, the plans are elaborate, and I am privy to only a small part of the details. The chain of command is obscure. My orders come from someone called the 'Exequatur'; I have no idea who they are. Your aunt knows far more than me. Ask her; ask her about what we did during the war. Ask her about what we did in Germany, Spain and Italy before the war even began. Europe will not be liberated without great sacrifice, never forget that, Stanley: freedom has a price, but the world I inhabit is dark and murky and cynical; sometimes I struggle to see the light.

I am fearful. Perhaps my fear is increased because we can now see an end to war, and we delude ourselves we might survive it; to fall now would seem a doubly cruel blow. But more than that, I fear betrayal. There are so many factions competing for the spoils. Mine is a world of duplicity and deception.

The British bulldog once straddled the world, but it is clear to anyone but a fool that he has grown old, and slow and tired. He has been in the ring too often. His body rebels against him, his cupboard is bare and his teeth are blunt. He still has some dignity, but the new world belongs to other animals.

The rats will endure, of course, they always do, but the real fight now is between the Eagle and the Bear. Theirs has always been an uneasy pact; now the beginning of the end is in sight, they will turn on each other. That is what I fear: I fear that I am nothing but an insignificant pawn caught in a much, much bigger game; a power struggle between the two likely victors. As you know, pawns are often sacrificed.

Alas, I must go now, Son; the aeroplane has landed. It is a Dakota. It is not really a war machine. In truth, it is little more than a stripped-down passenger plane; just one more deception in a world of deceit.

There is so much I want to say to you; so much you need to know, but I have no time.

If the content of the box does not give you the answers you seek, then ask your aunt; if she survives the war, ask your aunt about me. Ask her about the Angel of Saint-Emilion.

Your loving father, always,

B.B.

6

Decoration and Disguise

The farmhouse at Wellend, Great Malvern, January 1979

He has never had a bedroom of his own. He has never enjoyed that much privacy. Benedict is surprised when his aunt unlocks one of the upstairs doors and says, 'This will be your room, for now.'

To him, the room appears large and bright. He fears he will be lost in it. The ceiling is high, the plaster cracked, the paint fading, and a naked lightbulb hangs from the central ceiling mount. The velvet drapes have been tied back, and through the warped sash windows he can see the bedroom overlooks the kennels and outbuildings. He can see the Malvern Hills in the distance, the snow melting fast. It is not raining, but beads of water form on the inside of the windows and run in intricate rills, pooling on the window sill. As in every other room he has been in, there is considerable condensation and liberal patches of black mould on the walls.

This is the oak room, he thinks. Every object in the room is seemingly made from oak: the single bed frame and headboard, the chest of drawers, the wardrobe and even the lamp stand on the bedside table. There is not a single even surface in the room; everything slopes. The plaster on the walls was once painted magnolia, but the paint is flaky and peeling. There are no pictures on the walls, but there is a large oval-shaped mirror, discoloured by black spots.

He sits down carefully on the edge of the bed. He can feel the springs creak as he sinks into the mattress, but it is a lot more comfortable than his bunk bed ever was. It has been made up with clean white sheets, a heavy quilt and a colourful counterpane, and numerous rough blankets have been folded, army fashion, and left at the foot of the bed. There are even two pillows. He is not used to sleeping with pillows; it feels… luxurious.

'How would you like this room to look?' asks his aunt.

'How do you mean?'

She sighs, as if impatient to be back at her work. 'If this is to be your room then you must decorate it. You must decide how it should look. It should reflect your taste. This is your space to command.'

He has no idea what his taste is. He has never decorated anything in his life. He has never been in a position to make expensive choices like that.

'Perhaps you would like to experiment with designs,' she says, making an effort to encourage him, as Dr Goodman suggested. 'There are rolls of wallpaper and pots of paints in the outbuilding where you discovered the cricket bat. Help yourself to whatever takes your fancy. The choice is yours. You can look through some of the magazines in the kitchen; they might give you ideas.'

He has never had to make such choices. In their house, they could ill-afford mistakes. They did not have the luxury of 'experimenting'.

'I would like a rug,' he says, looking at the bare floorboards and fearing splinters in his bare feet, 'and I would like to get rid of that mirror.'

'You do not like looking at yourself?' she asks half seriously.

He looks away. 'No. No, I do not.'

'Why on earth not?' she asks, her face showing bemusement.

'I don't know. I just don't.'

She is silent for a moment, and he knows she is staring at him, judging him and finding his faults, just like his mother and father used to do. She will not let him have his own way. The appearance of choice is always an illusion. In reality, she will want the room to be exactly as she chooses.

He is surprised when she says, 'Very well, the mirror will go, and tomorrow we shall take a trip into Worcester and shop around for a rug, one that you like. What else, Benedict? What else does the room need?'

He has never been encouraged to make choices. It scares him.

'A lampshade and some pictures to hang on the walls,' he replies tentatively, not knowing the limits of what he can ask for.

'What kind of pictures?'

He doesn't want to say. He would like a photograph of his brothers, but he does not have one. There are no recent pictures of them; they could never afford to purchase the annual school photographs, not at the inflated prices they charged, and the family did not own a camera. His mother had a treasured photograph album, well thumbed, but she took it with her when she left. He had seen it once, when Silver-Sherry Nan was reminiscing and wistfully going through it. There was an old black and white photograph of a wedding in an elaborate card frame. He was surprised to find out it was his parents. They never talked about their wedding day. And he was even more surprised to see that his mother looked so different. She wasn't overweight. She was healthy, and smiling. That was not what she was like now. He only saw her smile when they had company.

'Wasn't she pretty, your mother,' said Silver-Sherry Nan, shaking her head sadly for all that had been lost. 'A most handsome couple.'

He did not want to admit it. It was not how he saw them.

*

When he does not answer her question, his aunt says, 'Do you know anything about art? Perhaps there are some artists' works you would like to hang on the walls?'

He likes her work, the little he has seen of it. When Dr Goodman had finally managed to navigate the Land Rover through the snow and return him to her house, they found that Gail had gone to bed, taking the dogs with her.

She had left a note on the kitchen table: '*We shall speak tomorrow. Eat the soup.*'

She had made French onion soup and fresh rustic bread. It was delicious. 'She is a far better cook than me,' said Dr Goodman, not from any sense of false modesty. 'It is a shame she does not cook more often, but her work, you know, it tends to consume her.'

As Benedict sat eating, he had noticed the new sculpture, abandoned on the table. It had intrigued him. It showed a twisted figure, seemingly hanging from a tree. The figure had wings, like an angel, but if that is what it was meant to be, it was the strangest angel he had ever seen. It was half-human, half-demon. One half of the face was beautiful and pure, like a Madonna. But the other half was tortured, full of venom and spite, and hideous. It was as if one being were metamorphosing into the other. The creature had two tongues, both sticking out, and one of them was forked, like a serpent. One foot had been replaced by a cloven hoof, and there was a bullet hole in the creature's head. A spider crawled out of it. One half of the sculpture looked ghastly and frightening, like a carving you might see on an ancient church pew, but the other half was sublime, even if the angel looked mournful, as if he had imbibed all the sadness in the world.

'What do you make of that?' asked Dr Goodman, seeing that the work of art had caught his attention.

'I like it.'

'Really, old boy, and why is that?'

'I don't know. I tend to like sad things. I find them comforting. I can't explain why.'

Dr Goodman did not dismiss his comments or seek to belittle them, not like his teachers would have done, not like his father.

'If you had to name the piece, what would you call it?'

The question surprised him, but, unbidden, a word sprang instantly to his mind: 'betrayal'.

*

'I don't know many artists,' he replies, answering his aunt's question honestly, if sheepishly.

'Did your parents not have paintings on their walls? Did they never take you to the London museums and galleries?'

Again, the implied criticism, this time of both of his parents. His temper begins to rise and his face flushes red.

'No, we never visited galleries. If you must know, we had three prints in the living room. My dad knew a lot about them.'

That does not surprise me, thinks Gail. *He considered himself an expert on everything*. But for once she holds her tongue. 'And what were they, can you recall?'

Of course he can, he has an excellent memory. '*The Hay Wain*, by John Constable, and two by Joseph Turner: *The Fighting Temeraire* and *Rain, Steam and Speed*. The steam one was Dad's favourite.'

Your father the romantic, who would have thought it, she muses. He adorned his walls with three of the most popular prints to be found in the country. *The Hay Wain* must hang in at least a fifth of the living rooms of England.

She does not consider herself to be a snob, but she laments the general public's lack of desire to explore art more widely. 'And what did *you* think of the prints?'

He shrugs his shoulders. 'I never gave them much thought. They were just there, in the background, covering the walls. The Constable was boring. Dad said it was a real place in Essex, and he had visited it once, and it still looked the same. But it always struck me as dull and sterile.'

She wishes he would elaborate. 'Why do you say that?'

He shrugs his shoulders for the second time, as if he cannot be bothered to explain. 'It was all a bit twee and rosy. For something that appeared to be so realistic, it seemed devoid of life. I preferred Turner's works, especially when I found out what they were about – the ghost ship *Temeraire*, the passing of an age; the way new technology transforms the world, blurring all the edges. I found *Rain, Steam and Speed* nostalgic; it reminded me of being on a steam train with Dad. I liked its gloomy atmosphere.'

She is surprised by his answer; she had not expected insight. And it is the first time he has spoken at length, and as he grows in confidence, he becomes more articulate. Perhaps she had been too quick to dismiss him. An idea occurs to her, but she decides to keep it to herself, for now. There are more immediate concerns.

'When we are in Worcester tomorrow, we shall need to purchase you a new wardrobe.'

He looks at the oak furniture. 'What's wrong with that one?' he asks.

For the first time since he met her, his aunt laughs aloud. 'No, I meant you need new clothes and new footwear. When we are abroad, we are judged by how we dress, Benedict, never forget that.'

'I have never been abroad,' he says mournfully. 'I haven't got a passport.'

'No, I didn't mean that… Oh, it doesn't matter. Remember this: even if you are poor you can give the illusion of wealth if you choose your wardrobe carefully. And that will open doors for you. I will ask Dr Goodman to accompany us; he will be better able to advise you. And perhaps you can visit a hairdresser, too.'

'Is Dr Goodman poor?' he asks, recalling his dapper dress. He had assumed he was wealthy, but perhaps it was a deception.

She laughs again. He thinks the look suits her.

'Good grief, no, but it is not considered polite to talk about such things. He ran his own aviation business, after the war. He was a pilot. He would still fly if he could. And his research has always had a certain… value.'

Benedict looks forlorn. 'I know as much about clothes as I do about art – nothing. The only new clothes we ever had in our house came out of a Littlewoods catalogue and were chosen by my mother. They were bought on credit. I think my dad is still supposed to be making payments for them.'

Making payments had always been a struggle for the family. They had saved the green Co-op stamps like they were gold dust, exchanging them for food. They had outcompeted the tramps, wandering the streets and parks collecting discarded glass bottles and recycling them for a few pence each. In November, they had made a Guy and hawked it around the houses, asking for a 'penny'. At Christmas time, they had tried carol singing. The family had a 'tab' at the local corner shop. Their mother never quite managed to settle it in full. On Thursday payday, their father would offer what he could. He sat in the kitchen while his wife berated him, wanting to know what had happened to the contents of his pay packet. 'How do you expect me to manage on this?' she would wail, bursting into tears. He said nothing. The next day, breathing heavily and looking flushed, she would present herself at the corner shop and pay off part of the debt. She always made excuses. Perhaps that is where her talent for telling tall stories began.

The tab never seemed to diminish, and more and more was purchased on credit. Final reminders for unpaid bills arrived almost daily. Two men came to repossess the television. The family hid behind the sofa, pretending they were not in. It was not the first time they had hidden from such men. But they forced their way through the front door and took the set anyway, their mother following them down the street, crying and making quite a scene, and shouting out how she had 'paid the bloody bill'. It was a lie, but Benedict had not known that then and he had felt sorry for her, and he had hated those men. 'Bailiff' became a dirty word.

More repossessions followed. He was sent to the corner shop almost daily, his mother visiting it less and less often in person. Young though he was, he knew why. He also felt the shame of asking for things on credit. 'Get half a pound of streaky bacon, a quarter ounce of Old Holborn pipe tobacco and ten No 6 tip cigarettes. Put it on the tab.' It was almost as bad as being sent to a neighbour to ask for 'a fiver' to see them through to the end of the week.

After his mother had left, the tab escalated. It was left to Benedict to cook for his father and elder brother, because, by his own admission, his father could not so much as 'boil an egg'. They lived mostly on boil-in-the-bag cod in parsley sauce, chips and peas, or some variant on that theme. The chip pan had lost a handle and was dangerous to use. After each outing, the lard was left to solidify inside the pan. When he came to use it again, it was like the smooth surface of the lard had been transformed into a fossilised dinosaur trackway. Benedict would scrape away the mouse droppings and trails of tiny feet that were evident.

The first time their father went to pay the tab, it had not been settled for a month or two. He was outraged to find it tallied to the best part of his weekly wage. He went berserk. When he got home he accused the shopkeeper of being a crook, and forbade anyone from ever shopping there again. A furious argument had followed when he discovered it was the elder brother's fault. He had been adding his own 'luxury' items to the tab. It was one more tiresome row in a lifetime of rows, but this one ended with his father kicking his brother out of the house there and then.

Benedict had not seen him since.

*

'Gail,' he asks, still finding the use of her first name awkward, and feeling reticent to ask for anything more, 'what I would really like is a bookshelf and a few books to read. And perhaps a picture of Donald Bradman to decorate the wall.'

7

Patient X

The Bristol University Hospital, summer 1978

'What have you been up to, Harriet?' says a nurse teasingly as they pass each other in the hospital corridor. 'There are two rather good-looking bobbies on your trail. I've left them in your office.'

'The police are after me?' She looks startled and hurries off in the opposite direction down the corridor.

'No sense of humour, that one,' says the nurse to a colleague, and they giggle like school children.

*

'Hello, I am Dr Marks,' says Harriet as she enters her office.

The two policemen look relieved to see her.

'Dr Marks, we have a patient for you,' says the senior officer, pointing to an elderly man sitting at her table.

The man does not look up, nor does he introduce himself.

The junior officer says, 'This... gentleman was found wandering along the railway track at Bristol station yesterday morning. He is suffering from amnesia. He doesn't seem to know what time of day it is.'

'He's on another planet,' agrees his colleague.

'We think he might have been assaulted. He has a nasty gash on his head and... other wounds... His wallet and watch are missing. He has no ID on him, so we have no idea who he is. We understand you are an expert in treating such cases.'

Dr Marks raises her eyebrows. 'Let me examine him.'

As she approaches the man, he speaks for the first time: 'The world is full of angels and demons, but how do you tell them apart? We must make sacrifices; the winning of the game demands it.'

The senior policeman rolls his eyes as if to say, 'Here we go again.' He lets his junior colleague speak for them both.

'We've exhausted the usual lines of inquiry – the care homes, the hospitals, missing persons – and his fingerprints have so far drawn a blank. We have no idea who he is. His accent sounds a bit foreign.'

'Where are his clothes?' asks Dr Marks, examining the patient's head.

'We had to issue him a prison outfit,' says the senior policeman, stifling a yawn. 'I'm afraid his clothes were covered in blood and his trousers soiled. Curious thing, he had "left" and "right" written inside his shoes, and "V.C." stitched into his jacket.'

'Angels and demons,' says the man, 'angels and demons.' He repeats it over and over, becoming quite agitated.

'Now then, sir,' says the senior policeman, raising his voice, 'let's just calm down, shall we?'

'The head wound is nasty; there could be concussion,' reports Dr Marks, after completing her examination. She beckons the two policemen to the corner of the room for a private consultation.

'The wound is unlikely to have caused amnesia. I am sorry to say, but I think this man has dementia, and it is quite advanced.'

'The poor sod,' whispers the junior policeman sympathetically.

'Right,' says the senior policeman, looking relieved, 'then we can leave him in your care?'

She nods. 'Yes, but you will need to put out an alert; we need to find relatives or friends, people who know this man. There will need to be something on the radio and television, and in the newspapers.'

'Leave it to me,' says the junior policeman. 'Let's call him Patient X, for now.'

As they make to leave, she whispers, 'You do realise Patient X has had extensive plastic surgery in the past; the face he shows the world is not his real face.'

8

The Ambassadors

London, March 1979

Benedict stops and listens to a man busking in a London Underground station. He sings a protest song. He sings it loudly and with passion. Benedict envies him his talent and wishes he could play the guitar and sing that loudly and with such conviction; then his voice might be heard and he could earn his keep. He wishes he had a penny to give the busker.

He has still not found paid employment, and strangely, his aunt has not complained about it, but the lack of work and the economic freedom he imagines it will bring weigh heavily on his mind. He supposes he has made himself useful enough around the house, but he despises his dependency on others.

Despite it being eleven o'clock in the morning, the underground train to Leicester Square is crammed full. There is standing room only. He clings to a tether hanging from the ceiling, holding himself rigid, trying not to bump into his aunt or Dr Goodman or any other passenger. The train is airless and noisy, and it has rendered everyone mute. He is thankful; it suits his temperament and his mood. As they rattle through a dark tunnel, he looks out of the window, but there is nothing to see. He wonders why they bother to have windows at all, unless it is to show people their own reflections. He catches other passengers taking furtive glances at themselves, as if they were consumed by vanity. He studies his own reflection; he thinks he looks forlorn, despite the new wardrobe and haircut. *Perhaps it takes more than a pair of suede boots, corduroy trousers, an Aran sweater and a checked shirt to hide our true nature.*

He has always looked glum, he thinks. Strangers would often say to him, 'Cheer up, it might never happen!' and laugh as they walked past. Today his sadness has a definite cause. It is his seventeenth birthday. He got up early to await the postman, but he received no cards and no presents, not one single happy birthday wish.

He wanted to be alone with his self-pity; he wanted to sulk, but to compound matters, his aunt had insisted he accompany her and 'Cyril' on a 'mystery outing to London'. They had taken the early morning train from Great Malvern to Paddington.

In honour of the trip, he had been obliged to take a bath. His aunt took one every day. That seemed luxurious to him, and a waste of water. In his house, there was only hot water if you boiled the kettle, and he had washed in the kitchen sink. But now his aunt insisted on a regime of regular ablutions, and he was told to make use of her expensive soaps and shampoos. He had even tried conditioner for his hair. He read the instructions on the bottle carefully before, with some apprehension, applying it to his scalp. She had lent him her nail clippers and he accidentally cut his nails to the quick. She bought him a toothbrush, and the first time he used it, his gums bled. For the outing, he was obliged to adorn his 'Sunday best', as Dr Goodman called it. 'Fashion is transient,' he had said, during their shopping trip to Worcester. 'Flares and kipper ties… they won't last. People will look back and say, "Good God, whatever was I thinking?", whereas good-quality clothing is timeless.'

He surreptitiously studies his aunt. She has undergone a considerable metamorphosis, as his mother would often do, at least in terms of her mood, whenever they had company. The casual work clothes have been replaced by expensive and elegant attire: a fashionable twin set and pleated skirt. She wears her hair down, uses subtle makeup and adorns a silver chain with a delicate pendant. Everything about her speaks of wealth and class, but more than that, she carries herself with such confidence, and such an air of entitlement, that in Benedict's eyes, she exudes supreme arrogance. It is the look he always associates with rich people. He finds it intimidating.

They alight at Leicester Square and make their way to Trafalgar Square. Despite being a Londoner, Benedict finds himself following his aunt, who strides forward purposefully, as he does not know this part of the city at all. They make their way to the National Gallery.

'Benedict,' says his aunt as they enter the building, 'I wanted you to see the permanent collection of artworks housed here. You will find your Constable and Turner; you can study the originals if you like. But I advise you not to spend too long on them. I want you to explore other galleries and find works of art that *you* admire. Take your time, but do not overthink your reaction to each piece. Never look at the titles until you have studied the work for a while. When you are ready, come and find us. We shall be in the square. Wait for us beneath Nelson's Column if we are not back by the time you have finished. We are meeting an old acquaintance nearby on a matter of business. It shouldn't take more than a couple of hours. Off you go now.'

His reaction is not what she expected. There is no enthusiasm, just a forlorn look. She had imagined he would welcome the outing and the chance to explore the famous galleries.

'What is wrong?' she asks, somewhat irked by his lack of gratitude. She had thought of this trip back in January, when they had first discussed his tastes in art.

Once more, the familiar shrug of the shoulders, the downcast eyes and the lugubrious look. 'Nothing,' he replies, without conviction.

She raises her eyebrows and sighs. She hands him a few coins from her purse. 'Here, buy yourself something from the café or shop. We won't be long, I promise.'

He takes the coins reluctantly.

'Enjoy yourself, old boy,' says Dr Goodman, with his usual joie de vivre and, trying to lift his spirits, 'This afternoon, we can visit any part of London you like.'

His aunt looks momentarily surprised by this revelation, but she quickly regains her composure and nods in agreement.

What can he say? He would like to go home, to his father's house, but he knows he can't. And anyway, his two frumpy companions would stand out like a sore thumb in that part of town. It would be embarrassing.

'It's alright,' he says, 'you don't have to do anything for me.'

He turns his back on them and mooches off towards the nearest gallery, not really caring where he is going, but just wanting to be alone and out of sight. He knows they are staring after him.

'And what do you suppose is up with him now?' says his aunt, shaking her head in disbelief. 'I told you he could sulk. I thought he would enjoy the National Gallery.'

Dr Goodman smiles sagely. 'Gail, old gal, you forget what it is like to be his age.'

She scowls. 'Will you please refrain from using that ridiculous expression. I am not that "old" and I am not a "gal". You know how incomplete his education is. He knows nothing of English grammar – have you seen his spelling and his handwriting? He cannot speak a foreign language, he has no Latin, his history is bitty, and his knowledge of culture, commerce, politics and religion, and a host of other subjects, is almost non-existent. He has no understanding of rhetoric and can barely articulate a sentence. How can anyone prosper on a fare like he was served at school? He should be more appreciative of my efforts.'

His look changes in an instant. Gone is the affable air of conviviality. His face hardens.

'Have it your own way, but I think you presume too much. This journalist we are meeting, do you know what he wants?'

'Of course; he wants to know about Cambridge. And he will want a hard drink, despite the early hour, journalists always do.'

'And what will you tell him?'

She laughs derisively. 'I will tell him what he wants to hear, provided he helps us in return. He has contacts at the American Embassy.'

*

It does not take Benedict long to realise that there are more artworks he dislikes than he likes – a good deal more. *It is like music*, he thinks, *people always claim they have eclectic tastes, but in reality, they can tolerate a very narrow range of sounds.*

He has no time at all for the religious depictions. Their constant wallowing in suffering and sacrifice leaves him cold, or he is simply baffled by the subject matter, not knowing the Bible well enough to appreciate the narrative. Many of the paintings are brutal, with the themes of beheading and crucifixion writ large, or they are about adoration, with ridiculous chubby cherubs floating about. He finds them tiresome.

He passes by the oversized paintings depicting Greek myths with little more than a casual glance. He knows none of the stories, and the actions of the gods seem cruel and vile. *Why would anyone want to glorify such barbarity?* he thinks. *Why would you want to hang such things on your wall?*

In each gallery, the unwelcoming uniformed attendants stare at him with suspicion and hostility, as if he were an intruder, and their eyes follow him closely around the room. There are guided tours in progress, mostly being delivered in foreign languages by listless instructors to bored-looking groups of students, their teachers scowling at the disruptive ones and sending them warning looks. The benches are taken up by unhappy and unhealthy-looking people with pallid complexions – 'London skin' as Benedict calls it – who seem to care naught for the art and who are determined never to relinquish their seats, and there is usually at least one well-spoken person talking overly loudly and expounding their wisdom about some artwork or other.

Some people just like the sound of their own voice, he thinks. *Pompous bags of hot air. Why can't people be quiet? Why do they have to make so much noise all the time? What arrogance makes them think other people want to hear what they have to say?*

Feeling profoundly bored and dispirited, he wanders aimlessly, his hands cast deeply into his pockets and his shoulders slouched, checking the clock from time to time to see if he can leave yet.

By chance, he happens across a gallery containing more recent works of art. The first painting that takes his interest is by a Joseph Wright of Derby, *An Experiment on a Bird in the Air Pump*. He is drawn by the painting's depiction of light, the gloom pierced by a candle, and the brilliant way the central figure, the natural philosopher conducting the experiment, has been illuminated. There is a girl in the painting turning to her father and crying, and he feels sympathy for her, for she is upset because a bird, starved of air, has died during the experiment. The natural philosopher has shoulder-length grey hair and looks slightly wild, like a manic preacher, like Isaac Newton, but he supposes he is depicted as the man casting light on hidden knowledge – we cannot survive without air and the plaintive cries of the dying bird cannot travel through a vacuum – and that such knowledge, such progress, comes at a price; it demands sacrifice. He wonders why he admires this picture and not all the others.

The next painting that captures his interest is very different: *The Boulevard Montmartre at Night*, by Camille Pissarro. He has no idea where Montmartre is, but he supposes it is in France. He finds in the picture a sense of dynamism and a vibrancy that was missing in the religious paintings and depictions of Greek gods. He can imagine himself wandering the streets at night, the gaslights piercing through the evening gloom. There is something evocative and romantic about the painting, a nod to the beauty of the scene, but he also detects a dark edge, an ominous quality. He senses purpose and opportunity and life portrayed in the dancing light of the picture.

And then he finds his way into the Rembrandt gallery, and he does not leave it for an hour.

He is mesmerised by the paintings, by their artistry and craft, by their brilliant realism and use of light, by the honest faces of the ordinary people depicted – people like him. His attention is drawn to a self-portrait, one showing the artist when he was sixty-three. He is speechless: he cannot fail to notice how much his father, Stanley Harrison, resembles Rembrandt. He has the same tufts of wispy hair emerging from beneath his cap, the same bulbous nose, the same rounded yet lined cheeks, and the same sad look in the eye. Here is a man that has been beset by tragedy and money troubles, and he looks resigned, and perhaps even a little guilty. Here is a man, he thinks, who feels the passing of time and the bleeding out of ambition; one who knows what life is really like, a man who does not need religious tales and Greek myths to depict the essence of human nature. He accomplishes that with his bold brushstrokes, and by showing people as they really are.

But more than that, he cannot deny that he sees something of himself in the artist's portraits.

Before he leaves the National Gallery he purchases four postcards from the shop, intending to hang them on his bedroom wall.

*

He is late for the rendezvous. He finds Dr Goodman and his aunt sitting stony-faced beside one of the giant lion statues guarding Nelson's Column. They are facing away from each other. He recognises the posture; they have been arguing.

'I am sorry I am late. I lost track of time.' He tries to sound cheerful, hoping the warmth of his greeting will start to thaw the ice that has developed between them. It is a trick that sometimes worked with his parents.

'It is no matter, old boy,' says Dr Goodman, smiling. 'Did you find something you liked in the gallery?'

'He is neither old nor a boy,' mutters his aunt.

'Yes. I bought postcards,' he says, trying to sound enthusiastic. He pulls them out of the paper bag and reluctantly shows them off, half expecting his selection to be ridiculed.

Dr Goodman looks through the postcards, feigning interest.

Despite her ire, his aunt cannot help turning to see what he has purchased. She is surprised to see a Rembrandt portrait, a Pissarro, a Joseph Wright of Derby, and *The Ambassadors*, by Hans Holbein the Younger.

'Why do you like the Holbein?' she asks sharply.

For once, he doesn't shrug his shoulders or cast his eyes to the floor. 'At first I didn't like it. I thought it another boring portrait of two rich men showing off their wealth. But then I noticed there was something odd about it, something that looked out of place: a white streak like a shard of glass intruding at the base of the picture. It made me curious.'

'The skull,' she replies, 'the skull which can only be seen in full from certain perspectives.'

'Yes, I saw other people looking at the picture from strange angles, tilting their heads and pointing, so I did the same. I thought the skull was a bit stupid and that it spoilt the picture. I overheard someone say it was a reminder of death.'

'Yes, a *memento mori*,' says his aunt.

Benedict nods. 'But I wondered why anyone would need to be reminded of that, especially if they were ambassadors to Henry VIII's court, as the information board said they were. But then I noticed other odd things and I began to wonder who these two men really were and why had they been shown surrounded by a globe and other instruments. I liked the puzzle of it.'

For once, his aunt looks impressed. 'That picture is well known and well studied. There has been much speculation about its symbolism, for example, the lute depicted with a broken string. One of the men is thought to be the French Ambassador to the Tudor Court, but even that is debated. What did you make of it?'

He looks thoughtful for a moment. 'I thought everything in the painting was about death, that's why the skull was unnecessary: the globe that is upside down, the broken string – the death of music – the crucifix; they all spoke to me of brokenness and endings. I thought the men had odd expressions. They looked a bit frightened. I didn't think they looked trustworthy. I wondered if they were spies. I wondered if the picture carried a hidden message; perhaps someone had been sentenced to death, or it was an instruction to assassinate one of the ambassadors.'

He saw the crucifix, she thinks, *and he noted the globe was upside down; not many see that. He may be taciturn and painfully shy, but he is observant. Yes, yes, he is no fool. Perhaps there is still hope; he might accomplish the task yet.*

She says, 'There are many hidden messages in paintings, and we have forgotten how to read them. Imagination is necessary, Benedict, but never allow yourself to be carried away by flights of fancy.'

'Is it really that fanciful?' replies Dr Goodman, coming to his defence and adopting a serious tone. 'Have you seen the news today? The British Ambassador to Holland has been assassinated, gunned down in the streets of Amsterdam by assailants unknown.'

His aunt looks away and adopts a pose every bit as stiff as the people occupying the benches inside the National Gallery, every bit as lifeless as the giant lions guarding Nelson's Column.

Of course she will have seen the news, thinks Benedict. She listens to daily radio broadcasts from the BBC, and broadcasts in other languages, too. And despite his reluctance, she insists they discuss world events during mealtimes. Unlike at school or at home, he is asked for his opinion. More often than not he has to disappoint her because he doesn't have an opinion to give. What does he think about the revolution in Iran, or the Chinese incursion into Vietnam? Did he think the government was doing enough to aid the Vietnamese refugees, the so-called 'boat people'? Did he believe that any footballer was really worth £1 million – the record transfer fee paid by Nottingham Forest for a striker? Could anyone really be worth that much? How much did he think he was worth? Which professions did he think should be valued most highly? Did he believe the state or the free market should decide the monetary value of people's work?

Often, his head would reel. She bought him a second-hand copy of the *Encyclopaedia Britannica*, an *Oxford*

English Dictionary and *The Times Atlas of the World* for his bookshelf. He spent ages looking up the places he had never heard of and reading about their history. Even so, he always felt out of his depth when discussing world events.

He knows his aunt reads the broadsheet newspapers daily, and constantly bemoans the fact that the *Times* and *Financial Times* have not been printed for nearly a year, not since the beginning of the labour dispute between the Canadian owners and the British staff. She refers to the *Guardian* newspaper as the *Manchester Guardian*, and proudly quotes George Orwell and his view that it was the only British newspaper that reported on the Spanish Civil War accurately.

When it became apparent Benedict had no idea what she was talking about, she lent him some of her books for his bookshelf: *Nineteen Eighty-Four*, *Animal Farm* and *Homage to Catalonia*. So far, he had only managed to read the book covers. She insisted they do the newspaper crosswords together and play Scrabble. She seemed to see it as her duty to extend his vocabulary and improve his spelling. She insisted he look up the etymology of unfamiliar words.

He wanted to tell her that he disliked hearing the news, that it invariably induced in him a feeling of gloom and despair, and that he didn't need to read it or listen to it to know how dreadful people could be. He found it biased and unbalanced, the editors deciding to focus almost entirely on political arguments and dissension, crimes and atrocities, and on all the dark things that were happening in the world. He found it too much. It was not that he wished to be ignorant or uninformed, he just wished the news could be happier.

*

Realising that Gail Miller is in a frightful sulk of her own, Dr Goodman decides it is wise to change the subject. 'Have you thought about where you would like to go now?'

Benedict nods. 'The Imperial War Museum.'

'Splendid. Do you know where it is?'

He shakes his head. 'Somewhere in London. I've never been.'

'It's in Lambeth,' interjects his aunt knowingly. 'We need to get to Charing Cross and then take the Bakerloo Line. It is an extensive museum. There has, after all, been no shortage of wars. Which part in particular did you wish to see?'

He is quick to answer. The Rembrandt portraits had made him think about his father and grandfather – what had Captain Harrison looked like? And the Ambassadors portrait was a remembrance of death; it had made him think about how his grandfathers had died during the war. He wondered why he had never thought to ask more about them. He was suddenly aware of how little he knew, and how little his parents had spoken about them. On some topics, the family's memory box was all but empty, as if the past were something best forgotten and buried away.

'I would like to know about the Blitz and the liberation of France during the Second World War.'

9

Six Weeks, B.B. Harrison, Six Weeks

London, March 1979

Benedict finds the images displayed in the Imperial War Museum more interesting than the paintings in the National Gallery – more interesting and far more shocking. Perhaps it is because they are more immediate and more real somehow; these are people, not unlike him. The content of the photographs and the eyewitness accounts render him speechless and sad beyond reckoning; he feels tearful. Some of the images are brutal and graphic, depicting executions and battles. He can hardly bring himself to look at them. They capture a world in flames and the atrocities of the Holocaust. And then there are the images of the air raids, the cities bombed, the firestorms and collapsed buildings, the wreckage of homes and lives, the deaths of civilians and the unspeakable horrors of the death camps.

The visit unsettles him. He feels physically sick. He wonders how his nans could have endured the war and how they could have borne their losses. And a new thought occurs to him: *How could any child grow up sane in such an insane world?*

The phrase 'mustn't grumble' comes into his head.

*

On the train back to Malvern he is subdued and even quieter than usual, lost in his own morose thoughts. Dr Goodman sits opposite him, his back to the engine and the seat next to him unoccupied. Benedict had claimed the window seat and was annoyed when his aunt invaded the space beside him. They are the only people in the carriage.

It is because it is first class, he tells himself. He has never travelled first class before. It makes him feel uncomfortable.

Dr Goodman respects his desire for solitude and buries himself in the *Daily Telegraph*. Benedict glances at one of the headlines, something to do with the death of Sid Vicious.

More cheerful news, he thinks. How hard it must be for his friends and family to see these sensational headlines all over the papers: '*Punk rock star dies from drug overdose*'. People should be left alone to grieve in peace.

He looks out of the window, but it is pitch black. He notices his aunt staring at him. She has a strange, unreadable expression on her face. *She has been uncharacteristically quiet,* he thinks, *ever since I came out of the National Gallery. Perhaps the business with the old acquaintance did not go well.*

'What are you thinking?' she asks.

'Nothing much,' he mumbles. 'I was thinking about Grandad Harrison. Nan never talked about him, nor did Dad. All I know is that he died in France.'

To his surprise, she asks, 'What would you like to know, Benedict?'

It had not occurred to him to ask her.

'What was he like?'

She smiles sadly. 'Stubborn, maddening, and quite brilliant.'

'Brilliant at what?' he asks.

'Anything he turned his mind to. You would have liked him; he was a keen cricketer and a very talented one. He taught me to play.'

'He was older than you?'

'By a few years, yes. You know, your father looks a lot like him.'

And suddenly he realises that he has seen a photograph of his grandfather in her house: the soldier sitting on a hospital bed in Spain. 'B.B.,' he mutters.

'Yes, Captain Kenneth B.B. Harrison, DSO, which was his full title.'

'What did the B.B. stand for?'

To his surprise, she laughs. 'Usually people ask what the DSO stands for. He won several medals for bravery; for his "distinguished service".'

'He was in battles?'

'Yes, but much of it was secret operations. I do not know the details.'

He has always been able to tell when people are lying; he has a sixth sense for it. He was the only person who ever saw through his mother's lies. He knows his aunt is lying now.

'The book you read when you first arrived at my house, *The Little Grey Men*, that book belonged to my brother. It was a favourite of your father's and he read it to him, often. During the war, he borrowed the author's initials, BB, and started calling himself "B.B. Harrison". Somehow the name stuck and everyone began using it.'

Now he understands why she was so upset that he had left the book on the kitchen floor. 'Who was the author?' he asks.

'The same man who was named as the original illustrator: Denys Watkins-Pitchford. BB was his pen name. He took it from the name of a type of lead shot.'

He recalls the pictures he has seen in the house, the ones signed by B.B.

'And so Grandfather must have been in Spain during the Civil War, and earlier, in Berlin, at the Olympics,' he says, thinking aloud.

She gives him a studied look. She had deliberately placed those images where he would see them. 'So, you notice more than you let on. Why haven't you asked me about the photographs before?'

He looks away shyly. 'I didn't wish to pry.'

This time, she speaks truthfully. 'Yes, he was fighting fascism. In Germany, he worked for the British Embassy, gathering intelligence about Hitler's growing war machine. Like many idealistic young men, he could see the way the wind in Europe was blowing, and he thought the only way to stop fascism was to fight it. He was appalled Britain didn't boycott the Olympic Games in Berlin in 1936. He joined an international brigade in Spain and fought in the civil war.'

He wonders whether he would have shown the same courage as his grandfather. 'But who were Helen and Jeanette?'

He appears grave, and she understands what he is thinking and what he is implying. 'They were… associates… allies your grandfather worked with. He knew Helen and Jeanette a long time before he married your grandmother.'

That is a partial truth, he thinks. She wants to allay his fears, he understands that. Captain B.B. Harrison was never unfaithful, not like Benedict's father, Stanley, was said to have been. At least, that is what his mother had claimed during the divorce proceedings, although his father had denied it, and no one else had any memory of it.

'What did Grandad do during the war?'

She does not answer immediately. She looks down at her pendant and fiddles with it. He thinks she looks tearful.

'Originally, he was an infantry captain, but after the fiasco that led to Dunkirk he wanted a change. He thought the British forces were being poorly led and that, without aid, we were likely to lose the war. He volunteered to join the SOE. You will have seen something about the work the organisation did, in the Imperial War Museum, although much of their work must remain secretive and classified, even now. He spoke excellent French, and so he was a natural recruit.'

He thinks back to the display he saw about the SOE. He wished he had paid it more attention. A look of uncertainty must show on his face, because Dr Goodman, who has lowered his newspaper, says:

'The Special Operations Executive, old boy. Churchill was a great fan. He told them to "set Europe ablaze", and by God they tried. Incredibly brave people; wireless operators would be lucky to last six weeks behind enemy lines. They gave great sacrifice but alas, they received little recognition.'

Yes, thinks Benedict, *that was it, the SOE*. He racks his brains; what can he recall? The SOE was made up of volunteers; it included civilians. Women had been allowed to join and fight, too.

A thought suddenly occurs to him, and his mouth falls open in amazement. 'Gail, were you in the SOE?'

She turns her head away from him, but even so, he can tell that she lies. 'No, Benedict, I worked as a nurse during the war.'

He closes his eyes and concentrates as hard as he can. What else can he recall from the display? There was a black and white image showing trained personnel parachuting into France. And another, showing agents smoking cigarettes and appearing relaxed, rifles casually slung over their shoulders, fraternising with resistance fighters. It was summer; they wore khaki shorts, but that was unusual as they usually dressed as civilians and carried fake identities. Another image: a suitcase that was really a wireless transceiver and a pen that doubled as a pistol. Everything was camouflage and deception. Theirs was a clandestine war. They worked with resistance groups and carried out acts of sabotage, blowing up railway tracks and disrupting communications.

What else? Come on, Benedict, think.

There was something about the Normandy landings, what was it? Parachutists dropped into France ahead of D-Day. They sabotaged Panzer tanks. It had greatly helped the invasion. Is that where his grandad had died? The dates fitted. Is that where he had won his medals?

'Did Grandad die in Normandy?' he asks, unable to disguise the excitement in his voice – the excitement and the pride.

'No, Benedict, he did not.'

He looks crestfallen.

She looks at him quizzically, as if she is weighing him up. To his surprise, she leans in closely and whispers, 'If I tell you what I know, then it must remain a secret. You must never tell another soul, not your father or brothers or grandmother – especially not your grandmother – do you understand?'

He doesn't understand at all, but out of curiosity, he nods his head.

'Gail,' says Dr Goodman, sending her a warning look, 'he is too young.'

She ignores him. 'Very well, Benedict, you should know that your grandfather was betrayed.'

'Gail, no!' protests Dr Goodman, throwing his newspaper down in disgust.

'What choice do I have?' she shoots back, her temper rising. 'We are running out of time.'

She turns to Benedict and speaks with a seriousness and urgency he has never encountered before.

'Your grandfather died during an SOE operation that went terribly wrong. Somebody betrayed them. Other people died too – many, many good people. The truth was suppressed. The guilty have never been brought to justice. I have spent a long, long time trying to find out what happened. I am very near to solving the puzzle. Dr Goodman has been helping me.'

For the first time since he has known her, she reaches out and touches his arm. To his surprise, he does not feel revulsion, not in the way he did when his mother tried to embrace him at the divorce hearings. He has never seen his aunt look so sad, so vulnerable, or so needy.

'Benedict, do you think… do you think you could help me too?'

10

The Fool's Mate

The farmhouse at Wellend, Great Malvern, spring 1979

His aunt had told him little more about his grandfather, or how he might help her discover who betrayed him during the SOE operation in France. She made him swear to secrecy once more and told him to ask no further questions, for now.

'Can you play chess?' she asked.

'I know how to play chess, but I'm not very good,' he replied.

'Then we must practise. You must get better; you must rise above the average. To reveal the truth of what happened to your grandfather you must unlock a box, and the key to that box is chess. We do not have much time. You must learn quickly.'

He had not understood, and she had said no more.

But once they returned from London, they had begun his training in earnest.

*

A wooden chessboard appeared on the kitchen table. 'You will play white,' said his aunt, taking up position opposite him. Dr Goodman looked on.

He advanced a pawn, and so did his aunt. He advanced another and she swept her queen diagonally across the board. 'Checkmate in two. That is known as the fool's mate,' she said disparagingly.

Dr Goodman laughed sympathetically. 'Never mind, old boy, we've all been caught out by that one when we've first started playing.'

His aunt was less kind. 'For heaven's sake, study what your opponent is doing. Consider all their potential moves. Think as many moves ahead as you can. Don't just think about your own strategy.'

He didn't have a strategy, that was the problem. He had no idea what he was doing.

'There are three parts to a game,' she said, 'the opening, the middle and the end. What do you imagine you should do during the opening?'

Her tone was severe, and he found it off-putting.

'I don't know.'

'Think about it.'

'I want to get these pawns out of the way so that I can attack with my bigger pieces.'

'Don't be absurd. Think again.'

Dr Goodman intervened, in a much kinder tone. 'Imagine you are a general commanding your forces. You have to protect the king, but you have to try to capture the opponent. What do you need to do first?'

He sighed. 'I don't know. I have never been a general.'

His aunt closed her eyes and nodded to herself. She needed to be patient. *He is naught but a beginner. He needs encouragement; he needs instruction.*

'During the opening, you need to develop your key pieces both for attack and defence. Your pawn deployment will help with that. Your knights are mobile and will command many spaces if you move them out like this.'

She demonstrated a move on the board.

'Do you see?'

'Yes, yes, I see.'

'Chess is all about commanding spaces,' she said, 'and you do that by connecting pieces. Connections and spaces, Benedict, remember that.'

'Just like taking the high ground in a battle, old boy, and ensuring your cavalry and artillery can back up the foot soldiers,' added Dr Goodman helpfully.

'It is also about maintaining the initiative. White usually attacks because white goes first and is therefore afforded initial advantage. If you play black, be more defensive.'

The second game lasted longer. Benedict played black. After ten moves his aunt stopped. 'I can see what you are doing. It won't work. I will have you in checkmate in four moves. It is not a bad ploy to mirror the opponent, Benedict, especially during the opening; it will help you counter my attack and develop your pieces, but you cannot win that way. We shall play again, and this time I want you to think for yourself, not just copy what I do.'

'You are doing a "Boris"', said Dr Goodman, smiling.

'What's a "Boris"?' he asked, feeling deflated.

It was his aunt who answered. 'One of Cyril's computer programs.'

'Really?'

'Yes, old boy, a prototype. It's not really mine, I am just helping out with it. We're rather proud of Boris at the lab. He plays chess.'

'*It* mimics playing chess,' said his aunt derisively.

'If you say so, Gail,' said Dr Goodman, laughing. 'Boris's memory has been programmed with thousands of famous chess games. We have developed an algorithm which enables him to recall every past move played in those games and use that memory to determine mathematically the best move to play against an opponent. You were doing a bit of a Boris then, old boy, because we have discovered that he often mimics an opponent's opening moves.'

'*It* is a copy-cat,' added his aunt. 'It replicates.'

Dr Goodman laughed aloud. 'Gail has played Boris several times.'

She scoffed, 'The computer cannot think, not in the way a human can. All I have to do is make an unusual move, one it is not expecting, one that has not been played before, and it doesn't know what to do.'

'But he's getting better, isn't he? He's learning. One day he will know every possible permutation and then he will be unbeatable. He does not make blunders. Not like humans.'

It was his aunt's turn to laugh aloud. 'Cyril believes our defining human characteristic is our ability to blunder.'

'It's the defining characteristic of all life,' he said. 'Blunders are written in the genes; they have a habit of mutating when they replicate. And unlike Boris, our memory can be faulty. How many moves ahead can you think, Benedict?'

'I don't know, maybe four or five.'

'And your aunt can do up to fifteen accurately, we've tested it. It makes her a superb chess player. She was the champion at university. A grandmaster can maybe do as many as twenty. Boris has no limit. If we give him sufficient memory and processing power, he has no limits. And grandmasters need a lot of time to think that far ahead. Boris can accomplish the same task in seconds.'

'Ten, nil,' said Gail, sending him a disparaging look and shaking her head. 'That is the score. I have defeated Boris ten times. Thinking is about more than recall. It is about seeing new possibilities. Boris is blind to those. *It* has no imagination.'

*

Throughout the rest of March and April he practised hard. His aunt played chess with him daily. He never won – didn't even come close – but he got better; little by little he got better. She dissected every game and showed him where he went wrong. Usually it was one move, one simple blunder that caused his whole defence and strategy to collapse. She demonstrated other possibilities, other strategies. He gained in confidence, in his ability to manipulate pieces around the board, in his ability to see the way he could control lines and spaces by connecting his troops together. She lent him *The Beginner's Guide to Chess*, and he read it avidly. He challenged himself to solve the chess puzzles in the newspapers.

He tried to avoid the many distractions.

At the start of April they feared letting the dogs outside. A nuclear accident at Three Mile Island in America; some news reports suggested leaked radioactive material was making its way across the Atlantic, blown on the wind.

'It is like the First World War,' lamented his aunt. 'My father was killed by a killing wind.'

For a while, they lived on frozen food and remained indoors. They boiled the water before drinking it and wore face masks. If felt surreal, like they were trapped inside a dystopian novel.

The equanimity of their lives was further disturbed by ongoing political unrest: the fear and shock induced by the death of the Northern Ireland Secretary, killed by a car bomb; the National Front meeting, provocatively staged in the ethnically diverse London borough of Southwark, and the anti-racist protest rally that had ended in tragedy when a demonstrator was killed during the unrest that followed, eyewitnesses reporting that he had been bludgeoned to death by a police truncheon. No one had been brought to book for the death of either man, although two Irish Republican groups had each claimed responsibility for the car bomb. Benedict had a growing sense that everything was falling apart.

'We should have been at the rally,' said his aunt, with regret. 'We should have lent our voices to the fight against fascists and racists.'

'It is better to avoid such trouble,' replied Dr Goodman.

Relations between the two adults were often tetchy, and not for the first time, Benedict wondered what exactly they meant to each other. They often bickered, like his parents had done, and the more he got to know them, the more he realised the only thing they had in common was nostalgia, a partial recollection of events and a shared but contested remembrance of the past.

But no, their arguments were never like the ones his parents had. There was no rancour, no resentment and no bitterness, and they always remained friends.

Towards the end of March, Dr Goodman had appeared in the kitchen and announced that 'It is all up for the PM! He's lost the vote of confidence by one vote. There will be a general election in May. Can you believe it? One of his own MPs was absent from the vote because he was ill.'

They discussed the conspiracy theories.

His aunt confided in him. 'Cyril is delighted, although he won't admit it. He rather admires Margaret Thatcher, the leader of the opposition. He thinks she will make a good prime minister.'

'I never said that,' he protested. 'I just think it is time for a change. Let's face it, she can't do any worse than the present lot.'

'Don't you like her?' asked Benedict, remembering the carping voice on the radio broadcast he had heard.

'I don't know her,' replied his aunt, 'but she has moved the Conservative Party further to the right. As for her policies, and as far as she has expounded any coherent political philosophy, I am not a supporter, and so no, she won't get my vote.'

'Why not?' asked Benedict.

'She is a neoliberal; she wants to reduce the role of the state and cut taxes. She wants no cap on how wealthy the rich can become.'

'What is wrong with that?' asked Dr Goodman, in all seriousness. 'She wants to unleash enterprise and innovation and encourage wealth creation. If the rich get richer then so will everyone; wealth will trickle down.'

'When has it ever done that, Cyril?' replied his aunt, stony-faced. 'Without constraints, wealth concentrates into fewer and fewer hands and the inequalities increase. I fear the Tories plan to privatise everything, even down to the very water that we drink.'

'And not before time,' said Dr Goodman, thumping his fist on the kitchen table decisively and causing Benedict's rook to topple over. 'You have no idea how much waste and inefficiency there is in the nationalised industries. Privatisation will bring investment and efficiency, and cheaper prices and better service for all.'

His aunt had laughed dismissively. 'The neoliberal dream; the neoliberal myth. Have you swallowed the Tory Party manifesto, Cyril? You know that is tosh. Prices will rise, as will unemployment, and many will no longer be able to afford basic services. The train and bus companies will cherry-pick the profitable lines and the rest will close.

The only winners will be the shareholders and those gluttons fortunate enough to work in the City.'

'The lines will close because they are unprofitable,' he responded, his colour rising. 'Why should tax payers have to fund non-profitable lines?'

'Because they are a service, Cyril. Don't you agree the state should provide basic services for *all* its people?'

'The state?' he said, with uncharacteristic disdain. 'I have seen what state control leads to, as have you! Do you forget Moscow?'

'You have been to Moscow?' asked Benedict, feigning surprise, remembering all too clearly the pictures on the wall.

His aunt looked sad. 'Yes, after the war. I worked for a while at the British Embassy. I had no illusions about the Soviet system, not like some.'

'The communist regime claims they have eradicated inequality,' added Dr Goodman, his ire rising, 'that there is freedom from want and poverty; they claim they have created a workers' paradise. But it is all propaganda, all illusion. It is a totalitarian state; a land of fear and brutal repression.'

His aunt looked angry. 'I have never supported that system,' she said, her face becoming resolute, 'but I have never been a neoliberal or capitalist either. I prefer the model of socialism followed in countries like Sweden, a mixed economy, with a balance between market freedoms and state interventions, with mechanisms in place to protect individual liberties and to redistribute wealth.'

He could tell that she had told him another partial truth; she had been in Russia, before the war.

'Redistribute wealth,' scoffed Dr Goodman, mimicking her tone. 'Who's swallowed a bloody manifesto now! You would steal wealth from those with the guile and graft to create it. Let's face it, there will always be inequality because, despite what you say, Gail, people are not born equal. Those with talents and those that can innovate should be allowed to reap the rewards of their industry and endeavours.'

My parents laboured hard all their lives, thought Benedict, *but they never received much reward.*

Dr Goodman was on his soapbox now and added, 'The American way is best; the cream should be allowed to rise to the top!'

His aunt had waved her hand petulantly in the air, as if to dismiss him from her presence. 'Oh, Cyril, you are a fool. You would leave too many bottles on the doorstep; we shall all drown in sour milk.'

11

A Pair of Teeth and the Librarian's Dress

In May, two unusual events occur. Benedict receives an envelope through the post – his first passport – and his aunt invites someone to dinner.

'This is very important,' she confides in him. 'You must make a good impression,' but she does not have time to elaborate.

The preparations for the evening are extensive. His aunt spends much of the day cooking and he spends much of the day cleaning. For once, Dr Goodman is absent.

By five o'clock the dogs have been locked away in the kennels, the cats have been encouraged out of the front door, fires have been lit in several rooms, the porch and kitchen swept, mopped and generally tidied, and the mould removed from the upstairs walls and ceilings. By six o'clock, Benedict has taken a bath and donned his

Sunday best, and the dinner has been prepared. By 6.15, Dr Goodman finally arrives, looking flustered but armed with several bottles of 'the finest plonk' and a bottle of Martini, and by 6.20, his aunt has unlocked two of the downstairs rooms that Benedict has never been allowed to enter.

The first is a large library, furnished with a tan leather sofa, an ornate Lady Chippendale writing desk and four Chesterfield-style Queen Anne chairs casually positioned around a low coffee table topped with Italian marble. The room is warm and smells of sandalwood; an antique Persian rug has been placed beside the fire. Several Art Nouveau lamps provide subtle lighting and colourful, if flowery, decoration. The walls are lined with cases and shelves which are filled from floor to ceiling with books, many of them leather-bound.

The second room has pretentions of even greater elegance. It looks out onto the garden through French windows, which are hidden behind red velvet drapes. There is a long rectangular table with eight leather and armless dining chairs stationed, like sentries, around it. It has been adorned with a white cloth and a candelabrum, and set for dinner for four people, with crystal glasses, fine china and a confusing array of silver cutlery. Against one wall there is an upright piano, the lid closed, and next to that, resting on a stand, a cello. Several picture frames and a few of his aunt's sculptures sit on top of the piano, competing for space with piles of fading sheet music. The opposite wall is covered by wallpaper depicting a William Morris design, a repeated pattern of birds and strawberries. There is a large and ornate Victorian fireplace. Two other walls are covered by regal red flock wallpaper, and one wall has been painted off-white. There are three pictures hung on the painted wall. One is a scratchy effort seemingly drawn by a child but rather pretentiously entitled *Sombre Welsh Hills*. One is a charcoal sketch showing the side profile of a man. Benedict imagines the drawing was done quickly as it looks unfinished. The man wears a beret. He raises a glass of wine to his lips. His hands seem to shake, and he looks full of remorse. The picture is entitled *Escape*, but it has no signature.

The third picture dominates the wall and is housed in a large, ornate and gilded frame. It shows a summer landscape of low hills and vineyards, with a medieval town on the highest summit. The artist's style reminds him of the Pissarro painting he saw in the National Gallery. The painting is full of movement and vibrancy, but there is nothing romantic or sweet about it. The landscape seems ominous and the clouds threatening. The farmhouses look derelict, abandoned and destroyed. The soil is flecked with streaks of red, as though it bleeds. The grapes look poisonous. There are some words scribbled into the bottom left-hand corner: '*Saint-Emilion, after the fall, Gail Miller, 1950*'.

They hear a car pull up in the courtyard. The dogs begin to bark. 'She's here,' says his aunt, adjusting her tweed skirt, spraying a mist of perfume on either side of her neck and rushing to greet the guest, an anxious look on her face. Dr Goodman follows her out of the room, hastily applying a comb to his hair as he goes. Not knowing what is expected of him, Benedict remains behind. It allows him a few moments to study the picture frames on the piano.

He is surprised to see a photograph of his father. He must be about seven and it must have been taken at the outbreak of the war. He is playing cricket in a suburban garden. A gasmask canister is being used for the stumps. The bat is too big for him. His father lobs him an easy ball to hit, but he appears to have missed it. Grandfather has a cigarette hanging out of his mouth. He wears khaki shorts and little else. Benedict thinks he looks thin – thin and unhappy. In the background, a woman wearing a scarf in her hair and a white pinny is hanging washing on a line. It must be Silver-Sherry Nan. There is an Alsatian dog chasing after the ball, but the movement is all a blur. Benedict wonders who took the photograph.

In another frame he sees a picture of a chess tournament. The two combatants sit upon a stage, surrounded by spectators. A banner with the words 'The Grand Final' hangs above the players. The audience are gripped by the encounter. With a shock, he realises that his aunt is one of the contestants. She is young, maybe no more than a university student. Her opponent is a much older man. He is dressed in robes, like an old-fashioned school teacher. He can see an enlarged version of the chessboard projected onto a screen behind them. From what he can see, the game is a stalemate.

The third frame houses an old black and white image taken in 1917. It shows four people posing for a family photograph. They wear frozen expressions. The mother is dressed in a nurse's uniform. She sits on a chair, a new-born baby in her arms. Beside her, there is a young boy dressed in a sailor's uniform. The father stands behind them. He wears a captain's uniform, and he proudly displays a chest full of ribbons and medals. Benedict supposes it is his great-grandfather and great-grandmother. He wonders why he has never thought to ask about them. He notices that there are some letters printed at the top of the picture. He does not understand what they say; they are written in French.

The final frame shows a scene in the courtyard of a farmhouse. It appears to be in a foreign country, for the architecture is unfamiliar. A gendarme guards four labourers as they load a large barrel onto the back of a lorry. The vehicle looks like a war waggon, and the steering wheel is on the left-hand side. The gendarme has a stern look about him. He is tall and wiry, with his hair cut short at the back and sides, and a black pencil moustache that makes his long face seem mean and untrustworthy. He has a rifle in his hands and a pistol in a holster. Benedict can't help but notice his prominent Adam's apple.

*

'You are holding your knife in the wrong hand,' says his aunt, not unkindly, as they begin dinner.

How can there be a wrong hand? thinks Benedict, but he knows he must be on best behaviour, and so he looks apologetic and dutifully changes the knife over to his right hand.

The female guest is nearly as tall as his aunt, but

nowhere near as well spoken. He recognises her accent; she is from the East End of London, although she has worked hard to disguise it. He finds it difficult to judge her age. She peers out at the world over the top of half-moon spectacles. If his mother had been present she would have complimented her on her professional and sober dress, but behind her back, she would have dismissed her attire as 'librarian'. Her hair is tied into a tight bun. She smells faintly of patchouli oil.

*

'This is Dr Marks,' says his aunt, when he has been summoned into the library for an 'aperitif' and 'introductions'.

The adults stop talking when he enters the room, and he knows why: he had been on their dissecting table.

'Please, call me Harriet,' says Dr Marks, proffering her hand towards him and smiling. She has a firm grip and a vigorous handshake.

'Pleased to make your acquaintance,' he says. He was hoping it would sound formal and correct, but it just sounds awful, even to his ears. He sounds like the Artful Dodger from the film version of the *Oliver Twist* musical.

Trying to rescue the situation, he asks, 'What's "a pair of teeth"?'

The adults burst out laughing. 'An *aperitif*,' corrects his aunt, 'is a drink we imbibe before a meal. It helps to open up the appetite.'

He doesn't need his appetite opening up, he is already starving.

His aunt then quotes something in a foreign language that he doesn't understand.

'Your French is magnificent, Gail,' says Dr Marks admiringly. 'Are you a native speaker?'

'Yes, my mother was French. She met my father during the Great War.'

Thinking of the horrific images he has seen in the Imperial War Museum, and before he can help himself, Benedict blurts out, 'What was so great about it? Every nation involved lost an entire generation of young men.'

The adults stare at him, as if considering his interruption rude.

'Great as in the sense of the scale of it,' offers Dr Goodman, 'as in Great Britain, or the Great Bahamas Bank, or the Great Australian Desert.'

He feels like an idiot and decides to say no more for the rest of the evening.

It is then that he ponders what his aunt has just said: his great-grandmother had been French. He had never known that. Why had no one ever mentioned it? Why was the collective family memory so full of holes?

'Harriet has something in common with your aunt,' says Dr Goodman, skilfully changing the subject.

'Your aunt and I share the same *alma mater*,' she says, taking a sip of Martini and turning to exchange a knowing smile with Gail.

Dr Goodman comes to his rescue and whispers into his ear, 'They studied at the same Cambridge college.'

'Oh,' says Benedict, not knowing what else to say. He can hear the grandfather clock ticking in the hall, the sound amplified by the awkward silence that has ensued. Despite his private vow of silence, he feels like he should ask her something.

'Are you a proper doctor, or are you like Dr Goodman?'

The women laugh, but Dr Goodman looks mildly offended.

'Yes, I am a medical doctor, but like Cyril, I work in research.'

'Dr Marks also runs a care home for elderly people in Malvern,' says Dr Goodman.

Benedict knows a lot about care homes, more than he ever cared to know.

Dr Marks laughs again. 'I don't *run it*, Cyril,' she protests, 'I merely advise on the medical side of things, as I do in several care homes. The local authority runs the place. I am still attached to the Medical School at Bristol University. That is where I conduct my research, Benedict.'

'Research into what?' he asks.

'Disorders of the brain.'

Dr Goodman can see that Benedict is struggling to connect the pieces. 'Unfortunately, many elderly people suffer from dementia,' he says meaningfully. 'Alas, many of those in Harriet's care are veterans from the war.'

*

'The dinner was wonderful, Gail,' says Dr Marks, once more praising his aunt's cooking. 'I love French food, and that was superior in every way to what the Michelin chef serves up at the Imperial hotel. I have to tell you, that place is overpriced and overrated. Your food was much more… much more authentic.'

'Thank you, Harriet,' she replies, looking pleased. 'It is nice for one's efforts to be rewarded. More wine?'

'Didn't you enjoy the meal, Benedict?' asks Dr Marks, holding out her glass for another refill.

'Yes, it was nice,' he replies. 'I never had anything like that at home. My mother wasn't a very good cook.'

'And why should women have to be good cooks?' asks Dr Marks, a half-amused expression on her face. 'I bet your father never cooked, did he?'

He shakes his head.

'I am sure your mother did her best. Did you ever volunteer to help?'

He feels under attack.

'Did your father ever compliment your mother, about anything?'

He racks his brains; he cannot recall one single occasion when that happened.

She is remorseless. 'Did you? Did you ever thank your mother for her efforts? Did you let her know she was appreciated?'

His remains mute. His choler begins to rise.

'I bet your father was one of those men who expect to be waited on hand and foot. Men like that want a maid, not a wife. I know his type; I grew up with them. They want a slave in the kitchen and a dolly bird on their arm. When they condescend to take you out, they expect women to wear makeup and put on a face. Why should I show the world any face other than my own, Benedict? Why should I hide behind a mask?'

She has worked herself up into a state, he thinks, and she seems to know a lot about his parents. What has his aunt told her? All he said was that his mother was not a good cook. He is too young to understand her ire.

'I take your point, Harriet,' says Dr Goodman, once more riding to his rescue, 'and you make it exceedingly well, but you have to admit, some women like to cook, take pride in it. My wife, Suzie, would never let me near the kitchen, God bless her, not until the end, when the illness took her – bloody cigarettes. And doesn't everyone like to look their best when they step out? Cosmetics give some people more confidence; I know they did for my Suzie, especially when… when…'

He cannot complete his sentence, and for the first time since he met him, Dr Goodman looks tearful. Dr Marks sends him a knowing and sympathetic look, and his aunt reaches out and pats his arm.

But Benedict is not in a sympathetic mood. Dr Marks makes too many assumptions. He feels his own anger rising. 'People wear masks all the time,' he says, 'like actors. They smile at you and then stick a knife in your back. What difference does a bit of makeup make? People are liars.'

The table falls silent.

'And are you?' asks Dr Marks. 'Are you an actor and a liar?'

He thinks about his mother. 'It depends on who I am trying to impress.'

12

The Solo School

After the contretemps at the dinner table, his aunt had taken charge of the conversation, skilfully steering clear of any potentially controversial topics, although Cyril had nearly blundered when he spoke enthusiastically about Margaret Thatcher's election victory and the impending privatisation of care homes. Gail could tell that Dr Marks was not a champion of the proposals.

'Do you like acting?' his aunt asked Benedict. 'Have you had any formal training?'

I have had a lifetime of training, he thought. 'I liked drama lessons at school. I was always cast in a lead role in school plays, despite my… stage fright.'

'And how did you overcome that?' she asked.

He turns red and he looks flustered; she knows he does not wish to talk, but he must, he simply must – everything depends upon it. She is relieved when he musters up the courage to say, 'I told myself not to think about the audience. I tried to lose myself in the role.'

To his surprise, he had found that he was good at acting and that he could make people laugh. Playing the fool on stage and playing cricket; they were the only things that had given him any kudos at school.

Dr Marks studied him carefully. He feared she might call him out as a liar, but when she spoke, she addressed his aunt on an entirely different subject. 'I like what you have done with the house, Gail. I understand the place was in quite a state when you moved in last year?'

Benedict had nearly fallen off his chair. It had never occurred to him, not once, that his aunt had only recently moved to the area. He had assumed the farmhouse had been in 'the family' for generations.

'Thank you,' she said, smiling, 'there is still much to do and much to sort out. You are my first proper guest.'

Dr Marks raised her glass. 'I am honoured. I was thrilled to receive your invitation and I was sorry to have missed you when you visited the care home. I have so wanted to meet you. I have always admired your art.'

*

After dinner there is a musical interlude, his aunt stationed at the piano. Benedict had no idea she could play, and play so well.

The first piece is surprisingly simple, a 'Study in A Minor', by August Müller, but she invests such sadness into it that Benedict recalls to his mind's eye the tragic images he had seen at the Imperial War Museum.

'Play Chopin's "Prelude",' says Dr Goodman. '"Opus 28, Number Four"; it was always Suzie's favourite.'

Dutifully, she obliges. By the time she has finished, tears are flowing freely down his cheeks. He reaches inside his blazer and removes a small wooden box. He opens the lid and, in tinkling and metallic notes, it begins to recite the 'Prelude'.

'I made this for her,' he confides, 'when she was bedridden. I should have put it in her coffin, but I couldn't bring myself to part with it; too many memories and all that.'

Trying to lift the mood, Dr Marks agrees to accompany his aunt in a duet, and, once the sheet music has been found, and after a few false starts, they complete a rousing rendition of 'The Arrival of the Queen of Sheba'.

His aunt then moves to the cello and begins the laborious task of tuning it. Another duet, this time a performance of Elgar's 'Cello Concerto'. As she plays the piano accompaniment, Benedict cannot help noticing how long Dr Marks' fingers are, and how fast they move.

'I think he might have enjoyed that,' says his aunt when they finish.

'Who?' asks Benedict.

'Elgar. His statue is in the town. He lived in these parts,' answers Dr Marks.

'We must do this again,' says his aunt. 'It has been too long since I last played. I am rusty.'

'Yes,' says Dr Marks enthusiastically. 'Yes, we simply must.'

*

'Let us retire to the library,' says his aunt, 'it is time for a digestif. Cyril, will you pour the brandy, please. Benedict, you can have a hot chocolate. Harriet, you will stay the night, won't you?'

They sit in the Queen Anne chairs. Benedict finds it uncomfortable. He feels out of place.

'Do you know how to play Solo, Benedict?' asks Dr Goodman, unwrapping a new pack of playing cards, removing the jokers and giving the deck a quick shuffle.

'Yes, Dad taught me. We often played, me, Dad and my brothers.'

'Yes,' he says, smiling, 'a game for four people, thirteen cards each.'

'Your father went to Solo School,' says his aunt adopting a friendly, conversational tone. 'Your grandmother took him. They played the game seriously.'

'Yes,' he replies, 'he often said anyone who talked during a game would get "drummed out of Solo School". We thought it was a joke.'

'It was no joke,' says his aunt. 'They played for high stakes. After each deal, if nobody was able to go, the players would call "pass" and they would all put money into a kitty. As you know, at the start of a new game each player tries to make a "call". They must state how many tricks they will be able to win or lose.'

'Yes, I know,' he says, 'to call "solo" you have to be able to win five "tricks" out of thirteen "hands", or rounds.'

'That's right,' she says, 'and for "abundance", nine from

thirteen; "abundance" or any higher call wins the kitty. If there had been a lot of "passes" then there could be a lot of money in the kitty. A real windfall. That is why they took it seriously. There were strict rules in the school: no talking during the rounds, no conferring and strictly no cheating. There was a minimum stake required to participate, and "heavies" on hand to ensure fair play.'

Is that where he learnt all the strange expressions he used to come out with during a game? thinks Benedict. *'Hand like a foot' and 'There's many a poor man living along the embankment who didn't lead with his trumps'.* He was a man who made little conversation and usually replied to any question with one of his stock expressions, his favourite being: 'Why keep a dog and bark yourself?'

A thought occurs to him. 'Dr Marks, do you think my dad will still be able to play Solo?'

She looks at him thoughtfully, and not without sympathy. 'Benedict, I hope you don't mind, but earlier this evening, Gail told me a little bit about your father. I would need to examine him to be sure, but I am afraid the prognosis does not sound promising.'

He casts his eyes down and concentrates on the hand Dr Goodman has dealt him: a hand like a foot.

He knows they all look at him with concern. He tries not to appear glum.

'Pass.'

'Benedict,' says Dr Marks, adopting what he assumes is her professional voice – it is how medical doctors have always addressed him – 'have you been to visit your father?'

Of course he has, first in the hospitals and then in the care homes. They have moved him four times. There is no point in visiting him again, he is… 'absent without leave', as one professional put it.

He nods his head and looks away.

Dr Marks says, 'There are several forms of dementia. As I understand it, your father has suffered a very severe stroke. There is extensive damage and paralysis. I am sorry, but I would be surprised if he made any sort of recovery, and even if he does, his memory may have gone for good.'

He supposes she is used to delivering bad news; she does it so nicely. He tries to appear brave. 'No more chess or Solo with Dad, then.' He had hoped to make light of it, but he thinks he sounds heartless.

Dr Marks does not castigate him for his crass remark, none of them do. They seem to understand his turmoil.

'I am sorry,' she says, and he thinks she means it. He finds that he cannot dislike her, however much he tries.

*

The evening settles down into a tense game of Solo. They 'pass' many times and the kitty – a pile of copper coins – grows and grows. Benedict is unusually talkative, chatting to Dr Marks about the school plays he starred in, and his brothers. He finds her easy to talk to. She is intrigued by the idiosyncrasies of his family, but even more intrigued by the workings of his mind. She marvels at how he can observe so much when his eyes are cast downwards so often. And his memory is prodigious, far better than hers, despite all the years of brain training she has undertaken. Time and again, towards the end of a game, he knows exactly what cards are left in their hands, something he has been able to deduce by remembering who has played which cards.

Towards the end of the evening, and after his aunt has claimed the kitty, Dr Marks turns to Benedict and says, 'One of our care home staff is leaving in the summer. There will be a vacancy, part-time, for someone to help "entertain the troops". Do you think you would be interested in applying? The pay isn't great, but it would give you some income, and I think you would find it interesting.'

'What would I have to do?' he asks.

'Talk to our patients and help out with the programme of entertainments. There is no shortage of games to play. The idea is to try to keep people active and occupied. We think it might help combat dementia.'

He looks uncertain. 'Will you be there?'

'Some of the time, yes. But when I'm not, just imagine the job is a part you have in a play in a school production. You said you can act.'

He nods. 'Yes, yes, alright, I will apply.'

She smiles encouragingly. 'Good for you. I will put in a good word for you,' she says, 'when the position becomes vacant.'

Unseen by either of them, Dr Goodman sends his aunt a sly and knowing wink, and she smiles inwardly in triumph.

13

The Two-Horse Citroën

Three weeks later, SW France,
summer 1979

Benedict and his aunt spend the morning in a leisurely climb, walking from the wine-making village of Pomerol towards the summit of Saint-Emilion. Towards the end of their pilgrimage, they ascend a steep, cobbled street, the medieval houses closing in all around. They are thankful for the shade. It is a hot, cloudless day, temperatures already in the mid-thirties, and by the time they reach the top, Gail Miller needs to rest. They find a table beneath an awning at a café conveniently located opposite the entrance to the ancient bell tower that commands Saint-Emilion's heights. From their vantage point, they can look out beyond the walls of the town and across the endless fields of vines, the clusters of grapes not yet visible. The sea of green is only disrupted by the occasional island, an isolated hamlet or a Gothic and fortified chateau, and

Benedict thinks there is something timeless in the vista. He recognises the landscape from the painting in his aunt's dining room.

'Try out your French,' she suggests as the tardy waiter eventually deigns to approach them. He has an aggressive and impatient mien, not at all welcoming.

'Good morning, sir,' he says, trying his hardest, trying to remember what she has taught him. 'I would like a glass of fresh orange juice please.'

The waiter pretends not to understand and shrugs his shoulders.

As he makes to turn away, his aunt says, 'I know "the Nose".'

She speaks quickly and in the local dialect. The man freezes, instantly, a look of fear crossing his face.

'You understood the boy,' says Gail. 'I'll have a glass of red wine, something full bodied, and not any of that rubbish you serve tourists. And bring me oysters. Make sure they are fresh. Be quick now, we've waited long enough.'

She dismisses him with a petulant wave of her hand.

The transformation in the waiter is immediate. He becomes attentive and efficient, fawning even. Benedict preferred his previous incarnation.

Satisfied she has put the churlish waiter in his place, she sits back in her chair and removes her straw hat and sunglasses. She uses a handkerchief to wipe beads of perspiration from her forehead.

'I'm getting a bit too old for that walk,' she confesses. 'There was a time when I could run that route in ten minutes.'

'When you lived here, before the war?' he asks.

She nods. 'Yes, Benedict, I am sorry I could not tell you the whole story at once, but I wanted you to see Saint-Emilion and the surrounding area, so that you could get a sense of what things were like. It has not changed much.'

'And you were a nurse, working in Libourne?'

'Yes, that's right. I think I was quite a good one, but I would have preferred to have been a doctor.'

'Like your… "friend", the man portrayed in the sketch in the dining room.'

'Yes, Dr Fronsac; he was a most valued colleague. He had good contacts. He helped me to escape France, just before the Germans invaded. He helped many people escape. Alas, he was captured and imprisoned. Nobody knows what became of him after that.'

'And this is where the SOE operation went badly wrong?'

'Yes, you will understand more this afternoon, when the guide shows us the caves.'

'The caves beneath the monolithic church?'

'Yes, that's right.'

Lies upon lies, he thinks; when will she ever tell him the truth? But then he recalls the conversation he had with Dr Marks, and he is reminded to show more gratitude. He says:

'Thank you for bringing me here. I enjoyed the flight, and I liked Bordeaux. It was kind of you to get me a passport. I will pay you back, I promise. I prefer the house you have here. It is better than Wellend, despite the mosquitoes.'

'They are particularly bad this year,' she says, scratching at a bite on her ankle. 'I don't ever remember there being so many of the blighters.'

*

After lunch, they join a party of tourists, and a local guide takes them on a tour of the caves beneath the medieval church. Benedict does not find it as interesting as he had hoped; the man says nothing about the war. His English is terrible, and he can barely understand him, but he seems to drone on almost exclusively about religion or wine. Benedict does not have much interest in either. The tour seems little more than an excuse for the adults to engage in yet more wine tasting – this time, underground, as if that novelty somehow improved the experience – and to purchase overpriced and overrated bottles of what Dr Goodman would no doubt have dismissed as 'second-rate plonk'.

On their leisurely descent back to Pomerol, his aunt decides it is time for illumination. 'There are cave systems carved into the limestone in many local places. They have been used for storing wine for centuries. During the war, some of them were used by the Resistance and the SOE to temporarily house escaped prisoners of war, Jewish refugees, and air crews that had been shot down. There was a secret network of people who helped get them south and across the Spanish border to safety. Dr Fronsac was part of that system, until his arrest. Later on in the war, the caves were used to hide ammunition and explosives.'

'And that is what Grandfather was supposed to do, hide explosives in the caves?'

She nods. 'Yes, as I told you, the plan was to open up a second front along the Atlantic coast and to take control of the port of Bordeaux. Your grandfather's operation was a key part of the plan. Bordeaux had been attacked earlier in the war when a group had knocked out the electricity substation serving the Italian U-boat pens. The Germans had carried out terrible reprisals after that. Your grandfather was supposed to co-ordinate the local resistance ahead of the invasion, working to knock out the railway lines, power supplies and communication systems.'

'But they were betrayed. The Germans knew all about it. They were waiting for him when he landed?'

'No, not the Germans, not at first; the traitor leaked information to the local gendarmes who collaborated with the occupying forces and carried out the arrests.'

He recalls the photograph in his aunt's dining room, the one showing a gendarme guarding a group of labourers. How could they have collaborated with the Nazis?

'The gendarmes handed over the resistance fighters and SOE operatives to the Gestapo,' she says, her voice choking. 'The SOE operatives wore civilian clothes and so were interrogated and executed as spies. The entire network was virtually wiped out in just one night.'

'And that is what happened to Grandad?'

It is painful for her to talk about it, even now, he can sense that, but so far, she has been telling him the truth.

'No, Benedict, when he landed, the gendarmes were

waiting for him, but he overshot the landing area, and so they could not capture him immediately. He tried to escape. There was gun fire. Several gendarmes were killed. He did not give up without a fight. Your grandfather was killed in action.'

He is not sure what he feels. He never knew his grandfather; he is a ghost, a stranger, a figure conjured up from fragments of other people's memories, and yet he cannot deny he has strong emotions: anger, sadness, loss and even a desire for revenge.

'How did you find this out?' he asks.

It is a good question, she thinks. *He should have asked it before now.*

'Cyril and I have contacts in the intelligence services, colleagues from our university days. They have helped us to piece the puzzle together. And there is a journalist we know who has good contacts in high places, and we have exchanged certain information with him. And of course, I still know people in Libourne and Saint-Emilion, and some of them have proven… most co-operative.'

It is a partial truth, he is sure of that. There is still something she is not telling him.

'And why is Dr Goodman so keen to help you?'

She tries to sound casual in her reply. 'Oh, has he not told you? I thought he would have done so by now. He is becoming rather forgetful. He and your grandfather were the best of friends at Cambridge. He was in the RAF during the war. He often flew missions for SOE operatives, although he would have preferred other assignments. It was Cyril who piloted the Dakota aeroplane that transported B.B. to France. He has been as keen as anyone to track down the traitor. He feels responsible for his friend's death, you see.'

*

Gail Miller's French house is located just to the north of the Dordogne river, just above its floodplain, and only a few kilometres to the west of the town of Libourne. It is an elegant villa, three storeys high, with prominent wooden shutters, flower-bedecked balconies and a roof covered in red clay tiles.

They arrived at the villa in the late afternoon, having taken the train from Bordeaux to Libourne, from where they hired a taxi. There had been a terrific electrical storm, the sky lit up by sheets of lightning, and thunder rolling along the valley. Hailstones the size of pebbles had battered the plants in the garden, cracked the windscreen of the taxi and smashed several of the clay roof tiles. The next day, his aunt had wasted no time in donning her dungarees, fetching out a ladder and setting about repairing the roof, reconfiguring the interlocking system of convex tiles to form a watertight structure.

He had been impressed by her practical skills. When they arrived, the electricity was off. She fetched out a torch and asked him to check the fuse box. He had no idea what to do. Patiently, she had shown him how to test and change the broken fuses.

In the garage was a Citroën 2CV. It looked like it had been left out in several hailstorms.

'It has not had a run in some time. Do you know anything about engines?' she asked.

'I am afraid not,' he admitted, a little shamefaced. 'My elder brother is good with motorbikes, but I am not mechanically minded.'

'Poppycock,' she replied. 'It isn't brain surgery, not like Dr Marks performs. Here, help me with this.'

She showed him how to adjust the tyre pressure, how to check the oil levels, how to remove, clean and adjust the spark plugs. He found it interesting, far more so than the pointless metalwork and woodwork lessons he had been made to do at school. When his younger brother had been subjected to the same curricula and had brought home yet another letter opener carved in a woodwork lesson, his mother had exclaimed, 'How many letter openers does that bloody school think I need! I don't need a sodding letter opener, wooden or otherwise, not for bills: they go straight on the fire.'

His aunt had shown him how to bump-start the car in second gear, and they had taken it for 'a spin' to charge the battery.

'Do you know what CV stands for?' she asked. '*Chevaux vapeur*.'

She gave him time to figure it out. 'Horsepower,' he replied, 'two horsepower.'

'Correct,' she said, beaming, proud of his progress. 'Low power, low tax.' She let him practise driving around her garden, caring naught if the parched lawn got churned up.

The extensive garden had turned out to be a delight, except for the mosquitoes. There was a seating area, shaded by several hazelnut trees, the soft nuts ripe and ready for eating. Benedict harvested them and his aunt added them to salads. There were tomato plants and lemon trees, and all manner of flowers Benedict had no knowledge of. It was like a new and private world to explore. There were dozens of startled lizards, scurrying up the walls and disappearing into crevices. He often saw deer in the garden, and once, after a storm, a savage-looking crayfish. Not knowing what it was, he had been wary of it. His aunt had gently chided him, saying he should have brought it in 'for the pot'. He was amazed by what people would eat: snails, frogs, oysters, mussels, eels, zander, pike and bream. He supposed it had something to do with poverty; that people had to make do with whatever resources they could acquire. But then he thought about his father's house and the available resources, and how they were never tempted to eat snails, worms or slugs, however hungry they were.

When his aunt was not in residence, the villa was looked after by the elderly neighbours, who turned out to be 'friends from my hospital days', although they treated Gail more like a member of their family. They spoke no English and spent much of their time in their garden, tending to their crops. Despite their advanced age, they were healthy and rugged, their skin well tanned and furrowed from long hours exposed to the sun. His aunt repaid their kindness by taking them to Libourne market, or to the medical centre or dentist, for they had no car and had never learnt to drive. They doted on Benedict, bringing him presents, including a Breton fisherman's smock and jumper which had once belonged to their son.

He wished he knew more French, so that he could thank them properly. As a gift for them, his aunt had helped him to make pots of hazelnut spread.

The villa formed part of a hamlet that stretched like a ribbon along the dusty road that led to Libourne. It was surrounded by vineyards, and higher up the valley, pine forests. There was an ancient church on the brow of a low hill. It had massive wooden doors, a spiralling tower, peeling plaster and heavily weathered white stone. They visited it one day, but Gail Miller kept from him that some of the pits in the lime were bullet holes.

Just outside the entrance to the church there was a war monument, a bronze statue of an infantryman in First World War uniform, the metal already coated by a green patina. He seemed to have been cast in the act of advancing across No Man's Land, a bayonet attached to his rifle. Benedict thought he had the appearance of a man who expected to be struck by a bullet at any moment, for his face was full of pain and remorse. The statue stood on a granite plinth, the names of local people etched into it. The letters were weathering badly and fading. There was a tribute written on a plaque, but it was turning to verdigris. Benedict could still make out enough to decipher its meaning: '*In honour of all the brave children of France who gave their lives during the two world wars.*' Fresh flowers had been placed around the base of the monument. The Tricolore fluttered in the breeze from an adjacent flagpole. It was a sombre scene, but a strangely peaceful one, thought Benedict: a fitting place to remember the sacrifice and suffering, a mark on the landscape, a permanent reminder on what happened here, 'Lest we forget'.

Gail Miller knelt beside the monument, seemingly lost in prayer. She had brought her own floral tribute. He saw her reach out and touch the plinth with a trembling hand, mumbling words to herself. She took out her handkerchief and wiped a tear from her eye. Unbeknownst to Benedict, it was a ritual she performed every year.

'Is this where he is buried?' he asked.

She took a moment to compose herself. 'No, Benedict, I'm afraid I don't know where B.B. is buried, not exactly. His body was taken to Libourne, where there was a German garrison. There were many executions that night. We think some of the bodies were taken to a nearby wood and buried in an unmarked grave, but nobody knows where. Despite our efforts, we have not been able to discover it.'

14

The Nose of Saint-Emilion

On the journey back from their excursion to Saint-Emilion, Benedict asks, 'Why can't I let Nan and Father know what happened to Grandad? Why must we keep it secret?'

His aunt pulls the car over to the side of the road and switches off the engine. He deserves an answer, she knows that.

'Benedict, you have to trust me. I cannot tell you everything I know, not yet. Your grandmother was told that B.B. had died fighting in France during a special operation, that is all, and she never pushed for more details, never wanted to know exactly what had happened. Does that strike you as odd?'

He thinks about Silver-Sherry Nan; she likes a quiet life. She had worked part-time in a hairdressers shop until she retired, and then, she had surprised everyone by purchasing an expensive flat in Brighton. The win on the football pools must have been very substantial. He supposes she was the compliant sort who didn't like to make a fuss – part of the 'mustn't grumble' generation.

But then he ponders how little he knows about her; how little interest he has taken in her life. He had assumed she had always been as she is now.

'I don't know,' he says. 'I don't even know what Nan did during the war.'

'She… she… entertained the troops. She kept your father with her in London, despite the Blitz. He was never evacuated, as he should have been. She exposed him to great danger. She has always been selfish.'

He thinks she is being disingenuous; perhaps she couldn't bear to be parted from her child. That's love isn't it, not selfishness. He holds his tongue.

'B.B. was furious when he found out,' continues his aunt. 'Your father's education suffered as a result. The school was bombed and the best teachers recruited for the war effort. The school had to bring staff out of retirement, and they had a terrible time trying to control those feral East End boys. He was bright, your father; he could have done well in academia, but he never really had a chance.'

'He never wanted the chance,' protests Benedict. 'He *wanted* to join the army. He wanted to fight a war. He was a marksman. Nan told me that he volunteered to fight in Malaysia, but he failed the medical and they pensioned him off.'

She nods her head. 'Yes, I know, he was quite bitter about it. I suppose many in his generation were sick of hearing about the heroic deeds of those who fought in the war; they needed a chance to show what they could do, too.'

'I don't think it was that,' he replies thoughtfully. 'He liked the camaraderie and the adventure of it. I think it was the only time he ever had real friends.'

Perhaps he is right, she thinks; perhaps she needs to be more honest with him. 'I never saw eye to eye with your grandmother. She was a dancer in the chorus line of a London show. That is where B.B. met her. She had many… admirers.'

He is astounded by the revelation. 'Nan was a dancer?' He can't believe his ears, but he has no sense that his aunt is lying. How was it that he had never known that?

'I must confess, I found her rather common, and I disapproved of the marriage. In my youthful arrogance, I thought my brother could do much better and that she wouldn't prove a good match. They had so very little in common.'

She refrains from adding that she found her manipulative, and that she was already pregnant when they married. She was never what she pretended to be.

'Is that why she dislikes you?'

'Perhaps, but your grandmother and your father got it into their heads that I was somehow to blame for B.B.'s death. I think they had visions of him dropping into France to rescue me, which was nonsense. No, Benedict, until we are certain of our facts, I think it is best that we leave the rest of the family out of this, for now. It could only reopen old wounds.'

*

They have not driven far from Saint-Emilion when his aunt pulls off the road for a second time. She stops in front of a pair of huge wrought-iron gates, which guard the entrance to a substantial chateau. A warning sign reads, 'NO ENTRY', the message repeated in several languages. Through the open car window, and above the pronounced ticking of the idling engine, Benedict can hear dogs barking in alarm. They sound savage. A gatekeeper is approaching, holding two of the beasts on a lead. He wears heavy boots and moleskin breeches. He is thickset and has a shotgun slung over his shoulder.

Undeterred, his aunt quickly darts out of the car and throws open the gates. She jumps back in and speeds off up the drive, nearly knocking the startled gatekeeper over.

They head uphill at an alarming speed, the two-horsepower engine protesting and sounding like it is about to rise up through the bonnet.

'Gail!' says Benedict in alarm, holding on to his seat for dear life. 'This isn't a getaway car!'

She doesn't respond. She guns the accelerator pedal to the floor.

Towards the top of the drive, more armed guards appear, blocking the way to the house and pointing their weapons at them menacingly. His aunt slams on the brakes and brings the car screeching to a halt.

'Damn!' she says.

She yanks on the handbrake and thumps her fist against the horn. It gives a continuous, angry blast.

The guards do not know what to do. Hesitantly, they approach the 'crazy old lady', their guns wavering in their shaking hands, calling out for her to switch off the ignition and get out of the car.

She ignores them.

'Quickly, wind up your window and lock the door,' she says.

He is just in time. The gatekeeper's dogs are upon them, snapping and snarling and clawing at the metalwork and windows. There is an angry thump on the bonnet, the choleric gatekeeper remonstrating with them and violently pulling at the door handle. Still his aunt presses the horn.

After what seems like an eternity to Benedict, an elderly man appears in the doorway of the chateau. He is portly and has a thick moustache. His greasy black hair is swept back across his head. He wears a collarless white shirt with black braces, with a black armband just above his left elbow. He holds a fat cigar between the fingers of his right hand. His expression is stern. Benedict wonders if the house is a casino.

The portly man looks at the car and he looks at Gail. To Benedict's surprise, he seems to recognise both. He gives a short, impatient wave of his hand and shouts something harsh. Within moments, the dogs have been called off and the path cleared. They drive past the astonished guards and on past the chateau, his aunt hardly taking her eyes from the man with the cigar, and he never once looking away.

Once they are out of sight, Benedict asks, 'Who was that man?'

Gail turns to him and laughs. 'That was fun, wasn't it? Admit it, you enjoyed that little escapade.'

It is the most animated he has ever seen her. He isn't sure he is enjoying himself; he is still shaking with fright.

'Congratulations,' she says, 'you have just seen "the Nose". Not many people have the honour.'

'The *who*?' he asks, completely at a loss.

She pulls the car over and applies the handbrake, this time correctly.

'The Nose, dear boy, the man with the cigar. During the war, he collaborated with the Germans.'

It is too much information and delivered too quickly. He struggles to keep up.

'Is he the one who betrayed Grandad?' he asks, after a pause, thinking that the man had looked evil.

She sighs, and looks at him kindly. 'No, Benedict. What you have to understand is that things are seldom what they seem. During the war, the vintners in this area had a terrible time. The Germans commandeered their wine and their source of wealth. There was dreadful hunger and poverty. And yet, despite the awful dangers they faced, a good many of them risked their lives to defy the Germans, as did many others.'

He looks confused. 'But you said the Nose was a collaborator.'

'And he was. Do you know what a sommelier is?'

'A wine taster; the guide in the cave said something about it.'

She raises her eyebrows in surprise. 'Oh, so you were listening after all. He was a frightful bore, wasn't he?

Anyway, the Nose is a master sommelier. Rumour has it that he can accurately detect up to thirty separate notes in a single glass of wine. During the war, many local vintners tried to hide their best wines from the Germans. Often, they deliberately mislabelled the bottles or casks. The Nose offered the Germans his services and they rewarded him richly for it. He could always tell a doctored wine or a substitute. He became wealthy; he still is, wealthy and powerful. The "heavies" you saw back at the house are only a small part of his army.'

She points across an abandoned field towards a derelict farmhouse. 'Do you see that building?'

'Yes, what about it?'

'The couple who lived there were caught out by the Nose. They were arrested and deported to a labour camp. The house was burnt down as a lesson to other vintners.'

'And do people know this?' he asks in outrage. 'How can they let that man continue to live here? Why hasn't he been charged for his crimes?'

She is impressed by his sense of natural justice. 'Because, Benedict, the Nose also saved many lives.'

Once more, his face registers confusion.

'He was a double agent. The Germans never suspected him, not once. He took great personal risks. He told them that wine was vintage or valuable when he knew it was not; it had been doctored, watered down, but who was going to question a master sommelier? His services were in great demand. He was invited to many parties with high-ranking German officials. He had access to top secret intelligence. And the network I told you about often relied on him. Sometimes, when people had to be moved in secret, they were hidden inside large casks. The Nose, working with the Germans, was responsible for inspecting those casks before they could be transported, and he allowed them to pass, knowing that he would be executed if the trick was ever discovered. He acted bravely, Benedict; he had to tread such a fine line, but in the end, he saved many, many people.'

He shakes his head in amazement. *Things are seldom what they seem.* 'Gail, the photograph in your dining room of the labourers moving a cask…'

'Yes, Benedict, they were part of the network. They were moving people in those barrels. The Nose gave me that picture.'

'But they were guarded by a mean-looking gendarme?'

She smiles sadly. 'Do you think he looked mean? Perhaps he did; perhaps it helped to make him such an excellent operative. We have learnt that he was the lynchpin of the network. Can you imagine that? He worked right in the heart of the paramilitary police force. He was an incredibly brave man, a truly heroic gendarme. He died the same night B.B. did. He was a cousin of the Nose.'

They are silent for a while.

'Why did the Nose let us pass?' he asks.

'Because he knows me and he knows about my brother. I have talked to him once before. He gave me useful leads.'

He looks baffled. 'But if he knows you, why didn't we just call at the front door? Why did we have to risk being shot?'

She laughs. 'We didn't risk being shot. I am not "crazy"! Those guards don't carry loaded weapons. It's all for show.

The Nose is a recluse. He does not like to be reminded about the war and he seldom accepts visitors. We would not have been allowed in. With a man like that, sometimes you have to force his hand.'

He is still confused. 'Is that how you got to see him last time?'

'No, it took months and months of negotiations with third parties. In the end, I had to pay a considerable number of bribes and agree to paint a portrait of his dogs!'

He is silent for a while, trying to still his racing heart. She has told him so many lies he struggles to sift out the truth. 'And why are we here? You didn't even call at the house.'

'I need to show you something. I would like you to drive.'

'Drive? Drive where?'

'Across the abandoned field towards the derelict house. If you take down a few vines en route, do not fear. The Nose can afford the loss.'

'But the 2CV will be shaken apart!'

She laughs. 'I see the lesson hasn't yet been learnt! This car was specifically designed for farmers, so that they could drive on unmade roads and farm tracks and get their produce to market. It is the engine that powers the French economy. It has wonderful suspension, you will see; it is far superior to the Land Rover and uses much less fuel. Now, drive, young man, drive.'

He obeys dutifully and nervously steers the car towards the abandoned farmhouse. He stalls the engine twice and kangaroo jumps several times, which causes his aunt to laugh aloud. He is relieved when they park and get out of the car. His hands shake badly and his legs feel like jelly. He notices that the internal mirror has been shaken loose and there is an awful smell like burning rubber.

'Well done,' she says, but he is not convinced. She is in a strange mood, he thinks: focused and yet detached somehow, as if she is in her own world and not really with him. He recognises the signs.

They spend a little time exploring the ruins. His aunt grows quiet and sombre. Despite the state of neglect, he finds it a peaceful spot. Beside a low, derelict wall, she stops and begins to carefully pull out a few weeds. Behind them, she reveals a simple faded red cross, painted onto the wall, with an inscription, in French, that reads: '*With eternal love, always, FF.*'

Gail kneels down before the cross. She whispers, as though she were in a chapel of rest, 'This is where they fell, Benedict; this is where they fell.'

In her hand she holds a small musical box, exactly like the one Dr Goodman made for his wife. Carefully, reverentially, as if handling a precious urn containing a loved one's ashes, she places it on top of the wall, directly above the cross.

He wonders what melody it plays.

15

Scripts

The Cedars Care Home, Malvern, summer 1979

Benedict has never worn brogues before. He had to use a shoehorn to lever them on. The unfamiliar and unyielding leather crushes his toes and rubs the back of his heels. He can already feel them blister. He hopes he does not have to walk far. The tie around his neck feels like a tightening snare. He inserts his index finger inside the collar of his pristine white shirt and tries to loosen it. He dare not remove it. He has no idea how to put it back on; his aunt had tied it for him. He can feel sweat trickling down his back and wonders if he should take off his jacket, his new woollen suit unsuited to the summer heat. He feels overdressed.

There are three other people waiting to be interviewed for the part-time post at the Cedars Care Home. None of them wears a suit. They are seated on creaking padded chairs in the cavernous atrium of an imposing Victorian building, a former grand hotel, trying hard not to make their surreptitious assessment of the competition too obvious. The large entrance doors have been wedged open. A whirling fan circulates lugubriously on the reception desk, its perpetual protest doing little to disturb the stifling air.

At one end of the atrium there is a broad, gently winding staircase leading to the upper floors. It has ornate wooden balustrades and rails, and a sage green carpet tread, fraying and worn. There is a redundant chandelier hanging from the ceiling. The walls are decorated with gaudy frames housing Restoration portraits of conceited-looking nobles in powdered wigs, or stern Victorians with bristling beards. Looking up to the first-floor landing, Benedict can see dark wood panelling, a pair of stag's antlers, and a small armoury of flintlock pistols, swords, shields and a full set of armour. He feels like he has entered a museum; he feels intimidated.

They hear a door slam shut on the first floor, and a woman swiftly descends the stairs, almost at a run. She is whistling to herself, her attitude and attire incongruous with the surroundings. She is dressed casually in shorts, T-shirt and flip-flops. She has a broad, welcoming smile. 'I'm Mrs Hart,' she announces, in a strong accent. 'Constance Hart, I'm the manager of the Cedars. I'll be part of the interview panel. Follow me, guys; let me show you the place.'

'Are you Australian?' asks one of the interviewees, a rotund woman in her thirties, who Benedict supposes must be a similar age to Mrs Hart. She has an open personality and a generous smile; her voice denotes genuine interest in getting to know the manager. Benedict immediately identifies her as the strongest candidate and his chief rival.

'Yeah, from Melbourne. Have you been?'

Their genial conversation continues all the way up the stairs and through the security doors and into the dining hall and recreational rooms of the care home. They exchange compliments like reunited friends.

'The living quarters are on the upper floors,' says the manager. 'Most of the residents are sunning themselves in the garden at the moment, but you will meet them later.'

'Christ, it stinks like a shithouse in here,' mumbles another of the candidates, a young man no older than Benedict, his face bedevilled by acne.

The manager pretends not to hear, but from the flicker of annoyance that crosses her face, Benedict reasons the competition has been reduced by one.

'We like to keep the residents busy,' continues Mrs Hart. 'We encourage visitors, and day trips out, for those that are able, and lots of games. We've got a croquet lawn and a pitch and putt green.'

'And table tennis?' asks Benedict. 'I've read that it is good for people with dementia.'

The manager beams at him. 'That's right, yeah, we've got an indoor table. Do you play?'

'Yes,' he lies. How hard can it be?

He feels pleased with himself; he has asked a question and shown interest in the job. His aunt and Dr Goodman insisted this was important. They have helped him to prepare, with mock interviews, advice on how to answer questions and scripts for him to learn – opening lines to initiate conversations with strangers. He has been diligent; he has learnt his lines well, because Gail Miller finally explained why he 'simply must get the job'.

'We don't use the D word in front of the residents,' whispers the manager, nudging Benedict conspiratorially, and then, addressing all the candidates: 'I'm afraid some have very severe memory loss. The nurses and care workers will take care of their basic needs: feeding, dressing, washing and medication. The successful candidate will be part of the entertainments team, assisting me.'

'I can play chess and cards,' offers Benedict, seeing an opportunity to impress. The manager smiles at him encouragingly, but the final candidate, a sour-faced young woman wearing large earrings and bright red lipstick, scowls, as if to say: 'The bloody interview hasn't started yet, sunshine.' She is chewing gum, and absentmindedly blows a bubble, which pops, loudly.

The 'living room' is a large, airy space furnished with comfortable sofas and armchairs. A colour television plays to itself in one corner, the sound intrusive and irritating. There are bookshelves and coffee tables bestrewn with magazines and newspapers – the crosswords half completed – and a record player with built-in speakers placed on a low table by the door, a selection of vintage LPs stacked next to it. There are three residents present: a man sleeping soundly on one of the sofas, a woman sitting next to him reading a book and a man sitting by himself playing solitaire. A bored nurse looks out of the tall windows, lamenting being indoors on such a fine day.

The manager cheerfully invites them to 'get to know the residents', whilst they await their turn for interview. The sour-faced woman is the first to go in, hesitantly following Mrs Hart through an oak-panelled door that leads to the interview room.

Benedict is nudged again, this time by the young man, whose eyes follow the sour-faced woman through the door. He whispers, 'I wonder who she's been "entertaining". Did you see the love bites on her neck?'

Laughing aloud, the youth turns his back on the residents and plonks himself down in front of the television, adjusting the channels irritably. The nurse stares at his back and then looks towards Benedict. She sighs and shakes her head in disapproval.

The middle-aged woman introduces herself to the room as Joan and starts talking amiably with the woman reading the book. 'Pleased to meet you, Joan,' she says. 'Forgive my husband; he likes to take a siesta at this time of day.'

'Don't we all, dear,' she replies, and they immediately strike up a friendly and easy conversation about the news, commenting on the 'scandalous' ten per cent rise in the price of milk, the 'shocking' rise in the price of petrol and the 'shameful' rise in unemployment. Joan observes that, 'The country had gone to the dogs under Labour; it's going down the bloody toilet under the Tories! Bleeding politicians!'

Benedict knows he is being judged; the nurse will report back to the interview panel. He needs to act.

He sits down opposite the man playing solitaire and delivers one of his memorised lines: 'Hello, I am Benedict. Would you like to play cards?'

The man does not look up. 'I am playing cards; by myself,' he replies grumpily. 'Can't you see?'

It is not an encouraging start, and it is not how the rehearsals had gone. He will have to 'play by ear'.

'It's a lovely sunny day. Wouldn't you like to go outside?'

'I hate the sun. If I wanted to go outside I would.'

Having been rebutted twice, he can think of nothing else to say. Feeling embarrassed and not knowing what else to do, he sits in silence and watches the man finish his game. When he has played his last card, the man sighs, leans back in his chair and looks up at Benedict for the first time.

'I am King Arthur,' he says, his face deadly serious.

He does not know what to say; there was no script for this. Is the man insane? Should he humour him, and say, 'Pleased to meet you, Your Majesty'?

The man laughs, suddenly appearing friendlier. 'Arthur King, if you must know, although everyone here calls me King Arthur. You are here for the interview?'

'That's right.'

'Why? Why would you want to waste your youth away in this house of death? Youth is the most precious thing you have, Benedict; don't spend it here amongst all this… this… decrepitude.' He waves his hand towards the other couple in the room.

'Don't you like it here?'

King Arthur looks sorrowful. 'The food isn't bad, and the staff try their best, and the accommodation is alright, but I would prefer to be back home, in my own house. That's where all my fondest memories are. I tell you, son, I fear if I stay here much longer I shall lose my mind. Here it all feels… like I am back in the army; back in the barracks.'

Benedict nods. 'I understand that.'

'I doubt it,' he replies sourly. 'My wife died last year and my children couldn't wait to get me into this home. They want the house, you see.'

He wonders if that is true. After she had left, his mother had wanted half of the family house. His father had refused. The battle had gone to court and the lawyers had a field day. In the end, his father had been forced to sell and release half of the miserable proceeds to his mother. The doctors thought the stress of it all had likely contributed to his stroke. When the ambulance had arrived to take him to hospital, the estate agents were putting up the 'sold' sign.

'Don't you have any friends here?' asks Benedict.

The man scowls again. 'I don't like the reptiles in residence. They are two-faced; they bitch behind each other's backs. I hear things most people don't. I believe there is one amongst us who is a truly wicked. Alas, I cannot point that person out to you, not unless they are present in the same room.'

Benedict looks down and notices for the first time that King Arthur uses braille playing cards.

*

His aunt is waiting for him in the Land Rover, parked across the road from the care home.

'Well?' she asks as he climbs in beside her.

'They haven't made a decision yet. They will let me know. I thought the interview went alright.'

That is not what she wanted to know. 'Did you meet him?'

He shakes his head. 'No, no, I didn't.'

*

That evening, whilst they are sitting at the kitchen table eating dinner, Benedict hears an unusual sound.

'Telephone,' explains his aunt, getting up and going to the library to answer it.

He has never lived in a house with its own telephone. When his father had his stroke, he had to run to the nearest telephone box to make an emergency call. It was quarter of a mile away, and it was the first time he had ever used it; he was not sure what to do. His face was as red as the telephone box by the time he arrived, breathless, and there was someone already on the phone and a queue of people waiting, impatiently, in the cold. For once in his life he managed to overcome his shyness and said to a woman with the kind face who stood in front of him, 'Please, my father has collapsed. I need an ambulance.'

The woman was forthright and wasted no time in leading him to the front of the queue and hammering on the telephone box with her umbrella. 'Get off the phone, now! We need to make a 999 call,' she shouted out, in a strong Jamaican accent. The man inside the box looked annoyed, but dutifully obliged, said a hasty goodbye to his girlfriend and hung up. The woman with the umbrella

things. From time to time he has agreed to fly missions for them, donning his disguise as an RAF pilot. He has worked at their research facility, helping to develop many of their secret weapons. The people he has met, civilians and professional soldiers alike, have had one defining characteristic: not amateurism, but courage.

And when called upon, Dr Goodman has also flown the Prime Minister to covert meetings. He has got to know him quite well.

'I'm afraid the SOE has the PM's full backing. They will have important work to do ahead of the Normandy landings, as I have already reported. Why don't you have more faith in them? They are brave people.'

'I don't doubt that, but they are also badly trained people, like the gentleman cricketers who used to turn out against professional sides and who regarded the whole affair as a silly game. Little wonder their wireless operators get caught so quickly. And the SOE doesn't communicate to us what they are doing. How many times have they trodden on our toes? Take this Bordeaux business, what do you make of it?'

Dr Goodman sighs. 'I don't know. There is something… something not quite right about it all. The details are vague to say the least. What do you think?'

'I smell betrayal. One of our best agents is at risk. They have worked in Bordeaux and Libourne since 1940. They have access to top military personnel, and they have provided vital intelligence. If one of the SOE plans fails, if one of them is captured and tortured, then the agent's cover could be blown. I cannot risk that happening.'

'Then what do you propose to do?' asks Dr Goodman, lighting his own cigarette.

'I don't know,' replies his friend, looking around like a startled rat, suddenly unsure of his bearings and the way out of the maze. 'For the first time in this bloody war, I don't bloody know.'

Encrypted message intercepted and decoded by British intelligence, Bletchley Park, 3 June 1944

> Tell Uncle Joe that the tour of the red wine region is a ruse. The vines are infested. Uncle Sam trains his eagle eye only to the northern coast. Advise: hand could be valuable but how should it be played?
> B.B.

Message from Françoise Fronsac to the Exequator, Lyon, 15 June 1944

> Go to hell, all of you. The Angel was put in the frame. I will avenge him; I will avenge them all. Do not look for me in Spain. I trust only my own people now. Be vigilant. If you sense someone behind you, run, and run fast, for I might be on your tail, and I never miss. Not once. Not ever.
> FF

17

Lost Wax and Locusts

The Dudley Forge and Foundry, summer 1979

The waiting room of the Dudley Forge and Foundry is little more than a glorified shed furnished with a tatty sofa, a reception desk which looks like it might have been salvaged from a collapsed building, a hand bell for customers to ring should they need to summon assistance, a faded list of prices attached to a filthy window with generous strips of yellowing sellotape and a vending machine which comes with its own 'out of order' sign. Every surface is covered in a healthy layer of dust. The air smells of wet clay, toxic chemicals and acrid smoke.

A poster nailed to the inside of the door claims that the firm are specialists in bronze casting, and a series of indistinct images purports to show the 'lost wax' process. Benedict had never imagined it was so involved. To turn his aunt's clay sculptures into bronze ones, moulds have to be made and lined with layers of wax. The initial layer – the first wax to be poured in – holds a memory for the finest detail of the piece. Then a structure resembling a stretched-out hand playing the piano has to be built and attached to the wax. This allows the liquid metal to flow freely through the piece and allows gases to escape. Before entering the foundry, the mould is dipped in ceramics to strengthen it. Large sculptures have to be cut into sections and then welded back together once the metal has been poured in and given time to cool. The hot iron mixture melts the wax, but it remembers the impression that it made.

After some time, and several forceful and impatient rings of the bell, an aged man dressed in brown overalls appears. 'Ah, Mrs Miller,' he says pleasantly, recognising his most esteemed customer. 'We've got three of your pieces ready, but the fourth is proving a bit tricky.'

She scolds him mildly. 'Really, Albert, doesn't anyone here ever answer the telephone? I tried to ring you, four times!'

Albert shrugs his shoulders, a little shamefaced, and points to his ears. 'You know what I am like, Mrs Miller; these old lugs are not what they used to be. Too much time in the forge.'

She turns to Benedict and introduces him. 'This is Mr Bronze, the proprietor of this establishment. Isn't it just the most appropriate name you could imagine?'

Albert laughs aloud. 'It beats being called Mr Hall! I am like Mr Baker who owns the delicatessen and Mr Butcher who… well, you get the idea. Anyway, I'll get the lads to bring your pieces through. You'll want to inspect them. I take it they are one-off pieces?'

'Yes, of course,' says Gail. 'I want to see the moulds destroyed, Albert, their memory erased, you know that.'

He nods and shuffles off into a warehouse that is attached to the back of the office.

'Let's wait outside,' says Gail, 'it is too stuffy in here.'

The Dudley Forge and Foundry occupies part of a busy industrial estate built inside an abandoned quarry. It is no quieter outside, and the air no more wholesome. All around them they hear whistles, thumps, loud bangs and clanging noises, and voices raised in greeting or alarm. Some workmen, enjoying a break, sit against a wall, smoking, and drinking from well-used flasks. They stare rudely and eye them with suspicion, making Benedict feel out of place, but Gail waves at them. They smile and wave back, not having the first idea who she is, but the action makes them seem less threatening.

'Why do you use this place?' he asks.

'It is quite simple: Albert Bronze is the best at what he does. I wouldn't trust my sculptures to anyone else.'

'And do you always turn the clay ones into bronze?'

'No, these are exceptions. I usually fire the clay in a kiln, but it can result in a loss of detail and changes in colour as compounds oxidise, and that is not always welcome. And clay, even when it is fired, does not always last well. Bronze feels more permanent somehow, but again, the casting process always results in some loss of detail, however carefully it is done. It is never a completely faithful replica.'

They wander over to the far side of the abandoned quarry, where a display board captures Benedict's eye. It has been erected next to a concrete statue of a creature that resembles a rolled-up woodlouse.

'*The Dudley locust*,' reads Benedict. '*A trilobite from the Silurian Period*.'

'An ancient fossil,' explains his aunt. 'The rocks they removed from this quarry were full of them. Mr Bronze has quite a collection. He'll gladly show them to you if you ask, although we shall be here until midnight if you do.'

Benedict reads on: '*They lived about 425 million years ago in a shallow sea around a reef. This species is called Calymene, an arthropod. It has a compound eye and hard exoskeleton. It grew by moulting. Many of the fossils are thought to be moults.*'

He cannot read any more because the display board has been vandalised. Someone has tried to set it alight. He looks up at the quarry face, which has been fenced off. The wire fence has also been vandalised and broken through in several places, and it serves as little more than a trap for other people's rubbish. He wonders if he could climb up and look for fossils.

Gail reads his mind. 'Mr Bronze will gladly let you have a specimen if that is what you are after. He is overrun with them – a veritable plague of locusts.'

She laughs aloud at her own quip.

Undeterred, he replies, 'I would like that. I find fossils interesting.'

'And what do you find so interesting about ancient dead things?' she asks, somewhat disparagingly.

'What they record and how we can tell so much from so little.'

'Like what?' she asks. 'What exactly can you tell from studying the Dudley locust?'

'That compound eyes, like insects have, evolved early on in Earth's history, and so evolution is not just a simple progression towards ever more refinement and improvement, and that species, seemingly well adapted to their environment, can still go extinct. The progression of life is not predictable. Fossils give us a glimpse into the past.'

She looks at him in startled amazement. 'Good God, Benedict, you sound like a bloody textbook! What have you been reading?'

He looks a little shy. 'I borrowed the *Origin of Species* from your library. I hope you don't mind?'

As quick as a flash she asks, 'The Darwin original or the abridged version by Richard Leakey?'

'The abridged version; I couldn't make head nor tail of Darwin's writing.'

She laughs. 'Nor could I, truth be told; the Victorians were nothing if not verbose.'

It is the first time he has ever heard her admit to any weakness. The rare show of humility makes his aunt seem more compassionate somehow.

An idea occurs to her. 'Benedict, would you like to study palaeontology?'

'Yes, yes, I think I would, but I have no idea where to start.'

She surprises herself with her reply. 'You have to do A-levels in science subjects. Then you must go to university and read geology. Listen to me... you start your job next week. If you like it, then you can carry on doing it whilst you stay with me, and in September, you can enrol at night school. That way, you can work and study at the same time.'

She sees uncertainty written in his face, and adds, 'Unless you have other plans, of course. You might want to go and live with your elder brother?'

He shakes his head and removes a crumpled-up letter from his back pocket. He hands it to her forlornly. The letter had arrived three days ago. She had presented it to Benedict saying, 'From the appalling spelling and illegible handwriting, I assume this is from your brother.'

He had not laughed, as she had hoped. Instead, he had taken himself off to open the letter in private, as if it contained long-expected exam results, or the outcome of a medical test, and he had not talked about it since. She has been anxious, wondering if the letter contained news of his father, or an invitation that would take him away from Malvern, perhaps permanently. She is reluctant to admit it, but she would miss his company.

She takes the letter and reads it through, mentally correcting the atrocious spelling and grammar, and struggling to decipher the handwriting:

Hail, Bones,
Have you grown any muscles yet? Get yourself to Norfolk; you can stay with me and Tracy. We've hired a caravan but we're on the waiting list for a council house. Let's hope they haven't all been sold off before we get one, eh! The baby cries a lot, but your used to cry babies, aren't you, what with our baby brother and

all. Have you heard from the irritating little sprog? I'm making good dough with this welding malarkey. There's plenty you could do: carrot topping in winter for the caning factory in Lynn and strawberry and apple picking in summer. You don't need qualifications for that. Have you heard from the old man? I've not been to see the miserable git, not since he kicked me out. I got a letter from the old woman. It contained a few quid. Guilt money, I call it. I sent it back to her. If you've still got the rail pass get yourself to Lynn station. I can pick you up on the bike from there, that is, if you don't shit yourself when I rev the engine. Ha, ha, bloody ha. Take care, Bro, and let me know what's happening,
Caesar

'Your brother seems to have adopted several… Norfolk expressions,' she says, not really knowing what to make of the letter.

He smiles sadly. 'He has always been like that. He only has to speak to someone with a strong dialect for a minute and the next thing you know, he is speaking just like them. My father says it shows a weak character, one that is easily influenced, but perhaps he just has a well-attuned ear? He was good at French and music at school, but the bullies ensured he didn't prosper.'

'I see,' she says, 'and he calls you "Bones" and himself "Caesar"?'

'They are nicknames the whole family uses. No one ever called me Benedict.'

'Was Bones a term of affection?' she asks.

He shakes his head. 'What do you think! It was bones as in "lazy bones", or "bone headed", or "he's all skin and bone", which was mostly true. I always felt hungry, always.'

She would like to ask why his brother is named Caesar, but she holds her tongue. 'And this baby, you never told me you were an uncle.'

'It's not his,' he replies morosely. 'I haven't met Tracy, but he told me she already had a baby when he met her. He's never been short of girlfriends. He's always been a charmer. He has the gift of the gab, but he always needs people to like him; he always feels a need to please them, however much they bully him.'

She senses she is on dangerous ground. 'But you are not made that way?'

'No, I have never really felt that I need people at all. I prefer to be alone.'

She needs an answer from him; she broaches the question she is reluctant to ask. 'And will you accept his invitation?'

He buries his head in his hands and sighs. 'It's not really an invitation at all; it's just his way of easing his conscience, to be seen to be doing the right thing. He doesn't really want me there, disrupting his little empire. We don't get on. We would end up fighting. Gail, I… I would prefer to stay with you, if that's alright, at least for now.'

*

Four labourers, dressed in identical overalls to Mr Bronze, wheel the sculptures into the office. The three pieces are strapped securely to an industrial trolley. None of them is particularly large, but they each weigh a ton. Gail Miller takes her time and inspects them with an expert eye, Mr Bronze looking on anxiously.

'These are a bit different to your previous works,' he says, rubbing his hands together as if he suddenly felt a chill. 'More… more… joyous, if you don't mind me saying so. I think this is some of your best work.'

She smiles and turns to him. 'Thank you, Albert, you have done a first-class job, as always.'

She hands Benedict the car keys. 'Would you open the Land Rover for Mr Bronze's boys, whilst we settle up the bill and discuss the last piece.'

Dutifully, he does as she asks, watching the labourers wrap each sculpture in layers and layers of protective wrappings, before placing them carefully in straw-lined crates, and then strapping each crate securely into the back of the Land Rover.

It takes an age for his aunt to appear.

'I was watching them break the moulds apart,' she explains. 'I always insist on that. There must be no copies made. These pieces are originals.'

They set off back to Malvern, the Land Rover coughing and spluttering and barely making it up the first hill.

'Well,' she asks, after they have travelled some way in silence, 'what did you make of the sculptures? Did you recognise the figures?'

'Of course,' he says. 'They are wonderful.'

He does not elaborate; he needs to be prompted. 'In what ways "wonderful"?' she asks.

He takes his time to answer, but when he does he answers truthfully.

'The two sporting ones had movement and energy, and captured something of the grace and significance of the moment.'

She looks pleased. 'Which did you prefer?'

'I liked them both. The one of Donald Bradman pulling a fast bowler to the boundary appealed to me at first, because he makes the shot look so easy, so dismissive, like he had all the time in the world to play it, and yet, there is a modesty about him. You've captured that moment really well. I didn't know you made sculptures of famous sports people.'

Nor did I, she thinks to herself, *the idea came from you. Perhaps I have finally managed to break out of the artistic box I have buried myself in all these years.*

'But I like the second one even more.'

'Go on,' she encourages. 'Did you recognise the figure?'

'Of course! Bobby Moore raising the World Cup aloft in 1966. In our house, the England players who were West Ham teammates – Bobby Moore, Geoff Hurst and Martin Peters – were venerated like the Holy Trinity. I like the way you have captured his face; the simple joy, relief, and humility he shows, as if he is saying to the nation, "This is how we should be; this is how we should celebrate. Rejoice and be proud, but don't gloat, don't bang the drum too loudly, and don't crow from the rooftops. There is no need for that; it is bad mannered."'

'You seem to approve of modesty and humility,' she says. 'How very British you are, Benedict.'

They laugh in unison.

'Will you sell them?'

'Yes, there is always a market for such things. I expect they will fetch a handsome price, and the critics will no doubt sustain themselves by writing many learned and torpid lines about Gail Miller's "latest phase", while the avant-garde will lament my sell-out to commercialism. What did you make of the third piece?'

'The archaeologist breaking into the Egyptian sarcophagus? I don't know, it was curious.'

'In what way?'

'The archaeologist looked greedy, maybe for knowledge or treasures, but the mummified remains looked sad, as far as a mummy can look sad. I couldn't decide if you had depicted a moment of triumph or tragedy.'

'Have you heard of Tutankhamun?'

'Yes, I went on a school trip in 1972 to the British Museum to see an exhibition of all the treasures they had recovered from his tomb. It was on loan from Egypt. We had tickets, but we queued for hours and hours and we never got in. My mum was furious when she found out, as we couldn't really afford the price of the trip.'

'I am sorry to hear that,' she says. 'I think you might have found it instructive. The gold mask of Tutankhamun is an astounding work of art.'

'You have seen it?' he asks, awestruck.

'Yes, once in London and once in Cairo. Like fossils, the archaeological artefacts allow us a glimpse of the past, but it can only ever be a partial glimpse. I am considering having a brass plate added to my coffin, a note to future archaeologists, which reads: "If I have been dead for more than 500 years and no family can be traced, then you have my permission to exhume me and study what remains, but please remember that you will only recover a fragment of all that has been.'"

*

By the time Gail Miller parks the Land Rover in the courtyard of the farmhouse at Wellend, Benedict has fallen asleep. He wakes up with a start and says, 'I have always found ancient Egyptian figures frightening.'

She turns off the ignition and stares at him. 'You nodded off just when the discussion was getting going. You have been asleep twenty minutes, and yet you carry on the conversation as if no time has elapsed at all. Curious, Mr Harrison, most curious.'

He shakes his head in an attempt to clear the fug; he has no memory of falling asleep.

'I have something for you,' she says. 'Two things, actually.'

She reaches into a leather bag on the back seat and removes two items. She hands the first one to him.

'As promised, a Dudley locust. Mr Bronze says he hopes that you like it, and that there are plenty more where that came from, if you're interested.'

The trilobite sits neatly in the palm of his hand, and he studies it with an expression of wonder on his face. 'What will we be like in 425 million years? What will remain of us?' he asks.

She scoffs. 'Oh, I imagine we shall have blown ourselves to kingdom come a long time before that. Our nature is to drive everything into extinction. I see the Americans and Russians have signed a new peace treaty, limiting themselves to only 420 rocket launchers apiece for their nuclear warheads! Can you imagine…'

'Dr Goodman says nuclear weapons are a deterrent that help to keep the peace, and that no side would really ever use them.'

'Does the good doctor forget Hiroshima and Nagasaki?' she says, raising her eyebrows in surprise. 'President Carter and General Secretary Brezhnev will never get the treaty approved, anyway. The hawks will oust them. There is too much vested interested in perpetuating the arms race. Cyril kids himself that his computer software will only ever be used in space rockets. Your trilobite has better eyes than he does, and more sense! Sometimes he wears blinkers.'

She sighs, clearly exasperated with the absent Dr Goodman. 'Here, this is for you, too,' she says, handing him another object. 'I realise I missed your birthday, and anyway, I wanted to get you something to celebrate your appointment at the care home.'

The object is heavy and wrapped in a rag. It is about ten centimetres tall. He recognises it at once. It is a sculpture, the fourth piece she was discussing with Mr Bronze. It shows another figure swinging a cricket bat, but this time it is not Donald Bradman or any other famous cricketer, this time it is Benedict Harrison. She has captured him perfectly. He is in the act of playing a front-foot drive.

The bronze is alive with movement, as if the metal were still molten. His face is a picture of concentration, and for once, his footwork looks correct.

It is just a shame he is wearing a duffle coat, fingerless mittens and bobble hat.

18

The Puzzle Cube and Fischer's Mistake

The Cedars Care Home, summer 1979

Benedict knows what he must do: befriend a certain resident in the care home, offer to play chess and commit to memory everything he says, however trivial. His aunt refers to the man as 'Patient X'.

'Gail,' he asks as he gets ready for his first day at work, 'why don't you befriend the man yourself, or Dr Goodman? You could pretend to be visitors.'

For once, she looks embarrassed. 'We tried, Benedict, we tried.'

'Your aunt ran a free art workshop for the residents,' explains Dr Goodman, 'not long after we moved here.'

'You have not lived here long either?' he asks in surprise.

'No, Benedict, we both moved here when we found out the identity of Patient X,' answers Gail.

'I helped out with the workshop,' continues Cyril. 'We encouraged them to paint portraits of each other, or of a favourite landscape. Patient X has dementia. We hoped the painting would trigger a memory. We had hoped he might paint Saint-Emilion.'

'What happened?' asks Benedict, intrigued as to why they have never mentioned it.

'Disaster,' replies Dr Goodman. 'Utter shambles.'

'We were recognised,' adds his aunt, 'or at least I think we were. Patient X must have known for a long time that we were looking for him. Something about us jogged a memory in his mind. He became agitated, started rocking backwards and forwards, shouting and screaming and ripping at his hair. And then he turned violent. He smashed up an easel and threw paints at me, all the while telling us to get out and calling me all manner of names. Cyril did his best to calm him down.'

'But he punched me in the face, a real haymaker. I never saw it coming, old boy; must be past my prime. He knocked me out cold. Had to spend the night in A&E. The junior doctor on duty scolded me like a teenager for engaging in a bout of fisticuffs.'

'In the end, the nurses had to sedate him,' says his aunt. 'Unsurprisingly, we have not been invited back. It is obvious that we cannot unlock his memories. That is why you must do this, Benedict.'

He looks thoughtful. 'You never mentioned that he could be violent.'

She tries to reassure him. 'His dementia is very advanced. It must be a frightening and confusing world he inhabits. Little wonder he lashes out in frustration. But Patient X does not know you and so there is no reason to suppose he will think you are a "wicked witch and wizard sent to possess him".'

'Dr Marks tells me he hardly talks at all anymore,' adds Dr Goodman.

'Except for when he plays chess,' says Benedict, repeating what they have already told him.

'That's right, old boy, and he will only play chess with someone he considers a worthy opponent.'

'He's good, Benedict, very good,' says his aunt. 'Dr Marks tells us that he could have become a grandmaster, were it not for the war. No doubt he would thrash Cyril's "Boris", even now, even with the vestige of memory he has left.'

'Like he will no doubt trounce me,' he replies mournfully.

'Play the game I showed you,' says Gail, 'and make sure you play white. You do remember it, don't you?'

He nods, not knowing if he can. There were a lot of moves, and there is no guarantee Patient X will simply replay a famous game.

'And this man, Patient X, he knows who betrayed Grandad?'

They nod, in unison. 'Yes, Benedict, he knows,' says Dr Goodman sadly. 'He is the only one who really does. It has taken us years to track him down. He has been protected and shielded by powerful people.'

'But how do I get him to talk about the operation to France, even if I do manage to befriend him and play chess?'

It is Gail's turn to look thoughtful. 'Often, when people near the end of their days, they begin to recall more vividly events from their distant past, significant moments that are so well entrenched in their minds that a shadow of them remains. They may be painful memories or fear memories that have been suppressed. Perhaps you can encourage him to talk about the war by using certain words or phrases. But you must be cautious. He will be wary of people, even now – it has, after all, been the habit of a lifetime; it has likely become a reflex. We have little time left before his memory completely goes, but even so, you must tread carefully.'

'What words and phrases should I use?' he asks, feeling out of his depth.

'Think, Benedict, think,' replies Gail Miller, handing him the photograph of the gendarme with the labourers, the lorry and the wine casks.

*

His first day at work goes well, after a fashion. He happily plays cards with King Arthur, until His Highness suddenly gets to his feet and accuses two residents – who have had the temerity to enter the living room laughing – of 'making off with the Holy Grail' and 'eloping with his beloved Guinevere'. A rumpus ensues, which is skilfully defused by Mrs Hart, the manager, who acts the part of Merlin the Wizard and confounds the King with a 'special charm'. It takes a while for the effects of the sedative to wear off.

He plays table tennis with an elderly woman who uses a crutch to walk. Out of consideration, he begins the game with a gently lobbed serve, which she smashes back at his head with a ferocious and ill-directed forehand. He has to duck to avoid the ball. After that, he shows no mercy and wins the game eleven points to nil.

He is invited to join in a game of Ludo with three residents who commend his good manners and admire his good looks. 'Oh, what a handsome chap,' says one of them. 'Oh yes, I bet all the girls are chasing after you.'

He does not recall an occasion when that has ever happened, not once, and he has never considered himself handsome. Inwardly, he feels pleased by the compliments, but then he assumes that their eyesight must be failing. He recalls an occasion in his last year at school when two girls brought in mistletoe. Giggling, and making a great show, they allowed the boys they fancied to peck them on the cheek. But not Benedict, never Benedict; they had laughed at the very suggestion.

He gets on well with Mrs Hart and finds her as easy to talk to as Dr Marks. But throughout the entire day, he never once catches sight of Patient X.

Two weeks pass by, and then three. He settles into a comfortable routine, but the man he is supposed to befriend simply doesn't appear. Gail Miller grows increasingly concerned. 'Perhaps he is moribund?'

'Or dead,' adds Dr Goodman gloomily.

There is excitement in the care home when the television news announcer informs the attentive audience that NASA's Skylab is falling uncontrollably towards Earth, and that they will offer a reward to anyone who finds parts of it. The residents demand to be immediately taken onto the hills to search for wreckage. They are disappointed when further announcements inform them that the spaceship is heading towards the Indian Ocean.

July gives way to August, but he never once catches sight of Patient X. Back at the farmhouse, Gail Miller insists he study a new book, *The Great Games of the Chess Grandmasters.*

He finds it impossibly hard going.

*

'Benedict, would you like to help me with an experiment?'

For once, Dr Marks is in attendance at the care home.

'Why not? I feel like a spare part today. No one seems interested in playing games, not even King Arthur. He said something about needing to "lance the bloody boil called Lancelot".'

She smiles. 'Come with me.'

She leads up to the third floor and through a series of security doors he has never been allowed to access.

'One of our residents lives up here. His name is Victor Cross – Professor Cross as it happens. He was at Cambridge University, a mathematical genius by all accounts. I'm afraid he has no relatives and no one to care for him but us. He has severe dementia and rarely gets out of bed. He has not spoken for several months, but I want to see if I can jog his memory.'

This is the man, thinks Benedict, his heart racing. *This is Patient X, it has to be.*

'What do you want me to do?' he asks, trying to still his nerves.

'I am going to be next door observing and filming what happens through the window. There is a microphone in the room, so I will be able to hear you even if you cannot hear me. I want you to sit down next to Victor and play with this.'

She hands him a multicoloured cube, ingeniously designed so that all the faces can turn in different directions.

'It's called a "magic cube". It is a puzzle. I picked it up at a convention in the States earlier in the year. It was designed by a man called Rubik. You have to work out how to rotate the pieces until each of the six sides contains just one colour.'

It looks impossible, thinks Benedict, and he wonders why anyone would waste their time trying to solve such a puzzle. 'And you think this might make him speak?'

She looks uncertain. 'Perhaps. Victor liked puzzles. I am told that he worked as a code breaker during the war.'

She unlocks the door to Victor's bedroom. Benedict is startled to see that the walls are covered from floor to ceiling in graffiti – black and red pen marks scribbled across the white, institutional paintwork. It resembles one of his aunt's abstract paintings. When he looks closely, he can see that the graffiti is made up of numbers, formulae and equations, some of impossible complexity.

'Victor's handiwork,' whispers Dr Marks. 'He does it at night, whilst he is asleep.'

He is sitting on the end of a hospital bed, fully dressed in a grey suit, white shirt and black tie, gazing at a wooden chessboard set out on the table before him. There are two stop clocks next to the board: one for the person playing white and one for the person playing black. The pieces have not been moved from their starting position.

A care worker sits in a chair in the corner of the room, knitting a woollen scarf. She looks up when they enter, nods at Dr Marks and says, unduly loudly, 'Welcome, Benedict Harrison,' and then returns to her knitting.

'Victor needs constant care,' says Dr Marks in hushed tones. 'His body is healthy, for now, but his mind is nowhere to be found.' But then she all but pushes Benedict into the room and raises her voice. 'Don't be frightened, Benedict Harrison, Victor isn't a monster.'

She closes the door behind him and moments later, her head appears at a window that looks through into the room next door. It resembles a television studio with a large floor-mounted camera and heavy-duty leads criss-crossing the room. She looks through the viewfinder, checks it is centred properly and begins filming. She gives him the thumbs-up.

Victor remains gazing at the chessboard, apparently oblivious to his presence. He can read no expression or emotion in his face, no animation. His body is frail and his shoulders bent, and he hardly moves, except for when he breathes or blinks. He retains a good covering of fine white hair, which matches the colour of his eyebrows. He has a large nose and a prominent dimple in his chin. Tufts of hair erupt from his ears and nostrils. Dr Marks would describe his face as that of a patrician, but to Benedict he just looks old, maybe in his late eighties or more. Old, and badly scarred.

He is sure of one thing: he has seen this man before, on a poster in the missing persons section of the police noticeboard in Great Malvern.

He forces himself to pull up a chair and sit down next to him. His nerves are on edge; there is something about the man he finds frightening. Victor still does not notice his presence. Dutifully, he starts to meddle with the magic cube, glad to have something to occupy him. He doesn't have the first idea how to solve the puzzle, so he makes a series of random movements. The colours on the faces become even more confused.

He looks up and sees Dr Marks nodding at him approvingly, and gesturing for him to continue. Victor has not moved a muscle; his fixed stare remains focused on the chessboard.

After a few more twists and turns he realises the puzzle is beyond him. He sighs and puts the cube down on the bed beside Victor.

Nothing happens.

He looks at Dr Marks and shrugs his shoulders, as if to say, 'There, I tried.'

She frowns.

Suddenly, Victor comes alive. With an agility that surprises Benedict, he picks up the cube and inspects it, turning it around a few times. And then his hands begin to move rapidly, at an astonishing speed given his age, and in under a minute, he places the completed puzzle back on the bed. He says nothing. He returns his gaze to the chessboard and re-enters a state of stasis.

Benedict and Dr Marks look at each other in amazement. 'Play again,' she says, and he understands her even though he cannot hear her.

He picks up the cube and puts it behind his back, making more random turns to create a new puzzle. He tries to make it as difficult as he can.

He places the cube back on the bed.

Nothing happens, not immediately.

But then, as before, Victor suddenly snatches up the cube and examines it, but this time, mimicking Benedict, he puts the cube behind his back. He performs a series of rapid twists and turns, and again, in under a minute, the puzzle is solved.

'How did he do that?' asks a startled Benedict, looking at Dr Marks through the window.

It is her turn to shrug her shoulders. 'Play again,' she says.

But Benedict has a better idea. He moves his chair and sits down on the opposite side of the chessboard. He says:

'Championship rules, forty moves allowed in the first two and a half hours. Then an adjournment.'

He starts his clock, plays white's first move, and hits the stop button on the timer.

Victor once more comes to life. He takes a moment to study the opening, and then decides on his defence, makes his move and stops his clock.

Benedict's hands tremble with excitement. Suddenly he remembers with astonishing clarity the game his aunt insisted he learn. He makes a series of rapid moves, each one countered by Victor, in just the way he expected they would be.

After fifteen moves the game is developing into a predictable stalemate. Boris the computer would already have offered a draw.

After twenty-five moves a miracle occurs: Victor speaks.

His voice is devoid of emotion, devoid of emphasis and inflection. He delivers his words in a flat monotone, like a computer-controlled voice simulator might do.

'Game one, World Chess Final, 1972, Reykjavik, Iceland, Boris Spassky versus Bobby Fischer. Spassky plays white. The USSR versus the USA, Cold War, KGB, CIA, political manipulation, the world watches on, the "match of the century", Fischer's antics and childlike tantrums. I was there. I won't make the same mistake the American did in this game.'

He reaches out his hand for Benedict to shake. It is the endgame and it is a draw.

He is so stunned by the sudden outpouring of words and by Victor's correct identification of the game they have been replaying, that he does not think to respond. The care worker is quicker on the uptake. She puts down her knitting and asks, 'Victor, you were there? In Iceland?'

He ignores her. It is as if she does not exist.

'Do you speak German?' he asks.

Fortunately, Benedict is slow to respond.

'We shall play again tomorrow. I shall play white. Let us speak in German. It will irritate the KGB and CIA who are listening in. Is that not so, Dr Marks?' he asks, turning to stare at her through the window. 'Angels and demons. Unlike Fischer, I have no objection to being filmed whilst I play chess. Spassky made an error when he agreed to play game three of their contest behind closed doors. Fischer had never beaten him up to that point, but he beat him after that.'

He says nothing more. He rearranges the chess pieces, lies down on the bed and falls into an instant catatonic state.

19

The Dying Seahorse

Dr Marks and Mrs Hart sit him down in the manager's office and feed him tea and biscuits. Benedict's hands still shake badly after his extraordinary encounter with Victor.

'So, he solved the puzzle but never spoke?' asks Mrs Hart in astonishment. 'My goodness, what is going on inside his head?'

'That's the great unknown,' replies Dr Marks, helping herself to a Rich Tea biscuit.

'These are great for dunking, aren't they?' says Mrs Hart, allowing her biscuit to soften and expand rapidly in her teacup. She mistimes her move and the soggy end of the biscuit disintegrates into her tea before she can retrieve it.

'Cripes!' she says merrily, and Benedict cannot help but laugh.

'Chess remains the only activity which stimulates his

memory and allows him to talk,' says Dr Marks as she spoons a teabag out of her cup and absentmindedly lobs it in the bin, splattering tea up the wall, 'although, he has not been as lucid as he was today, not once in all the time we've been making observations. That game you played, Benedict, it must have really meant something to him. And you are the only person who has ever managed a draw.'

'I don't understand,' he replies. 'I don't understand how he could solve that puzzle and remember that game, and yet, he has no memory of anything else. Will he remember I have been to visit him today? Will he remember he offered to play again, and to speak in German?'

'Time will tell,' says Mrs Hart cheerfully. She takes a giant and uninhibited slurp of tea.

'Yes, it will,' adds Dr Marks. 'You must visit him again.'

Benedict shakes so badly his tea spills into his saucer. He feels too embarrassed to pour it back into the cup.

'What exactly is wrong with Victor?' he asks.

Dr Marks sits down next to him, takes out a pen, helps herself to a sheet of paper from Mrs Hart's desk and begins to draw a human brain.

'I don't know, not exactly,' she answers. 'Victor has a common form of dementia known as Alzheimer's disease. It attacks a structure in the brain called the hippocampus.'

She draws something that resembles a seahorse and labels it 'HC'.

'The nerve cells or neurons in Victor's hippocampus are dying. We don't know why. Perhaps it is something to do with the action of certain proteins, but studies are in their infancy. The hippocampus plays some role in memory. In studies with mice, the hippocampus has been stimulated to produce new neurons, and this has improved memory. Exercise might do a similar thing in humans, which is why table tennis is so useful for patients with dementia.'

He makes a mental note of that; he must let the residents win more points so that the games last longer.

'Tell him about the man with no hippocampus,' says Mrs Hart, her mouth full of biscuit crumbs which she projects across the room. She lifts up her cup and drinks spilt tea directly from the saucer.

'Come on, Benny,' she says, encouraging him to do the same. 'Don't be shy.'

She is the only person who has ever called him Benny; he finds he likes it, but he wouldn't take it from anyone else. His natural reserve prevents him from upending his saucer.

'There was a famous case of a man who suffered terrible epileptic fits,' says Dr Marks. 'Do you know what they are, Benedict?'

He nods. 'My younger brother, he…'

She smiles in sympathy. 'Well, in an attempt to cure his epilepsy his doctors removed most of his hippocampus and some other parts of his brain. The operation destroyed his ability to remember new information. But he could remember things that had happened up to the moment when his hippocampus was taken out, which means that memories must also be stored in other parts of the brain.'

She adds a note to her diagram; it reads 'neocortex', and she links the hippocampus and the neocortex with a prominent arrow. 'During sleep, the hippocampus sends messages to the neocortex, relaying information.

Perhaps it is telling it what to remember. The man with no hippocampus still had old memories stored in his neocortex, but the link to the hippocampus had been severed, so he could lay down no new memories.'

'I'm lost already,' says Mrs Hart. 'I was only ever good at sport at school. Give me a bat or racquet and I was happy. I won trophies and medals.'

'You wouldn't win any medals for dunking,' says Benedict, and she laughs aloud.

'Oh, Benny, you're such a wit. Don't you just adore British humour?'

He looks at Dr Marks' diagram. She has added more structures and notes: the amygdala, the basal ganglion and the cerebellum.

'These all play a part in memory,' she says. 'Victor's body still functions, even though he has no conscious control of it. He breathes and his heart beats. These structures regulate his bodily functions.'

She points to the cerebellum and basal ganglion. 'They remember what to do even if Victor cannot. And the amygdala is somehow involved in the formation of fear memories.'

'I wish I could forget some of mine,' says Mrs Hart, her face for once growing serious.

They are quiet for a while after that and lose themselves in their tea.

'I saw a picture of Victor outside a police station,' says Benedict. 'It referred to him as "Patient X".'

'Yes,' replies Dr Marks. 'We had no idea who he really was until quite recently.'

'Thank heavens for Gail Miller,' says Mrs Hart. 'We have your aunt to thank for the breakthrough. She identified him as Victor Cross. Apparently, he taught her when she was at university.'

Benedict recalls the image in her dining room showing the university chess final, the man in the robes – was that Professor Cross? He had a passing resemblance to Patient X, but it was not an exact likeness.

'I wish I had been here when your aunt and Dr Goodman ran their art workshop,' says Dr Marks. 'Victor would not usually have attended such an event, but for some reason, that afternoon, the security system failed, and his care worker was suddenly taken ill. He was left on his own, only for a moment, but unfortunately he managed to find his way to the living room. We usually try to isolate him from large gatherings as he can be quite… volatile.'

'And what an appearance he made,' adds Mrs Hart. 'He was in his birthday suit! He accused your aunt of working for the KGB and Dr Goodman of working for the CIA!'

They never mentioned any of this, thinks Benedict. *They lied to me. And Gail knew who Patient X was all along. Why has it taken them so long to find him?*

'I'm afraid he suffers from delusions and paranoia,' adds Dr Marks, 'and I am not sure how much of his memory is simply an illusion.'

'What does a memory look like?' asks Benedict. 'I mean, inside my head, what shape and form would it take? How can neurons remember?'

'I don't know,' replies Dr Marks truthfully. 'Nobody does. There are 100 billion nerve cells in your brain, give or take a few million, and each one can probably connect to 10,000 other neurons. That is a lot of potential connections, and somehow those connections make memory.'

'Then neurons are like pieces on a giant chessboard,' he says. 'All the pieces are connected.'

She shakes her head. 'No, Benedict, the human brain is so complex it is pointless trying to make analogies or to reduce it to a simple metaphor.'

'Oh, that's a shame,' says Mrs Hart, ripping open a packet of custard creams and offering them around. 'I liked the car analogy. I could just about figure that one out. The brain has these different parts, just like a car, and each one does a certain job, useless by itself, but when you connect the parts together the blessed machine begins to motor!'

Dr Marks laughs aloud. 'I've not heard that one before, Constance, you are a gem.'

She takes up her pen and adds another part to her diagram. 'Neurons connect across synaptic bridges, and we think each new memory is recorded as a new connection or circuit. It might even be that a memory is formed when new synapses grow. When we recall a memory, the synapses seem to fire in a certain order.'

'Think of your memory as a pair of shoes being tucked away inside a tiny shoebox in a giant shoe store,' says Mrs Hart.

'If you must,' says Dr Marks smiling, 'but the store would have to be the size of a planet.'

'Just like your brain, Harriet,' says Mrs Hart.

They both laugh. 'A dwarf planet in my case,' she says. 'Pluto, perhaps.'

'To retrieve the right box you must follow the correct path or else you'll end up in the wrong department, or on an empty floor,' adds Mrs Hart meaningfully.

'The shoebox being the new circuit, the connection between certain neurons that records a particular memory,' says Benedict, trying to keep up.

'Yes,' confirms Dr Marks, finally conceding the need for a visual analogy. 'The more often you wear a certain pair of shoes, the stronger your recollection of that box and its contents becomes. But if you don't wear a pair often, you might forget about them and find it difficult to locate the box. The neuron circuits work in a similar way: they fade if we don't revisit them. Different groups of neurons seem to be involved in different types of memory, and perhaps different memories are made in different ways.'

'Memory is just remembering where you stored your shoebox and what you put in it,' adds Mrs Hart helpfully. 'But I have so many shoes, I get them muddled.'

Dr Marks laughs again. 'Technically, memory is a reactivation of specific neural pathways, and every time we recall a memory, we may inadvertently change it.'

'But what causes the reactivation?' asks Benedict. 'Why can't I forget bad memories?'

It is clear from the look on his face that he would dearly like to.

'It's difficult to throw out old shoes,' says Mrs Hart sympathetically, 'however much they give us blisters. We get attached to them; they are part of the furniture.'

'But why do certain memories come into my head even when I don't ask them to?' he asks.

Dr Marks shakes her head. 'I don't know. Using Constance's car analogy, I suppose the vehicle needs a driver, or an exequatur. Our brain creates an inner eye, a consciousness and an ability to think, and thinking requires a retrieval of memories – memories which must be judged and acted on by the driver. When we are awake, we need to be mindful. Perhaps our subconscious mind sends our inner eye messages, to keep it alert, to remind it of potential threats and dangers, and that is why troubling thoughts enter our heads unbidden. Or maybe something in our environment or in our interactions with others inadvertently triggers the synapses, and the memories invade our inner eye? In a way, it is a mistake to compartmentalise the brain; it functions as a whole. It is all the connections working together that produce the inner eye. Our sense of ourselves does not belong to any one part of the brain.'

'The driver is the soul,' says Mrs Hart meaningfully, 'and our souls can be tortured by angels and demons.'

Dr Marks gives her a puzzled look, as if she had not quite appreciated the extent of the manager's spiritual convictions before. Her reply is gentle, not wishing to offend the sensibilities of her friend:

'I think it is a mistake to separate the mind and the soul from the structures and processes of the brain; our essence lies in the brain's chemical reactions and the way it changes in response to environmental stimuli, which includes our cultural memories and social interactions.'

There are so many questions he wants to ask; so much he wishes to understand. 'Our memory can be faulty. I can remember times when I was sure my mother had lied, but my brothers remembered it differently. Their memories were delusions. Our recollections are like fossils; they only ever give a partial glimpse of the past.'

'Yes, there is much we don't understand,' concedes Dr Marks. 'Memory is imperfect. It might turn out that the neural pathways are not fixed, that they are able to forge new connections, and that our brains have a plasticity that generates our imagination. Memory and imagination are often at odds, as they are in dreams.'

She has lost her audience; they look dumbfounded. She feels the need to summarise:

'What is clear is that Victor's hippocampus is badly damaged, his neurons are dying and his synapses no longer fire as they should. His brain is shrinking away. The degeneration is irreversible, and we have no way of slowing it down. We do not even understand the risk factors in Alzheimer's disease. I believe Victor has reached a stage where he can no longer make permanent memories or readily recall past memories. In terms of shoeboxes, he will soon go barefoot. But somewhere in his neocortex, or some other part of his brain, a vestige of memory survives, and the act of playing chess seems to fire these circuits. It is all he has left. You must play every day, Benedict; we should try to help Victor remember what he can, while he can. It is the humane thing to do.'

Mrs Hart wants the last word. 'When the shoeboxes are all gone, Benny, the store closes for good. The empty building no longer knows what it is.'

20

The Memory of Ice

The French Alps, summer 1944

The Alpine passes connecting France to Switzerland are guarded. There are troops, watch towers, electric fences, barbed wire, landmines and Alsatian dogs. Françoise Fronsac will have to climb high to avoid them, up onto the roof of Europe; it is the only way through.

It is as well she is physically fit, and determined. It will be a hard climb, and a dangerous one. She sets off before daylight. As the day warms, the snow and ice will melt, and they will feed water to the braided rivers. They will swell, become turbid, and become impassable. The snowbanks will saturate and lose their strength. She will sink in if she walks on them. The icefalls upon the glaciers will warm causing their seracs to topple. The crevasses will gape wider and the moulins will fill with torrents of water. The ice holding the fragile slopes together will thaw, loosening its grip on weathered rocks and boulders, and they will come crashing down the mountainsides without warning.

Travelling in the high mountains is best avoided, but if it must be done, it is best done before the day heats up; before the treachery of the sun works its evil.

Françoise Fronsac knows this.

Before daybreak, she crosses the River Arve and climbs from the Chamonix valley to the terminus of the Glacier du Tour. Cold air drains from its surface, but despite the chill, she sweats from her exertions. She wears hobnail boots and thick woollen socks, moleskin breeches, a cotton shirt and woollen sweater, and a Burberry jacket. She carries a canvas metal-framed rucksack on her back and a walking pole in each hand.

The glacier descends the mountain at a steep angle, fed by several smaller cirque glaciers, their basins choked with snow and ice. That is the way she must go.

Above the glaciers, the mountains form a ring of sharp needles and horns which point vertically up into the sky like a set of ferocious teeth. As far as she knows, they have never been conquered. A lake has formed in front of the glacier, its water uninviting and murky green. It is fed by a stream flowing out of a subglacial tunnel. Her way would be blocked were it not for a lateral moraine, a large mound of sediments that have formed between the glacier and the northern side of the valley. She climbs up onto the mound. It is made of gravel and sharp boulders, and difficult to walk along, but it is easier and safer than walking on the ice. She begins her ascent in earnest.

The sun begins to rise into a cloudless sky and daylight fills the valley. Eagles appear above her, circling on thermals. She knows they spy on her. She hears rocks fall, and the slopes around her rumble and groan. Here and there she sees stones rolling or sliding down the mountainsides. The glacier wakes up and starts to stretch, its crevasses cracking and breaking. Startled by the noises, chamois and marmot scurry and take flight. She looks back behind her to see if she is being followed. Down in the valley, below the treeline, she sees something move. Thankfully, it is only a bear chasing off a lone wolf.

She feels quite alone, abandoned, betrayed and vulnerable. 'Go south,' the Exequatur's message had read. 'Use the network; make for Spain.' But it was a trap. The network was gone, and the Exequatur must have known it. The gendarmes were waiting for her at her house.

'Thank God for the Nose,' she says to herself. 'Without his tip-off, I would have been taken.'

She had taken refuge in a church, but the gendarmes had found her there. They had exchanged gunfire. She was surrounded. It was a miracle she had escaped by using a concealed tunnel which connected to the crypt. They had pursued her all the way to Saint-Emilion. She had never run so far or so fast. She was hunted, like a fox. More caves, more gunfire, and many of her friends left for dead. The anger of the memory drives her on.

The lateral moraine begins to peter out as she approaches the snowline. It is time for a rest. She opens her rucksack, removes a metal flask and takes a long drink of water. She eats a little stale bread with some cheese and sausage, and a shrivelled apple. She has no other food with her. She attaches crampons to her boots, dons a pair of fur mittens and puts on her sunglasses. It is time to walk on ice.

She uses her walking poles as probes, checking to see if the betraying snow covers a moulin or a crevasse. She makes many detours, and her progress is slow. All the while, the disturbing noises continue: boulders and stones chase each other down the slopes, the ice creaks beneath her, and far below, the sound of rushing water. To her far left, she hears a distant rumbling noise and she knows an avalanche has broken out. She can see the trail of powder racing down the mountainside.

This is such a dangerous place, she thinks. *Utterly beautiful, but dangerous, like Raymond used to be.*

She knows that during the Great War, Alpine troops had fired cannons into the mountains to deliberately start avalanches, sending them down against their enemies. She had often wondered if they had not inadvertently disturbed something buried in the ice. Ice has memory; it retains objects and information in its frozen chambers: bits of metal, fragments of shells, wreckage, dust, chemical signatures from the atmosphere, and carcasses. Glaciers remember their past mass, the configuration of a colder regime, and like the clothes of a man who has lost weight, they struggle to readjust to the new conditions. Glaciers are not dead environments; they are infested by microbes, like every other surface on Earth. She has a vague, childhood memory of the Spanish flu pandemic that claimed so many lives. It had taken her mother and she had been raised an orphan. Some medics claimed it started in Austria, towards the end of the Great War. Did the soldiers disturb a virus long entombed in the ice with their cannons? Did they inadvertently unleash the pandemic?

At one point, the slope steepens alarmingly, and the glacier thins and breaks up into an icefall. In front of her are towering slabs of ice, stacked up like a deck of playing cards that have been turned vertically and allowed to slide, one over the other. She knows the ice blocks are called seracs and that they are dangerous to climb, for the ice is brittle and prone to breaking away, and the entire block can topple over. When they fall, they can crash so violently to the ground they initiate avalanches.

Breathless and tired though she is, she has no choice but to climb; there is no other way to go.

She ties her poles to her rucksack and removes two ice axes, one for each hand. She has no rope or harness and no one to belay her. What she is about to attempt would seem foolhardy and reckless in the extreme in times of peace.

She looks up at the ice in front of her, inhales deeply, tells herself to have courage and to remember how strong she is, and plants the first ice axe into the serac. She digs in her crampons to get a hold, and she begins to climb, laboriously, like a snail pulling itself up a wall.

Before long, her muscles burn and tear with the exertion, her heart beats so fast she fears it will hammer its way out of her chest, and her lungs scream out for her to stop. She feels cramp in every fibre of her being – her hands, her wrists, her thighs and her calves. She is wreathed in sweat, and regrets not leaving the rucksack behind and taking off the 'stupid' Burberry jacket. She catches herself shouting out curses. She bewails her fortunes; she cries for Raymond and the Angel; she vows vengeance on the world. She begins to feel dizzy. Stars appear in front of her eyes and she fears she will faint. *Dear God, let me make it. Don't let it end here.*

In the event, she is lucky, and her perseverance and years of training as an athlete pay off. When she finally attains the top of the icefall, she collapses in a heap, her body spent. She lies there motionless for some time, allowing her heartbeat to slow, her lungs to fill and her temperature to fall. She physically shakes from head to foot.

Water, I need water, she thinks, reaching for her flask. She takes a long, refreshing drink and eats the last of her food. Above her, the slope of the glacier evens out. It splits into several streams, each connecting to a separate cirque basin. She needs to keep to the left and climb as high as she can. The glacier adjoins the Col du Tour. There is a way up and over it. To the north-west and south-east of the col the mountain slopes rise towards summits along knife-like edges the French call '*gendarmes*' or arêtes. If she can climb over the col, she will descend into another ice-filled basin and pick up the Trient Glacier, in Switzerland. It flows all the way down the valley towards freedom.

Towards the back of the cirque basin there is a permanent snowbank adjoining the col, which affords easy access to the path she seeks. As she prepares to climb it, something catches her eye: a bright light; something shiny and reflective. As she gets nearer to it, she realises what it is.

'Oh dear God,' she says, falling to her knees.

It is a ring, a gold ring, attached to a finger which reaches up out of the snow. There are six bodies dumped unceremoniously one on top of the other. The cadavers show unmistakable signs of torture, and they have been shot in the back of the head. They have been dropped here, deliberately, maybe from an aeroplane, the snowbank an unmarked icy grave. She recognises their dress: simple farmers, a railway worker and a school teacher.

New snow has buried the bodies. In time it will be compacted and converted to ice. It will become part of the glacier, and the glacier, remembering the input of snow, will take the mass and move it down the valley. In one hundred years' time, or maybe two-hundred, the bodies will be released at the glacier terminus, but by then, the memory of the people will have faded.

She is glad she still has her rucksack with her. It contains her sketchbook and pencils. She takes them out and spends a long time recording the faces of the six dead men as accurately as she can. She makes note of their ages and heights, their build and their hair colour. She carefully removes the ring and other identifying objects, and stores them in her sack. She draws a map of the glacier, and marks on the position of the bodies as carefully as she can.

'They will be remembered,' she says as she utters a prayer over the grave. 'Remembered and avenged, I promise you.'

21

Snow Angels

Reykjavik, Iceland, February 1972

It is such a simple calculation, a matter of adding two numbers together, but he cannot solve the sum. His mind can no longer see the solution.

What the hell is up with me? thinks Professor Cross.

It is as if a fog has formed in his mind.

'Think, damn you,' he says aloud, tapping his fist against his skull.

He feels like his brain has been hidden beneath a trapdoor, and the trapdoor is locked. Or like Einstein, his brain has been removed.

'Perhaps I am just getting old?'

He looks at his face in the car mirror. His eyebrows have turned white. They have grown long and they turn up at the end. He must remember to trim them. He thought he had. Unseemly white hairs protrude from his nostrils. He must remember to pluck them out. He thought he had.

And then he notices that he is wearing a wig, its brown hair at odds with the colour of his eyebrows. He doesn't recognise his face. It is horribly scarred; it belongs to someone else. He has a vague memory of surgery – painful and drawn-out surgery.

He looks down at the floor and realises his bootlaces are undone. He has left his fur hat in the hotel. At least, he thinks he has. There are remnants of food spilt down his front. His clothes smell of cigarettes and alcohol.

What is happening to me? he wonders. *This fug in my mind is getting worse.*

He forgets names. He forgets appointments. He goes out without his wallet. He leaves his binoculars on the roof of the car and drives off, only to watch them bounce along the road in his rearview mirror. He forgets birthdays and anniversaries. He leaves the oven alight and the lights on. He drives from A to B and has no recollection of the journey. He forgets to stop at traffic lights. He can never recall where he left his spectacles. He re-reads chapters of books without realising it. And of late, he forgets what he is supposed to be doing.

Why am I here? he thinks. *Am I supposed to meet someone in the park?*

He shakes his head, trying to clear the fog. He gets out of the car and goes to tie his laces, but he cannot remember how. He looks at his watch, but he has forgotten how to tell the time. Feeling utterly bewildered, he wanders aimlessly towards a large, frozen lake. He forgets about the keys and leaves them in the ignition.

How did I get here? he thinks. He has no memory of

his flight the previous day from London to Keflavik, the dramatic landing in a blizzard, the aeroplane rapidly dropping altitude and being blown sideways across the runway. Then the white-knuckle drive to the capital along a road banked high with snow; the inspection of the docks; the cheap hotel where the shower water stank of sulphur; and the needless drive to the park, which is only a stone's throw from the city centre.

It is a clear day, but the sky is steely and threatens more snow. He sees a few disconsolate ducks and geese standing on the edge of the lake, looking forlorn, as if, like him, they don't know why they are here or what they are supposed to do. A couple walk past holding the hand of a well-wrapped-up young child. The adults smile at him sympathetically, and he greets them in Icelandic. He had no idea he could speak the language.

The young child points at him as though he were something out of a horror movie. The mother looks embarrassed and apologises, telling the child it is rude to point.

'You've left your engine running,' says the man, pointing towards the car.

He smiles back in gratitude, and says something about his age, as if that explains everything, and goes to retrieve his keys. He notices that there is a name and telephone number written on the fob, and that there are several other keys attached to it. The name reads Dr Walter Smith. It rings no bells. Why on earth would he have a set of keys belonging to a stranger? And why would he be driving his car?

He examines the number plates: Icelandic, an expensive Mercedes, kitted out with studded snow tyres.

Feeling more bewildered than ever, he makes his way aimlessly back to the lake. The couple with the child are lying in the snow, making snow angels.

Angels… there is something about that word that triggers a memory: angels and demons… For a fleeting moment he thinks he will have a breakthrough, that the fug will lift, but the dullness closes in again and everything goes blank. His mind is a blizzard, his memories a box buried deeply beneath a snowdrift.

'Dr Smith?' says a voice behind him. 'Dr Walter Smith?'

He turns around and sees a thickset man wearing an oversized parka, hood up, hands thrust deeply into the side pockets. He speaks with an American accent.

He doesn't reply; he doesn't know the answer to the question.

'Have you been to the Island of Heimaey?' asks the American.

For some reason he finds himself answering the question. 'Yes, and I have seen the Icelandic fishing fleet hauled up there.'

The stranger nods, satisfied that he has the right man.

'We were supposed to meet an hour ago, on the other side of the lake. Where the hell have you been?'

'I'm sorry,' he says. 'I… I am not feeling well.'

'You could have rung. I've been freezing my nuts off.'

'I am sorry,' he repeats, 'for you and your nuts.'

The man stares at him for a moment, and then laughs. 'Well, to business: will you do it?'

Do it? Do what?

'I am not sure; tell me the plan again.'

The man looks incredulous. 'Jesus, my colleagues have been over this a dozen times!'

'Humour me.'

'The Cod Wars,' says the stranger, in exasperation, and a memory floods into his mind.

The ongoing dispute between Britain and Iceland over access to Icelandic fishing grounds, the Royal Navy escorting ships to the areas where the British have enjoyed historical fishing rights and the Icelandic Navy sabotaging their nets; ships being rammed, the growing international dispute and Iceland threatening to withdraw from NATO, the North Atlantic Treaty Organization.

'Yes, the Cod Wars,' he replies. 'Very troubling.'

The man looks at him as if he were an imbecile. 'We can't let the Icelanders leave NATO, that's the bottom line. We have a bilateral agreement with them, and we've had troops stationed here since '49. Iceland is strategically important; it is from here that we aim to block the Soviet nuclear submarines and to stop them marauding across the Atlantic. The Brits need to settle this dispute, and fast.'

'It will decimate our fishing communities,' he says, not knowing where that idea came from.

'You still consider yourself British?' asks the man in surprise. 'You've lived here since '46; you've got an Icelandic passport. Your wife was Icelandic, and I'm told you've been working for us for some time.'

I was married? I live in Iceland? I work for the Americans?

He has no recollection, none whatsoever. *Damn the fug, damn it. Think, man, think.*

A vague impression begins to form in his mind, and he latches on to it.

'I was in London, yesterday.'

'I know. We sent you.'

'My contacts are not opposed to the plan, but it must be done… discreetly. And later, they want your backing when they set up their own exclusion zone around British shores. If the Icelanders are allowed to dictate who can fish up to 200 nautical miles off their shores, then we want the same privileges, and not just for fish. We want exclusive rights to the mineral and fossil fuel resources, too.'

'Agreed. So, *you* will help us to broker a settlement, behind closed doors, of course; we can't be seen to be getting involved, although no doubt there will be leaks. There are no end of spies and double agents in this city, but I guess that's true of every major port. You are well known to the security services here; the Icelanders trust you, and I assume MI6 still think you are their man?'

MI6: the name is familiar. It has been a large part of his life. Suddenly, he finds himself invaded by memories.

'Section Six, Military Intelligence. MI6, yes.'

He is suddenly gripped by a fear memory: a fall from grace, a change of identity, the need to leave Britain, the demon on his tail…

'Have they ousted all the Commies yet?' says the American disparagingly. 'I mean, for God's sake, Kim Philby, the former head of the anti-Soviet section during the war, and then your Chief of Intelligence in the USA, turns out to be a Soviet spy and ends up defecting to Moscow in '63. Before he does, he tips off two other double agents about their impending arrest, his friends from his Cambridge University days, Burgess and Maclean, and they defect in '51. Your whole intelligence service is a laughing stock – Kim Philby, the Cambridge spy ring; MI6, the leaking ship. We're told there was a fourth man in the spy ring, another Trinity College recruit… Has he ever been identified?'

'I can't say.'

Of course he can't, the man is an establishment figure. To extract a confession, MI6 had to offer him indemnity from prosecution. But it must be kept secret; MI6 could not stand further public humiliation and loss of confidence. It is still reeling from the embarrassments of the 1950s and '60s. And there were probably other traitors involved; others who were never identified, but who passed secrets to foreign nations during the war and afterwards.

He decides the best form of defence is attack. 'This upcoming chess championship, will Bobby Fischer turn up?'

The American shrugs his shoulders, surprised by the sudden change of subject. 'Who knows, the guy is a loose cannon. He's demanding a bigger pot of prize money.'

'But you will want him to be victorious; you will hail it as a triumph of Western ideology over the Soviet system, and its champion, Boris Spassky. You will want that every bit as much as the Soviets will want their man to win. Tell me: is it true that you investigated Fischer's mother for her alleged communist sympathies? I understand she lived in Russia, before the war, but she was forced to leave because of the rising number of attacks against Jewish people. And yet Fischer is said to be anti-Semitic and a Holocaust denier. Is that really who you want representing the "free world"?'

'I can't say,' he replies, mocking his English accent. 'I understand you're something of a chess demon yourself, Dr Smith; that you could be a grandmaster, but that you refuse to play in public after your… your… accident.'

Accident? Accident? What on earth is the American talking about?

'I wouldn't let a little scarring put you off. There are other fellows your age with Hurricane rash.'

22

The Warlord

The farmhouse at Wellend, summer 1979

After his meeting with Patient X, Mrs Hart, the manager, insists Benedict go home early to recover and to prepare for his next game of chess.

He is in an odd mood, his anger dampening any sense of elation. His aunt has lied to him or told him half-truths, repeatedly, and Dr Goodman has colluded. He feels rebellious.

When he gets back to the farmhouse he discovers his aunt unloading the motorcycle sidecar, carrying her easel and paints into the house. The dogs are sprawled out upon the kitchen floor, panting hard from their exertions chasing after the bike.

'You're back early,' she says by way of greeting, casting him a suspicious glance.

Wondering what the matter is, she blocks the entrance.

He doesn't speak; he pushes past her.

It is unlike him. He is never intentionally rude.

'What happened?' she asks, her voice rising in concern.

'I met Victor Cross.'

She makes him sit at the kitchen table. She hands him a glass of homemade lemonade. He doesn't touch it. She can sense his resentment.

So can the dogs. They have moved to the far side of the room. He is smouldering, like a volcano, like his mother used to do.

'You knew who Patient X was all the time. Mrs Hart told me it was you who identified him. He taught you at university.'

She does not try to deny it.

'Why didn't you tell me? Why didn't you tell me he accused you of being a KGB agent?'

Mrs Hart has a big mouth, thinks Gail Miller.

'He is paranoid, Benedict; it is the illness. He believes everyone spies on him. What difference would it have made if I told you who he was? I am afraid he has not been the Professor Cross I knew for many years.'

That at least is the truth, he thinks.

'Who is he? I mean, how is he connected to Grandad's death?'

She sighs. What should she tell him? How can she make him understand? The world was so… so different back then.

She sits down beside him at the kitchen table and speaks quietly and calmly, because, when people are in a rage, they never hear properly.

'Listen to me,' she says gravely. 'Listen carefully and please don't interrupt.'

He looks at her, his face surly, but he complies.

'The Great War was fought between competing empires, but it ended with revolutions and a shift in the balance of power. Then came the Great Depression; capitalism had failed. During the 1930s, many bright young people, many of our finest minds, could see that a consequence of that failure was a Europe sliding towards fascism; it was on the rise in Germany, Italy, Spain and Britain. Intellectually, students like B.B. gravitated towards different political systems, and they knew that they had to fight the fascists. The intelligence services have always actively recruited agents from places like Cambridge University, placing gifted graduates in the Foreign Office and military intelligence. Professor Cross has been a life-long advocate of our liberal democracy; he too feared the rise of fascism. During the Second World War, he became a senior member of MI6, but he was helping to recruit students to the cause even in the 1930s. He recruited B.B., but at the same time, others were recruiting students to different causes. Some favoured the Soviet system, others were fascists, and they worked as double agents. And so you see, the traitor who betrayed the SOE mission could have belonged to one of several competing factions. Victor knows who they are, and he knows the identity of the Exequatur.'

'The Exequatur?' asks Benedict, a bewildered look crossing his face.

'Yes, the Exequatur was the person in charge of the SOE missions in the Bordeaux area at that time. The operation B.B. was involved in was not the only one that

tried to re-enact the battle scenes they showed. She said the soldiers "kept us out of mischief". The "Desert Rats" were our favourite troops. We'd spend hours setting up the pieces and then have gigantic battles, running around making actions and war noises, and killing everyone off. The battles never lasted long.'

'How… entertaining. It must have disturbed your grandmother's sherry time.'

He ignores the barb.

'My elder brother once got an Airfix model of a Spitfire to make. He treasured it, hung it from his ceiling like a lucky charm. He always wanted to be a pilot. Mum had a tantrum one day and smashed it to pieces.'

'I am sorry to hear that. You played at "war" a lot?'

'All the time. We'd make Sten guns out of old pieces of wood and pretend to fight battles in the garden, digging trenches and making imaginary tanks and planes.'

'And you were always heroes; you always triumphed against evil?'

He is surprised by the question; he had never thought about it that way. 'I suppose so; the world was divided into goodies and baddies. We were always the goodies.'

She smiles sadly. 'Some psychologists would say you were sharpening your edges, building your ego and developing a sense of yourself. Others would say you were being inculcated into a culture that glorifies war and violence; a culture that demonises others.'

It had never occurred to him that he was demonising anyone. 'We were only playing,' he says.

'And how do you think you learn, Benedict?' she asks.

He thinks about his synapses and his neural networks and all the things he must have learnt without realising it, all the impressions and illusions. There must be ways of overcoming his childhood memories and the reflexes they encourage; there must be a way of retuning his brain, otherwise he will end up like his parents; he will share their habits of mind. Is that what Dr Marks had meant by plasticity: an ability to rewire synapses? Is that how people get brainwashed?

'Did you never play at war?' he asks.

'No, Benedict, I never *played* at war.'

*

'In all likelihood, Professor Cross will have no memory of your meeting today,' says Gail Miller encouragingly. 'You have no need to speak German. You may get away with playing the same game. You did well to remember it.'

He looks uncertain.

'Very well, Benedict, we shall spend this evening teaching you a different game.' She sits down at the chessboard. 'Victor may insist on playing white, after all. If he does, you must prepare for a rapid attack like this.'

She demonstrates a brilliant set of opening moves. 'It was always his favourite, but like a Blitzkrieg, it is a limited strategy if you can counter the initial advance.'

They are interrupted by the ring of the telephone. Looking concerned, she goes to answer it.

He can hear her muffled voice speaking quietly and urgently on the phone, but he cannot make out what she says. When she returns to the kitchen she is buttoning up her coat, and he notices the colour has left her face.

'I must go to the Royal Worcester Infirmary,' she says hurriedly. 'There has been an accident.'

*

Hospitals are amongst his least-favourite places. Benedict associates them with pain and suffering. He refuses to accompany her.

Aged eleven, he had spent a lonely night in a hospital recovering from an operation to remove a rogue tooth from his upper jaw. It was growing upwards towards his nose bone and dislodging his two front teeth, which were growing crookedly. After the operation, they had made him wear a plastic mould in his upper palate, with two metal prongs which jutted forwards and kept his two front teeth evenly separated whilst they grew. He wore it for three years – three years of shame and ridicule. It was gruesome and made him feel like a freak. Every time he opened his mouth, the two metal prongs stuck out. He felt like a monster; he felt like Frankenstein's monster. There were other people in his class sporting mouthfuls of metal – the medical and dental professions were barbaric – but braces never looked as bad as his prongs, and they were not suffered for the same duration. He learnt not to open his mouth. He learnt not to smile.

Aged six he had an operation to save the sight in his left eye. His elder brother had accidentally struck him with a wooden rod whilst they were playing in the garden. The rod had metal ends and belonged to a set his father used to unblock the drains. He had left them, unscrewed, stacked in a pile in the back garden. To the boys, they became an arsenal of weapons. For six months it was touch and go. He had to wear an eyepatch. He remembers the kind nurse saying, 'You have been in the wars, my brave little pirate', and his mother saying nothing. Instead, she scowled at his brother as if to say, 'Look what you did, with your stupid clumsy antics.'

He was lucky, said the doctor; another fraction closer… the macular… blindness…

His mother liked to embellish the tale, and her role in 'saving his vision'.

His left eye is weak. He is supposed to wear spectacles, thick-rimmed NHS spectacles, the broken arm held together with a strip of Elastoplast, but he left them behind, at his dad's house. He took the plastic mould with the metal prongs to the end of the garden and smashed it to pieces using his father's hammer.

*

Dr Goodman lies in the hospital bed, his head and chest wrapped in bandages and his face badly bruised.

'Had you been drinking?'

It is the first question Gail Miller asks. Her tone is unsympathetic.

'No… well, yes, just a couple of stiff ones before leaving the club. The police breathalysed me. I wasn't over the limit.'

She shakes her head. 'You are getting too old for whizzing about in a sports car.'

'I wasn't whizzing. Somebody took a pot shot at me.'

Her tone and mood change instantly from exasperation to concern. 'What do you mean?' she says, drawing up a chair.

'Just what I said. As I was heading towards Wellend someone fired at me. I heard the shot. A twelve-bore, I think. They hit my front tyre and it blew out. I skidded and ended up hitting a tree. Fortunately, I wasn't going fast, but the Aston is probably a write-off.'

She looks behind her to check no one is approaching, and then she leans in and whispers, 'Did you see who it was?'

'No, it was getting dark. Fortunately, a farmer saw me and helped to cut me out of the wreckage whilst his wife telephoned for an ambulance.'

'Did you tell the police about the gunshot?'

'Of course.'

Suddenly, he takes a sharp intake of breath and groans, as if he is in pain. He holds his hand to one of his chest contusions and winces.

'Gail... Gail... you can't think this has anything to do with B.B. Not after all this time. I am sure it will turn out to be an accident. We are no longer warlords. I have had nothing to do with the intelligence services since the war ended. Why would anyone consider me or you a threat now?'

She looks behind her for a second time. 'We are close, Cyril; there are still those who would bury the truth.

Benedict met Victor today and they played chess. Victor spoke, something which was observed by the care worker and Dr Marks, and related to Mrs Hart. Don't you think it a coincidence that you were shot at on the very day Benedict achieved a breakthrough?'

'What are you implying?'

'I'm implying that any one of them could be working for the intelligence services. Think about it: when we ran the art workshop the security system conveniently fails and Victor's nurse is suddenly taken ill. He is able to wander around freely and accuse us of being spies. Someone sabotaged us; someone did not want us getting our foot through the door. And now this… accident. This is a warning, Cyril, a warning for us to back off. We must be on our guard, Benedict too.'

23

The Equations of Life

When Benedict arrives at work the next day, he finds King Arthur remonstrating with Mrs Hart in her office. Residents and staff have gathered on the stairs to listen in to the argument. Like those watching a fight in a playground, most of them revel in the confrontation.

'I won't have it,' he says, his face puce with anger. 'I want to be moved to a different room, and I want to be moved today.'

Mrs Hart bats him away. 'Arthur, lower your voice; you'll upset the other residents.'

'I don't care,' he replies, his rage boiling over. 'I've asked you repeatedly to move me and now I'm demanding it. I can't stand being in that room a moment longer. It is torture.'

Benedict joins the assembly on the stairs and catches the eye of one of the nurses. She whispers, 'Patient X has been at it again.'

'Been at what again?' he whispers back.

'Writing equations on the wall whilst he sleeps and talking to himself all night long. Arthur's room is next door. It's keeping him awake and driving him mad.'

She pauses for a moment's thought and adds, 'Well, madder than he already is.'

'He talks in his sleep?'

Why didn't Dr Marks mention that?

The nurse laughs. 'Does he talk in his sleep! He delivers full-blown lectures and sermons, all in foreign languages. He drones on and on about numbers and equations. It is so boring I wonder it doesn't send Arthur to sleep, but the scribbling must be annoying, like mice scratching at the skirting boards.'

They hear Mrs Hart ask, 'Have you tried the earplugs and headphones we gave you?'

'They don't work!' replies Arthur, thumping his fist against her table. 'How many times do I have to tell you? I have sensitive hearing. I hear things others don't. I want to be moved somewhere quieter. He's a demon, Patient X, a demon.'

'I'm afraid there *is* nowhere else just now,' replies Mrs Hart resolutely.

'Then I'll sleep in the ruddy living room!' replies Arthur, storming out of the office. 'I won't listen to one more of his threats!'

The assembly on the stairs disperses hastily as the King storms the atrium.

*

'I am sorry you had a bad night,' says Benedict, sitting down in the living room opposite King Arthur. He has an idea, and he needs to speak to him.

'Why are you sorry? It wasn't your fault and it didn't affect you,' he replies tersely.

'Well, it's affecting me now because I have to round everyone up for lunch, and you're the only person missing.'

'I'm not hungry. I want to be left alone. I have an exclusion zone around me; I'm cold Icelandic waters.'

'Yes, I can tell. Can I ask you something?'

'Will it make a jot of difference if I say no?'

'I would respect your wishes.'

'You shouldn't, they are unreasonable. Why should you put up with unreasonableness? They don't pay you enough for that. That's Hart's job. I hate it here.'

'So I gather. Do you speak German?'

'*Ja.*'

'And did you learn it in the army?'

'That's right, sonny; I was in Signals. The world was dimming even then, but my ears have always been tip-top. I listened in to "Jerry".'

'And Victor speaks German, in his sleep?'

'Victor! Don't mention that bastard's name to me. And anyway, Victor's not his real name. It's Walter Schmidt.'

He emphasises the V sound at the start of Walter.

'How do you know that?'

'Because he introduces himself that way, every bleeding night during his ruddy lectures. He calls them the "Equations of Life series". Don't ask me what they are about, it's all Double Dutch.'

'And he makes threats, in German?'

'Yes, when I bang on the wall and tell the git to shut his lousy trap! He calls me sergeant, the blind sergeant. He says, "Do not interrupt me again, Sergeant Blind, or I will cut off your signals permanently."'

Benedict is appalled. He has no sense King Arthur is lying.

'What does he mean by that?'

'Use your imagination, sonny.'

'Have you told Mrs Hart or Dr Marks?'

'What do you take me for, a tell-tale tit? I can fight my own battles. If the bastard ever comes out his room I'll show him a signal or two, Sergeant Blind or not. I give as good as I get. I call back, "Shut it, Adolf, or I'll remove your other ball!"'

Benedict has a moment of inspiration. 'Does he ever mention the war?'

King Arthur does not answer. 'Why would you ask me that?'

'I understand he worked as a code breaker. I'm interested in codes, that's all.'

'I try not to listen. I put my fingers in my ears and my pillow over my head.'

'I see, it must be awful.'

'You've no idea. It's like sleeping next to a perpetual snorer. Nothing you do can stop the infernal racket.'

Benedict's mother had snored; he is sympathetic.

'He did give one lecture, something about France during the war. I don't remember the details. He was talking a load of bollocks about probability theory and the sacrifice needed to make Jerry believe in the invasion. I assumed he was talking about D-Day. He kept mentioning Eisenhower and Stalin, and angels and demons. As I say, it was all Double Dutch, but I'll tell you this for nothing: he was no bloody code breaker during the war. More likely he was a German spy.'

*

It is not until mid-afternoon that Benedict is permitted to enter Victor's room again.

'Dr Marks cannot make it,' says Mrs Hart, unlocking the security doors, 'but she did insist you play chess every day.'

Professor Cross is sitting on the end of his bed. He is wearing striped pyjamas. He rocks backwards and forwards, scratching at his hair as if he has an infestation of head lice. The room smells befouled. A care worker and nurse are in attendance. The care worker wipes food from the wall. The nurse wants a word in private with Mrs Hart.

'No visitors today, Constance. Victor's having "one of those days". He's very... agitated. We've had to send his clothes to the launderette. All his clothes. If he soils the bed again, I don't know what we shall do. We have no more clean sheets.'

'Oh dear,' says Mrs Hart sympathetically, but before they can call him back, Benedict goes and sits down at the chessboard.

'Tournament rules,' he says. 'Forty moves in the first two and a half hours and then a break.'

He swivels the board around so that Victor can play white.

The transformation in Patient X is immediate. He stops rocking and scratching his head. He turns to face the board, makes a move and punches the clock.

It is exactly the opening Gail Miller predicted. He responds as she had showed him. They had spent half the night going over the game – over and over. They never got to the ending; the best he can hope for is a 'good show'.

The attack is swift and deadly. He defends as she showed him. He 'castles' his king and positions his bishops in front of his pathetically weak monarch. The holy men are stationed side by side, his knights providing additional cover, and his powerful queen providing the keystone to his defensive arc of pawns.

The opening is rapid and decisive; white gains a better position and retains the initiative, but black defends stoutly.

They are entering the middle game. One blunder, one tiny mistake and his defence will crumble. Soon, there will be an exchange of pieces. He must get the sequence right, or he will lose, and lose badly.

'You play well, Kurt,' says Professor Cross, 'but you will not beat her. None of you will. Gail Miller is too strong for you.'

His tone has changed since yesterday: there is a sing-song quality to his voice, and it is imbued with inflection and emphasis. His accent is foreign.

It is chilling to hear him mention his aunt's name, and in the context of a past encounter with a man named Kurt. He will need to act; he will need to improvise.

'Thank you, Professor,' he replies.

'I am not a professor yet, just a lowly doctor. Perhaps if you exercised more, Kurt, your mind would improve. You drink too much. I know you are a talented musician, but try to stay sober, at least during matches.'

He needs to keep him talking; he needs to know about the war. 'Does Gail Miller exercise?'

'Of course, she is an athlete: a fine runner and an excellent shot. She has boycotted the Games, did you know?'

'In Berlin?' he ventures.

'Of course in Berlin! Really, Kurt, lay off the bottle. I rather admire her stand. The Nazis will make great capital from the Games. It will be a sham. Gail is going to work as a reporter, nothing more. I will leave for England soon; it is becoming too dangerous here. Where will you go?'

He had assumed he was talking about Cambridge. Where the hell does Victor think he is?

'Berlin,' he offers, for want of something to say.

'You would stay here?' asks Victor, raising his white eyebrows in surprise. 'They will close down your little cabaret and then they will hunt you down. Leave now, Kurt, whilst there is still time.'

He recalls something his aunt had told him. 'We must fight fascism.'

Victor nods. 'Yes, that is self-evident, but there are many ways to do that, Kurt. You will try to do it with words and songs that appeal to our emotions and higher sentiments, but patriotism will trump you every time because it appeals to the baser instincts of the fascistic mind. Your protests will not be enough. Art has a role in the struggle, not least because it embellishes our propaganda, but intelligence will be more important. Do you understand?'

No, not at all, but he needs to say something. 'Then I will go to Spain?'

'Don't be a fool, Kurt; you are no B.B. You have his brains, but not his brawn. Leave Spain to men who can fight. Anyway, it is already a lost cause. The Left will turn on itself, like a pack of hungry wolves. The agitators will see to that. Stalin will eliminate all rivals.'

'Then what about France?' says Benedict, hoping to turn Victor's mind to the war.

'France will fold as easily as a deckchair. I have told Gail, but she is obstinate; after the Games she intends to return to Bordeaux.'

'Why?' he asks.

'Isn't it obvious, Kurt? She misses her husband and child.'

He is so startled by the revelation that he only just avoids making a catastrophic blunder on his next move. Gail Miller was married and had a child, in Bordeaux. Why has she never mentioned it? Why are there no pictures of her husband or child in her house near Libourne?

Victor has stopped talking; the middle game has begun in earnest. He offers to exchange queens, and Benedict accepts. Victor nods in approval.

They are approaching uncharted waters. This is as far as he got with his aunt. He has no idea how the endgame is supposed to go. He tries to stall for time by asking another question. 'What will you do in Cambridge?'

'What I have always done, Kurt: I will carry on my research and I will bore undergraduates to death with my legendarily dull lectures.'

'You have been there before?'

'Of course, I have been a visiting lecturer for some years. They are offering me a permanent position as a professor of mathematics.'

'Does Gail Miller find your lectures dull?'

'Why don't you ask her? I know you are sweet on her, Kurt, everyone knows; it is painfully obvious. But you should leave her well alone.'

'Because she is married?'

'And because she is dangerous, Kurt. She gives nothing away, but she is sharp, and deadly, far deadlier than her brother.'

'In what way?'

'Have you never seen her race? There is a ruthlessness about her. A cold-hearted ruthlessness. I have never seen anyone so determined to win. Ruthlessness and determination; she has the mind of a killer, Kurt.'

He finds it hard to accept what he is hearing, but it is clear that Victor believes every word he says. He cannot take all the information in at once, but he knows he must keep him talking.

'The equations of life, I bet she found those interesting.'

Victor looks towards some of the numbers, formulae and equations he has scribbled on the walls.

'She is one of the few who appreciates them. She sees the need to understand life at the cellular and molecular levels. Only mathematics can give us the tools to frame the terms of our biological existence. She has produced some interesting work on the pathology of certain diseases and their rates of division, mutation and spread. She has some novel ideas about the flu virus.'

'Gail is a nurse.'

He laughs scornfully. 'Is that what she told you? Oh, Kurt, you are a fool. She is no more a nurse than I am a Nazi. I joined the party so that I could maintain my position at the university and continue my work – work that the British will find very useful when I hand it over to them.'

'Then what is she?' he asks, unsure that he wants to hear the answer.

'At heart, a pathologist. Did you know she fled Cambridge and took her research with her? She intends to bury it away because it is too dangerous. She does not wish it to fall into the wrong hands. She will take it to France, but it will not be safe there. Liesle will find it.'

Who on earth is Liesle? he wonders.

'Do you miss her, Kurt?'

'Liesle?' he offers.

'Of course Liesle! How many other dancers have you proposed to at that cabaret of yours? If you don't mind me saying, she wasn't your type; I think you will find she is a faithful daughter of the Third Reich. I understand that she turned you down and went after B.B. instead; followed him all the way to London where she starred in a West End show. Liesle Swann became Sarah Swan, and then later, Sarah Harrison. Were you jealous, Kurt? Would you like a West End show of your own?'

He stares at Victor in disbelief. Has he just referred to his nan as Liesle Swann?

He feels like he is drowning. He needs to get out of the room.

He tips his king over, the universal sign of resignation.

Victor looks surprised. 'You concede too early,' he says. 'The outcome is uncertain. You had a good chance of forcing a draw. You must work on your endgame, Kurt; you fold too readily.'

24

Liesle Swann

The farmhouse at Wellend, August 1979

The bus is late, again.

The nurse looking after Professor Cross stands three spaces behind Benedict in the queue, but she does not acknowledge his presence. He tries to make eye contact and smile, but she ignores him, a sour expression on her face. She is short of stature and overweight, her swollen feet bulging out of her shoes and dark sweat patches expanding beneath her armpits. She reminds him of his mother.

He knows why she is in a bad mood. His shift had ended with another altercation at the care home, this time between the nurse and Mrs Hart. They had argued over the care of Victor.

'I said no visitors. Is my medical opinion to be ignored?' ranted the nurse, barging her way into Mrs Hart's office uninvited.

'Dr Marks gives the medical directions, not you,' she replied tartly, an uncharacteristic edge to her voice.

'Perhaps his visitors would like to help clean up his shit! He's been nothing but trouble since the lad started playing chess.'

'If you don't like it, Sandra, you can sling your hook. Unemployment is predicted to top 3 million next year, good luck finding a new job!'

After that, the door was shut and he could only make out the odd word, threats mostly, and something about getting the union involved. Thinking about it, he can't recall ever seeing Nurse Sandra at the care home before.

A beaten-up Land Rover draws up at the bus stop and the passenger door flies open.

'Jump in,' calls out Gail Miller. 'I'm just back from visiting Cyril. I'd hoped to be in time to give you a lift.'

The bus draws up right behind her, the driver angrily sounding his horn and gesturing rudely for her to move out of his way.

'Don't you shake your fist at me, you silly little man!' she shouts back at him. 'My taxes help pay for these bloody roads and *you* don't own them!'

It would seem to be a day for altercations. He wishes he could be alone; he knows he is about to have another.

'So,' she says, deliberately taking her time to pull away from the bus stop, 'did you play the game?'

It is time for the truth. There has been too much mendacity.

'I will not tell you. Nor will I play Victor again. I am fed up with being your pawn. Either tell me everything you know, or forget it. I'm sick of your games.'

She keeps her eyes upon the road and does not reply, not until they reach the farmhouse.

*

'Come with me,' she says, not bothering to lock the car door. 'There is something I wish to show you.'

He follows her into the house. She unlocks one of the upstairs rooms, one he has never been in. The room has no source of natural light. The walls are lined with metal shelves, each one colour coded. They are stacked neatly with box files, each one precisely numbered. It looks like a records office.

'What is this?' he asks.

'My history and my research. Come in, quickly. Close the door.'

'Your research into viruses?'

'What?'

'Professor Cross, or Walter Schmidt, whatever his real name is, said you were a pathologist.'

She looks puzzled, but only for a moment. 'Benedict, tell me what happened today and what you have heard. Leave nothing out. I will listen and not interrupt. When you have finished, I will answer your questions and show you evidence to back up what I claim to be true.'

He recounts everything Victor said. True to her word, she listens and does not interrupt, not once, not even when he mentions her husband and child. Her face reveals no emotion.

'Where would you like me to start?' she asks.

'Victor, who is he really? Was he a German spy?'

She fetches down a box file, rummages through a few papers and withdraws a copy of a birth certificate.

'What's this?' he asks.

'Read it, carefully.'

The certificate registers the birth of a Victor Cross, born in the parish of Dore in the city of Sheffield, to Reginald Cross and Doris Cross, nee Blackburn. Victor is not German.

She hands him a newspaper cutting. It announces the appointment of the eminent British mathematician Victor Cross to a professorship at Cambridge University. There is a brief résumé of his glittering academic career, firstly at the University of Sheffield, and then at Leeds University. Victor had never been in Berlin.

'I don't understand,' he says. 'He called me Kurt, he talked about being a member of the Nazi Party, and he speaks German and talks with an accent.'

She turns her back on him and fetches down another box. She hands him her passport and asks him to note her date of birth.

'How old was I in 1936, the year of the Berlin Olympics?'

'Twenty.'

'Old enough even by the standards of the day to be married and to have a young child, admittedly, but it is not true, Benedict. Read this.'

She hands him a letter written by a medical doctor. It gives condolences; she will never be able to have a child.

'I am sorry,' he says, feeling utterly bewildered.

'And read this too.' She hands him another certificate, this one from Cambridge University, confirming the completion of her studies in fine art.

She has never been interested in diseases or pathology.

'I met Victor at university but not because I studied maths. He ran the chess club.'

'Does Victor suspect me?' he asks. 'Has he deliberately fed me lies?'

She shakes her head. 'No, he no longer has that capacity, of that we are sure. We cannot know what goes on in the remnants of his mind, but it would seem reality, fiction, fantasy and illusion have all become muddled; he can no longer tell them apart. Perhaps he did work as a spy in Germany during the early part of the war, or perhaps this Walter Schmidt is an alias he used after the war when he went into hiding. You must not take everything he says at face value.'

He looks at her glumly. 'Then how will I ever find out the truth?'

'Listen to me,' she says, replacing the papers carefully in the correct files and returning them to the shelves, lifting down a small box and ushering him out of the door. 'There will be fragments of real memories in every tale he conjures up. We just have to work out which bits are true.'

'Is any of what he told me today true?'

She points to the box in her arms.

'Yes, your nan was called Liesle Swann.'

*

She knows he will need time to digest the information. She lets him study the contents of the box whilst he sits at the kitchen table.

'My father is half German and I am quarter German? I never knew.'

'Does it matter?' she asks.

'It matters that I never knew. And just think of all the imaginary battles I've fought against "Fritz the Hun".'

She smiles sadly. 'Your nan came to Britain in 1931 to audition for a part in a new West End production. She was successful and became an overnight sensation when the show premiered.'

She hands him a fading brochure from the opening night of the show. He can't see the name Liesle Swann anywhere, but he recognises her picture.

'For publicity reasons your nan was named in the cast list as Sarah Swan. She was granted a residency visa in that name. She pursued B.B. with a dogged determination and they married in 1933. Has your nan ever expressed any political views?'

He sighs in frustration, throwing the papers back into the box. 'Half of this stuff is in German or Russian; I can't make head nor tail of it. Nan hates politics; she has no interest in it.'

'Are you sure, Benedict? How well do you know your nan?'

He hardly knows her at all. All he has is childhood memories of Silver-Sherry Nan, a slightly frail, reserved and snobbish woman with haunted eyes. He didn't even know her first name was Sarah. She never visited the family, and they seldom visited her.

'We have learnt that your nan was investigated both before and during the war by the intelligence services. She was always under suspicion. We have assumed that she was worked as a double agent. This was not uncommon during the war. British intelligence often tolerated known spies if they could use them to feed false or misleading information to the enemy.'

He can tell from the tone of her voice that she has doubts. 'But now you think your assumptions were wrong?'

'She may not be German at all,' she says, taking up one of the sheets of paper from the box and pointing to the Cyrillic script. 'In the village where she allegedly grew up, we have been unable to find anyone who remembers her. We have found no friends or relations, no family graves, no birth certificate or school records. We know very little about her. But we recently discovered that she may be Russian by birth.'

His head whirls. And then he recalls the business meeting Cyril and Gail had with an old friend in London; they were meeting someone with intelligence about his nan.

'A contact of ours was able to gain access to a Russian general who defected to America. This man had access to many secret Kremlin files. It would seem a woman resembling your nan was known to him. She was sent to spy on the German Communist Party, and then ordered to Britain in the early 1930s to perform a similar task.'

Benedict throws his hands up in exasperation. 'Nan

always had a funny voice. She didn't sound like she was from the East End, but the family excuse was that she was a "bleeding Northerner".'

'Her English has always been excellent,' concedes Gail, 'but she is not a native speaker. The accent never disappears entirely, and there are grammatical errors.'

She thinks about her own accent. Try as she might, she has never been able to eradicate it. At the hospital, Cyril had told her that he had once found it exotic, but that now it just irritated him, like so many things in life. His spirit was low and his body a wreck, like his car.

'You have never trusted her, have you, but don't tell me you believe she betrayed her own husband?'

What can she say? She knows what he is really thinking: how could she have betrayed the father of her child? But Stanley Harrison might not have been B.B.'s child, although, in truth, he resembled him. There were other men at the time who claimed to be the father.

'Your nan has never been short of money. Have you never wondered at that?'

'She had a big win on the pools.'

'No, Benedict, she did not. We have checked.'

He buries his head in his hands. 'Then where did her money come from? She only ever worked part-time in a hairdressers.'

'She claimed that B.B. had left her money, a very great sum of money, but it has never been clear where that came from. And then she had another windfall, allegedly an inheritance payment from a relative in Germany. We have not been able to trace that relative.'

'You think some foreign power has been supporting her?'

'Perhaps. Liesle Swann would have known that in the early 1930s B.B. was an active and leading member of the British Communist Party, and maybe she was sent to spy on them. Stalin was paranoid: the only version of communism he would accept was one that was subservient to him.'

'So B.B. *was* a communist?'

'To begin with, yes. But after the Spanish Civil War, he became disillusioned, like many young men who fought there. He detested Stalin and the totalitarianism of the Soviet regime. He began working for British intelligence, even before the Second World War. I don't believe Liesle Swann ever knew that. He may even have been her handler, the agent responsible for passing her information.'

She will not say it, but she has often wondered if B.B. had realised precisely who and what she was even before they married, and that he took up with her because he always intended to work her as a double agent. Had he become disillusioned with Stalin's regime even before he went to Spain? Had he fed Liesle false information about the British Communist Party, too?

She hands him one final piece of paper from the box.

'What's this?' he says.

'Read it, and then tell me your nan has no interest in politics.'

It is a copy of a membership card for the British Conservative Party, and a recent picture of Silver-Sherry Nan stares back at him. He can't help but notice the hard glint in her eyes.

25

Obstruction

The next time Benedict goes to work he finds everything has changed.

Mrs Hart is absent, on indefinite sick leave, the care home rumour mill rife with theories but unable to establish anything definite. Nurse Sandra has been appointed temporary manager.

She is waiting for him as he enters the building, and she invites him into 'her office'. She does not smile or offer him tea and biscuits. She doesn't even offer him a chair to sit on. Her voice is curt. 'There will be no more chess with Victor, not for the foreseeable future.'

'But Dr Marks said I should play him every day.'

'Dr Marks isn't here, is she? In fact, she seldom is. Anyway, I understand she left for America, yesterday – some medical conference in Washington.'

'When will she be back?'

'I don't know, I am not her secretary,' she replies in clipped tones. 'She puts her career before her patients, that one.'

'No she doesn't,' he replies, his temper rising. 'You're the one who moaned about having to look after Victor. You have no right to stop me playing chess with him.'

She opens the door and shows him out.

'I have every right, sonny. If you are not prepared to accept my rules then you can – how did Mrs Hart put it? – oh yes, "sling your hook".'

He doesn't like being told what to do. He is obstinate. Under his breath, he mutters something his father used to say: 'The only hook I'll be slinging is a left hook.'

And then, 'I'm going to see King Arthur.'

As he barges past her he says, 'You remind me of someone.'

She looks surprised.

'The stationmaster at Great Malvern,' and, when he is out of earshot, 'I give you the Hitlers, Mr and Mrs Hitler; they were made for each other.'

*

For once, King Arthur is not in the living room. It takes Benedict a while to find him. He is outside in the garden, standing stock-still in the middle of the manicured bowling green, apparently staring up at a yew tree. The bowls players have given up asking him to move, and pursue their game by playing around the obstruction.

'Arthur? Arthur, are you alright?' asks Benedict.

'Does the tree have a horizontal branch about two feet above head height?'

'Arthur, what is wrong?'

'Take me to it, Benedict. I would like to touch the bark.'

'I thought you hated the garden.'

'Please, Benny, do this one thing for me.'

He has never heard King Arthur ask for anything nicely. He finds the change in mood unnerving.

'Here, take my hand.'

'You're a good lad, Benny, despite what they say.'

'And what do they say?' he asks, trying to make light of the remark.

'That devil Nurse Sandra, Mrs bloody bossy-boots, she says you're about as much use as a "fart in the Mersey tunnel".'

'The feeling is mutual. I don't think she was at the front of the queue when brains were dished out.'

He feels it is a suitable put down; it places Nurse Sandra in an appropriate box – a box that can be buried away. It is a something that has been said about him, more than once.

King Arthur nods. 'But she's been clever enough to land the manager's job. A lot of the other staff are narked off about it. They've been here years, but they've been overlooked. There hasn't even been an interview. Nurse Sandra's been here five minutes, but now she's the big cheese. She must have pulled a few strings. Just proves the old adage, it's not what you know…'

'How long *has* she been here?' asks Benedict.

'Too bloody long! She arrived with Patient X.'

Benedict stops beneath the yew tree. 'There is a branch just above your head.'

King Arthur raises his hands and clings on to it. He pulls himself up, testing the strength of the branch. It bends but doesn't break.

'It will do.'

'It will do for what?' asks Benedict. 'Arthur, what *are* you doing here?'

'I'm plotting my death.'

'Be serious, please.'

'I am serious.'

*

'Do you recall I told you one amongst us was truly evil? That person has now become the manager: Sandra Morgan, Morgana if you will, my nemesis. I must bring her down, Benedict; the witch can only fall if I sacrifice myself. I have a plan.'

'Arthur, let's go inside.' He needs help. The King is psychotic. 'Have you been taking your medication?'

'The poison pills!' says the King, clasping his own throat with one hand. 'I fed them to the slugs. Last night I slept well. The best I have slept for ages. Do you know why?'

'You slept in the living room?'

'No, Patient X was moved to another room. I heard them moving him during the night. He was heavily sedated.'

'Then you should be pleased.'

'No, I feel nothing but remorse, nothing but guilt.'

'Why?'

'Because Patient X deserves my help, not my ire. I should champion the cause of all my subjects. Nurse Sandra is always by his side. I hear what she says, when she thinks she is alone and no one can hear her. She whispers to him, endless stories, told in German. She reads from a script. Do you know they only bother to get him dressed when Dr Marks visits, and they never allow him outside, never. His room doesn't even have an external window. I suspect they drug the poor bastard and keep him in a straightjacket.'

He begins to feel scared. He has never seen the King this paranoid or delusional.

'She is lazy and wants an easy life, Nurse Sandra, and the powers that be want Patient X's secrets to die with him. I told you he was a German spy.'

'Arthur, please, let's go and get a brew.'

'I think about my death all the time, Benedict. I imagine my body dangling from a tree. Every time I recall something I have done wrong in my life, I imagine the rope pulling tighter and tighter around my neck. It is a fitting punishment for my sins. My waking hours are consumed by such thoughts. My sacrifice will bring down Morgana.'

He does not know what to say, but an idea springs into his head.

'No, Arthur, you must retune your mind and cast out those wicked thoughts. They were put there by Morgana to torment you.'

The King looks puzzled; young Benny may have a point.

'I guard memories of my children,' says the King thoughtfully. 'In my mind they are perpetually young. I do not wish to think of them as adults and yet I cannot help it. Do you think Morgana attacks my memories like she attacked Merlin?'

'Of course she does. We will find another way to fight her, Arthur, I promise you. I also know people who can pull strings. Let me see if we can't break the power of Morgana.'

'Will you do me a favour?' he asks in a whisper. 'Help me liberate the helmet from the suit of armour on the first-floor landing? I should wear it. The King needs his armour! It might help keep Morgana out of my mind.'

*

Benedict finds the episode with King Arthur depressing. He hadn't appreciated the extent of his illness. But it wasn't just that; he was upset by the talk of suicide.

The first Christmas after his mother had left, and before Caesar had been evicted, his father had done something out of character. He had tidied up the house and helped Caesar cook Christmas dinner.

He had made a Bird's trifle, studiously following the directions on the packet with an expression of growing bewilderment. He had purchased a bottle of Asti Spumante, spuds, Brussels sprouts and a piece of meat. A desultory and artificial silver tree had appeared in the corner of the living room, decorated with red tinsel and a few splintering glass baubles. There was a plastic angel on top; it had a weathered face and fraying wings. Some wit had drawn a patch over one of its eyes. The coloured lights were abandoned when he realised half the fuses were blown and he had no spares. Three of his fisherman socks were hung from the sideboard and filled with an assortment of satsumas, walnuts, a cheap cracker, some toiletries and a few penny toys: a plastic donkey on a stand that collapsed when you pressed its base, only to stand up again when you released the trigger; a cylinder which mooed like a cow when it was inverted; a pope soap-on-a-rope; a bottle of Matey bubble bath; a soft fabric ball covered in glittering threads which appeared to have no useful function whatsoever; an equally useless plastic monkey suspended between two poles who did a backflip when the poles were pressed inwards. To Caesar, a packet of tobacco and some Rizlas, and a lighter made out of a bullet shell.

'They made lighters like that in the trenches, during the First World War,' he had said knowingly, as Caesar unwrapped his gift.

To Benedict, a plastic statue of Bobby Moore, his hair a jaundice yellow, and a packet of playing cards which depicted famous cricketers. There was a stocking for his younger brother, too, but they never discovered what it contained.

Between them, Benedict and Caesar had saved up some of their penny-for-the-Guy money and their earnings from carol singing, and bought their father a packet of pipe tobacco and a second-hand book about angling. He considered himself something of a 'specimen hunter'.

Their father had got it into his head that their mother would visit on Christmas Day. Surely she would bring the younger brother around to visit, and she would want to see her boys? He waited for her, watching silently out of the window, his mood becoming gloomier by the minute. He had hoped for reconciliation, but she never showed up. After dinner, he became maudlin, and took himself off to bed with the bottle of Asti.

And there he would have died had it not been for the want of a fifty-pence piece.

The electricity meter ran out. Benedict was playing cards with Caesar, who was smoking a roll-up and drinking shandy. His brother went upstairs to cadge fifty pence for the meter from 'the old man'.

He had overdosed on pills, and he was comatose. Caesar ran to the phone box and rang for an ambulance. They took him to A&E and pumped his stomach. Caesar went with him.

Benedict remained in the house, quite alone. He found a Christmas card in his father's bedroom addressed to him. He opened it. There was a picture of a jovial Santa on the front delivering a sack of presents to two sleeping children. Inside the card read: 'Benedict, why is everything with you so black and white?'

There was no signature, no warm greetings and no Christmas wishes.

He did not visit his father in hospital. That evening, he left home, determined never to return. He walked and he walked and he walked. He spent the night asleep on a bench in a railway station waiting room. In the morning, he awoke to find he had been visited by Santa. A cup of tea and mince pie had been left on the bench beside him.

He remembered to thank the stationmaster, who was bleary-eyed and still wearing a paper crown and cotton wool beard, before he left.

*

There was little they could do to counter the orders of Nurse Sandra Morgan. Gail Miller spent a long time on the telephone, but they could not get hold of Dr Marks. Bristol University finally confirmed that she was on a sabbatical at Harvard University, not attending a conference in Washington, and that she was not expected back much before December. She had more success with the local authority, who agreed to mount a surprise inspection of the care home, following her reported concerns about the treatment of Patient X. They assured her that Nurse Morgan's qualifications and track record were exemplary. They couldn't comment on the situation with Mrs Hart for reasons of confidentiality, but no, they were not expecting her to return any time soon.

They were at an impasse, and Benedict could sense his aunt's frustration. She tried to make light of it. 'Oh well, it will give us time to work on your chess game.'

She bought him more books and made him practise daily. He still could not match her.

In September, Benedict enrolled at night school and began attending biology and chemistry classes two nights a week. Most of his classmates were mature students, and he found he flourished in the amiable and productive atmosphere in a way he had never done at school.

His pay was minimal, but he insisted on giving the better part of his wages to his aunt to help with his keep. She didn't refuse the money, not because she needed it, but because she knew it was important to him to give it. He was parsimonious and managed to squirrel away a few coins each week. He didn't drink and he didn't smoke, he had no interest in buying clothes or material goods, and he never expressed a desire to go out. She worried he was becoming a recluse. He had no friends, except Romulus and Remus, to whom he had finally grown accustomed. He walked a lot in his free time, happily taking the dogs on long excursions on the hills, or he read. He read and he read and he read. He spent more time in the library than she spent in her studio.

In September, Cyril was finally discharged from the hospital. Gail Miller decided that what they all needed was a break.

'We are going on a road trip,' she announced one evening mealtime. 'We shall leave on Friday lunchtime after Benedict has finished work and return Monday morning.'

*

'Where are we going?' he asks, looking uncertain. 'I don't think the Land Rover will get very far.'

'Where would you like to go?'

He looks down at the floor. 'I don't know.'

'Come on, Benedict, you have a whole weekend ahead of you, surely there is somewhere you would like to explore or someone you would like to visit?'

'As long as it doesn't involve too much walking, old boy,' adds Dr Goodman, holding a hand to his cracked ribs.

She needs to say it for him; he cannot bring himself to ask: 'Would you like to visit your father and your brother?'

He nods his head.

'Very well, we shall head for London tomorrow afternoon, but then we shall head north. I feel like seeing some different hills.'

She does not add that she is bored by the Malverns, as in truth, she has always been, even when she visited the area some years back and painted *Sombre Welsh Hills*. She had always found them underwhelming when compared to the Alps and the Pyrenees.

'On Sunday, we can go to Norfolk and visit Caesar. Benedict, we need to go shopping. You need winter clothes and walking boots.'

'But the Land Rover…' he asks with concern, convinced it will never make it to London.

'At least it hasn't got shot-out tyres,' says Dr Goodman gloomily. 'Can you believe the police investigation revealed two teenagers were responsible for my accident? Yokel boys without a brain cell between them – got hold of a shot gun and went hunting rabbits. Bloody awful shots!'

It does not sound like a convincing story, even to Cyril.

'Perhaps they mistook you for Bugs Bunny,' says Gail. 'I mean, your ears are getting larger.'

He frowns. 'Apparently, the little devils had been shooting at crop dusters too!'

Since being discharged from hospital, Dr Goodman has developed a bitter view of his fellow human beings.

'Benedict,' says his aunt, ignoring Cyril's outburst and handing him a bunch of keys, 'go to the outbuilding next to the workshop and unlock it. You will find something inside. I want you to test it for me. Use the garden if you need to.'

Intrigued, he does as she asks. Inside the outbuilding he finds a car covered by a tarp. He smiles to himself, hoping it will be another Citroën 2CV. When he uncovers the vehicle, he discovers it is a Morris Minor Traveller, almond green in colour with a wooden panel frame made from ash. It is an estate car, comfortable and in good condition. There are doors that open outwards at the back and space for the dogs in the boot. He notices that the tax disc was purchased in Hayfield. He makes a mental note to look it up in his encyclopaedia.

As she taught him to do with the 2CV, he checks the condition and pressure of the tyres, the oil level and the coolant level in the radiator, the adjustment of the spark plugs and the security of the distributor connections. He wonders if the battery has any life in it and when the car was last used.

Cyril appears by his side and shows him how to prime the oil pump. He tells him to put the car in neutral and pull out the choke. As instructed, he turns the ignition switch to the on position. At the front of the car there is a crank. He inserts the handle and turns it, pulling hard on the upstroke to fire the engine into life. To his surprise, the car starts first time.

'Let it idle for a few minutes until it has warmed up, and then push in the choke, otherwise you'll flood the carburettor,' advises Dr Goodman.

Benedict puts on the seatbelt, adjusts the internal mirror, eases the car into first gear, removes the handbrake and carefully drives forward onto the lawn. He spends the next half an hour driving slowly around in circles and practising manoeuvres.

Gail Miller watches him out of the kitchen window. She suddenly realises what he is saving up for: he wants driving lessons. Before they depart for London, she takes him to the post office, purchases a set of L-plates and helps him to send off his application for a provisional driving licence.

26

The Worst of Roads

London and Norfolk, autumn 1979

The visit to London proves to be a mistake.

It is an unusually warm September day, and they get caught in rush-hour traffic. Even with the windows slid fully open at the back, and wound down fully at the front, it is uncomfortably hot inside the car. Benedict feels himself sticking to the seat. The dogs pant excessively in the back.

'I'll take the boys for a walk,' says Gail, abandoning the driving seat without warning and leaving Cyril to negotiate his way through the jam of traffic. 'Come on, Benedict, stretch your legs.'

The traffic is at a standstill. Gail has time to open the back doors, attach leads to Romulus and Remus, fetch out a bowl and pour them water and let them slurp it up before Cyril has moved an inch.

'Catch us up,' she says to him as she leads the dogs along the pavement towards a nearby park.

It takes him an hour to move 200 yards.

'I'd forgotten how much I despise London,' he says when they get back in the car.

'It is like a furnace in here,' she complains. The heater is on full blast, blowing out hot air.

'Sorry about that,' says Cyril, 'but look at the temperature gauge. This crate is overheating badly. The cooling fan won't kick in unless we get a bit of speed up. One day some bright spark will invent air conditioning for cars and a better cooling system.'

'Have you tried turning off the engine?' asks Gail.

'Afraid to try,' he replies. 'Damn thing is unlikely to start up again.'

'Cyril, we can't sit in this, it is intolerable. Pull over and turn the engine off for a while.'

'It won't restart!' he says, exasperated by her stubbornness. 'It will be too hot. And anyway, we are not allowed to stop here.'

'Says who? Since when have you been so ruled by regulations? Let's park up and take the underground.'

'Are you mad? If you leave the car here you'll have no wheels left when you return. And the dogs won't like it on the tube.'

'Cyril, please pull over. It is the dogs I am thinking of.'

Scowling, he does as she demands. He switches off the ignition, but the engine refuses to die. It ticks over for several heated seconds before finally switching off with a worrying shudder. It sounds like a death rattle.

'I'll pull the bonnet,' says Cyril. 'It'll help cool it down faster.'

They sit in the car for thirty minutes, angry traffic growling past them. A traffic warden appears and threatens to write a ticket if they don't 'hop it, pronto'.

Cyril is apologetic and tries to start the car. Nothing happens. It is as if the battery has died.

'I told you,' he mutters under his breath. 'I told you it wouldn't restart, but you never listen to me, never.'

'Oh, do be quiet,' she says petulantly. 'Come on, Benedict, let's go Morris dancing.'

He looks perplexed.

'The car… the Morris – let's give it a push.'

Without fear, she steps out into the road and holds up her hand, bringing the car behind them to a halt. There is a sounding of horns, and angry gesticulations from the other cars in the queue. The traffic had just begun to move a little faster.

Two young and bearded men wearing white shirts and kippots exit the halted car and rush to their aid, bending their backs as they help to push the heavy Morris Minor Traveller forward. They are joined by another young, bearded man wearing a turban. Between them, they get up sufficient speed to jump-start the car. The three men smile delightedly, and Gail thanks them kindly for their help.

'You see, Cyril,' she says as they start off along the road, 'not all young men are out to steal your wheels.'

*

The Eden Gardens Care Home, where his father is a resident, is on the northern side of the river, to the east of 'the Tower' and to the west of the River Lea. Like the area where Benedict grew up, it is run-down, overcrowded and beset by poverty. The Victorian slums were bombed during the war or demolished by a wrecking ball shortly afterwards. They have been replaced by an imposing ring of ugly new tower blocks which block out the sky. Damp and black mould is visible on the external walls, the jerry-built chicken hutches already falling apart. The surrounding streets lack greenery, and the houses lack gardens. They appear to be always in the shade.

'Good God, what a dump,' says Dr Goodman, frowning. 'It's like some Stalinist estate.'

'I'm sure if architects and city officials who dream up these monstrosities had to live in them, they would come up with something more humane,' observes Gail Miller.

The litter competes with the graffiti for dominance, the broken glass bottles just winning out over the abandoned prams and television sets for abundance. Benedict wonders how many have been dropped from the top of the tower blocks. On the corner of the street there is a burnt-out car and next to it, a torched sofa. A gang of feral children, some mounted on Raleigh chopper bikes and dressed in colourful tank tops, watch them with mischievous curiosity as they drive by, unused to seeing a working vehicle on the roads.

'Would you like a moment alone with your father before I come in?' asks his aunt as they finally draw up into the car park, Cyril doing his best to weave between the shards of glass and abandoned washing machine that has been dumped behind the care home.

He nods his head, grateful for her consideration.

Dr Goodman says, 'We can take the dogs for a walk around the block, maybe find a watering hole. Don't worry about us, old boy, take all the time you need.'

'I think you should wait here,' he says, noticing that the gang across the street are arming themselves with missiles. 'I won't be long.'

But he is mistaken. Gaining entrance to the care home is like trying to break into Fort Knox. There is razor wire on the roof and a series of metal security doors to pass through. It takes ten minutes to make it through to the reception desk.

'Can I help you?' asks the woman behind the counter, in a voice that clearly indicates that she either cannot, or she has no interest in trying.

'I'm here to visit Stanley Harrison.'

'Visiting time finished five minutes ago. You'll have to come back tomorrow,' she says, concentrating on filing her nails.

He tries to be polite. 'We got stuck in traffic. We've come a long way. I won't stay long, I promise.'

'I ain't in the habit of repeating myself, sunshine,' replies the woman, stifling a yawn.

He will not be denied, not by this obstacle.

'I'm sorry,' he says, 'I thought this was a care home, not an "I couldn't care less home".'

'Do I have to call security?' she says, putting down her nail file and casting him a vicious look.

He knows his sarcasm is inspired by a lack of respect, but he surprises himself when he says:

'I'd be surprised if you could muster the energy.'

She stands up to her full height, her face turning red. 'Why, you cheeky little monkey. Come here and say that!'

Something in him snaps. Without realising it, he finds himself singing, '*Lazy bones, sitting in the sun...*'

'Don't you raise your voice at me!' she hollers. 'I don't take that kind of shit from anyone.'

At that moment a pair of double doors swings open and a stern-faced nurse appears. 'What is all this noise?' she asks in a sharp voice.

'This... this... little monster won't leave,' says the receptionist meekly.

'My name is Benedict Harrison,' he says in his sweetest tone. He tries to remain calm, but he is shaking with rage. 'I have come a long way to see my father, Stanley Harrison. My great-aunt is in the car outside, her name is Gail Miller, perhaps you have heard of her? She is with a friend of the family, a Dr Goodman. They will be here soon. I'm sure they will write a fulsome report of this establishment and its level of care.'

He has never name-dropped so shamelessly in his life, nor had the temerity to use such language, but it has the desired effect. Even the receptionist grows quiet.

'And why hasn't Mr Harrison already been allowed through?' asks the nurse, sending the receptionist a severe look.

'Visiting time is over,' she replies shamefacedly.

'Oh, for heaven's sake,' says the nurse, 'don't be absurd! Mr Harrison, kindly follow me.'

*

The care home resembles a geriatric ward. His father is propped up in a hospital bed. He is attached to a drip. There are seven other residents on his 'ward'. He has nothing but a screen for privacy, and a small chest on wheels in which to store his worldly goods. It is smaller than a diddy box. His false teeth sit in a jar on top of the chest. His hair hasn't been combed and he remains unshaven. He wears hospital-issue pyjamas, despite it barely being teatime. They are stained with soup around the chest and navel. It is intolerably warm on the 'ward'. None of the windows have been opened. The view outside is of a tower block. The windows are protected by metal grids to prevent the local gangs smashing through them with bricks. The man in the next bed moans constantly, as if in excruciating pain. A television plays to itself in a corner. There is a large 'no smoking' sign posted above each bed, alongside a cross and a banner saying 'Jesus loves you'. The ward smells of Dettol.

By comparison, the Cedars Care Home is luxurious, but then again, muses Benedict, its residents are all wealthy.

Good God, is this what we are reduced to after a lifetime of toil?

There is not even a chair for visitors to sit on, not that Stanley Harrison gets any visitors. Not his work colleagues, his neighbours, his 'good friends from his army days', his ex-wife, not his sons and not even his own mother. Silver-Sherry Nan claims she is too frail to travel. He knows this because she has written it inside the one 'get well soon' card that decorates his chest on wheels.

He goes to the nurse's station and helps himself to a jug of water and two plastic cups. He takes one of their empty chairs and returns to his father's bedside. He wishes one of the laconic and listless nurses would challenge him; then he would give them a piece of his mind. In every hospital and care home he has ever visited it has been the same. The reception staff have advanced qualifications in rudeness, obstructive behaviour and sheer obnoxiousness, and an armada of nurses drift around aimlessly, as if they have been separated from the fleet during a storm.

His father doesn't recognise him, and he doesn't speak. He stares into space, a dull look in his eyes. His body has wasted further since he last saw him.

'Do you want a drink, Dad?'

There is no reply, not a flicker.

Gently, he tilts his head forward and pours a little cool water into his mouth, making sure he has swallowed it.

What can he say? It would seem foolish to ask, 'How are you?' He spends a few minutes telling him about the family gossip, about Caesar and himself, but he finds it hard to talk to someone who gives no response. He opens a drawer in the chest on wheels and removes his dad's comb and shaving kit, and spends a few minutes smartening him up.

The severe-looking nurse stops by and smiles approvingly. 'Benedict, it is time to turn your father.'

He understands; if he lies too long in one position he gets pressure sores.

'I'll help,' he says. He's done it before. He is shocked at how little weight his father has.

He realises the nurse looks tired, and then he recalls the endless shifts they work at the Cedars Care Home and the impossibly difficult jobs they have to do at times. He admires the skill with which they deal with King Arthur. He knows he has been unfair in his previous judgement of nurses. Even Sandra Morgan has a genuine care for her patients, he grudgingly admits, and the receptionists probably have to deal with some right 'headcases'.

'How is he?'

He recognises her look: professional sympathy combined with a hard edge; tell the relatives the painful truth. It must be a horrible job.

'I'm sorry, Benedict, but your father has had more strokes. He is in a coma now. His body is shutting down, his organs failing one by one. I am afraid there is little else we can do.'

He feels like he is choking. His eyes fill with tears.

'We have him on a care pathway to manage his… pain. Soon he will be unable to swallow. The drip will help to keep him hydrated and a nurse will visit him when she can to feed him ice cubes. If you know of other relatives and friends, please urge them to visit soon.'

He wishes he had a time machine.

'How long does he have?'

'I don't know for sure, maybe two weeks, three at the most. I am sorry, Benedict. Has your father made a will?'

He laughs scornfully. 'What for? He doesn't have anything worth leaving. I assume the money from the house sale will go to my mother. At least I'm not first in line to inherit the family debts.'

Gallows humour; it is all he is capable of.

'Debts die with the debtor, Benedict. Ask your great-aunt to help you. You may be entitled to part of his estate.'

What estate? he thinks, but he remembers to thank the nurse for her care.

Before he leaves, he feeds his father more water and takes out his pipe, fills it with tobacco and leaves it on the pillow beside his head. He places his small transistor radio next to it.

'I bought new batteries, Dad, with my first wages. You'll be able to listen to the horse racing on Saturdays.'

He takes hold of his hand one last time, squeezes it gently and says a silent goodbye. He leaves a framed photograph on the top of the chest of drawers. His aunt gave it to him. It shows B.B. playing cricket with Stanley, during the war. He writes a few words on the back:

'I see plenty of colours in the world now, Dad. You take care of yourself. We won't forget you, even when they put you in the box. I know you tried your best. Bones.'

*

They head north on the M1 motorway and stop at a Little Chef café for a plate of what Dr Goodman describes as 'working-class nosh'. Fortunately, it has grown dark, and they cannot see the industrial tip on one side of the road and the sewage works on the other.

But they can smell them. *Perhaps that is why everyone smokes*, thinks Benedict.

He has hardly spoken since leaving the Eden Gardens Care Home, and they have not badgered him with questions. After he returned to the car, Gail Miller went to visit his father, to pay her respects and to talk to the nurses. Benedict saw the little shake of the head she gave Dr Goodman when she returned.

Despite the late hour, they press on north. En route, the car's radio plays the usual mixture of sad and frightening news: more terrorist bomb attacks, the deaths of children, the Pope cancelling a visit to Armagh.

'Can you put some music on?' asks Benedict from the back seat.

His aunt rummages around in the glove compartment and finds a tape. She bangs it a few times and tightens the spool before inserting it, uncertainly, into the car's seldom-used cassette player. The sound quality is poor, and on a few of the numbers he wonders if it is playing at the wrong speed, but it is better than listening to the endless bad news.

It is a tape of folk songs, some utterly ridiculous and childish, with female lead singers with unpleasant, shrieking, warbly and high-pitched voices, accompanied by groups of men who sound like a drunken choir belting out monotonous and predictable refrains. Or they are lengthy and exceedingly dull instrumental pieces whose melody is exhausted after the first verse, but whose performers insist on attempting twenty more equally boring variations before they finally take pity on the audience and give up. It is like the jazz his aunt often listens to, or the tedious guitar solos of the rock songs Dr Goodman prefers – self-indulgent performances that are nowhere near as interesting or moving as the knowing audience, nodding in appreciation, would have you believe. Such works always call to mind the fable of the 'Emperor's new clothes'.

He dismisses the folk tape as 'merry music'; it doesn't suit his mood.

Only a few of the songs does he find more interesting, mostly the ones that are overtly political. There is one called 'The Father's Song' by Ewan MacColl, performed live by an artist called Dick Gaughan. He admires the lyrics, and the passion and the craft of the singer.

Dr Goodman sighs and tuts all the way through the political numbers, shaking his head and mumbling to himself, 'Nonsense, poppycock; oh, come on, that's ridiculous!'

After an hour the cassette player protests and mangles the tape.

'Thank God for small mercies,' mutters Cyril.

*

In the small hours of Saturday morning they finally arrive at their destination, an expansive cottage overlooking the River Sett in the heart of the Derbyshire village of Hayfield. The dogs, familiar with the surroundings, bound out of the car and race each other towards the front door. Despite the dark, Benedict can see that the house is old and stone built, and that it extends over several floors. At the rear, the kitchen doors open out onto a small patio, which sits just above the level of the river. A short distance downstream the water plunges violently down a large weir.

'It used to be a mill,' says Dr Goodman by way of explanation, fetching their luggage out of the boot.

'Do you own this too?' he asks his aunt as she unlocks the front door.

'Yes, this was my home until I moved to Wellend.'

*

The next day they take a leisurely drive to the Derbyshire village of Castleton and park outside the George Inn, near to the old marketplace. They take a seldom-used path that runs below the ruins of a Norman keep called Peveril Castle. Romulus and Remus run about excitedly, glad to be back amongst the haunts of their youth, whilst Benedict and Gail search for fossils in a small, abandoned quarry. Dr Goodman, feeling breathless, sits on a table slab of limestone and smokes a cigarette.

They return to the inn for lunch and, afterwards, they leave Cyril in the pub to 'enjoy the afternoon in convivial company', because, after all, 'Gail will be driving us back to Hayfield', and so he can enjoy a 'pint or two, and a warming fire'.

'Simple pleasures, Benedict,' he says, knowingly, as they depart. 'That is the secret to a happy life.'

Outside the inn, Gail wraps herself up against the autumnal weather and says, 'Are you sure you want to do this? You can stay with Cyril if you prefer. Really, I won't be offended.'

'I've got my new walking boots on,' he replies, 'so yes, I want to try them out.'

He is loath to admit that he doesn't really like pubs; there is too much noise and smoke, and he can't abide the smell of stale beer. He has always found them intimidating places, like churches; he has never felt welcomed.

She smiles, and leads him out of the village, striding confidently uphill and the dogs running ahead of them. To his surprise, she walks in the middle of the main road, the A625 which links Sheffield to Manchester.

After a short while he sees a large Ministry of Transport notice which explains the absence of traffic: '*Danger, no access: this road is now permanently closed*'.

'A landslide,' explains Gail. 'They've had trouble with it for years. The ground we walk upon is seldom solid.'

After a steep climb, he begins to see sections of the road which have been taken by the slide, and angry fissures in the tarmac. There are a few other curious people milling around, taking photographs of the damage. Up to his right he can see a towering sequence of rocks which seem to have fed the slide. The arc-shaped scarp rises to a prominent peak, as dark and sombre as Gail's *Welsh Hills.*

'That's Mam Tor,' she says, '"the shimmering mountain". It's not technically high enough to be called a mountain, but it's a bit more dramatic than the Malverns, wouldn't you say?'

He has to agree, although the steepness of slope is no different. They climb towards the top of the hill, where an incongruous triangulation point marks the summit. They face into a stiff southwesterly wind and watch the dark clouds scud across the sky. He is impressed by the vista.

'You should find this panorama interesting geologically,' says Gail. 'That great chimney you can see belching out smoke – the chimney everyone can see – is a cement works, the Hope Valley cement works. They are burning lime which they quarry from the "White Peak", the hills made out of limestone. Peveril Castle is built on such rock.'

'I thought this was a national park,' he says, surprised to see such heavy industry despoiling the landscape.

'It is, but the quarries and cement works were here a long time before it became our first national park. People can't live in a museum, Benedict; there has to be work. This landscape is not really natural; it was fashioned by human endeavour. I suspect it will all become part of the heritage industry soon enough. That seems to be the only industry thriving these days.'

He finds it hard to catch his breath in the violent gusts of wind. 'And what's over there towards the north?'

She turns her back to the wind and points. 'That's the Edale Valley, and the hill beyond is part of the Kinder Scout Plateau. It's a bit wild up there sometimes, an expansive peat bog – very easy to get lost when the fog comes down. It's the highest point hereabouts. We stand at a geological boundary: that area is called the "Dark Peak", and the rocks change to sandstone and shale, very prone to slipping and sliding, just like Mam Tor. B.B. loved it up there.'

He is not sure he caught her last sentence correctly. 'B.B. came here?'

'Yes, when he was a student. After the First World War, we lived in France. We grew up near Libourne. But B.B. came back to England to study, and he loved walking these hills. He often stayed at a friend's house in Hayfield. He was part of the Kinder mass trespass.'

Benedict looks nonplussed. 'The what?'

'Workers in the factories of the industrial cities were forbidden to walk amongst their own hills. "England's green and pleasant land" was not for them to enjoy. In 1932, a mass trespass was organised on Kinder Scout. The protesters gathered at Hayfield. The police and gamekeepers were waiting for them, and there were scuffles and arrests. Five hundred people braved the moors that day, and the protest eventually led to the establishment of better rights to roam. Sometimes, the law has to be challenged if we are to tackle injustice and have a fairer society. B.B. knew that. I fear we take our hard-won rights too much for granted nowadays and forget the struggles of our forebears.'

Once again he admires the courage of his grandfather and wonders if he will ever be able to match it.

'Even now, there are landowners hereabouts who resent walkers following footpaths that cross their land. "Why can't you walk on the roads?" they will shout at you, or they deliberately block off the paths or put dangerous bulls in the fields to ward you away. They would have the countryside privatised; "Private, keep out, no entry" is their favourite sign. They do not understand how privileged they are to live amongst such scenery, and that is why they wish to deny access to the less fortunate masses.'

They continue their walk, moving along a prominent ridge towards a lesser summit called Back Tor, and then onto another summit, appropriately called Lose Hill. They stop and rest for a while, enjoying a flask of milky coffee and a slice of pork pie. He begins to realise how tired he is. It is a pleasant tiredness though, and he is sure he can walk the remaining few miles back down to Castleton. The day draws in and the light begins to fade. It starts to rain in earnest.

'A good test for our waterproofs,' says Gail, merrily zipping up her wax jacket. The walk seems to have lifted her mood.

There is no one else around; they have the ridge and the hills to themselves. The solitude suits Benedict. He feels at ease and becomes more animated.

For no apparent reason, Gail Miller begins to holler into the wind. She stands up, spreads her arms out wide and screams at the top of her voice, a long, sustained scream.

The dogs join in, howling in unison.

She turns to him and says, 'Try it, Benedict. You will feel better, trust me.'

He doesn't know why, but he takes a deep breath and screams. He screams as loudly and for as long as he can. He screams until he loses his breath and his voice hurts. He screams so intensely he worries that the Lose Hill will begin to slip and slide.

*

Early on Sunday morning, they leave Dr Goodman sleeping off a hangover and walk the dogs beside an abandoned railway line that once linked Hayfield to the nearby town of New Mills. The line followed the gorge-like Sett Valley. Benedict knows why it closed: his dad never stopped talking about the 'bloody Beeching Axe'. The restructuring of the railways recommended by Dr Beeching in the 1960s to 'improve efficiency' – following the cut in national subsidy and increased competition from cars – had led to his father being made redundant, alongside many other rail workers, and the closure of many branch lines.

'Railways are like a river,' his father had said, 'they need tributaries to feed them. If you cut off the tributaries, the trunks will die. It is a short-sighted policy, and the country will live to regret it, mark my words. If we put a fraction of the money into the railways and our manufacturing as we put into the bloody nuclear industry and military, this nation would thrive.'

It was his most militant subject, not that his dad was ever remotely active in politics. Unlike his own father, Stanley Harrison was not a man who would ever consider defying authority. He took his severance pay without protest.

In New Mills, the River Sett joined its waters to the River Goyt, which flowed on towards Manchester where it was joined by the flow of the River Tame, to eventually become the mightier River Mersey. The confluence of the two rivers occupied a shady gorge, and a series of ingenious and prominent weirs had been constructed to harness the power of the water. All around them, Benedict could see the remains of abandoned textile mills, bereft monuments to a once-thriving industry. The mills now resembled lidless boxes with empty windows and sad, crumbling interiors. They had been ransacked. The dereliction put him in mind of the bomb damage he had seen in pictures of the Blitz, except that green moss was taking hold of the stone, as it does in graveyards. Here and there were the remains of substantial pieces of industrial machinery, the metal turning to rust, and he wondered what they were and what function they had served. On top of the impressive bluffs he could see the workers' terraced houses, some of them precariously perched on slabs of fractured sandstone. He imagined the gorge filled with black smoke and metallic clangs, the water dyed red and yellow, and the ghosts of the worn-out workers leaving the mill at the end of their working day when the works' whistle finally signalled their release from toil. He thought about the incongruous name of the town, New Mills; 'abandoned mills' would seem more appropriate.

The gorge was now empty and quiet, and even the dogs took no interest in the desultory buildings.

*

By mid-morning they are heading east, towards Norfolk, following the A57 to Sleaford, or, as Dr Goodman puts it, 'We're risking the worst road in Britain.'

He winds his window down, despite the rain, because he is feeling 'delicate'. The draught of cold air and water that blows into the back of the car is unpleasant, but Benedict does not wish to complain.

'Something I ate,' explains Dr Goodman.

Benedict catches Gail's eyes, just as she rolls them and shakes her head. 'It wouldn't have anything to do with the alcohol, would it?' she replies sarcastically.

The farther east they travel, the flatter the landscape becomes, and the sky grows in proportion to the ironing-out of the topography. By the time they hit the Lincolnshire Fens near Spalding, they are all feeling gloomy, oppressed by the monotony of the landscape and the dismal panorama.

'Good God, what a desolate place,' says Dr Goodman. It was becoming his favourite expression.

In all directions there is nothing to see for miles except an occasional stand of poplars, an isolated hamlet, drainage dykes and endless fields of black soil. At one point, there is a spot height located on the top of a ten-foot-high artificial drainage embankment, positioned next to a pumping station.

'Are we below sea level?' asks Benedict.

'I don't know,' replies Gail. 'The fens were marshes and wetlands drained and reclaimed by ingenious engineers several centuries ago, many of them Flemish. In Cambridgeshire, it was a seventeenth-century Dutch engineer called Cornelius Vermuyden who designed the plan to drain the Ely marshes, and it was funded by a group of wealthy men called the "Gentlemen Adventurers". Their descendants have owned most of the land ever since.'

'The fens,' intones Dr Goodman, sighing, 'an endless expanse of monoculture which turns into a dust bowl when the soils dry out and the wind howls. There was a time when sheep farming was the main industry, but in their greed, the new landowners have grubbed out the trees and hedgerows and converted to arable, so now there is nothing to break up the fetch of the wind. The soils are only productive because they plaster them with so much artificial fertiliser.'

'I never knew you took an interest in agriculture,' says Gail, in a tone of voice that suggests he should change the subject.

At that moment, he pulls out to overtake the car in front of them. It is an underpowered vehicle optimistically towing a caravan, and they have been stuck behind it for several tortuous miles. Hastily, he pulls back in when an approaching articulated lorry on the other side of the road blasts its horn in angry warning.

'Cyril, just be patient!' says Gail.

'I'm trying to be,' he replies grumpily. 'This road is bloody awful. It winds too much and there is nowhere to overtake. These bloody caravans ought to be banned from the public highways. Why doesn't the idiot pull over and let the queue pass? Bloody inconsiderate. It's typical of caravan drivers; they are too mean to rent a holiday let or book a hotel like everyone else. Oh no, they have to clog up the roads with their damn homes on wheels.'

She turns to stare at him. 'Have you finished?' she asks.

He doesn't reply. He suddenly slams on the brakes and performs an emergency stop, skidding to a halt only inches from the back of the caravan. The driver in front had slowed unexpectedly because, unknown to Cyril, a tractor was carelessly parked on the verge, narrowing the width of the road. The caravan driver intended to wait for vehicles on the other side of the road to pass the tractor before he moved out to negotiate his way around the obstruction.

Dr Goodman hammers on the steering wheel in frustration. 'What's wrong with him? You could get a bloody tank through that gap!'

'Cyril, you could get a tank through any gap,' points out his aunt dismissively. 'That is, after all, what they are built for.'

Dr Goodman looks furious. 'Alright,' he says, 'have it your way.' He leans his head out of the window and shouts, 'Come on, man! You could get a supertanker through that gap!'

He looks back at her, a smug grin on his face.

'Pull over,' she says. 'I'm driving.'

*

Caesar is not at home when they finally locate the static caravan he is renting, but his girlfriend Tracy and her young baby are.

'You must be Bones!' she says by way of friendly greeting, standing in the doorway semi-dressed, the baby wailing in her arms. She has a broad Norfolk accent, and he has to bite his tongue, trying not to laugh at some of her pronunciations. 'You're the spitting image of Caesar!'

It is what everyone Caesar knows says to him, always, when they meet him for the first time, and Caesar never stops pointing out the likeness. He cannot deny the similarity, although his brother has a longer face and is taller, but he has always found the comparison annoying. It denies his individuality; it is as if he can only exist in Caesar's shadow.

Tracy invites them all in, but Dr Goodman and his aunt politely decline, saying they are taking the dogs to Sandringham for a run, and to find a place to stay for the night. They promise to call back later, to collect Benedict and to meet Caesar.

The caravan occupies a narrow strip of fen sandwiched between a drainage ditch and a busy road, about five miles south of King's Lynn. The field is muddy, and Benedict's shoes get coated in wet earth.

'Just leave them by the door,' says Tracy. 'Do you fancy a beer?'

'No, thank you, it's a bit early for me,' he lies, not wishing to appear 'a total square'.

The caravan is horribly cramped, and smells of chemical toilets and unburnt gas.

'Tea? Coffee?' she asks, motioning to the baby and adding, 'Excuse me a mo; he needs changing.'

'Changing for what?' he replies, his delivery deadpan.

Tracy laughs aloud. 'Oh, you're just like your brother.'

He hopes it is not true. 'Coffee, please. I can make it if you're busy.'

'It's no trouble, Bones. You just make yourself at home in the living room,' she says, squeezing through the door that leads into the tiny bathroom.

The living room is an L-shaped seat positioned around a Formica table. More squeezing is required to access it. He notices the holes in the cushions and fabric seats. Caesar has been up to his old tricks.

There are a few colour photographs propped up on the ledge by the picture window, their edges curling. They show Tracy and Caesar at Cromer pier eating candy floss and wearing 'kiss me quick' hats; Tracy and Caesar swimming in the sea at Hunstanton, the raw sewage outlet pipe visible in the background; Tracy and Caesar sitting on a motorbike, dressed as Hell's Angels and surrounded by similarly clad bikers.

'They were taken with an instant Kodak camera,' says Tracy proudly, switching on the kettle and handing the baby to Benedict. 'Caesar bought it me for Christmas, but we can't afford any more film at the moment.'

'Very nice,' he says, not knowing how to hold the baby and not wanting to look at the swimming photograph too closely; in it, Tracy appears to be showing more of herself than she perhaps intended.

'Sugar?' she asks. 'Caesar has at least four.'

'Not for me,' he says. 'I'm trying to lose weight.'

She howls with laughter. 'Good God, you're all skin and bones as it is! You're a funny boy, Bones.'

He laughs, although he doesn't find it funny. He tells himself to stop telling white lies. He cocoons himself in them, trying to project a false personality and shielding who he really is. He fears he will end up like his mother.

*

'What was the worst lie she ever told?' his aunt had asked, on the journey to Norfolk.

He had reeled off several, each whopper bigger than the last. 'Caesar was a gifted linguist and will marry a wealthy French aristocrat; his younger brother was a virtuoso tenor and will enter the Royal Academy; she had once dated a famous musician; she had written the lyrics to one of his famous songs; she had driven a lorry to Asia to bring aid to Vietnamese boat people; she had sky-dived for charity; she had canoed down the rapids of Niagara; she had been in a camel race in Timbuktu; she had skied in the Norwegian fjords; she invented the inflation device that enabled stricken lifeboats to right themselves; she was a qualified nurse.'

The list went on and on. The lies were always told with utter conviction, and so people were naturally convinced by the tales, although those that knew her better suspected the details may have been embellished. Benedict knew for certain she had no passport and had never left the country, and the idea of her sky diving, skiing or canoeing was preposterous: she hated heights and feared water.

When he was younger and knew no better, he had found some of the stories boosted his ego. He had wanted to believe they were true, even if he knew they were not. But then, later, he had thought how sad her life must be, to have to embroider the truth so much, to try to make her life seem more significant and meaningful than it appeared. He felt she lacked modesty, for her stories always had to trump everyone else's for drama. He thought she must be frustrated with her existence.

But then he had thought: who the hell was he to comment on the unfulfilment of another person's life?

In time, the lies became more frequent and more outrageous; sympathy had given way to despair, and amusement to cringing embarrassment: his mother was mad, plain and simple.

'I think your mother has been very ill for a long time,' said Gail. 'It is sad her illness has gone untreated for so long.'

Perhaps it was true of him, too; he fears he suffers from the same malaise.

*

'Where is Caesar?' he asks, trying to drink the undrinkable instant coffee she has placed before him, the out-of-date milk curdling into sour lumps in the prized, but chipped King's Lynn Speedway mug she has generously offered him, and wondering if the insanitary smell of the baby will infect his clothing. 'Does he work on Sundays?'

'Nah, not since he got the push.'

'He was made redundant at the welders?'

She shakes her head. 'Nope, they sacked him 'cos he was always bleeding late for work. He can't get out of bed in the morning. He's looking for employment at the moment. Right now, he's out with the Crows.'

She points to the photograph of the Hell's Angels gang.

'They like to go for fish and chips and a beer in Hunstanton on Sundays, and then ride about causing trouble. I'm a bit fed up with them to be honest, so I stayed at home this weekend. He'll be back soon.'

'Why are they called the Crows?' he asks, trying to keep the conversation going.

'I don't know,' she says, wondering why she had never thought to ask the same question. 'Rumour has it that they have an initiation ceremony – you have to bite the head off a crow – but it's all bollocks. Maybe it comes from "stone the crows"? Most of them are on the wacky baccy, but I don't want that stuff around the baby. I've told your brother that. If I catch him smoking it again I'm turfing him out, and for good this time.'

*

In the event, Caesar does not return for several hours, and when he does his mood is dark and maudlin. He doesn't greet Tracy or the baby with any warmth or enthusiasm, and Benedict feels sorry for her. He helps himself to a beer from the tiny fridge and uses the table edge as a bottle opener, chipping the Formica in the process. He lights a roll-up cigarette.

'Not in the house!' says Tracy, her good humour evaporating. 'Think of the baby.'

'We're not in a sodding house, are we,' he replies morosely.

She scowls at him and takes the baby into the bedroom, slamming the sliding door shut.

'What are you doing here?' he says, by way of greeting. His tone is cold and uninviting.

He wears a leather jacket, purchased second hand, its tassels fraying from the sleeves, and a crude skull and crossbones studded into the back. His jeans are coated in engine oil. He wears a white T-shirt, a heavy silver-painted chain around his neck and a fake onyx signet ring. A garish bracelet hangs loosely from one hand, the words Caesar and Tracy etched into the metal either side of a crudely drawn love heart. He had always liked to adorn himself with trinkets. He wears his hair long, unkempt and greasy, and his leather belt is buckled by another skull and crossbones.

He has never been intimidated by his brother. Never. He could match Caesar in a fight, and they both knew it, and when it came to brains, they both knew who stood ahead in the queue.

'Dad's dying,' he replies. 'Two to three weeks, that's all he's got left. If you want to see him, you need to visit soon.'

'He's been dying for years, Bones. Can he speak?'

'No, he is in a coma.'

'Then there's no sodding point in visiting him, is there? I suppose the old woman will get the house.'

They sit in silence for several minutes, in which time Caesar downs two beers and belches loudly. From the bedroom, he can hear the muffled sounds of Tracy and the baby crying.

'You been chatting to Trace?' he asks.

No Caesar, he thinks, *we have sat here in silence all afternoon, you moron*. But he says:

'Yes, I've been here a while, waiting for you.'

'Do you like her?'

The question isn't accusatory; Caesar is so insecure he needs to be liked, and he needs people to like his girlfriends, too.

'She's been friendly,' he replies noncommittally.

He had liked her well enough; he had found her honesty refreshing, and he could tell she had a kind heart. The conversation hadn't been forced, and they had laughed naturally together.

He leans in and whispers, 'She probably fancies you 'cos you look like me. Take her out if you want, I'm getting tired of her anyway. Time to move on. Plenty of fish in the sea.'

He picks out a piece of fluff from a cushion, rolls it into a ball, places it in the bridge between his thumb and index finger, puts his thumb in his mouth and inhales, slowly drawing the fabric fibres up his nose – the motion he has always called 'snuggling'.

Benedict recalls why his brother's moniker is Caesar. His father had known a work colleague who owned a bulldog of that name who was famed for his flatulence. He started using the nickname for his eldest son at a time when, unbeknownst to him, the school bullying reached its zenith and, as a consequence, Caesar was experiencing digestive troubles of his own.

His brother suddenly stretches and yawns, as if he is already bored by their conversation. Benedict cannot help noticing the angry wounds on his wrists, three jagged red marks on each arm. They are recent and healing badly.

27

Voices

London, autumn 1979

The Loving Heights crematorium is conveniently located only a stone's throw from the Eden Gardens Care Home. Some residents get to view the black smoke rising endlessly from its red brick chimney through their bedroom windows.

Unlike ancient churches and graveyards, the modern funereal building and gardens lack space. There is a small waiting area, where visitors can hear and see glimpses of the preceding funeral service taking place inside the main hall of condolence. The assembly is then ushered out of a back door with unseemly haste, whilst the next group are ushered in. Some people protest and claim it is like a production line, but to Benedict, it feels more like an abattoir.

The preceding ceremony is crammed full: a young child, well loved and keenly missed. Relatives, family friends and schoolmates queue patiently to gain admittance to the sad hall, but some are to be disappointed and have to wait outside. By the time the service is over, the crematorium is well behind schedule, and mourners and hearses are beginning to pile up in the car park.

There are only a handful of people present to say goodbye to Stanley Harrison. His aunt had accompanied Benedict on the train journey to London, purchased flowers and a card, and dressed in black. His brothers and mother are absent. The only other people present are the severe-looking nurse from the care home, an elderly man named George who was in the army with his father, George's wife and Silver-Sherry Nan, who is accompanied by a care worker of her own. She looks frail. She sits in a wheelchair and wears sunglasses, despite the autumnal weather. She is wrapped in a tartan blanket.

The man leading the service is neither a priest nor a vicar, a friend or a relative, and it soon becomes clear that he hasn't the first idea who Stanley Harrison was. He hurries through a few well-worn prayers and plays a hymn or two on a record player, the stylus jumping over the scratched LPs. He stands at a wooden lectern placed on a dais. The coffin rests on a stand beside him, the lid sealed. Gail's bunch of flowers sits on top. Benedict has placed his inheritance there too: his father's pipe, the photograph of him playing cricket with B.B. and his set of false teeth.

The wooden seats remind him of the chairs they used to sit on in primary school. They are hard and uncomfortable. Nothing about the hall is welcoming or intended to invite a prolonged stay, except for the deceased, who remain eternally. The brick walls are furnished only with cheap mustard-coloured drapes, low lighting and a few amateurish oil paintings of seascapes. It would be a suitable place for a séance, thinks Benedict.

George gets unsteadily to his feet and moves forward to read a short eulogy. He rests upon a Zimmer frame, which has an oxygen canister strapped to it. A tube reaches up to a mouthpiece which hangs by a strap from his nose. 'Emphysema,' he had explained. 'Bloody cigarettes.'

'I first met Stan at Aldershot. We did our National Service together. We were sent to Germany, to Berlin. Stan was a clever beggar and worked in the typing pool doing admin. He was wasted there. He should have been in Signals, but he wouldn't have it. He could be stubborn, Stan.'

He pauses for sombre laughter, a coded response that signals the assembly remember with affection the stubbornness of Stanley, and to clear his lungs of phlegm.

'He was a hell of a marksman. He could hit a milk bottle half a mile away. He wanted to fight in Malaysia, but someone grassed him up and told the authorities about his worsening health. They made him have another medical and he failed it. He left the army after that, and we lost touch.'

Another pause, more lung clearing; a large intake of oxygen through the mouthpiece.

'He picked up quite a bit of German in Berlin, which impressed the ladies. Stan was always popular with the ladies. In his youth, he had been the leader of a Teddy Boy gang. He was quite nimble on his feet and liked going to dances.'

The revelations are startling. Benedict had never known his father had been to Germany, or that he liked dancing. He struggles to recognise the man George describes. He recalls his slightly upright and pigeon-toed walk, a sort of slow military march, and he cannot ever imagine him being a 'ladies' man'.

'The lads used to call him "snake-hips Harrison".'

A third pause, but this time, no laughter. Another intake of oxygen. The man leading the ceremony takes an obvious look at his watch and emits an ill-concealed sigh. Noises of dissatisfaction begin to penetrate the hall, the gathering masses in the waiting area growing rebellious.

Silver-Sherry Nan snivels loudly, drawing attention to her suffering, and holds an embroidered handkerchief to her eyes, rubbing underneath the square-framed sunglasses.

'But what Stan really loved was sports. He was a damn fine goalie and had a trial for West Ham seconds. And he was a good opening batsman – solid, not flamboyant, but reliable – and a good mate, the best of mates. What a time we had.'

He turns and places a hand on the coffin lid, the man leading the ceremony looking relieved that the eulogy is coming to an end. 'God go with you, Stan. I'll join you soon, mate, and we can play merry hell in heaven.'

Another LP starts playing and the drapes hiding the entrance doors to the furnace are drawn back. As they file out of the hall, the coffin begins to slide off the table and into the fire. The doors and drapes have barely had chance to close again before the next group are ushered in.

'Goodbye, Dad,' says Benedict as Gail Miller places her hand gently on his shoulder and steers him out of the back door.

*

'Have you ever seen the First World War graves in France?' asks George as the funeral party make their way to the crematorium's gardens of remembrance. 'They look like this. Rows and rows of white crosses. It is the saddest place on God's earth.'

'Yes, I have seen them,' replies Gail. 'My father is buried in one of those war graves.'

Silver-Sherry Nan is being wheeled ahead of them. She has shown no interest in engaging in conversation, or even greeting them. Benedict wonders if she conceals a hip flask under her blanket.

'Will they spread the ashes here?' he asks.

Gail nods. 'Yes, you must remember the plot number. The little white cross will have your father's name on it and the date of the funeral, and it will mark the spot where his ashes are buried.'

'It seems very… crowded,' he says. 'Crowded and impersonal.'

'I know, and I am sorry,' she replies. What can she say? Funerals cost money, even this farce of an affair, and Stanley Harrison was broke. Unbeknownst to Benedict, she has paid for the cremation and funeral arrangements herself, because nobody else would.

With some difficulty they pass the huge crowd of mourners from the preceding service, who are blocking the garden path, the mother wailing and the father angrily gesticulating because they had not realised they would be unable to mark the child's plot with the flotilla of flowers the mourners have donated, many of the elaborate wreaths spelling out the child's name. Some of the schoolchildren had brought toys with personal messages attached that they had hoped to leave behind.

'I am sorry,' said a bespectacled crematorium employee in 'librarian dress', 'but we have nowhere to store flowers or toys. That was made clear when… when the arrangements were made. Perhaps they could go to a care home or a hospital?'

The severe nurse shakes her head and whispers to Gail, 'They won't take them; some of the patients are allergic to pollen.'

Allergies, thinks Benedict; his mother had once claimed she suffered from total allergy syndrome and had spent six months of her life in a sanitised room at Addenbrooke's Hospital in Cambridge, unable to speak. To this day he is convinced it was an act designed to make Stanley give up smoking. He never did, and when his mother returned home, she developed an allergy to life.

'Go and talk to your nan, Benedict,' says Gail as they approach the marker, the cheap piece of wood which is little more than a glorified lollipop stick, that has Stanley's name already seared into it. 'She won't talk to me, but perhaps she will want to say something to you.'

She is sitting very still, and he wonders if she has fallen asleep. Reluctantly, but dutifully, he goes and stands next to her.

'Hello, Nan.'

'Which one are you?' she asks in a feeble voice.

'Benedict,' he replies.

'You don't resemble your father, not in any way.'

'Thank you,' he says.

'Don't be sarcastic with me, young man. Where is your mother?'

He shrugs his shoulders.

He cannot help but notice how badly her hands tremble. He has seen similar cases in the care home, some residents unable to drink their tea without spilling it everywhere. 'Parkinson's disease,' the nurses always say by way of sympathetic explanation. 'Very advanced.'

'She always did have ideas above her station, that one,' says his nan. 'Always thought my Stanley wasn't good enough for her. She insisted they move into their own house instead of coming to live with me.'

And suddenly he knows with crystal clarity that it was her who informed the military authorities about Stanley's failing health. She did not want him to leave her side, not ever. He must have known it too, and that is why he was always distant from her. Her selfishness drove him away.

She looks over towards Gail Miller and asks, 'What's that evil bitch doing here and why are you with her?'

He finds her voice grating and unpleasant, and he can contain his anger no longer. Despite her condition, and despite the sombre occasion, he finds himself saying, 'Keep your vicious tongue to yourself, old woman.'

He says it in German. He has no idea where it comes from.

He turns his back on her. He wants nothing more to do with Silver-Sherry Nan, not ever.

*

The wake is a private affair held in a backroom of a local pub. It is a modest rectangular building with two large and frosted picture windows – one recently vandalised and temporarily boarded up – redundant hanging baskets, red bricks and green tiles. Benedict thinks the tiled entrance resembles a public toilet.

The dingy backroom is set out with a trestle table. A white cloth has been draped over it, like an altar. The cloth is old, fraying and badly stained. Two plates of sandwiches have been left out, the edges of the white bread curling upwards. There is an urn of coffee, a flask of hot water, a saucer full of teabags, mugs and paper plates, some stale-looking biscuits, a few cold sausage rolls and some slices of pork pie. The carpet smells of stale beer and is perforated by numerous black cigarette burns. The ceiling might once have been white, but it has been stained yellow. There are pictures on the walls, but they have been discreetly covered by tea towels. Benedict idly wonders what they depict.

George offers to buy the first round. It does not cost him much. Benedict has lemonade, and Gail and George's wife have a whisky. He has pale ale. The severe nurse just has a cup of tea as she regrettably 'can't stay long'. Silver-Sherry Nan does not attend the wake. She was met by a private taxi at the crematorium gates and left without saying goodbye to anyone.

The only other person present is the woman who had once helped Benedict telephone for an ambulance when his father had his first stroke. 'I'm sorry I missed the ceremony,' she says, by way of introduction. 'The damn bus never came.'

She stands at the entrance to the room, uncertain of her welcome.

'Thank you so much for coming,' says Benedict, moving forward and embracing her, an act that is spontaneous and imbued with genuine warmth. He embraces so few people. 'Can I get you a drink?'

She smiles radiantly, and he introduces her to the assembled party, although he has to ask her name.

'I'm Winifred,' she says, 'call me Winnie,' and the severe nurse smiles at her, recognising a fellow professional, and says, 'I'm Mary. Which hospital do you work at?'

*

The conversation is amiable, and they do their best to eat some of the food. George has two more pale ales and raises his glass 'to Stanley'.

'To Stanley,' they all repeat.

'He was such a lovely man, your father,' says Winnie. 'So charming and well mannered. I didn't know him long, but I visited him several times after he had his first stroke. He was still able to speak a little then. It was more difficult for me to visit once they moved him here, but I was with him at the end, did you know that?'

Benedict had not known that, but he was glad his father was not alone. How frightening that would have been.

'I held his hand, Benedict, and spoke words of comfort. I know he is up in heaven now.'

He smiles sadly, too choked to reply.

'That was very kind of you, Winnie,' says Gail. 'You must be a wonderful nurse.'

'A true angel,' adds George.

Gail lets the comment pass; this is not the moment for a political rant about the male objectification of nurses.

'It has always been my calling,' says Winnie. 'My own boys, my twins, were taken to God before their first birthday. I hear their voices, every day, and they remind me to be a Good Samaritan and to be kind to others. Your father was very proud of you, Benedict.'

'Was he?' he asks, surprised by the revelation. He wants to doubt the truth of it; the idea makes him feel uncomfortable.

'Of course he was. He said you were the brains of the family. He regretted that he had not been able to help you more, but he knew you would land on your feet. He worried about your other brothers, though, all the time. He wanted you to have this.'

She reaches into her handbag and fetches out a black and white photograph. It shows his father dressed as a Teddy Boy, with drainpipe trousers and suede creepers, a long jacket with a velvet-trim collar and large side pockets, a white shirt and narrow black tie. There is a cigarette hanging out of his mouth. His wiry hair is curly, but he has swept it back and plastered it down with grease. A woman in a black pencil skirt hangs on his arm, but it is not Benedict's mother. They appear to be at a dance hall.

'Such an elegant man,' says Winnie admiringly.

'Those clothes cost him a packet,' says George. 'Wouldn't surprise me if he was still paying for them.'

'The Teddy Boys were notorious, weren't they?' asks Mary, a concerned look crossing her face.

'Yeah,' says George, 'some of the gangs were right hooligans and thugs. They were involved in the Notting Hill race riots and attacks on immigrants.'

Benedict recalls his father's often casual racism, the same thoughtless racism that his mother would show, and Caesar, and his nans, and his classmates. It would manifest itself in words rather than deeds, and stupid comments and jokes they had heard and repeated from television programmes. But if you had asked Stanley, he would have claimed he wasn't a racist. He couldn't abide the idea of slavery, he boycotted South African goods in protest against apartheid and he championed the cause of Nelson Mandela; his favourite musicians were Big Bill Broonzy and Fats Waller; he greatly admired Sammy Davis Junior and acknowledged how much harder he had to work for recognition than the rest of the 'Rat Pack'; and his favourite cricketer was Gary Sobers. He talked affectionately about his West Indian teammates at the local cricket club, and he regretted that he could not bat with the same flair as they did. Many of his work colleagues were immigrants, and he was genuinely interested in their religions and cultures. He didn't socialise or have close friends with them because he was, at heart, an antisocial man. He didn't like injustice and he would champion the rights of all people, at least intellectually.

'Stanley was never in any of those gangs,' says Winnie. 'He told me that himself and I believed him. He was only interested in the look, and the dancing, and the music.'

'To Stanley,' says George, once more raising his glass to the heavens, and signalling to the bartender for another pale ale.

*

'How do you feel?' asks Gail Miller on the train journey back to Great Malvern.

It is a question she often asks him, and he always struggles to answer it. He has no idea how he feels, and he has no desire to spend time trying to find out.

'I don't know. I am glad the funeral is over. It was good of Mary and Winnie to come, and George and his wife.'

'Mabel, her name was Mabel. She certainly liked a whisky or two.' Gail Miller smiles to herself.

'George said the four of them were going to make a night of it, in remembrance of Dad.'

'A proper East End knees up, eh,' she says, chuckling to herself. 'I think your father would have approved.'

'Do you think Winnie and Mary will remain friends?' he asks thoughtfully.

'Yes, yes, I do, they got along famously. I have all of their addresses, should you wish to write to them in future.'

'I should do that,' he muses. 'Send a thank you card or something.'

'That would be most thoughtful of you,' replies Gail, thinking how far he has come in such a short space of time.

'But I thought Caesar would be there, and even perhaps my mum with our younger brother. I can't believe she wasn't. Just think of how many years they lived together.'

'I am sorry, Benedict, but are you sure that she received the invitation?'

'I sent it to Caesar; he's got her address, he would have passed it on.' He screws up his face in consternation. 'I mean, I know he can be an idiot, but he would have done the right thing. Why do you think she didn't come?'

She can sense his hurt, the poison of neglect coursing through his veins, the venom making straight for the heart.

'I don't know. Sometimes, when relationships die, people just want to forget. It is hard; they need to move on. They don't want reminding of a life which has failed. What would you have said to her?'

He looks away, out of the train window. She notices that he clenches his left fist. 'I don't know. If she had started telling fibs I would have run away from it, or I would have confronted her with her lies. Honestly, I don't know what I would have done.'

She pats him on the arm. 'The Benedict of a year ago might have run away, but this Benedict would have confronted her.'

Maybe she is right, he concedes; he seems to have been making of habit of confronting people of late.

'Do you ever hear your mother's voice in your head? Do you ever have imaginary conversations with her?'

What a peculiar question, he thinks. 'No, never. Should I? Do you hear your mother's voice?'

She looks thoughtful. 'Yes, sometimes. She tells me to forgive.'

'Forgive what?'

'All the unintended blows life delivers.'

It sounds like spiritual nonsense to him. 'Was she religious?' he asks.

'Yes, Catholic, like my father.'

'Like my mother,' he snaps. 'I thought Catholics weren't allowed to divorce.'

'It can be granted, in special circumstances, but it is not encouraged. How did the divorce make you feel?'

There she goes again, always asking him about his feelings.

'Glad,' he says, and he means it. 'All they did was argue. It was a blessing when she left.'

'And is your maternal grandmother also a Catholic?'

'Yes, very devout.'

She nods her head in understanding. The daughter's divorce would not have pleased her. There would have been another rift within the family.

'I wonder if Nan hasn't travelled to Dublin to see the Pope,' says Benedict. 'She might be praying for a miracle. He's going to address a huge rally.'

Gail points to the headline in her newspaper. 'The Pope has made a powerful speech calling on the children of Ireland not to listen to the voices of hatred and division. How do you feel about that?'

He throws up his hands in exasperation. 'I don't know. I don't know how I feel about anything anymore.'

28

Afternoon Tea with Jasmine

Great Malvern, November 1979

In November, Dr Marks finally returns from her sabbatical, and Mrs Hart is well enough to resume her management duties. Conveniently, the day before they return, Sandra Morgan is promoted to a permanent managerial position at a new care home in Stourbridge.

'They never found anything against her,' says Gail Miller, when Benedict reports the news. 'The surprise local authority inspection found Victor to be well cared for. I was asked for my sources. I'm afraid they may have suspected you as the whistleblower.'

He shrugs his shoulders. 'Maybe she got a tip-off about the inspection? I think they knew King Arthur was the source. They've put him on lithium now; he seems less delusional.'

'So, you will play chess again tomorrow,' she says, her face registering excitement. 'Which opening will you use?'

'I have been thinking about that,' he says. 'Can I show you something I've been working on?'

*

That evening, at night school, the biology class requires students to work in pairs, measuring each other's pulse and recovery time after a series of short exercises. Benedict is paired with the only student in the class who is a similar age to himself. He has noticed her before, but he has never summoned up the courage to speak to her. She has dark, straight hair, worn in a short bob with a straight fringe. She wears dark liner to accentuate her eyes and large gold earrings. She has a small gold stud on the left side of her nose. He thinks she resembles a figure from an Egyptian hieroglyph, but for once, he does not find the apparition frightening.

Previously, he has thought about how to begin a conversation with her, perhaps even muster up the courage to ask her out. But he rejected the idea; she would probably just laugh at him, finding him unattractive.

She is more outgoing than him, or at least, she hides her shyness better.

'I'm Jasmine,' she says. 'I wish I was as good at biology as you are, Benedict.'

It is an encouraging start: she knows his name.

'Hello, Jasmine,' he replies, feeling tongue-tied and sensing his pulse quicken. 'I'm not that good really.'

'But you're top of the class! You know all the answers.'

It is not a criticism; she says it with admiration. 'You

work things out much faster than the rest of us. We find it a bit intimidating.'

He had never considered that he could intimidate anyone. 'Well, people say I have a big head. Perhaps there are some brains in there after all.'

She laughs, and he finds her smile radiant.

'I don't think you have a big head. It's rather a nice head.'

She looks at him in an unusual way, and he is nonplussed. He has always found it difficult to read people's signals.

He flushes red and looks away.

She finds his humility delightful. It is such a refreshing change from all the brash and arrogant types who try to flirt with her. And he is so old-fashioned, both in his dress and his manner, and so reserved. But there is something about him that intrigues her.

She giggles. 'Do you like acting, Benedict?'

'Yes, I was in all the productions at school.'

She is surprised by his answer, and she smiles again. 'Would you like to join our drama group? We meet at the theatre on Sunday afternoons. This Christmas, we're putting on a production of *Fiddler on the Roof*. We're still looking for people to join the chorus.'

'Yes,' he says. 'Yes, I would like that.'

'Good, then why don't you meet me at the Turkish coffee shop on the high street at two o'clock? We can have something to drink and then go on to the theatre.'

He only has a vague idea where the high street is, and he wasn't aware there was a Turkish coffee shop, but he is sure he will find it.

'I had better take your pulse first,' he says, feeling his heart skip a beat.

'So, that's a date then,' she asks, her face breaking into the broadest of smiles.

*

'I'm sorry I couldn't give you any warning about my trip,' says Dr Marks. 'It was all rather sudden. A colleague was taken ill and I was asked to step in. It was too good an opportunity to miss.'

Benedict smiles. 'I'm glad you are back, both of you.'

They are sitting in Mrs Hart's office. The manager looks unwell, but he is too polite to ask what the trouble has been.

'Thanks, Benny,' says Mrs Hart. 'I hear you've been holding the fort pretty well.'

'I haven't been allowed to see Victor, or play chess.'

Mrs Hart exchanges a concerned look with Dr Marks.

'Yes,' replies the doctor, 'that has been… regrettable. It is true that Victor does not enjoy being outside, and that, if he has an external window to look out of, he becomes agitated. Nurse Morgan did what she thought was best for her patient by restricting him to the one room, but she was wrong to ban the chess games. I have to warn you that Victor has declined further since you last saw him. I am told he has not spoken since you last played him at chess. He uses a wheelchair now. He has forgotten how to walk. We fear he may soon forget how to swallow. I am afraid his vital signs are fading. He may not live to see another Christmas.'

Good Lord, thinks Benedict, *he has less time than they imagined.*

'Can I play him today?' he asks.

'I am sorry, Benny, but he's sick. Why don't you try again next week,' says Mrs Hart.

*

He arrives early at the Turkish coffee shop. One hour early; he didn't want to be late. He is so excited he hardly slept. His aunt insisted on giving him a lift and insisted on taking him to Worcester the previous day to buy new clothes. He wears a black polo neck jumper and a woollen blazer, jeans and his suede boots. He carries his recently dry-cleaned duffle coat in his hands, his hat and gloves shoved into the pockets.

'Very smart,' said Gail, carrying out a troop inspection in the kitchen before they left. 'A proper gentleman. You have had a bath and washed your hair?'

'Yes.'

'And cleaned your teeth?'

'Of course, twice.'

'And gargled?'

'Yes, Gail, and I've put the eau de Cologne on too, although it stinks.'

'And you have the present?'

He nods. His aunt had suggested flowers, but he had preferred a book. It was not a bad idea, she conceded, and so they visited a bookshop.

'No, not that,' she had said as he held up a copy of *The*

Selfish Gene by Richard Dawkins. 'Let us try for something a little more… romantic…'

*

'Come in, Benedict, come in,' says an aged, stocky man with receding white hair and a thick moustache. His left eye is brown, but his right eye is opaque. His accent is thick, and it takes Benedict's brain a moment to understand what he says. 'You are Benedict, aren't you?'

'Yes,' he says, intrigued as to how the man would know.

When he arrived, he had found the coffee shop closed. His heart sank. Had Jasmine played a cruel trick on him? He had waited half an hour, but the shop remained unlit and the door locked. He nearly turned around and walked home. He had knocked on the door window only tentatively, not really expecting an answer.

'Come, come in, please.'

The man seems to be the owner and he seems to be expecting him.

'Does Jasmine work here?' he asks, peering into the shop and noticing it is empty.

'Yes, yes, sometimes, when she is not studying. We live upstairs. I am Ozan, her father.'

'Oh,' says Benedict, finally cottoning on. 'I am very pleased to meet you, sir.' He holds out his hand. He tries to surreptitiously wipe it on his jeans first, because he is sweating with nerves.

Ozan laughs. 'Jasmine said you were typically British

and very formal. I am not a sir and there is no need to stand on ceremony.'

He says it in a kindly way, and they shake hands. 'Welcome to our home, Benedict, welcome. You are early. Jasmine is upstairs with her mother and sister. They will be an age getting ready; it is how we men learn patience. Would you like a Turkish coffee?'

'I have never had one of those,' he admits, 'but I would like to try it.'

'Good, good man,' says Ozan. 'Sit, please, make yourself at home. I'll be right back.'

The Turkish coffee shop has an ornate wooden serving counter running parallel to the back wall, which is almost entirely covered by a large glass mirror. There are copper kettles and ingenious-looking coffee-making machines set out on the counter. Everything looks polished and scrupulously clean. There are several low tables positioned around the shop, next to elegant divans and settees. The walls are decorated with photographs of Turkey, some of which are for sale. The landscape looks magnificent, and he wonders what it must be like to visit. The floor is covered in beautiful rugs of red and black thread. There are potted plants everywhere, including an enormous yucca tree in the middle of the room. There is a menu displayed by the till; he tries to pronounce some of the unfamiliar names: falafel, hummus, baklava. A bookcase fills one corner. It is full of vintage, hardback tomes. Beside it, hanging from the wall, is an oud.

'Here we are,' says Ozan, placing two tiny cups of coffee

on a table and inviting Benedict to sit down opposite him on a divan. He can't help but notice how bent and twisted his fingers are.

Ozan takes a sip of his coffee, and Benedict follows suit. The coffee is strong, the strongest he has ever tasted, and bitter. But he finds it aromatic, and after a few more sips, it begins to grow on him.

He notices the table has a chessboard carved into it. 'Do you play?' he asks.

Ozan smiles, revealing several gaps in his teeth. 'Yes, do you?'

He nods.

'Good, good, I think we have time for a quick game.'

They spend the next hour engaged in a close match. Only occasionally does Ozan break his concentration by asking a question, about his job, his studies and his career plans.

'Geology,' he says, nodding thoughtfully. 'There is a lot of money in oil, but it is a dirty business. It tars everyone who touches it.'

'I'm more interested in fossils,' he replies.

'Is there money in fossils?'

When they hear someone coming down the stairs they shake hands and call the game a draw.

'You play well, Benedict,' says Ozan. 'I play against many of our regular customers, and no one has ever managed so much as a draw against me.'

'You should play my aunt,' he says. 'She wipes the floor with me every time.'

He raises one of his bushy eyebrows in surprise.

'Really? Then your aunt must be a genius. You must bring her here; I would love to meet her.'

'You would love to meet who, husband?' says a voice behind him.

He stands up and beams. 'Benedict, this is my wife, Susan. She is the artist who took all these wonderful photographs,' he says proudly.

Ozan's wife is tall and elegant, and some years younger than her husband. Jasmine takes after her in looks. She smiles and shakes hands with Benedict.

'I am pleased to meet you at last,' she says. 'We have heard a lot about you.'

'You British,' chuckles Ozan, 'always so formal. Benedict was just telling me that his aunt is a chess genius. I would like to meet her.'

'I might know your aunt,' says Susan. 'I am from Malvern originally, although I have lived abroad a lot.'

'She only moved here recently,' he says. 'She is called Gail Miller.'

Susan's eyes open wider. 'Not *the* Gail Miller?' she asks. 'The artist?'

'Yes, technically she's my great-aunt.'

'Then you must bring her here,' says Susan. 'Please, Benedict, I have been a great admirer of hers for as long as I can remember.'

*

Jasmine wears black jeans and an oversized green jumper, the same outfit her younger sister, Roxanne, wears.

Benedict cannot fathom why it has taken her so long to get ready, but he knows when she is about to appear, for his pulse quickens and his fingers tingle.

'Hello, you,' she says, smiling and affecting a casualness she doesn't feel. Her sister wraps herself around one of her legs, and peeks out at him shyly.

'Hello,' he says. 'I bought this for you. I hope you like poetry?' He feels awkward and clumsy as he stands up, nearly knocking over the chess pieces, and passes her the book. He knows that all eyes are on him.

'Only those with no soul have no poetry,' she replies, her tone serious. 'Thank you for the present, that was kind of you. Look, Papa, look what he got me.'

Ozan beams. 'A good choice, Benedict. We should venerate the soul of the poet above all others.'

'Would you like some English tea and something to eat?' asks Susan diplomatically.

'Yes, he would,' replies Jasmine, before he gets chance to answer. 'Can we have something sweet, Mama, please?'

Susan smiles indulgently and ushers Roxanne into the back kitchen. 'Ozan,' she calls out behind her, 'we shall need a hand.'

'Oh,' he says, smiling, and he dutifully skips off after her.

They are left alone in the coffee shop.

'You've made quite an impression on my dad,' says Jasmine, once she is sure the door to the kitchen is closed. 'He doesn't usually like any of the boys I bring home.'

'Oh,' he says, sounding just like Ozan, and trying to fight down a pang of jealousy. It had not occurred to him that there had been previous boyfriends.

She laughs at the look on his face. She moves over close to him and whispers, 'Benedict, my father is very protective of me. Those boys were just friends, nothing more. My father wanted to meet you. That is why I have taken a while to "get ready". I think he was impressed by your gift. Pablo Neruda is his favourite poet.'

He is relieved and smiles, but worries that his emotions are so transparent.

'He is good at chess,' he says, wondering if the family are eavesdropping on their conversation.

'And so are you. I hear you managed a draw. I've never managed that.'

She begins whispering again: 'He hasn't always run a coffee shop. He was a musician, in Turkey, and a gifted songwriter. That is where he met my mother. She was a journalist and photographer. He was persecuted by the regime for his Christianity and for his political beliefs. He was imprisoned, without trial, and tortured.'

Benedict thinks about his missing teeth, his blind eye and the twisted fingers. 'That is awful,' he says with genuine feeling.

'When he was released, they fled the country and he sought asylum. He has never been allowed to work, not properly. The coffee shop is my mother's; Dad just helps out now and again.'

'And were you born in Turkey?'

'Yes, although I was only a baby when they fled. It was hard on Dad; he had to leave his relatives behind. He has never been able to go back.'

'I am sorry,' he says. 'I like him, and your mum.'

She takes hold of his hand and squeezes it, and he notices that her hand is every bit as clammy as his.

'You are so sweet,' she says. 'Do you mind if my sister walks with us to the theatre this afternoon?'

He shakes his head; he wouldn't mind who accompanied them as long as she kept hold of his hand.

She raises her voice and says, 'Roxanne has a part in *Fiddler on the Roof* as one of the young urchins. She is only seven. I think the fame has gone to her head.'

'I heard that!' comes a high-pitched squeal from behind the kitchen door. 'You're the one with the big part – big part, big head!'

They hear Susan say, 'Hush, little one.'

'It's true,' concedes Jasmine, laughing, and speaking loudly: 'I am playing the rebellious daughter who defies her father and marries against his wishes.'

They hear Ozan say something in Turkish. It sounds like a curse.

And then she whispers into his ear, 'Dad doesn't really approve of us acting, but Mum insists we follow our dreams. Dad is a bit like you, old-fashioned, but he has a good heart and he wants what is best for us.'

'You find me old-fashioned?' he asks despondently.

'Of course! Oh, Benedict, you are such a square, but that is what I like about you.' She squeezes his hand again, and only lets go when they hear the kitchen door opening.

*

They sit around one of the low tables drinking tea and eating homemade Turkish delight. Benedict finds it irresistible, and Ozan encourages him to 'eat his fill'.

'Jasmine,' says Susan, 'why don't you sing Benedict a song before you leave for the theatre?'

'Would you like to hear a song, Benedict?' she asks, smiling.

'Yes, I'd like that very much,' he says, trying to surreptitiously wipe a dusting of icing sugar from his lips.

'Very well,' she says, standing up and fetching the oud. 'Papa is teaching me to play. I'm not very good yet, so don't laugh.'

*

He is surprised to find that the amateur dramatics group is made up of people of all ages and backgrounds; he had assumed it would be a youth theatre. The director is a striking-looking middle-aged woman called Mrs Shakespeare, who invests enormous energy into everything she does and runs the company like a military unit.

The afternoon begins with warm-up exercises, the troop sitting in a circle. Mrs Shakespeare has them make strange vocal noises, mirror the actions of their neighbour and improvise scenarios she gives them.

'Benedict,' she says, 'walk in a furtive manner.'

He has never been more grateful to his aunt. He is one of the few younger people in the theatre who knows what furtive means.

Everyone watches him. He gets up and walks into the centre of the circle. He can feel Jasmine's eyes on him. And then he acts furtively. He stops, suddenly, and casts a suspicious glance behind him; he pretends to follow someone in front of him, stopping when they stop, and turning around to look in an imaginary shop window. He makes them laugh with his performance, and Jasmine beams at him.

'I think we have a natural here,' concludes Mrs Shakespeare, leading the enthusiastic applause.

Later, whilst the company are in rehearsals, she has the musical director run him through his paces. 'Not bad at all,' he concludes, 'although we need to sort your breathing out. You have a good ear. I think there is a decent voice in there somewhere waiting to get out.'

After a brief discussion, they offer him a part in the chorus. He accepts, without hesitation. It will mean that he gets to see Jasmine every Sunday afternoon.

*

It is dark by the time they finish, and it has snowed. Susan arrives before the end to collect Roxanne, and to bring her daughters warm coats and scarves to put on. She says to Jasmine, 'Benedict can walk you home if you like, but don't be late. Your father is anxious enough as it is.'

She smiles and kisses her on the cheek. 'Thank you, Mama,' she says.

He feels like he could walk forever, arm in arm with Jasmine. Gravity no longer weighs him down. Everything about the late afternoon is perfect: the cover of snow, the half silver moon, the yellow halo of the streetlights, the winding paths and stone-built houses, the illuminated shops with their pretty picture windows which catch their passing reflections. He feels like being bold; he feels like shouting into the wind.

'Watch this,' he says, suddenly running forward and tying to leap over a privet hedge. He lands badly on the other side and bangs his knee. It hurts like hell, but he tries to show no pain.

She can't help but laugh at his antics. 'Benedict, I never took you for a fool! I preferred you when you were being furtive.'

He lies in the snow, laughing. 'I have no idea why I did that.'

'Did you think to impress me, Superman?'

He begins to make a snow angel.

'I think it was a leap of joy,' he replies, hoping she won't laugh at him. 'You should try this. Come on, let's leave our imprint in the snow.'

She laughs, but lies down next to him and does as he does. When the snow angels are complete, they lie still and stare up at the stars.

'So, you enjoyed the afternoon then?' asks Jasmine.

'Yes, yes, I did. You have a lovely singing voice, even if I couldn't understand a word you sang.'

'Do you think so?' she asks thoughtfully. 'It was one Papa's songs. Maybe I'll translate it for you one day. It is very beautiful. Did you notice how it made him cry?'

*

Time passes too quickly and before they know it they are back at the coffee shop. Ozan waves to them through the window, a look of relief on his face.

'I have to go,' says Jasmine, brushing snow from his duffle coat. 'Are you sure you will be able to get home alright? You could ring your aunt from here if you like, Dad won't mind.'

'I will be fine. It's really not far to walk and I like the snow.'

'Here, take this.' She removes her scarf and wraps it around his neck. 'It is cold, Benedict, I wouldn't want you freezing to death.'

She reaches up and kisses him on the cheek.

'*Ciao*,' she says, turning to leave. 'I will see you in Biology on Thursday.'

'*Ciao*,' he calls back after her.

He is still standing where she left him some moments later, waving to an empty coffee shop.

The walk home would be daunting were it not for the elation he feels. He doesn't register the miles or the cold. Images of the afternoon replay constantly in his mind. He touches his cheek and recalls her warm kiss. He buries his nose in the scarf, and he is reminded of her scent.

By the time he makes it back to the farmhouse, he has composed his first poem. He calls it 'Snow Angels' and it is dedicated to Jasmine, Ozan's daughter.

29

The Turncoat Bird Takes Flight

Salford Docks, December 1946

Night or day, the docks are seldom quiet. There are always ships waiting at the quays. They come from the Americas, along the Manchester Ship Canal, loaded down with raw materials – cotton, sugar, rum and tobacco – or they sail out to what remains of the empire, to deliver textiles, machines and finished goods to the colonies, wealth-making products that fuelled an industrial revolution at home and wrought havoc to indigenous industries abroad. 'Cottonopolis' they called Manchester, the world's first modern industrial city, but already it shows the signs of decline. For now, the cranes work ceaselessly, and the high-intensity floodlights do their best to pierce the thick smog and winter gloom. In time, the docks and the dockers will become ghosts, and they will fade from memory.

At first light an army of hungry-looking men press against the dock gates, waving their work cards, hoping to be selected by the foreman for loading or unloading duties. Some of them are old hands who have worked throughout the war. They remember the shortages and the stricken vessels. They remember those who have not returned. And they remember the bombs.

To the south of the docks lies Trafford Park, the world's first purpose-built modern industrial estate. It was a site where they manufactured Lancaster bomber engines, and so it was an inevitable target for Luftwaffe raids. The night sky has been lit before with high-intensity lights, the phosphorus bombs dropped by the pathfinder aircraft to mark their targets. Then followed the bombers with their high explosives and incendiary devices. The red glow of the fires could be seen across the Pennines in Sheffield, another doomed industrial city targeted by the Luftwaffe. The bombs were indiscriminate; they did not give a fig where they fell. They fell on cathedrals, hospitals and schools, on football grounds, on homes and workplaces, on factories, on roads, on bus stations and train stations, on docks and dockers. Christmas 1940, the Manchester Blitz, the city on fire, the city crippled, 2,000 injured, one for each incendiary bomb dropped, and 684 innocents dead.

Some of the hopeful dockers are soldiers, recently returned from the war, part of the demobbed masses, eager for peacetime employment – eager for peace. They are viewed favourably, but only a lucky few make it through. The rest are turned away from the gates, unpaid and empty-handed.

'What did we fight for?' mutter bitter voices. 'For rationing and empty bellies, for wreckage and ruination? For lives torn apart, so that Mr bloody Churchill can crow in triumph? Good riddance to him,' they mumble. 'I'm glad we voted him out.'

But there is one man who will make it through the dock gates; it has been pre-arranged. Françoise Fronsac knows this; it is how they always work.

She waits for him, for one single sight of him. One shot, that is all she needs.

He wears a donkey jacket, collar turned up, a flat cap and hobnail boots, but the disguise will not save him. He hopes to blend in, to become another match in the matchbox, but he is a fool. The shift is long and the work arduous. Despite the winter season, he will overheat. The dockers always do. He will strip down to his braces and grandad shirt, and then even that will be removed. The heat, the sweat, the constant shifting of crates; he is not used to such labour. It is not unknown for the men to brave the waters of the quays, even in winter, when dirty ice forms on the surface. That is how much they overheat.

That is all she needs: one sight, one shot.

The security around the docks is weak. If she had been an enemy agent during the war, she could have attached limpet mines to every ship at the quays and blown them skywards. She witnessed such an event in Bordeaux, in December 1942.

It inspired her plan. Using the cover of night, she kayaked along the ship canal. She scuttled her vessel and made for a warehouse near to Ontario Basin. There were no searchlights, patrols, guard dogs or barbed wire. She climbed an external fire ladder and attained the roof. By daybreak, she was in place, watching from her eyrie.

He knows she is after him. He has known it since the 9th June 1944 when she evaded capture. He knows who is to blame for the death of the Angel and Raymond. She needs to talk to him.

No, that is too nice a term; she needs to interrogate him.

She adjusts the sights on her rifle and checks the silencer is secure. The rifle has a swastika etched into the wooded butt. She recently acquired it in Svalbard, a leftover from the German occupation – a sniper's rifle, lethal over a distance of three kilometres and powerful enough to fell a polar bear.

She does not intend to kill him, not yet. First, she must delay his departure. He will load himself on a ship bound for America, a stowaway, his passage uncharted and unrecorded. There will be no official record of his departure or arrival. Then he will change his name and change his face and disappear completely. It is how the Americans do things, and Victor Cross has been their man for a long time.

He is a betrayer, just like any other. The Americans and Soviets were both allies, so why is he considered a traitor of a different hue to those who spied for the communists? Why hasn't he been arrested, interrogated and imprisoned? Why hasn't he faced public humiliation and shame? The intelligence services will let him slip away; they will not want a scandal. But hasn't he colluded with a foreign power, passed on secrets, and in so doing endangered the lives of field operatives and compromised missions?

No, she does not wish to kill him, not yet.

I must clip the wings of the turncoat bird as it takes flight.

They will take him to Salford hospital to treat the gunshot wound. And there he will be vulnerable. She has been a nurse; she knows how to navigate such buildings. A night-time visit, a syringe and an injection, a wheelchair to move him, and he will be hers.

She waits, patiently, for many hours, with only a few greedy pigeons for company. She passes the time filing away the swastika and replacing it with a Tricolore. She studies the vessels through her sights. She knows which are being loaded, and which are bound for the USA. The dockers are like ants stripping a carcass and taking it piece by piece to the colony. Towards evening, a vessel bound for the Americas makes ready to sail. As they prepare to draw up the gangplank, a man darts forward, a kit bag slung over his shoulder. During his travails, he has overheated and unwisely removed his cap and coat.

She would recognise him anywhere: Victor Cross.

He is nearly at the gangplank, two sailors urging him to hurry. The ship's whistle sounds, and the shore workers and deck hands begin to remove the last of the hawsers holding the vessel in place.

It takes her only a moment to line him up, to assess the condition of the wind, and to mark her target. She factors in his motion and pulls the trigger. The rifle recoils against her shoulder with great force, startling the pigeons into flight.

The bullet smashes into his left leg and he crumples to the ground like a stricken deer.

'I have you now,' she says.

But she is mistaken.

To her horror, sailors race from the ship and surround him, shooing away the dockers who would help the man and take him to hospital. She cannot get another clean shot. They haul him up the gangplank and to safety.

'Damn!' she says. 'That ship must be full of agents.'

The gangplank is hauled in and the last hawser released. The ship turns slowly away from the quay and into the canal, and begins its journey towards the Americas. As it is swallowed up by the gloom, the captain gives a long blast on the foghorn.

It is a mocking sound, the sound of a metal container sliding into oblivion. It says, 'You won't catch me now, Françoise Fronsac; I will become a ghost, like the cranes, like the docks, and the dock workers. Search all you like, you will never find me. I will leave no trace. My secrets will bleed into the shadows.'

30

Doodlebugs Over Malvern

The farmhouse at Wellend, November 1979

His aunt is waiting for him when he gets in.

'Well?' she asks, offering him a warming mug of hot chocolate and encouraging him to sit nearer to the kitchen range. 'How was your date?'

He gives a brief account of the afternoon but reveals nothing of a personal nature. She notices the borrowed scarf.

'And do you like Jasmine?'

He nods. He doesn't want to say it aloud because he fears he might jinx things.

'And did you tell her so?'

He shrugs his shoulders. 'Not in words, but I think she guessed.'

'And did you arrange a second date?'

He was anticipating an interrogation, but he is confounded by this question. 'She said, "*Ciao*" and "I will see you in Biology on Thursday."'

Gail Miller laughs, but not unkindly. 'Oh, Benedict, you really don't understand the rules of the game, do you?'

'What game?' he asks.

She does not answer. Instead she beckons him to follow her. They go to the library, where the telephone is. She flicks through the *Yellow Pages* and finds the number for the coffee shop.

'There,' she says, pointing to it. 'Ring Jasmine.'

'Why?' he asks anxiously.

'Why do you think?'

He is not sure. 'Perhaps she will want to know I got back in one piece?'

She shakes her head. 'No, not that, but why you didn't ring me for a lift heaven only knows. Try again.'

'Perhaps I should thank her for a nice afternoon?'

She laughs aloud. 'Oh, Benedict, what are we to do with you? "Nice" is not going to cut the ice, remember that! You need more powerful words to convey your feelings.'

There she goes again, he thinks, *everything is about feelings.*

'Jasmine will want to hear from you because it will show her that you are interested in her. She will be waiting for that signal; she will be expecting it. If you do not contact her, she will think you cold and disinterested. She will want you to arrange a second date. She will want you to show some initiative. You must suggest something, and before the biology class on Thursday.'

She sees the look of utter panic in his face. What could he offer? A game of chess, a walk with the dogs, a fossil hunt, or a reading session in the library? He never goes out, anywhere.

She takes pity on him. 'Tomorrow is November the 5th. You are not working and there is no night school. It says here that the coffee shop closes at 5 pm. Why don't you invite the family over here? We could build a bonfire and get Cyril to bring some fireworks over. It might be fun. Why don't you suggest they come over for about seven o'clock?'

She sees the doubt in his face. 'Bonfire night is a bit childish, isn't it?'

'Do you have a better idea?'

'What if she doesn't want to come? What if she has other plans?'

'Ring her, and find out.'

*

They spend the morning building a huge bonfire down the bottom of the garden. There is no shortage of wood to burn.

'Should we make a Guy to put on the fire?' she asks.

He tells her about Ozan's suffering, and they decide against it. They take the dogs for a long walk and leave them in the care of a neighbour. The cats are rounded up and locked indoors. They spend the afternoon making toffee apples and parkin, and par-boiling potatoes. Dr Goodman arrives with two boxes of fireworks and half a dozen packets of sparklers. Benedict helps him nail the Catherine wheels to a post and build a low brick wall to support the milk bottle rocket launchers. They change the batteries in the torches and put out a bucket of sand and a bucket of water, just in case. Gail makes two punches: one for the adults and one for the young people.

Seven o'clock arrives, but the guests don't. Benedict stares out of the kitchen window, anxiously.

'They are not going to come,' he says morosely.

'Give them a chance, old boy,' says Cyril. 'This is not such an easy place to find in the dark.'

By a quarter past seven he is beside himself. 'That's it, they are definitely not coming. Why haven't they rung?'

Five minutes later, they hear a car engine approaching.

'They're here!' he says, trying to hide the excitement in his voice, and trying not to run to the door like a lapdog to greet them.

The car is a Mini Traveller, nearly as beaten up as the Land Rover. Susan gets out of the driver's seat. 'I am sorry we're late,' she says, 'we ran through a large puddle and the distributor got wet. The engine conked out. It took a while to get it going again.'

*

The fireworks prove to be entertaining, but not in the way they were intended. Two of the three Catherine wheels refuse to spin at all and just burn out in a shower of sparks, and the other spins completely off its axis. The Roman candles emit a sorry glow and a feeble putt, the traffic lights seem to be permanently stuck on red, the bangers refuse to bang, and the rockets, lifting from their launchers with a frightening fizz, disintegrate into nothingness. On one occasion, a milk bottle launcher tilts over just as the rocket fires, and they have to duck to avoid it. They laugh so much their bellies hurt. They laugh at Cyril and his animated attempts to get the fireworks to light, and they laugh at the pathetic display they offer when he does, each one proving more of a dud than the last.

With one exception: there is a hand-sized firework shaped like a cylinder with wings attached. It launches into the air at terrifying speed but then turns back on itself like a boomerang. It makes a screaming sound. They run from it, but it chases them, like a heat-seeking missile, like an angry mosquito, before it finally lifts into the air and explodes.

'Good Lord,' exclaims Dr Goodman, 'it's a doodlebug!'

'Let's have another!' squeals Roxanne in delight.

Despite the drizzle, the fire burns vigorously. Yellow flames flicker and curl into the air, and they are transfixed by their primitive beauty.

'It's like dragon's breath,' says Jasmine.

'How hot is it at the centre of the fire?' asks Benedict.

'Just under 1,000 degrees,' says Dr Goodman, 'judging by the colour of the flames.'

'Hot enough to burn a book,' says Ozan thoughtfully.

'Or a witch,' says Roxanne gleefully.

They cover the potatoes in silver foil and place them in the embers at the edge of the fire. Gail challenges Roxanne to an apple-dunking competition. They fill a metal pail with water and float apples in it. They put their hands behind their backs and try to pick out an apple using only their teeth. Despite Benedict's fears, Jasmine eagerly joins in, and he follows suit. Ozan insists on having a go, and Susan.

Not so childish after all, thinks Benedict.

Jasmine adores the sparklers, they all do. They wave them around like wands, casting spells and making ephemeral patterns in the air. Benedict spells out his name with the incandescent light, and then he spells out Jasmine's. The two words briefly meld together. He looks up, hoping she witnessed it, and she smiles, just for him. Roxanne makes a love heart and blows it towards her parents. Jasmine's spell is altogether different: a bird in a cage, taking flight. Between them, they use up every packet of sparklers, lighting one after another from the end of each other's wands.

When they tire of the cold and damp, they return to the kitchen for a feast. Warm punch, jacket potatoes with butter, falafel and pitta bread – a present from Ozan and Susan – parkin and toffee apples, and baklava, a gift from Jasmine to Benedict.

'I know you have a sweet tooth,' she says, recalling his demolition of the Turkish delight. 'I made these myself. I hope you like them.'

'I have thirty-two sweet teeth,' he replies, in his deadpan way, and they all burst out laughing.

'Very droll, old boy,' says Dr Goodman, 'very droll.'

'These are wonderful, Jasmine,' says Gail, before adding pointedly, 'aren't they, Benedict?'

He must not forget his manners; please God, do not let him say they are 'nice'.

'They are… divine,' he agrees, helping himself to another.

*

After the feast, a Gail Miller masterstroke: she suggests Benedict and Jasmine go and retrieve the dogs from the neighbours. Ozan looks doubtful, but Susan readily gives her permission before he has chance to deny them his.

'Take the torches,' says Dr Goodman as he escorts them to the door and whispers to Benedict, 'Don't be long, there's a good chap. Old Ozi is a bit anxious about his daughter.'

When they are gone, Gail shows Susan some of her art, and they discuss photography. Dr Goodman shows Ozan a fix for the car. 'These are good little motors, but the distributor is badly placed. It's far too low and prone to getting wet. Tie a plastic bag around it, like this.'

Afterwards, Gail plays Ozan at chess. Dr Goodman shows Roxanne and Susan another of his music boxes, and they are so enchanted by it he makes a gift of it to them. The chess game does not last long, despite the distractions.

'You really are a genius,' says Ozan admiringly.

As soon as they are outside, Jasmine takes hold of his hand. 'Thank you for inviting us here. No one has ever invited our family anywhere. Dad gets lonely sometimes. He's really enjoyed himself this evening, Mum too. Your aunt is wonderful, and Cyril is so funny.'

'I am glad you came. I couldn't wait till Thursday to see you.'

She leans into him and kisses his cheek. Her lips feel warm and sensual.

'I have something for you,' he says, 'a surprise, but don't laugh.'

He retrieves a sheet of paper from his duffle coat pocket and hands it to her. He has copied out his poem in his neatest handwriting.

She reads it through quickly, by torchlight, her hands shaking with excitement.

'Oh, Benedict, this is… wonderful.'

She reads it through again, more deliberately, taking her time to digest the imagery and sentiment.

'Would you mind if I showed this to my father? It is so beautiful it deserves to be set to music.'

*

He is good to his word, and they do not take longer than necessary to bring the dogs back. When they enter the kitchen, they are content in the knowledge that they will soon see each other in class and at the theatre, and that Benedict will ask his aunt if she can give them a lift to the pictures on Saturday evening; they are showing a re-run of *Fiddler on the Roof* and Jasmine is keen to see it.

They find the atmosphere has changed; they both sense it as soon as they enter the kitchen. The adults look at them with concerned faces.

'What's wrong?' they ask in unison.

It is Gail who answers. 'Benedict, I am sorry, we had a telephone call from Tracy. It's your brother… Caesar… There's been… an accident… a terrible accident.'

31

The Suicide Ward

Lodge Moor Hospital, Sheffield, November 1979

'Do you know what Sheffield has in common with Rome?' asks the jovial conductor of the number 81 bus, which takes a route from Sheffield city centre westwards, towards the wealthier suburbs and the cleaner air, the greener woods and the dark edges of the Peak District.

The bus is crowded, and Benedict has been standing for some time. He doesn't feel in the mood for conversation.

'Two mediocre football teams?' he answers.

He laughs heartily. 'Well, I can't argue with that. But they are also built on seven hills. I live in the east end, near the River Don. The wind blows all the smoke and filth over us. It's hardly worth hanging your washing out. By the time you take it in, it's dirtier than when you started. There was a cricket match abandoned in the summer at the Tinsley steelworks ground: smog stopped play.'

Looking through the dirty windows at the thick layer of smoke drifting along the valleys to the east, he can believe that is true. The bus has been climbing for a while, and they have now attained quite a height.

The conductor follows his gaze. He seems to be in no hurry to collect fares. 'Welcome to Steel City,' he says.

'How much is the ticket to Lodge Moor Hospital?'

'Tuppence,' replies the bus conductor. 'All fares are tuppence, wherever you want to go within the city, and whatever time of day.'

No wonder the bus is so crowded, thinks Benedict. 'How come it is so cheap?' he asks.

'Have you never heard of "the People's Republic of South Yorkshire", son?' says the conductor merrily. 'The local council charges the wealthy folks that live in the west end high rates and uses the money to subside public transport. Robbing the rich to support the poor, only proper when you think about it; Robin Hood was Robin of Loxley, a Sheffield lad, and we're heading west towards Loxley forest. We've a proud tradition of redistributing wealth.'

'The wind blows mostly from the south-west towards the north-east?' he asks, looking down into the valleys at the drift of smoke from the factory chimneys.

'Exactly, although there is another foul wind blowing from the south, from London. I fear for the future of this city.'

It takes Benedict a moment to understand what he refers to. 'You mean the Tory Government is a foul wind?'

'Right first time, sunshine – "Maggie Thatcher the milk snatcher", and her odious cronies. They are coming for us.'

His mood darkens, and his tone becomes serious.

'First it will be the coal mines, and then it will be the engineering and steelworks. No investment, subsidies removed and no protection from cheap foreign imports. I ask you, which other nation in the world removes protection from its steelworks? Within a generation the east end will become a wasteland, a ghost town, and the mines of the South Yorkshire coalfield will close too, and all so the government can offer the wealthy tax cuts and put the country up for sale. I'm glad I'll be retired by then, but I worry for my grandchildren.'

He pulls the cord above his head and a bell rings, signalling for the driver to pull over at the next bus stop.

'This is Lodge Moor,' he says.

'But I haven't paid for the fare,' replies Benedict, rifling through his pocket for some change.

'Keep your tuppence, son, who is going to miss tuppence? You're not worth robbing.'

*

Lodge Moor Hospital sits atop one of the seven hills of the city, on its western extremity, a location where the keen wind is at least fresh – an ideal site for an institution originally designed and built in the nineteenth century to isolate smallpox victims.

It takes Benedict a while to locate the reception, and even longer to find the ward his brother is on. The hospital is extensive, with many wings, all of which look identical: low-level grey buildings, not unlike army barracks, with long and empty corridors, soulless, echoing tunnels that go on forever, and offshoots which lead to cavernous wards of identical design.

The DNA of the building has been replicated, perfectly, over and over again.

He asks a trainee nurse for directions. She looks puzzled and calls out to a balding porter in lead-grey overalls, 'Arthur, do you know where ward 17A is?'

'Suicide ward,' he calls back.

The nurse looks at Benedict sympathetically. 'Follow me,' she says.

The ward contains twenty beds, all identical, all occupied by young men aged between seventeen and twenty-one. They have come from all over the nation to recuperate in the spinal injuries ward of the hospital, a specialist facility where they will learn to live with their disability, their broken backs, their severed spines and the loss of their limbs. Most are paraplegic, and so they will learn to use a wheelchair, to navigate the corridors, to get in and out of bed from the chair; they will learn how to use the commode, and how to manage their leg bag and their enemas. They will learn about pressure sores and involuntary muscle spasms, about restricted circulation and the need to develop greater upper-body strength. The most enlightened nurses and doctors will encourage them and help them to see what is possible. No one focuses on what they can no longer do.

Later, when they are more skilled and more used to their condition, they will be accompanied out. The new world will be frightening, and they will need a chaperone. It is the unexpected that will fox them: the cars double parked on either side of the streets that block off the pavements, meaning they will have to risk wheeling into the busy roads; the dog shit, so liberally left on the pavements by thoughtless owners that they will wheel through, especially at night when they cannot see it to avoid it so easily – tell them to wear gloves, say the professionals – the steep slopes that will require considerable hand strength to control the wheels and to prevent a catastrophic runaway; the public who will ignore you and the public who will insist on pushing you, even when you do not ask for it; the young children that will point and stare; the bloody doors you will not be able to fit through; the stairs, the endless bloody stairs; the broken-down lifts; the special treatment and obvious fuss needed to move from A to B by any form of transport; the bloody pub that is so crowded and badly laid out you cannot even get to the bar; and the self-deprecating humour of your ward mates: 'I'm armless; I'm legless, again.'

It can take a year to recuperate, but eventually they will be ready to go home; to go home and prosper, because, despite their hard blow, the world remains full of possibilities. They have their lives ahead of them, these young men, and the specialist spinal ward will help them to make the most of it. Should they relapse, there are counsellors and mental health professionals on hand to intervene.

The positive message the nurses and doctors give is not always heard by the patients. In the immediate aftermath of the car or motorbike accident responsible for their condition, they are prone to concentrate only on what has been lost. They feel robbed, despite what the medical profession tells them. They feel robbed of life, of their youth, of their vitality. It is so unfair, they feel cheated; their memories haunt them.

And so they are watched, constantly, day and night. The staff look for signs. Upon the suicide ward they mount an ever-vigilant suicide watch. Shaving is only allowed when supervised, cutlery is counted out and counted back in, medication is strictly controlled and visitors are closely monitored. It is not the first few weeks that are the worst – most patients remain in shock or denial, or there is still hope that sensation will return to their legs; it is the period following that when the risk level rises, especially when there are triggers: the sound of a motorbike passing by; a car being revved by joy riders; a football match on the television; an advert showing a handsome couple walking hand in hand along a beach; a groom standing next to his bride.

*

Before he is admitted to ward 17A, Benedict is vetted by the ward sister.

Here we go again, he thinks, *more obstructiveness*. His hackles rise and he clicks into sarcastic mode.

'You are alone?' she asks.

'Really?' he replies, looking behind him as if he is surprised to be unaccompanied. 'Oh yes, I remember now, I came by train, and then bus, from Worcestershire.'

She is not impressed by his attempt at humour and scrutinises him more carefully. Has he been drinking?

'That is a long way to travel by yourself.'

'I didn't feel like company.'

'And what is in that?' She points to a book he holds in one hand.

'A book,' he says. 'They contain words. You can read them.'

She doesn't laugh. 'A book about what?'

'Card games. I have a pack of cards, too. I think my brother might appreciate them.'

She doesn't respond. 'And what is that?' she asks, pointing to a crumpled white paper bag he holds in his other hand.

'Elephant's feet.'

'I beg your pardon?'

He opens the bag to show her. 'I got them in a baker's in town. The shop owner called them elephant's feet.'

Inside are two large hand-sized buns made from choux pastry, filled with cream and topped with melted chocolate.

'A Viennese pastry it is not,' observes the sister disparagingly. 'It will clog up your brother's arteries.'

'I don't think he'll care, do you?'

His casual attitude causes her to visibly stiffen. 'Very well, but no smoking and no alcohol.'

'And no laughing either,' he mutters, under his breath, peering into the joyless ward.

She hears him and speaks sternly. 'This is no laughing matter. Do you know what happened to your brother?'

'He had an accident, came off his motorbike.'

'That isn't the full story. Ask him; ask him what happened.'

*

'What the hell do you want?'

Caesar sits upright in a hospital bed, trying to hold down his left leg, which has gone into spasm. He wears a hospital gown and very little else. It falls open at the back, and Benedict can see how twisted his spine has become. Welded vertebrae bulge from his skin, like dinosaur bones extruding from a crumbling layer of rock. He has a name tag around his wrist, like babies are given in the maternity ward. There is a clipboard at the end of the bed, full of notes and red marks. His leg bag is full of dark yellow-brown urine. It looks like peat water.

'I brought you something,' says Benedict, trying to remain upbeat and placing the paper bag on the bedside cabinet. He sits down in the cumbersome institutional wheelchair placed by the side of the bed.

'If it's not baccy or booze I'm not interested. I could murder a pint.'

'It's a bit early, isn't it, even for you?'

'It's never too early. Christ it's boring in here. There's sod all to do. And the hospital radio is crap. All they sodding play is "Cool for Cats" by Squeeze.'

Looking around, he would have to agree. It is the middle of the day and most of the patients are up and about. Some are exercising at the swimming pool or gym; others have gone into the city with friends or relatives. Only five other beds are currently occupied by young men unsure of what to do with themselves, and an air of ennui and boredom prevails.

'Can't you talk to your neighbour? Maybe you could play cards?' He hands him the book and pack of cards he has brought.

He gives a surreptitious shake of his head and mouths the words, 'I don't like him.'

'Don't get too comfy in that chair,' he says, 'I need a piss.'

He had not appreciated how difficult an operation it was to get from the bed and into the wheelchair. Caesar levers himself up, sideways and then down, using a ceiling-mounted hand bar for support. Benedict would like to help, but he cannot see what to do. He feels useless, even more so when it becomes clear that the motion brings Caesar pain.

'Push me,' he instructs, after he arranges his legs on the footplates and removes the brakes. He wraps a hospital dressing gown around his shoulders.

'Push you where?'

'To the "bridge of sighs".'

*

The corridor leads past a games room, where there is darts, table tennis, bar football and board games, including chess. It is empty.

They pass the television room, also empty.

They pass a sign for a sports hall.

'They have a wheelchair basketball team,' says Caesar morosely.

'That sounds fun,' he replies. 'Maybe you could join.'

'You need a special sports wheelchair to play. You couldn't manage the turns or acceleration in this iron horse. They cost thousands to buy. The little prick in the bed next to me is getting one. It's all the twat talks about. His mummy's buying it for him. Speaking of which, the old woman visited; brought baby bro along. Can you imagine the yarns she's going to spin out of this one? No doubt I'll be winning gold at the Paralympics. Bloody crocodile tears at the bedside. She makes me sick.'

They pass two nurses and Caesar insists they stop to talk with them. He becomes animated, and more his old self. 'Who does this strapping fellow remind you of?' he says, pointing at Benedict. 'He could be my twin, couldn't he? Only he got the brains and I got the looks. I'm taller than him when I stand up.'

He flirts with them for the next five minutes, and they giggle and make a fuss of him before they insist duty calls, but they promise to visit him on the ward later.

'That Abigail's a right good looker,' observes Caesar, waving to the departing nurses and grinning. 'Lovely personality, too. You know I finished with Tracy?'

'No, I'm sorry to hear that.'

He knows what he is thinking, that he has acted magnanimously and chivalrously in some way, by letting her go.

'Ask her out yourself if you like. I didn't want her and the kid coming up here screaming the place down. I think she's been shagging someone else behind my back anyway.'

He doubts that is true, but he holds his tongue.

*

The corridor terminates in a small conservatory which overlooks a dismal garden – a fountain with a concrete angel, a patch of municipal grass, a flowerbed of roses and a few wooden benches. To access the garden from the conservatory, they have to cross a small ramp.

'We call it the "bridge of sighs",' says Caesar. 'The garden is the only sodding place we're allowed to smoke. Well, we're not really meant to, but the nurses turn a blind eye. Some of them like a puff, themselves. That Nurse Abigail is always out here – forty a day, that one. When we go back in, we sigh, because we're heading back into prison.'

Caesar reaches into his dressing gown pocket and removes a lighter, cigarette papers and a pack of tobacco. He hands them to Benedict. 'Here, roll us a ciggie, will you. I need to empty my bladder.'

He wheels himself over to the rose bushes and releases the content of his leg bag against their stems.

'Best insect killer on the planet,' he boasts. 'Never could stand roses anyway. Bleeding plants, what are they good for? They just give you hay fever.'

Benedict hands him the rolled-up cigarette. 'Where do you think tobacco comes from? Or beer?'

He's not listening.

'Jesus, Bones, this is rolled up tighter than a duck's arse! You're supposed to put some baccy inside the sodding paper! Honestly, if you want something doing, you have to do it yourself.'

It is time, thinks Benedict; he has put what capital he had in the tolerance meter but now the time has expired. He feels nothing but sympathy for his brother, and he knows he should humour him and try his best to help him, but twenty minutes, that is usually all it takes before they are arguing. The meter ticks faster where his mother is concerned.

'What happened, Caesar?'

'What do you mean?' he asks, lighting the cigarette.

'The accident, what happened?'

He sniffs, leans back in the chair and blows smoke through his nose. He evades the question. 'Do you know I can't even "snuggle" in here. They've got me seeing a head shrink.'

'What happened?'

'Does it matter? Bad luck, mechanical failure, the brakes locked on and I went over the handlebars.'

That is not what the ward sister implied.

'I don't remember much, Bones. I blacked out.'

'But you'd been at a party. It was night time.'

'I'd been at the pub! Bloody Norfolk country roads; it was pitch black. I was lucky someone found me. I wasn't pissed if that's what you're thinking. I'd only been able to afford a pint.'

No, that is not what he had been thinking. The ward sister said the motorbike veered from the road. It collided with a tree. No brake was applied, and the bike was accelerating. His brother had always had a recklessness about him, a self-destructive recklessness.

'Take me back inside, Bones. This is my day for a crap.

I'll be on the bog all afternoon. You might as well sod off now.'

'What really happened, Caesar?'

'A crap, Bones, I need a crap.'

32

The Saint-Emilion Attack

The Cedars Care Home, December 1979

He is little more than a skeleton dressed in a suit. The fedora hat is too big for him. His frame is so wasted he looks like a child in a giant's wheelchair. Victor Cross stares vacantly into the distance.

Benedict plays white. Victor does not respond.

He glances through the window towards Dr Marks, who looks concerned. She shrugs her shoulders as if to say, 'Perhaps he is beyond reach now.'

Benedict begins to say, 'Championship rules…' but, to their surprise, Victor cuts across him.

'I know the rules, Guy; I wrote some of them. Let me think.'

Dr Marks stares in amazement, and then remembers that she should be filming everything. She switches on the camera.

'Do you think to play the Cambridge variation,' says Victor, studying Benedict's lone pawn advance. 'It is a risky strategy, but then again, you young men are so privileged, you can afford to take such risks.'

An idea occurs to Benedict.

'Anthony Blunt has been revealed as a Soviet spy.'

The newspapers had recently been full of the story. Margaret Thatcher had stood up in the Houses of Parliament and revealed Sir Anthony Blunt, an advisor to the Queen on matters of art, and a former professor at Cambridge, as the fourth man in the infamous Cambridge spy ring. He had worked for the Soviets in the 1930s, recruiting students to the communist cause. The intelligence services were riddled with spies; it was a national scandal. The Palace had already withdrawn his knighthood.

'That does not surprise me. You young men drink too much and have loose tongues. They will never reveal all the spies, Guy, do not fret.'

He makes a move and, quick as a flash, Benedict counters.

'What's this?' asks Victor. 'You play with abandon, Guy; that is not like you.'

'I don't have much time; I have an aeroplane to catch. I'm going to France.'

Victor does not appear to have heard him. He studies the board for a long time, in silence. Eventually he makes a move.

Once again, Benedict counters almost at once.

The game continues in this vein for three more moves, by which time Victor has used up nearly forty-five minutes of his time allowance, and Benedict not even one.

'I do not recognise this game,' says Victor, for once sounding perturbed, and rubbing at a liver spot on his trembling hands.

'It's a new play. It's called the Saint-Emilion attack. B.B. showed it me.'

'B.B. is dead, Guy,' replies Victor, removing his fedora and using a handkerchief to wipe beads of perspiration from his forehead. 'The mission to Saint-Emilion was a disaster.'

He can hardly contain his excitement. At last, Victor Cross is talking about his grandad and France. He must choose his words carefully. He sees Dr Marks' puzzled face appear at the window. She holds her arms out as if to say, 'What on earth are you talking about?' He ignores her with studied indifference.

'Yes, I know,' he says to Victor. 'He was betrayed.'

'He betrayed himself,' he snaps back, as if he had just been accused of the crime. His response is irritable, and menacing.

At the window, Dr Marks draws her finger across her throat, telling him to stop what he is doing. He ignores her for a second time.

'How do you mean he betrayed himself?'

'He wrote a letter to a known German spy, a solicitor called Anderson, and he left details of the plan in a strongbox at a bank for him to find.'

Benedict cannot believe what he has just heard, but then he recalls Gail Miller's warning that Victor is liable to confuse reality, fantasy and imagination.

'Why would he do that?' he asks. He notices Dr Marks turn off the camera and make her way towards the room, her expression angry.

'Because he was ordered to. The second front was a ruse; even the German High Command knew that. The Americans had no intention of invading Bordeaux. But we needed to sow doubt, just enough doubt to make certain field generals withdraw their armoured divisions away from the Normandy coast. If we could make the invasion plans realistic enough, maybe they would reinforce the south-west with those Panzers. That would give the D-Day landings more chance of success. The best way to sow doubt was to make sacrifices.'

He struggles to follow his logic. Dr Marks enters the room scowling.

'Benedict, what are you doing?' she asks, her voice for once unfriendly.

He ignores her for the third time. 'What kind of sacrifices?'

'Angelic ones,' replies Victor. 'There are angels and demons in this world, Guy. Sometimes, only by sacrificing the angels, can we convince the demons of our intentions. B.B. understood that. The plans were deliberately leaked to every known German informer. The SOE missions were allowed to go ahead and some of our agents sacrificed. In this way we hoped to convince the field generals that the second front was not a ruse.'

'Stop this, now,' says Dr Marks. 'Can't you see how agitated Victor is becoming?'

Benedict turns to stare at her. 'He is reminiscing, I thought that is what you wanted, to get him to remember the past. Or are you scared of the past, Dr Marks?'

He turns back towards Victor. 'So you are saying B.B.

deliberately sacrificed himself, knowing the Germans would be waiting for him and the mission was doomed to fail?'

'Of course, Guy, that is the way of the world, you know that. The Saint-Emilion attack had to fail. It endangered one of our best spies. If a certain member of B.B.'s team had been captured, they would have been interrogated, and the identity of the Nose revealed.'

'Benedict, I don't know what you are playing at, but this stops now,' says Dr Marks, wheeling Victor away from the chessboard. He instantly becomes passive and listless, all animation and lucidity leaving his face.

'Check!' says Benedict, making a move and hoping to incite a reaction.

But there is nothing. Dr Marks points to the door, making it clear that he should leave.

'Checkmate in three,' says Benedict.

With astonishing speed, and taking Dr Marks by surprise, Victor wheels his chair back towards the board. He needs only a moment to study the move and its consequences. 'Well played, Guy,' he says, nodding thoughtfully.

'Will you please get out, now!' says Dr Marks, once more latching on to the handles of the wheelchair.

'No!' shouts Victor, suddenly tipping the chair backwards and pushing her away. The footplate rises up and bangs into the table. The chess pieces fly everywhere.

Victor starts laughing manically. 'There will be no record of that game, Guy. It will be erased, like so much has been erased. But they will come for you, in time, my clever little friend. Do as B.B. did: jump with a cyanide capsule in your mouth. Do not let them take you alive.'

'Out, now!' orders Dr Marks, pulling the wheelchair back towards the bed.

He turns and makes to leave. As he opens the door, Victor speaks for the last time. 'B.B. didn't need the cyanide capsule. His own sister shot him in the head.'

33

The Saint-Emilion Defence

He runs and he runs and he runs. He runs as if he is being hunted by gendarmes. He runs as if a spectre chases him through the woods. He runs as if Jasmine's life were in danger. He runs along railway tracks, heedless of the danger. He runs across fields, covered in deep snow. He runs in the middle of the road, ignoring the angry horn-blasts of motorists. He runs with the same reckless abandon that drove Caesar into a tree.

When he makes it to the farmhouse he doesn't stop to even greet the dogs. He runs upstairs and kicks open the locked door to his aunt's archive store. He begins to rummage through the files, showing the same urgency and desperation a thief will show, in the short hours when the night is darkest, as they rummage through a set of unfamiliar drawers looking for something valuable.

He cares not where the boxes fall or how mixed up the

papers become. After a while, he finds what he is looking for: a box containing his aunt's personal effects. He spends a moment sifting through them.

He hears a floorboard creak. He looks up, a savage fury in his eyes, and he sees her, standing in the doorway, her hands held behind her back. Her face is a mask, her expression unfathomable. He has no idea how long she has been there.

'Françoise Harrison,' he shouts accusingly. 'That is the name on your birth certificate. And there is a marriage certificate here, too. I know my French is rubbish, but even I can see it is a union between a Françoise Harrison and a Dr Georges Fronsac. You are FF; you are Françoise Fronsac!'

When she speaks, her voice is quiet and even. 'So it would seem. I have been known by many names, Benedict, Helen and Jeanette amongst others.'

'You worked for the intelligence services, like B.B. You were there, that night, in Saint-Emilion. Why didn't you tell me?'

She doesn't answer him directly. 'You have played Victor again. What did he say?'

He moves towards her in a state of blind fury, not knowing what he should do. 'You were scared Victor would remember what you did and that the world would find out. That's why you sent me in there: to find out if he remembered! Gail Miller, the artist executioner! Victor told me; he told me it was you who shot your own brother in the head!'

She swings her arm up from behind her back. It is a

leisurely motion, almost casual. In her hand she holds a revolver. She holds it to her right temple, her arm steady and her eyes locked on his. She lowers her finger to the trigger and pulls.

*

Dr Marks uses a public telephone box on a quiet street corner and calls an ex-directory number. She uses the correct code word and asks to be connected to the 'Operator'.

'The line is not secure,' reports a secretary who answers the telephone. 'I'll put you through now. Please speak briefly and then hang up.'

'Yes, what is it?' asks a muffled voice.

'V had another lucid moment. Nothing useful regarding activities across the pond, but he spoke to BD about the mission. He revealed what the sister did to the brother, but nothing else of value.'

'I see,' says the voice. 'Where is BD now?'

'He ran home.'

A long pause, the silence only broken by the crackle on the line.

'Hello, are you still there?'

'Yes, of course. How much longer does V have?'

'I can't say. I was amazed he spoke at all.'

'No more games. It was always a risky gambit, but V has said nothing useful and we cannot allow BD to know the truth.'

'But... but...'

'But what?'

'It is a fascinating case… from a research perspective. This could really define my career.'

'If you wish to have a future career, you will do as instructed. I am told your recent work in America was exemplary. Please do not let yourself down now, not over this.'

The man hangs up and the line goes dead.

*

Gail Miller sits in the kitchen rocking chair, the dogs sitting obediently at her feet and the unloaded revolver sitting obediently on her lap. Benedict sits at the table, his head buried in his hands. He cannot bring himself to look at her.

She speaks quietly.

'That is how it would have ended for me, had I been caught. Interrogation, torture and a bullet in the head. Better to take your own life, on your own terms. B.B. knew that.'

He doesn't want to listen to her anymore. She lies as freely as his mother. She has spent her life telling lies; she can no longer break the habit.

She speaks without emotion, as if she were a talking clock relating nothing but naked facts.

'I married Georges two years before the war started. I was training to be a doctor in Bordeaux. He was captured in the first month of the war, betrayed by a quisling. We had already established an escape network for victims of the Nazis. They tortured him to death. The body they hung in the prison courtyard was already lifeless. I was under suspicion too, but I had been warned, a tip-off on my way home from the hospital. I worked for MI6. The intelligence came via the Nose. I owe him my life. I went to ground and changed my name – my name and my identity. I did what I could in Bordeaux to organise the resistance, but by 1943 it was becoming too risky for me to stay. I returned to Libourne and ostensibly worked as a nurse. In reality, I ran the network. I took up with Raymond. He was a brave man, truly, and I loved him every bit as much as I had loved Georges. On the night of the failed mission, he shot himself in the head with a revolver just like this one. I know, for I saw him do it. B.B. was too slow. He tried to run, but he was just too slow. The gendarmes would have caught him and he would not have been able to resist the interrogation of the Gestapo. He would have betrayed the network. I had to shoot him; it was the merciful thing to do.'

He shakes his head, the anger building inside him.

'He had a cyanide capsule, Victor told me. They would not have captured him alive.'

For the first time she speaks with emotion.

'No, he didn't, Benedict, that is a lie. I urged him to run faster, Lord knows I did. I have replayed that scene in my mind so many times, wishing for a different outcome. Can you imagine what my life has been like? I have endured only because I am stubborn, and because, even now, I want revenge on the person who betrayed us. I accept that the plans for the second front were willingly leaked to fool the Germans into believing the invasion was a reality – I have long suspected that was the case – but B.B. never betrayed himself. He was no lamb walking meekly to slaughter. Victor knows who sent that letter to Anderson, the solicitor.'

'Why didn't you tell me the truth from the start?'

She sighs. 'Would you have believed it, Benedict? And anyway, perhaps there are elements of my past I wish to forget. Would you believe me if I told you there were other firefights that night, near Libourne and in Saint-Emilion? That I fought off the gendarmes and German troops with a Sten gun and hand grenades, and only escaped because I knew the cave systems better than they did, and because I had help from other brave resistance fighters. All of them fell, Benedict, in the defence of Saint-Emilion's cave. Would you believe it if I told you I walked to freedom by crossing the Alps? Would you believe me if I told you I took revenge on the doctor who betrayed Georges, and on a Nazi general responsible for ordering a massacre of innocents? I know what it is like to have young eyes and to look upon people like me; we are dismissed because of our wrinkles and growing frailty. Nobody believes what we were once capable of.'

He shoves back his chair angrily and begins to pace the kitchen. 'You used me. You invited me here just because you wanted me to get close to Victor.'

She doesn't deny it. 'Perhaps, at the start that was true, but I am not the only one. Dr Marks has used you too.'

He turns on her. 'What do you mean?'

'She works for MI6. When she visited this house she was spying on me and Cyril. She wanted to know what we intended. When she discovered you played chess, she decided to use you. She had tried playing Victor herself, but she is not in your league, Benedict; she lacks your memory. Do you have any idea how good you have become? No, I suspect not, you are nothing if not modest. She tried using other players – some of them very good – but all to no avail. After he became agitated when he saw me and Cyril at the art class, she had the same idea we did: maybe playing a "Harrison" at chess might just unlock Victor's mind, and she was right. She hoped he would reveal other secrets, secrets about his dealings with the Americans. But she knew it was a risky game, for he might also reveal the truth about B.B. It was Dr Marks, not Nurse Morgan, who left the instruction to prevent you playing chess with Victor whilst she was in America.'

He fetches a jug from the sink and pours cold water into his hands. He splashes his face with it. 'Is nothing in this world what it seems?' he asks.

She replies with uncharacteristic passion: 'Jasmine, Jasmine is what she seems. Have faith in her.'

He turns on her again, his face red with anger. 'Don't, don't you mention her name, not ever. You soil everything you touch with your damn lies, so keep your hands off Jasmine.'

She nods; he has a right to be angry. 'Benedict, have you ever wondered how Victor ended up at the Cedars Care Home, conveniently under the care of Dr Marks? Has it never occurred to you to ask why she put out a national alert about him? There were two reasons. Firstly, it was a message to placate the Americans telling them not to fear because they had managed to extract nothing useful from their spy. Secondly, it was a message to me.

They wanted me to find him. They lured me here because they thought I might be able to unlock his mind. They have this great double agent in their midst, every bit as valuable as a defector, with all these priceless secrets in his head. Even now they want to penetrate the fug that clouds his memories. I do not know how many operatives work in and around the care home, but there is a reason Victor never leaves that room. They fear even now that the Americans will try to take him back. The day we ran the art class, he was deliberately released. They wanted to see how he would react when he saw me. They wanted to know if my presence would spark a remembrance.'

She stands up and walks towards the door. She opens a cupboard and removes a box of bullets. She loads the revolver.

'What are you doing?' he asks, suddenly fearing she has lost her wits.

'I am going to call on Dr Marks. We have reached the endgame, we both know it.'

*

The telephone rings ten times before it is answered.

'Come on,' urges Benedict, 'pick up the damn phone.'

'Conservative Club,' says a disinterested voice.

'Hello, is Dr Goodman there please, Dr Cyril Goodman?'

'Who wants him?' asks the curt voice.

'A friend… Tell him Gail Miller needs to speak to him, urgently.'

'Women are always after Cyril!' says the voice sarcastically. 'Wait a minute; I'll see if he's at the bar.' The voice does not sound in a hurry.

Another five minutes waiting, this time on hold.

'Hullo.'

'Dr Goodman?'

'Benedict old boy, is that you? What's up?'

'Gail has gone to call on Dr Marks. She took a revolver with her.'

'Where are you?' His voice is suddenly alert and full of urgency.

'At the farmhouse.'

'Hang up now. I'll be there as soon as I can.'

*

Dr Marks' apartment forms part of a gated community in a fashionable area of Cheltenham. It boasts all the latest security paraphernalia to keep out undesirables. There are regular patrols, an undercroft car park protected by a security barrier, an entrance only accessed with a security code, a concierge service and a security camera trained on the entrance lobby.

She has worked a long shift. All she wants is to relax in a hot bath with a chilled glass of wine.

She knows something is wrong the moment she opens the door to her apartment. Even though it is dark she knows there is someone waiting for her, an intruder; she catches the faintest whiff of her perfume and the smell of dogs.

'I hope you haven't been waiting too long, Gail, or would you prefer I call you Françoise?'

A lamp in the corner is switched on. She is sitting in an armchair, the revolver on her lap.

'Call me what you like, Harriet, it makes no difference to me. Do come in and shut the door. There is a draught.'

'What do you want?' she asks, trying to remain calm. How on earth did Gail Miller gain access to her apartment? Someone in security has been lax; someone will pay for this. The woman's exploits are legendary in the service, but even so, this should not have happened.

'I want to talk to you about Benedict.'

'I'm all ears,' she says, walking casually to the fridge to help herself to a glass of wine.

Gail laughs, an icy and chilling sound. 'Perhaps you should rephrase that, given the unflattering hairstyle you insist on wearing. Your pistol isn't there, Harriet, I removed it from the vegetable box. Use the wine bottle as a weapon if you must, but I would prefer if we didn't have to fight. You should know that I have swept the apartment for bugs. I found two. Did you know about them? Perhaps you are not trusted? I have disposed of them for you.'

Dr Marks studies her with grudging admiration. How long have the listening devices been planted in her apartment? She feels resentment, but strangely, it is not directed towards Gail Miller. 'Would you care for a glass?' she says, offering up the wine bottle.

She shakes her head and says:

'Benedict can make Victor talk. You know this. But you will not allow him to reveal what I want to know. Even now, the service protects itself. But I take it Victor has not told you anything about the Americans. The Operator grows impatient. Has he told you to shut Benedict down?'

'Yes, this afternoon. There will be no more chess. It is deemed too risky.'

'And do you always do as you are told?' asks Gail.

'I have my career to think of.'

'Yes, yes, you do. Just imagine how it will prosper if you get Victor to reveal what he knows. Let me put a proposition to you.'

Dr Marks takes a large swig of wine. 'As I said, I'm all ears.'

'What if Benedict is able to get Victor to focus on America. He could do it, you know he could. Victor may reveal what you want to know.'

She takes another swig of wine and refills her glass. 'And why would Benedict do that?'

'Because, on Christmas Eve you will allow him to play his Saint-Emilion attack one last time. Really, it is quite brilliant. And he will try, at last, to elicit the truth about what happened to his grandfather.'

Dr Marks does not answer for some time. She stares into the distance, swilling the wine around her glass, absentmindedly. When she replies her voice is full of doubt. 'I don't know, Gail, Victor may not have that long left and I have never liked the way a sick man has been manipulated. And Benedict might not be as pliable as you believe. I have never liked the way he has been used either.'

She nods her head. 'He is harder than you think, and he is tenacious. He will not give up, not ever.'

34

The Unbreakable Seal

Bristol, summer 1978, eighteen months earlier

The speed dial on the Ford Cortina reaches one hundred miles per hour, but Victor Cross does not seem to notice. He stares ahead, blankly, as he has done every day for the last three weeks.

The driver weaves in and out of the traffic with great confidence, clearly used to such motion. The car has been supercharged and it has false number plates. Victor sits in the back, sandwiched between two heavily muscled thugs. He is sitting on a beach towel. There have been accidents before, and already he has soiled himself.

For three long weeks they have held him below decks on an unmarked ship stationed just off the coast of the Isle of Arran. They have used every trick in the book to 'encourage' him to talk. But the silent man, Patient X as they call him, has resisted all invitations to do so. It was as if his memories had been locked in a box and the box had been sealed with a Gordian knot. It was unbreakable, the most resistant lock they had ever encountered. Worse still, the man seems unable to care for himself. The interrogators ended up playing nanny.

The operation had gone so well up to that point. Following a tip-off, they had abducted the man from a hospital in Iceland. It had been an outrageous act. It had taken stealth and daring to overpower the two armed guards protecting his private room, and to smuggle him out on a fishing trawler, right under the nose of the American forces stationed at Keflavik, and the ever-watchful Icelandic navy. There had been a political stink afterwards, of course, but the service denied they had anything to do with the abduction.

But now they realised the man was a liability. There was talk of returning him to Iceland, or of dropping him overboard, but the Operator has decided on a different play. They are to hand Patient X over to a different agent, one more skilled than they at unlocking the secrets of the mind.

'We've tried drugs,' they said petulantly, annoyed that their professionalism was being questioned, but the Operator simply rang off.

'Next left,' says the chief thug, and the driver slows down so he doesn't miss the turn. They drive down a backroad for several miles, until they reach an unmanned railway crossing.

'It's here, pull over,' he grunts.

They check that no one is around. They open the back door of the car and haul Patient X out of it. He seems to have forgotten how to stand up. He has a tell-tale wet patch around his groin. The chief thug hits him in the head with the handle of his pistol and he falls to the ground, unconscious.

'You sure you placed the call?' he asks.

'The Operator did,' replies the driver. 'The police will send a car. The sergeant knows where to take him.'

'Good riddance to bad news,' says the thug with the pistol.

'God help the poor bastard,' says the driver.

35

Brain Box

Extracts from the case notes of Dr Harriet Marks

Subject: Patient X

10 July 1978: …Patient X remains in a secure unit for his own protection. All tests confirm advanced Alzheimer's disease (as I understand it, this was previously determined by Icelandic and US medical teams but access to their files is restricted)…

…The progress of the disease is as aggressive as any I have ever witnessed. I have ordered another toxicology report. I suspect new drugs were previously trialled on Patient X, but they have not proven efficacious. The subject hardly speaks. They have no conscious memory of who they are. Faces, voices and odours are forgotten as soon as staff leave the room. Nothing I have tried triggers the subject's memory, not music, photographs, maps or objects. Physically, Patient X recovers slowly from his many previous mistreatments. The cranial indentation caused by the application of a blunt object was responsible for concussion. The subject's face is scarred, but this relates to previous experimental plastic surgery…

13 July 1978: …The toxicology report suggests blood poisoning by an unknown alkaloid. Patient X has no appetite and does not willingly self-feed. Vomiting is frequently observed…

16 September 1978: A breakthrough: Patient X played a game of chess. He spoke rapidly, and in German. He revealed nothing sensitive, but mentioned a relative called 'G'. He referred to 'G' as the 'queen of the heart'. He only spoke for as long as the game lasted. A rematch was refused. It seems he will only play a capable opponent…

17 September 1978: …The most remarkable case I have yet observed. During REM sleep, the alarm on Patient X's heart rate monitor sounded: 170/90. His body was convulsing. He cried out in several languages, including English, Icelandic, Russian and German, 'Angels and demons; angels and demons.' I puzzle at Patient X's religious and spiritual beliefs. He reacts violently to any suggestion of medical treatment. Perhaps this is a legacy from the aforementioned plastic surgery.

Despite our attempts at restraint, the patient arose from the bed and began to write numbers and formulae on the wall. All the while the subject lectured us, in German, about the 'equations of life'. At no point was the subject awake…

...It would seem that he retains many memories, but not when conscious. The chess game earlier in the day may have triggered this episode of recall by exciting some vestige of the hippocampus. The disease appears to erase the driver of the brain; it attacks the inner eye. The game of chess perhaps excites other pathways and excites an almost dream-like state, allowing specific synapses to fire, and for certain memories to be recovered...

18 September 1978: ...Patient X has no memory of the previous chess game. I was able to offer another challenge, but once again conversation and recall lasted only as long as the game. I was dismissed as an inferior opponent. Patient X referred to me as 'no GM'...

10 October 1978: ...Patient X lectures in German most nights and freely writes complex calculus on the walls. It is exhausting to witness. During the day he appears catatonic. The first of the chess volunteers arrived today. They played one game. It lasted longer than previous games, but Patient X revealed little and hardly spoke. We have tried triggers during the game – images, music, names and objects from the war – but nothing induces moments of lucidity...

10 December 1978: ...Instructions were issued to move Patient X to a care home in the Midlands. This will be a secure unit, closely monitored. Patient X continues to decline, rapidly. Weight loss is becoming critical, and a drip has been applied. Frequent vomiting has resulted in dental issues: fungal infections, ulcers and dry mouth syndrome...

13 December 1978: …Patient X was deliberately exposed today to 'external forces.' This elicited an instant reaction. For the first time in some weeks the subject became vocal and violent. Both outsiders were recognised, despite their age and attempts at disguise. Perhaps there are fear memories here and the amygdala fired constantly? This may be a route to unlocking secrets. It would seem strong emotions excite synapses that allow snapshots of memory to emerge…

21 January 1979: …Patient X has declined further. It is with difficulty that they now rise from bed. Help is needed in dressing and feeding. Various medications have been tried, but none elicit a response. Further games of chess have proved fruitless…

1 March 1979: …Patient X developed a severe fever, possibly associated with the onset of organ failure. At times, rapid breathing observed in excess of 35 breaths per minute. Oxygen administered…

1 April 1979: …Exercise regime stepped up. Muscle weakness becoming serious…

10 May 1979: …A possibility of a new chess partner, one linked to GM. This will require preparation. Instructions issued to 'read' to Patient X in German and to reiterate opponent's name and close links to GM. This may prove most effective during sleep…

2 July 1979: …Another fever. These are becoming too frequent. Nausea and vomiting continue. Weight loss is now critical. Patient X refuses to use exercise equipment. Regime of daily massage and yoga prescribed. Dental visit; three teeth extracted…

4 August 1979: …The ground has been prepared. Patient X's fevers have finally abated and so he was introduced to the new opponent. He has been told, repeatedly, that the opponent is a maths prodigy and chess champion…

…The opponent was given the 'magic cube.' Patient X has never seen this so has no memory of it, and yet, they solved the puzzle in under a minute with no instruction. Somewhere inside his head there is a memory of what a puzzle is and an algorithm for reconfiguring a cube. It is extraordinary how quickly this memory surfaced and how the inner eye was able to work that memory into their imagination and 'see a way' to solve the puzzle. An unplanned game of chess followed. Patient X became lucid, far more lucid than they have yet been. Patient X revealed an extraordinary awareness of their surroundings. He referred to me by name and knew he was being filmed. Given their apparent catatonic state, it is baffling how much awareness Patient X exhibited. I suspect 'GM' dictated the choice of game, selecting one they knew has strong resonance with Patient X. The opponent proved to be an able actor. There is much potential here for unlocking hidden secrets, but it is a potentially dangerous path…

13 December 1979: …The opponent is every bit as remarkable as Patient X. He possesses one of the keenest memories I have ever seen. Game after game they have played (or more precisely, replayed). He never falters. They play for hours, sometimes four hours non-stop. Neither shows sign of fatigue. They are evenly matched.

The opponent is skilled at eliciting responses. He listens well, despite never making eye contact; he detects emotional clues from words and silences rather than from body language. He has great intuition. He has learnt to use vocal triggers to elicit specific memories. We have learnt so much, far more than we ever dared to dream. The opponent has their own agenda, of course, but alas, despite his best efforts, Patient X never quite remembers what he wants to hear…

…More shallow and fast breathing, vomiting, chills and weakness; the organs definitely begin to fail. Regression to early years is now evident. Lucid moments return less frequently…

20 December 1979: …He tries and tries and tries – he has the endurance of a marathon runner. The opponent has used every vocal trigger imaginable, but the memory they seek refuses to surface. Perhaps it has been erased, permanently. It is a dancing game that they play. It is remarkable how the inner eye – the exequatur – still seeks to protect itself, even at the end…

…Patient X has visibly deteriorated, irregular heartbeat, total loss of appetite, almost constant fast and shallow breathing. I fear it will not be long now…

…I feel sorry for the opponent. He has shown remarkable resilience and patience. He knows the task is impossible. I believe he identifies strongly with Patient X. They have much in common, not least their stubbornness and ingenuity…

…The opponent challenges the tenets of my discipline. He challenges everything I have been taught to believe about memory. He confounds cognitive science. He can concentrate for hours, he effortlessly recalls every detail of a game, and he holds hundreds of potential moves in his head at any one time. He is driven; he blocks out all external noise; he focuses only on the endgame… I have come to believe his prodigious memory is allied in some way to his intentions, but what they are, I cannot say for certain… I am not convinced he knows his own mind at times… Why does he continue the fruitless endeavour? Is it sheer cussedness?

36

The Endless Game

Father Christmas wears a green outfit and a garland of holly around his head. He is neither corpulent nor jovial. If anything, he seems to scowl at the residents as they enjoy their festive repast in the Cedars dining room.

Mrs Hart and her team of helpers have done wonders, transforming the dining area into a winter wonderland. There is a real Christmas tree in the corner, festooned with golden lights. Presents have been left beneath it. Stockings hang from the mantelpiece and yule logs burn on the fire. Paper rings run around the coving, and there are real candles lighting up the table, which has been covered in a red cloth. Carols sing out from the record player, and hundreds of cards have been tied to red ribbons and hung from the walls. Every available surface is covered in twinkling fairy lights, and the windows have been decorated with artificial snow. A wreath hangs from the entrance door, and silver pine cones and sprigs of holly with red berries decorate the table. Some of the more optimistic residents have armed themselves with mistletoe.

'I am not that creature invented by a certain American drinks company,' says King Arthur; I am the traditional English Green Man.'

'You look more like a character out of a Dickens novel,' says Benedict, 'another invention of Christmas.'

'Nothing wrong with Dickens,' he replies. 'He wrote a damn fine musical called *Oliver!*'

Sometimes, he cannot tell if the King is being serious.

'I thought you would have known that, Benny, you being an actor of some repute.'

He laughs then, partly in relief, knowing that the King is pulling his leg. 'You enjoyed *Fiddler on the Roof* then?'

The previous evening, most of the residents had attended the final performance. Mrs Hart had organised it and led the enthusiastic applause which punctuated the show.

'It was dire, Benny, tedious and overly long, although you were good, and your girlfriend has one heck of a voice. Such a pretty damsel, too, I'm told, but then again, I understand you're something of a picture gallery yourself these days, although I hear you yawning a lot. They are working you too hard. The lead was stuck in a real ham sandwich and the woman playing his wife was a turkey. She hurt my ears. She could be sued under the Trades Description Act for claiming she was singing.'

That is what he has always liked about the King: his delusions are honest ones. He always tells the truth as he sees it.

'I suppose I had better hand out these presents,' he says, heaving a sack onto his shoulders unsteadily. 'I helped to wrap them. It's all cigarettes, booze and chocolate liqueurs. This lot will be asleep by three o'clock; you'll be able to sneak off early. I hope you're taking that lovely damsel of yours somewhere nice.'

He bursts out laughing. 'Nice doesn't cut the ice, Arthur, I would have thought a king of your renown would know that. And yes, we are meeting up later. It's her birthday today. Jasmine is eighteen. She is ten weeks older than me.'

The King does something he has not done for a long time: he beams. 'I'm glad for you, Benny; no one should be on their own, not ever. My son and daughter are coming to see me tomorrow. I haven't thought about the noose in a while.'

It is Benedict's turn to smile, and they shake hands with genuine warmth. 'Merry Christmas, Arthur, you take care now.'

'Merry Christmas, sonny, you have a good one. And give my regards to that fair maiden of yours. Tell her… tell her she's welcome to sing at my court anytime she likes.'

*

At three o'clock on the dot he meets Dr Marks in the atrium.

She has changed of late: she wears her hair down and has different spectacles. She wears less sober outfits. He thinks the new look suits her.

'Are you ready?' she asks not unkindly.

What they are about to attempt has been forbidden by the Operator, but she no longer cares to do as he instructs her. When they are done, she intends to leave the service. She has been offered a promotion, at a university in America. She will write a learned paper for an academic journal – maybe several papers – about the extraordinary case of Patient X, about how memory can be fired by habitual actions, even when the hippocampus is all but defunct, about mental blockage, loss and compensation, about the plasticity of the neural networks which can still produce moments of lucidity even when the functionality of normal memory is all but gone. The New Year is full of promise.

'I feel nervous,' replies Benedict, 'like the first time I met him.'

She touches him reassuringly on the arm. 'You will be fine. You have played him so well up to now.'

And it was true. He had done such good work for them over the last few weeks, even the Operator had been impressed by the intelligence they had gained. Skilfully, he had turned the conversation towards America, and they had been amazed by Victor's awareness of recent political events.

'President "peanuts" Carter will fall within the year,' said Victor, 'and that third-rate actor Ronald Reagan will take his place. The SALT Treaty will never be ratified; the hawks in Congress will not allow it. The military-industrial complex has too much invested in the nuclear arms race.'

He sounded like Gail Miller; he sounded exactly like Gail Miller.

It had scared the hell out of them.

And then he talked about spies and contacts, double dealings, plots and intrigues; the surveillance of Charlie Chaplin and other movie stars; the paranoia of the McCarthy years; the coups and covert operations overseas. It was dynamite, a treasure trove of memories that should help to bring the culpable to heal. Dr Marks filmed and recorded every word. The leaks in the ship of state were about to be caulked and tarred over.

And towards the endgame she switched off her recording devices and allowed Benedict time to steer Victor back to France. That was the deal they had made; the Operator didn't have to know. As far as she could tell, Benedict would willingly do their bidding if she allowed him the chance of questioning Victor about his grandfather, not because his aunt wanted it so, but because establishing the truth had become so very important to him. The world of deceit he had been raised in had left its mark like a brandishing iron: he burned with a desire to find the truth, to see through the mendacity and dishonesty that enveloped him, and to triumph over the likes of Victor Cross.

'He's so resistant,' says Benedict. 'It is like trying to wear down a sea wall with a pebble. You know how hard I have tried to get the truth out of him. But that memory is buried so deeply, I think he can no longer recall it.'

'Perhaps his control centre still prevents it surfacing,' she replies thoughtfully. 'Maybe you just need to find the right trigger.' And then she thinks, *Here is another subject I should write a paper about, one blessed with an extraordinary ability to learn, remarkable concentration, and the most formidable memory and intuition.*

He sighs. 'I've tried everything I can think of. You know how much he has declined, even in the last week. I think this evening may be our last chance. And…'

He hesitates. 'And what?' she asks kindly.

'And I am not sure I want to know the truth anymore. I mean, let's say I discover what happened to B.B… I fear what Gail will do if she ever finds out who the traitor was. I may have to keep it from her. I may have to lie to my own aunt.'

*

'I have something for you,' says Dr Marks as they make their way to Victor's room. She hands him an envelope.

He opens it. It is a card with a photograph glued to the front. It shows all the residents of the care home – with the exception of Victor Cross – waving at the camera. Dr Marks is there, and Mrs Hart too. King Arthur is dressed in the suit of armour. On the back there is a message: '*Happy Christmas to our favourite son*.' Everyone has signed it. He smiles in gratitude. 'Thank you,' he says.

Inside the card is a cheque made payable to 'Master Benedict Harrison' from the Cedars Care Home. It is a generous sum – way too generous.

'We know you want driving lessons,' says Dr Marks. 'That should cover the cost.'

She will keep from him the contribution made by the state in recognition of his valuable service. It is one thing she had managed to agree with the Operator and Mrs Hart.

*

Victor is lying on the bed, in his pyjamas. He rests on top of a plastic protective sheet. His breathing is rapid, shallow and erratic. He is no longer able to access the wheelchair. They have placed a teddy bear by his side. He hugs it, as a small child would do. It seems to bring him comfort.

It won't be long now, they can all sense it. He seldom eats and he is seldom awake. He no longer calls out in the night, gives lectures in German or writes on the walls. During the last few chess games, he has spoken less and less. His lucid moments are waning, like the winter sun.

For once Dr Marks accompanies him into the room. She has no intention of filming this last game. She tells the care worker in residence that she can go, and the woman picks up her knitting and smiles gratefully. Dr Marks sits down in her still-warm chair.

'Good luck,' she says, and she means it.

Benedict sighs, steels himself, and moves the table with the chessboard on and a chair nearer to the bed. He gives the habitual announcement, 'Tournament rules...' and then he makes his opening move.

Slowly, and with great difficulty, Victor turns his body over so that he can study the board. He holds the teddy bear under his arm. He speaks to it. 'Greta... fret... no... do not fret my love. Gone... not long. Hope... still hope... for a donor.'

He struggles to make words now, and his sentences are often confused or incomplete. They have to fill in the gaps.

Benedict looks to Dr Marks and she mouths the words, 'Greta was his wife.'

'Edgar, this… isn't American… this move.'

It is time to push things to a conclusion for there is no more time. Victor has visibly aged since yesterday, and his voice has grown feebler. There is nothing for it; he must be bold.

'The scores are even,' he says. 'This is the *last* game in the championship. Everything rests on the outcome of this match.'

It has felt like he has played a real championship or run a marathon every day. He feels exhausted, physically and mentally. In the last month, when he has not been with Jasmine, chess has consumed him. But he is dogged; he will see this through to a conclusion. He doesn't like to be defeated, not by anything.

'I thought to play the Saint-Emilion attack again.'

'Never wise… repeat the past,' replies Victor, straining to lift up his arm and move a pawn. 'I won't repeat… mistakes.'

Benedict makes his second move. 'B.B. never made a mistake and he never betrayed himself. Someone else sent the letter to Anderson, the solicitor. And he never jumped with a cyanide capsule in his mouth.'

'I… am unwell… I… don't recall.'

Again, he responds to the opening much faster than before, and with an unusual move of his bishop.

Benedict plays his third move, a slight doubt forming in his mind. He might just have blundered.

'MI6 was concerned about the SOE operation. There were too many leaks. It was likely a certain operative would be captured and tortured, and the identity of the Nose revealed. They could not afford for that to happen, not with the valuable intelligence he was feeding them; intelligence that would help to secure the Normandy landings.'

Victor's response is equally swift. Benedict senses his attack is failing before it has even started. He stops to ponder his next move. It takes him forty minutes. His brain feels so tired he struggles to hold the permutations in his head. His concentration begins to wane.

Come on, think, he tells himself, *think*.

Dr Marks shifts around uncomfortably. The clock ticks forward. Patient X begins to rub at his liver spots and his breathing deteriorates into a series of sawing noises. He sounds like he is drowning.

Benedict feels an itch inside his nose and sneezes. The action elicits a response from Victor:

'Françoise Fronsac… the key… she… only one… only she knew… the Nose… spy… she… worked him… the Nose… often reluctant… she was… persuasive… always persuasive… she… was… main contact for us… everything… everything came via Fronsac.'

He is distracted by the use of his aunt's real name.

'Exequatur… wouldn't order… execution… I… had… to take charge.'

'Who was the Exequatur?' he asks. 'And who was to be executed?'

It takes another thirty minutes before he replies, and Benedict has to repeat the question over and over again. He feels wretched, like an interrogator. Eventually, Victor says:

'Brigadier… SOE top man. Françoise… I must… we must… eliminate Françoise.'

He is struggling to make sense of Victor's narrative. 'Are you saying you ordered the execution of Françoise Fronsac because the SOE brigadier would not, and because she was the one agent who knew the identity of the Nose?'

He nods. 'Angels and demons… Raymond a demon… informed him… B.B. communist spy. Eliminate… network compromised… bury Françoise.'

'You ordered Raymond to kill Françoise? But he wouldn't do it. They loved each other, didn't you know that?'

'Intelligence… failure… Françoise… too good… spy… top spy… kept… kept truth from us.'

Benedict plays his fifth move, not really caring what happens and no longer concentrating on the game. 'Us? Who are "us"? Do you mean military intelligence?'

He doesn't answer immediately. He closes his eyes and holds his hands to his chest. 'Water,' he says, 'water.' He sounds just like Benedict's father. It frightens him.

'I think we may need to adjourn,' says Dr Marks, helping Victor sip a glass of water and putting her hand to his forehead. 'He's fading fast. Another attack of fever, I think.'

But slowly, with trembling hands, Victor makes his move.

'There… Greta… I… have him… now.'

Benedict feels agitated; he has been endlessly patient, but they are getting nowhere and Patient X is all but spent. For the first and only time he loses his temper with Victor

Cross. He raises his voice. 'Who sent the letter to Anderson the solicitor?'

Victor's response is immediate. He freezes, his body turning ridged, his eyes fixed and unblinking, his chest no longer rising and falling. All colour and animation leave his face. He loses control of his bladder.

Dr Marks quickly examines him. 'Victor? Victor?' she calls out, gently slapping his cheek, but he doesn't respond. 'I don't think this is a catatonic state,' she says, shining a torch in his eyes and then listening to his chest. 'I think his heart has stopped.'

She runs to the door and calls for a nurse to assist her. 'Call for an ambulance,' she shouts.

Benedict slumps back in his chair, feeling utterly defeated. 'I am sorry,' he mumbles to no one in particular. For all his efforts, for all his hours of endeavour, for all his ingenuity, the truth will die with Patient X. He looks at the ruination of his body and he can feel nothing but pity for the man. 'Go to Greta, Victor, and rest in peace.'

Suddenly Victor's eyes become alert and he takes a deep rasping breath, like a man who has just been saved from drowning.

'Greta… Greta… I am sorry… you are… right… I… am guilty… the guilt… it torments me… I… must confess… seek absolution… ask Françoise… forgiveness… it was I… I sent the letter… If… Raymond… kills Françoise… then… the Nose is safe… mission has… has then to fail… erase… erase all trace… Raymond… B.B… whole network… blame… blame won't… fall on me.'

Benedict is stunned into silence. He sits in the chair,

his mouth agape. After all his probing and the endless games of chess, the truth has been revealed at last. A memory that Victor tried to bury has finally resurfaced. His own neurons have betrayed him. All he needed to do was utter his wife's name.

What a filthy world of double dealing they inhabited. It sickens Benedict to the bone.

What should he feel now? This is his moment of triumph and yet he feels no elation. His pity begins to evaporate; sitting opposite him is the man responsible for the death of his grandfather, and for many brave men and women of the network. He doesn't know what to do with himself.

'Hold the ambulance,' calls Dr Marks, placing a stethoscope to Victor's chest.

In anger, Benedict makes his last move. He doesn't even look at the positions on the board. He simply moves his queen a few spaces diagonally. It is an instinctive act. He wants to lose, and lose quickly. He wants to get out of the room as fast as possible. He needs to breathe fresh air. He never wants to set eyes on Patient X again.

To his astonishment he sees Victor topple over his king. He looks at the board; a 'discovery check', a move that has placed his opponent's king in check without Benedict realising it. In fact, it is even better than that; it is checkmate.

'A… brilliant… move… Kurt… Guy… Edgar… congratulations to you all… you see Greta my love… how we are defeated… at the last.'

37

The Body's Prisoner

What is the car registration? She cannot remember it. A minor irritation. There was something she was meant to do, but she cannot recall what it is.

It is the anxiety, Gail Miller tells herself; it is always like this when she is waiting.

And this has been one of the worst waits of her life. They have parked the Morris Traveller outside the care home. They are powerless; all they can do is pray for Benedict.

Perhaps he will come soon, and they will finally have an end to it. He has done so well, better than they could ever have hoped for.

And suddenly, he is there, opening the back door of the car and getting in. His face gives nothing away.

He tells them everything Victor said. He does not embellish the tale or provide undue emphasis. It is a clear repetition of facts.

From his office in London, Victor Cross played at war, as if it were nothing but a game of chess. The Nose was a valuable piece protecting the king, and he would do anything to protect the king.

They do not interrupt, not once. She looks out of the driver's side window, her breathing steady and her face showing no obvious emotion. Cyril holds her left hand.

'They were betrayed from the start,' repeats Benedict. 'I think there was more than one leak, and some of the leaks were deliberately made by MI6. To protect the Nose, Victor believed he had to eliminate you and sacrifice the network.'

'Had Raymond eliminated Françoise then the world would never have known about his betrayal,' mutters Dr Goodman. 'How haunted he must have felt when he discovered you survived.'

Still she looks out of the window and does not speak. Cyril says:

'I suppose Victor devised the whole plot by himself. He probably felt another agent could be sent in, after the fall-out from the bungled operation, and work the Nose as you had done.'

She scoffs, 'No one but me could work the Nose. No one else knew him the way I did. And Victor Cross never worked alone, not ever. He is a traitor, a clever traitor.'

'You were wrong about my nan,' says Benedict. 'I knew she couldn't have betrayed Grandad.'

The implication is clear; "you were wrong about her, you could be wrong about Victor, too."

She brings to mind snapshots of how his nan was back then, fragments of conversation, the tone of her voice, the impression she made. She never loved B.B.; she used him like a ladder. There is more to this, she is sure of it. Victor has only revealed a partial truth.

But perhaps, in the end, that is all there ever is to recall.

'If your nan did spy for the Ruskies,' says Dr Goodman, 'then she may have inadvertently betrayed B.B. She may not have realised the Soviets would inform the gendarmes. Stalin would have wanted to stall the American advance on Berlin; he would not have welcomed a second front in France. There were good reasons why she was under suspicion, Benedict.'

'But you were wrong about her. You two have spent your lives cursing and maligning an innocent woman. No wonder she is so bitter.'

'You forget the Americans,' says Gail pointedly. 'Victor Cross always sided with the Americans.'

Benedict shakes his head. 'Do you know who you sound like? Arthur King! Why would the Americans want the SOE operation to fail? We were allies.'

'Because of the Commies,' replies Dr Goodman. 'The network was full of them. The Americans may not have known B.B. was MI6. They may have believed he was still an active member of the Communist Party. By that juncture in the war, attitudes were hardening towards the Soviets. They may have wanted to kill two birds with one stone. By leaking the plans, they convince the German generals that the second front is a reality, and by working with Victor, they eliminate an active network of potential future enemies.'

Benedict laughs. 'This sounds like paranoia, Cold War paranoia. Victor has just confessed that he sent the letter.

I had no sense that he was lying. Why can't you accept the simple truth?'

'Because the truth is seldom simple!' replies his aunt, her temper fraying.

Dr Goodman is conciliatory. 'Perhaps he is right, Gail? Perhaps it is time to put this to rest. It has consumed too much of our lives. Raymond was faithful to you, and we know who betrayed B.B. and why. I find some comfort in that.'

He tries to squeeze her hand reassuringly, but she withdraws it.

'What will you do now,' asked Benedict, a note of concern in his voice, 'about Victor?'

'What can I do?' she snaps. 'He is a prisoner of his own body. Dr Marks tells me he is unlikely to see in the New Year, and you tell me you will not play him again. It is over. I just need a little time to come to terms with that. You two can drive to the coffee shop. I'll meet you there. I want to walk for a bit and clear my head.'

She does not wait for a reply. She exits the car, taking a large shoulder bag with her. She glances up briefly towards the third floor of the care home and walks off down the street.

'She'll be alright, old boy,' says Dr Goodman, firing up the engine. 'You did well, Benedict, she will come to see that, in time.'

*

The easiest way to penetrate any vault is to walk in through the entrance door. It is Christmas, a season for excuses, understaffing and lax security. Gail Miller all but lets herself into Patient X's room.

She waits in the shadows on the opposite side of the street for over an hour. She sees Dr Marks and Mrs Hart depart. She waits until she observes the receptionist leave her post to visit the lavatory. The atrium is deserted. She quickly enters, rummages behind the counter and helps herself to an ID lanyard that reads 'Temp', and then runs up the stairs with surprising agility. Through a window in a door she sees most of the residents and staff drinking heavily in the dining room, or asleep in the lounge, one of the endlessly repeated television 'specials' playing to itself in the corner, although what is so special about it, she cannot imagine.

The codes on the security doors are a potential barrier, but Benedict is observant, and he told her what they were some weeks before. They do not care to change them very often.

She walks into the room like she owns it. There is an aged and heavily bespectacled care worker sitting on a chair, idly flicking through a well-thumbed and glossy magazine. Victor is asleep on the bed, his face turned towards the wall, the teddy bear at his side.

'The party is just getting going downstairs,' she says, affecting a Bristolian accent. 'I'll sit here for a bit if you want to go and get a drink.'

She is in disguise – a few props from her shoulder bag: a blonde wig, contact lenses that turn her eyes blue, a little makeup. Superficially, she looks younger, and Nordic.

'Oh, that's kind of you,' says the care worker. 'I don't mind if I do. It's always a lively affair. There's bound to be a few sore heads in the morning. You have to watch out for the devils with mistletoe! Are you from the agency, dear?'

'Yes, I'm covering over the Christmas period. I don't mind, I need the money.'

'Oh yes, it's getting harder by the day to make ends meet, isn't it? I'll not be long. Victor's no trouble, although he gave us a bit of a scare earlier when it seemed his heart had stopped. Turned out to be a false alarm; just call me if he needs changing.'

When she has left, Gail Miller locks the door. She pulls the curtains, blocking off the view of the adjacent room. She stands in the corner, as far from Victor as she can get. It is thirty-three years since she last saw him this close to. The plastic surgeons did a botched job; he is still recognisable. She removes her revolver from her overcoat pocket. She speaks to him sharply, and in German:

'Wake up, Greta is here.'

His eyes open immediately, as if a bolt of electricity flows into him. He turns to face her.

'Greta? My Greta? How… how… is… the grave?'

'You will know soon enough. Why did you not help me?'

He tries to get up, but he lacks the strength and she will not aid him. He tries to reach out to her, tears forming in his eyes. He proffers the teddy bear towards her – a gift, a token of his affection.

'No… donor… kidneys… diseased… I tried, Greta, I tried.'

'No, weasel, you failed. Why did you not give me one of yours?'

She suspects she knows the answer. The Victor Cross she knew did not believe in medical interventions. He believed the body should never be opened up by the scalpel and that it should be buried whole. They must have drugged him and held him down when they changed his face.

'God… did not… permit me.'

'So you watched me die in pain. Your god is cruel.'

'No… he… is… merciful.'

'No, Victor, you are mistaken. There are no angels and demons; there are only people like me and you. There are those who make sacrifices and those that are sacrificed. The ones you sacrificed want revenge.'

'Please… Greta… hold… me… please… so… so… lonely, so… very… lonely.'

She raises the revolver to eye level and fixes his forehead in her sights. She will make his ending swift. Here is the man complicit in the death of her brother, whom she loved dearly and whom she has missed, every day, and Raymond, whom she loved every bit as much. She may never discover the complete truth, but she knows enough now to condemn the traitor. She has waited for this moment for thirty-five years. How she has prayed for it and longed for it, her need for revenge all-consuming. Time out of mind she has imagined this scene and the bitter-sweet taste of justice it will give her. She will willingly pass sentence on the man responsible for the death of the two men she loved the most in this life.

She puts her finger on the trigger and begins to apply pressure.

'Lonely… Greta… so… lonely…'

'Goodbye, Victor,' she says.

But her voice sounds shaky, and inexplicably her hand begins to tremble. Her vision begins to blur. Images of B.B. begin to dance before her. He is falling, from the sky, with wings outstretched like an angel. He spreads out his arms as if to protect Victor Cross. He is joined by a second ghostly figure. He is dressed as a gendarme. He holds up his hand as if to halt a vehicle, as if to protect Patient X. His hand has a bullet hole running through it, like a stigmata.

'No,' she mumbles, 'no… get out of the way… run… run, my love…'

B.B. points to his forehead, as if inviting her to shoot him for a second time. Half his face is angelic, half demonic. A large spider crawls out of the bullet wound in his head and drops towards the floor. It dangles from a silk thread, which is attached to the angel's forked tongue. It resembles a parachutist, hanging in the air, its legs groping the void, searching for firmer ground. She recoils in fear.

'Fronsac… I am sorry…' says Victor, 'but… the plan… was a… success… a complete… success… Eisenhower… Churchill… they approved… Panzers… divisions of Panzers… turned away from… Normandy… the Nose… reported… the sacrifice… made a difference… I… I have no regrets…'

The trigger resists her, as if an unseen hand holds back the hammer. She does not have the strength to pull it. Looking at him now, seeing him so desperate and alone, she feels nothing but sympathy – sympathy and sorrow. In spite of her rage, she cannot bring herself to pull the trigger.

'Damn you!' she cries. 'Damn you to hell!' She smashes the revolver down on the chessboard, breaking it in half and scattering the pieces everywhere. She picks up the two kings and flies from the room.

In the living room on the first floor, King Arthur has a sudden vision and cries in alarm that there is an angel in a blonde wig running down the stairs being pursued by a giant, demonic spider. Everyone laughs at the blind king.

She leaves the doors to Victor's room wide open and unguarded. The noise from the party filters up to the room: peals of laughter, merry voices, snippets of carols, and squeals of outrage and delight. Victor Cross no longer registers the sounds nor recalls the function of the doors. He lies down on the regulation hospital bed that is covered in a plastic sheet, holds the teddy bear tightly to his chest, and falls into a deep and entirely dreamless sleep. The last memory that ever surfaces is of his late wife.

'Read… to… me… my Greta… my love… read to me… of iron masks… and Venice balls… of secrets… of intimate secrets… remind me, my love… of our sweetest joys. For I have been careless… and I have forgotten them.'

EPILOGUE

Benediction

St Anne's Church, Great Malvern, midnight, 24th December 1979

He has never really believed in God, but he has always enjoyed singing carols. It is not the first midnight mass he has ever attended, but it is the most joyous. For once, Benedict finds a church inviting, despite the crowds. He wonders how many of the congregation are, like him, non-believers.

He occupies one of the front pews, Jasmine, Ozan and Susan to his left, and Gail and Cyril to his right.

They had rendezvoused, earlier, at the coffee shop. They had been invited to dinner. Roxanne was sent to bed early, so that she could attend midnight mass later that evening. She was reluctant to leave, and only did so when 'Auntie Gail' agreed to read her a bedtime story.

She welcomed the distraction.

It turned out to be a musical evening to celebrate

Jasmine's birthday. Gail had brought her cello along and Jasmine played the oud. She sang a duet with Benedict, a song of their own composition called 'Angels and Demons', which the adults applauded with heartfelt enthusiasm.

'You two are really good together,' said Susan, smiling with pride.

I know, thought Benedict.

'You put that bloody awful folk tape to shame,' said Dr Goodman, thumping him playfully on the arm.

Ozan was overcome by joy and hugged them both for a long time. 'Such divine music,' he said, weeping.

A selection of Christmas favourites followed, Gail playing the 'Coventry Carol' with great feeling and melancholy. She seemed to become lost in the melody, as if she were away somewhere else entirely, her mind recalling some past tragedy. Benedict recognised the signs.

'We have a surprise for you,' said Jasmine, handing the oud to her father.

'I don't play so well these days,' he said apologetically, holding up his bent fingers, 'but Jasmine insists, and because it is her birthday...'

He was modest; even with his tortured hands he played magnificently. Jasmine sang along, an enchanting melody that lifted their souls, the words coming straight from Benedict's heart.

'Benedict,' said Gail, filling the stunned silence that followed the performance, 'you will be wasted as a palaeontologist. Your words... they are a gift; they are your gift to the world.'

*

The midnight mass began with a rendition of 'Once in Royal David's City', the first verse sung by a solo chorister who turned out to be Roxanne. She appeared from behind a screen, two similarly aged choirboys either side of her, carrying large candles in heavy candleholders to provide illumination. The innocence and purity of the scene invoked a collective and heartfelt sigh of adoration from the congregation, and Susan, Ozan, Gail and Cyril all waved to her.

Later, the vicar had taken to the lectern for a reading from the Bible. The candle bearers stood either side of him. Much to the mirth of the congregation, the two young boys became sleepy, and the candles weighed increasingly heavy in their hands. They began to sway and lean inwards, the flames from the candles approaching the vicar's sideburns with alarming speed. He accelerated, moving through the reading with unprecedented gusto.

Just before disaster struck, the service was interrupted by a drunken man, recently turfed out of a nearby pub. He burst into the back of the church singing, 'I'm Henry the Eighth, I am...'

Fortunately, the disturbance jolted the candle bearers from their slumber, and the flames were withdrawn from the nearly singed sideburns of the vicar. He looked upwards towards the heavens and mumbled thanks to his Maker, a clear case of Divine intervention.

*

After the service, they briefly returned to the coffee shop to say farewell and to exchange presents. Cyril was the first to depart. 'A long journey tomorrow, old boy,' he said to Benedict. 'I go to Cambridge this time of year. My daughter lives there.'

He was puzzled as to why he had never mentioned his daughter, not once, in the twelve months he had known him.

On the way back to the farmhouse, Gail had explained. 'Unfortunately she was born with severe brain damage. She needs constant care. I'm afraid she doesn't know who Cyril is, but of course, he visits her anyway. He takes her a new musical box, every year.'

The learning machine, thought Benedict, his heart going out to Dr Goodman. *That is why he is developing the learning machine, to aid his daughter.*

He would have liked to have spent the whole of Christmas Day with Jasmine, but he knew it was impossible. 'Papa will want me here,' she said, 'and to be honest, this is where I want to be too.'

He understood, really he did.

She told him about their traditions. They recorded a film on a hand-held cine camera. It was packed in a tin and posted to their family in Turkey in October. The family there did the same. On Christmas Day, at an agreed hour, they each fetched out a projector and put up a screen and aired the footage for the first time. In their film, Ozan insisted they sing a song for his mother, and the girls danced and showed how happy they are in their new life. And then Ozan would use the telephone and speak to his relatives, the whole family chipping in. It always ended in floods of tears – tears of joy and tears of sadness, for what is life after all except a journey marked by tears?

They had exchanged presents and cards and agreed not to open them until later in the day. His aunt insisted they opened hers there and then. Two pictures, two original Gail Miller masterpieces, likely worth a fortune in years to come. For Jasmine, a sketch of her family at the farmhouse on bonfire night, Cyril lighting fireworks, Gail and Roxanne bobbing for apples, Benedict writing her name with a sparkler and she casting a bird in flight, and Ozan and Susan embracing.

They had all gasped at its simple majesty. 'Thank you,' said Jasmine, hugging Gail like she was a long-lost relative.

For Benedict, a portrait of him and Jasmine: a close-up of their faces and expressions. They look bright and intelligent, and full of hope, despite the suffering they have witnessed, the affection between the two subjects made plain for all to see. Privately, she considered it the best work she had done in years.

*

After a few hours' sleep, Gail and Benedict load up the Morris. It is still dark. It takes them the best part of three hours to drive the hundred miles or so to Hayfield. It is mid-morning by the time they arrive. It is a bright day, full of promise.

'I intend to go home and live out what remains of my life in my house near Libourne,' says Gail as they approach the village. 'There are people there who are very dear to me, and I have been away too long. You have become very dear to me, too, Benedict. You are welcome to join me, anytime, whenever you wish, Jasmine too, and Caesar. There will always be a room set aside for you. Cyril will move back to Cambridge. His lab is still based there. I don't suppose he mentioned it. I don't really care for Malvern, and Hayfield no longer feels like home.'

She sees the panic in his face. 'But I won't move yet, not until you have finished your studies.'

'Thank you,' he says, and he means it. 'Jasmine wants to go to art school, to study graphic design. We are going to apply to the same universities, but not Cambridge; we're not bright enough for that.'

She pulls up in front of the house and switches off the ignition. She turns to look at him, and says, earnestly, 'Benedict, you are far brighter than most of the people I ever met at Cambridge. What they have is privilege; what you have is integrity. Never forget that.'

He doubts it is true, but he smiles anyway, and remembers to thank her, for everything.

When he is alone, he opens his present from Jasmine. It is an exercise book containing some of her drawings. He recognises her in many of the images, and there are portraits of him, too. She has annotated the pictures with lines from poems and thoughts that have occurred to her. It is a personal and intimate gift, and the best present he has ever received. He telephones her immediately to thank her. He hoped she liked his gifts: for her eighteenth birthday a bottle of French perfume his aunt had insisted he purchase because 'She will simply adore it.' He had misgivings – the smell of it made him sneeze – but in the end, he accepted her advice. For Christmas he gave her a book of his poems. She can't speak for long, Ozan is hovering by the phone: 'I love the perfume, it is so romantic. And I haven't studied all of your poems yet, but I will; you know I will. I can't wait to see you. Hurry back, won't you.'

They are soon on the road again, heading east towards Sheffield, another hour's drive, but Gail Miller seems inexhaustible. Ward 17A of the Lodge Moor Hospital is all but empty, many of the patients having returned home for the holiday period. But Caesar is there, waiting for him, Nurse Abigail sitting on the end of the bed. She is off duty. She wears a denim jacket and fake reindeer antlers, as Caesar does. Her presence has a transformative effect on him; he is charm personified.

'Here is a present for you,' says Bones, proudly pushing a brand new sports wheelchair forward. 'It's from Silver-Sherry Nan and Aunt Gail, although I chipped in too. She contacted me out of the blue. She heard about your accident. She wanted to help. She hopes you will be able to visit her soon. We're both invited to Brighton.'

'Then you'd better pass your bleeding driving test soon!' he replies, lifting himself into the new chair and testing it out.

'Abi, this is much easier to move than the iron horse. You could sit on my lap and we could do wheelies down the corridor.'

Benedict laughs. 'Oh, don't encourage him,' says Abigail, smiling. 'He's incorrigible enough as it is.'

'I'm going to build a trike, Bones, and then I'll be able to take Abi for a proper spin. I'm going to become a stunt rider, see if I can't get into the film industry.'

*

It takes some effort for Caesar to get from the sports wheelchair and into the front passenger seat of the Morris, but he does it eventually. It is the first time he has left the hospital grounds since his accident, and Benedict is glad Abigail agrees to come with them. They left the dogs back in Hayfield, which is just as well, for the wheelchair takes up much of the space in the boot.

'Do you mind if I smoke, Gail?' asks Caesar. 'I've not been on the road since… well, you know.'

'If you wind the window down you can smoke as much as you like.'

She drives with exaggerated care, westwards, towards the Derwent reservoir. The roads are all but deserted. 'The Dambusters practised here, during the war,' says Gail wistfully as she pulls up beside a Victorian aged masonry dam, a tree-lined reservoir stretching out like a silver hand behind it.

'Shall we have a winter picnic?' she asks.

With some difficulty, Caesar gets back in the wheelchair and Benedict takes a hamper from the back seat. The road is deserted, and they make their way along it for about a mile or so. It is winding but only slightly undulating. Benedict walks alongside his brother, who wheels ahead from time to time, testing out the speed and manoeuvrability of the sports chair.

'This is great, Bones, you should have a go.'

He can tell that his brother is glad to be outside again, to breathe fresh air, to smell the resin in the pine trees to his left, and to see the open water to his right. The wide-open spaces are intoxicating. 'I'm going to offer my body to scientific research, see if some brainbox can't implant some gizmo into my spine that helps me to walk again. When I marry, Bones, I want to walk down the aisle with my bride.'

Benedict tells him about Dr Goodman and his computer that learns, and they both see hope in the research, although they share an unspoken fear that progress may not come fast enough.

'He is doing better than I imagined,' says his aunt, to Abigail, who walks with her, about ten metres further back. 'He is surprisingly cheerful. He seems to be looking ahead. I suppose he puts on a mask.'

'He's up and down,' says Abigail. 'It's to be expected; he's approaching the real danger period. I fear what will happen when his mood crashes.'

*

They stop by a glade and spread a tarp on the ground. They open the hamper and enjoy turkey sandwiches, mince pies and Christmas cake. There is a Christmas cracker each. They ridicule the pathetic jokes and don the paper crowns, although Caesar is reluctant to remove the antlers Abigail gave him. Gail uncorks the champagne. They drink from plastic flutes.

'A toast,' says Caesar. 'To Silver-Sherry Nan, a true diamond bird.'

'To Nan,' they all repeat. Even Gail Miller joins in, although the words choke in her throat.

'To stunt riders,' says Abigail, and for the second time they all raise their glasses.

'To our loved ones,' says Benedict, feeling unusually bold and sentimental, and they all join in. For once, Caesar does not mock him. Abigail smiles sweetly.

'To memories,' says Gail wistfully, and nobody knows quite what to say.

*

On their way back to the car they take a short detour along a well-made path that leads them to the edge of the reservoir. Caesar is hesitant at first, but emboldened by Abigail's encouragement he risks the track. They still wear their paper crowns and carry their champagne flutes in their hands. The sun has begun to set and a mist forms across the water. It seems like they have the entire valley to themselves.

At the water's edge, Gail removes two objects from her coat pocket and shows them to Benedict. He recognises them at once: the two kings from Victor's chessboard. He does not ask how she acquired them; he does not wish to know. He takes the white king in his hand and he looks her in the eye. They both know what will happen next. They nod to each other, turn to face the water, and hurl the pieces as far into the reservoir as they can throw them.

They skip across the water before they sink, like bouncing bombs.

They look back at one another and smile. It is over; it is finally over. He knows what she will do next.

Gail Miller begins to scream. She takes a deep breath and hollers with all her might. She screams until her whole body shakes. Benedict joins in.

Abigail and Caesar look startled and cast anxious glances at each other, but then, caught by the fever, they too begin to scream.

They scream for all the blindness and madness in the world. They scream for all the blows and suffering and frustration they have faced. They scream to release all the hurt, each of them trying to outdo the other for volume and sustain. They scream loud and they scream long; they scream until tears flow down their faces, four voices joined in unison and grief, a royal abundance of sorrow.

When they are sated, when they can scream no more, they begin to laugh, great, joyous belly laughs, the likes of which they have not experienced in years. They embrace, and hold on to each other, as if they never want to be parted. They laugh so much it hurts, and new tears appear in their eyes. The sound carries down the valley and makes contact with the concaved surface of the stone dam. It rebounds, and the echo comes back to them, reinforcing their joy, and reminding them of its ephemeral nature.

They will endure, that is what the screaming and the laughing signify. It is a benediction. They will make their way through life and mark their passage with tears of joy and tears of grief, for that is what memory is, a remembrance of tears.

It has taken Françoise Fronsac a lifetime to realise that.

If you have enjoyed *Emilion*,
please consider leaving a review
on your preferred platform.